This signed edition

has been specially bound by the publisher.

all summer long

ALSO BY DOROTHEA BENTON FRANK

All the Single Ladies

The Hurricane Sisters

The Last Original Wife

Porch Lights

Folly Beach

Lowcountry Summer

Return to Sullivans Island

Bulls Island

The Christmas Pearl

The Land of Mango Sunsets

Full of Grace

Pawleys Island

Shem Creek

Isle of Palms

Plantation

Sullivans Island

all summer long

Dorothea Benton Frank

WILLIAM MORROW
An Imprint of HarperCollins*Publishers*

 For information, address HarperCollins Publishers, 195 Broadway, New York, NY 10007.

HarperCollins books may be purchased for educational, business, or sales promotional use. For information, please email the Special Markets Department at SPsales@harpercollins.com.

FIRST EDITION

Designed by Bonni Leon-Berman

Library of Congress Cataloging-in-Publication Data has been applied for.

ISBN 978-0-06-239075-2 (hardcover)
ISBN 978-0-06-256622-5 (BAM signed edition)
ISBN 978-0-06-256635-5 (B&N signed edition)
ISBN 978-0-06-256623-2 (Target signed edition)

16 17 18 19 20 RS/RRD 10 9 8 7 6 5 4 3 2 1

In memory of our friend Pat
with great love

All that glitters is not gold;
Often you have heard it told:
Many a man his life has sold
But my outside to behold:
Gilded tombs do worms enfold
Had you been as wise as bold,
Young in limbs, in judgment old,
Your answer had not been in'scroll'd
Fare you well: your suit is cold. Cold, indeed, and labour lost:
Then, farewell, heat and welcome, frost!

—*The Merchant of Venice,* Act II, Scene VII
William Shakespeare

contents

prologue

Easter Monday, April 6, 2015
Manhattan

Whether the subject of change was partners, possessions, or places, some people had an easy time letting go. A fixture in the crown of Manhattan's classic interior designers, Olivia Ritchie was not such a person.

Over the years she had enjoyed the privilege of observing the private and personal habits of the *one percent* through her work. She was surprised to discover that there were people—many of them, in fact—whose closets weren't jammed to capacity with twenty-year-old garments thcy thought would come back into vogue. Hers bulged with a kind of weird ferocity, as though the closets were populated by tiny, possessive museum demon docents that guarded the history of her style. These same people with the organized closets, whose clothing and accessories were usually spread over their other residences, which helped to explain why they were so neat, actually replaced the contents of their spice cabinets and pantries annually, and over-the-counter medicines were tossed out by their expiration dates, just because it seemed like a good idea. Actually, someone on their payroll did it for them. Olivia didn't do any of those things. To begin with, she had only one home. And only a part-time housekeeper.

Olivia Ritchie wasn't technically a hoarder, but she loved her collections and the precious possessions she had amassed over decades. She saved garments and linens simply because she loved the fabric or the workmanship. You could find them wrapped in acid-free paper and packed in acid-free cardboard boxes under the bed and stacked in the very top of the linen closet and armoires. There were scores of handbags and scarves and mountains of costume jewelry that had been out of style for a very long time. Sometimes she would use a detail from one of them to represent a motif in a custom wallpaper or fabric. Sometimes she used the object for color. She squirreled away all sorts of things because they could be an honest catalyst for inspiration. And if she truly tired of something, she managed to sell it to a client.

Olivia had dozens of objets d'art and curiosities from all over the world, ranging from a sixteenth-century Italian saltcellar sometimes attributed to the school of Benvenuto Cellini to dozens of ivory Japanese netsukes. She had miniature cloisonné boxes that played sweet music, tiny French clocks that chimed assertively on the quarter hour, and dozens of hand-carved Chinese puzzle balls. The intricacies of the puzzle balls never ceased to amaze her. They seemed impossible to her—impossible to envision as an artist and impossible to render. All of these belongings, down to the most humble buttons in her button box, were poised to ignite her creative spark. These tools inspired Olivia's magic. She made the dreams of other people come true. At least that was the pleasant rationale to keep them all.

But she couldn't keep her first husband, the philandering, financially irresponsible medical student she had married in her mid-twenties against the pleading of everyone she knew.

Two years into it she came home one night to an empty apartment. All he left her was a note on the kitchen counter along with ten milligrams of Valium. The note read: *Sorry. I can't do this anymore. You're too demanding and controlling. You really ought to get some help.*

He took every stick of furniture, the contents of the kitchen and linen closet, and needless to say, all the music. Oh, he left the wedding album on a windowsill in the living room, a choice that stung. She ripped the pictures into shreds and threw them off the balcony, watching as pieces of her dream floated down to 73rd Street. It took her a while to get over it.

Olivia buried herself in work and built her business, one gnarly client at a time. After being single and, she would admit, very lonely, Olivia achieved extreme success and married again, this time with the blessing of everyone she knew. But she vowed never to answer to anyone again. There would be no mingling of resources this time around. She was in charge of it all and the happiest she had ever been. People said she had dreamed Nick into her life—Olivia was a lucid dreamer, something that drove her crazy because her dreams were so vivid it was hard to tell the difference between a dream and reality. Nick teased her without mercy about them, comparing her to a New Zealand tribe of indigenous people who confused them also.

Her safe and jovial (much older than her) second husband—darling, poetic, professorial, and ever the perfect gentleman—Nicholas Seymour, was a lifelong student and teacher, and he didn't particularly care about power. Well, he was happy to cede control of their money as long as things went well. For fourteen years of bliss they had been flush and pretty much able to do as they pleased because her business thrived.

Nick was like Olivia in that he also collected things. Nick had shelves upon shelves of gorgeous handmade leather-bound books whose spines were hand tooled in gold leaf. His small study that held these treasures had a tiny woodburning fireplace, a luxury in their type of building. The combination of the lingering ghosts of wood fires over the years and old leather laced with the occasional Montecristo smelled better than any perfume on this entire earth. And Nick had an army of tiny cast lead Confederate soldiers placed in battlefield dioramas on a few shelves, lit and protected by glass walls that looked like small aquariums. To his everlasting delight, the Union troops of General William Tecumseh Sherman did not and would never reflect actual history in *his* depictions.

"It's a mighty powerful feeling for a modest man like me to be able to change the outcome of a war," he would say with a wink to a guest. "May I offer you a measure of my oldest bourbon?"

Who could refuse? He and his visitor, usually a colleague or a graduate student, would sink into Nick's well-worn and cracked leather armchairs and sip away into the evening telling stories about the South or European wars or just about the great beauty to be found in a line of Seamus Heaney's poetry.

Nick, who could have been the prototype for Oscar Madison, was a man of many interests. The walls and file drawers of his study were filled with ancient rare maps used by explorers in ages long gone. His favorites were classified as *cartographic curiosa*, a term that referred to maps with geographical inaccuracies such as misshapen continents or ones that showed places like California as an island.

"Look at this," he said to Olivia one night, carefully lifting the brown paper away from a new acquisition—a seventeenth-century map detailing North America. "This fellow de Lahontan was a French military officer stationed in Quebec. After he fought the Iroquois, he made this map."

"Amazing!" Olivia said. "Gosh, honey, didn't you wear that shirt yesterday?"

"Yes. Is it a capital offense to wear a shirt a second day?"

"No, but it's wearing yesterday's lunch." Olivia said and touched the rather large stain left by the drips and splatters of the red sauce from spaghetti Bolognese they had shared the prior day at a charming neighborhood restaurant.

"Oh. I'll change it in a moment."

"No, you won't. I know you. It would take an act of Congress."

"I *will!* But listen to this." He shuddered and thought, *Women!* "What's truly amazing is that the literature he published along with it described a mythical place, one inhabited by a large and lavish tribe of Native Americans."

"Mythical? You mean it's a lie?"

"Yes! Yes! Yes! In those days, who could call you out?"

"Well, they didn't exactly have Google Earth in the 1600s," Olivia said, and smiled.

"No, they surely didn't." Nick shook his head and looked at Olivia. "God, I just love this stuff."

Although she didn't quite understand his fascination with old maps, Olivia and Nick shared an appreciation for fine craft in any discipline. Their treasures were an extension of who they were professionally and spiritually. They were an ideal couple, except that he was truly a bit of a slob and she wasn't exactly forthcoming about their finances.

They forgave each other their indulgences and almost anything really, but unfortunately for Olivia, the dreaded moment of truth had arrived. It was time for her to downsize with Nick, which meant selling their apartment and moving. *Downsizing.* It was a terrible term, one that woke her up in the middle of the night with visions of misery along with her serious financial problems and gave her cold sweats. Downsizing. Even the sound of it was depressing. It implied all sorts of terrible things. Failure to maintain their lifestyle as it was. Getting out of the game. Yesterday's news. Done. Finished. Old. Down. What was down? Hell was down. She was going to hell.

This terrified her, and for good reason. Nick thought they could both afford to retire, but Olivia knew they could not. And if the concept of downsizing didn't fill her with enough dread, they were moving to Charleston, South Carolina. She, a fourth-generation New Yorker, was walking away from the bright lights of the center of the universe. Her fingernails would be found embedded in the cement in front of the Decoration & Design Building. This could easily prove to be the worst decision of her life. It was professional suicide.

In the minds of her clients she would be washed up. Moving away from New York would surely be a death knell! *It tolls for thee, Olivia.* Why in the world would a client in Manhattan hire an interior designer from anywhere else? New York still had all the edge, didn't it?

But this was the agreement she had made with Nick, a confirmed bachelor, when they married fourteen years ago. They sold his studio apartment and he moved in with her. When the time came, they would retire to Charleston, the land of his ancestors and his boyhood. He was beside himself, giddy with joy.

"I'd go anywhere with you," she'd said fourteen years ago, and meant it.

Then.

"By God, you're wonderful. You'll love a simpler life!" Nick bellowed with thunderous affection on so many occasions, and he always meant it too. "You're an angel! And I am a lucky man."

But Nick, with his salt-and-pepper closely clipped beard and blue eyes filled with mirth, lived in the world of poetry and history and didn't have an inkling about how money or the world worked. He depended on Olivia's business acumen to manage their money, and she had done a splendid job of it. She said all their success was due to being lucky. And she was. Until recently.

It didn't take too many mistakes to throw her business into a downward spiral. And even though the mistakes weren't always hers, she ultimately took the fall. First, there was the thirty-thousand-dollar sofa that came in two inches short that the manufacturer wouldn't take back and the client wouldn't accept. That sofa was now in a storage unit in Secaucus along with other problematic items, and they all irritated the living hell out of her every time she saw them.

"Some people are just dreadful," she'd think to herself every time she made a delivery.

Truculent behavior was one of the ugliest characteristics of the entitled and vastly wealthy. Sometimes her clients were completely unreasonable just because they could be.

Next, there was a contract for a total renovation of an eleven-room apartment on upper Park Avenue. The profits from that job would have covered their living expenses for two years. But then the sudden stunning news of that client's explosive, tabloid-documented, acrimonious divorce hit the news as though a gigantic rogue meteor had crashed in Time

Square. From every corner of Manhattan tongues were wagging like those of dogs galloping toward an overturned street vendor's pushcart. All of that anticipated income and all those deposits for fabrics, furniture, lighting, and rugs slipped right through her fingers and dissolved into a nasty puddle of her growing anxiety and despair. The identical thing happened when a major client was transferred to London and another to Sydney. Plans had been drawn by an award-winning architect to reconfigure the footprint of their apartments, in addition to plumbing and electrical plans. Fixtures had been ordered, exotic wood floors and paneled walls had been bought at auction, and then wham! The rug was unceremoniously pulled from under her feet, like Lucy with Charlie Brown's football. No one cared how this would impact Olivia professionally or personally. She gave the impression, because it did not pay whatsoever to ever lose your cool, that her business was so successful their cancellations wouldn't change a thing. It wasn't true. And she never told Nick.

Bad things come in threes, she said to herself.

No, they didn't. They came as frequently as the fiendish gods of trouble could hurl the disastrous lightning bolts to earth.

To round out her worries, their apartment on East 86th Street sold for much less than she anticipated. While the apartment, as you would expect, was a metaphoric jewelry box, the building itself was an unrenovated post–World War II ugly white brick monstrosity with low ceilings, clanging pipes, and no parking garage. These days, people wanted a view, a media room, and a health club in addition to every other amenity you could name. Dog walkers and concierge services? Yes. These days, people flocked not only to the West Side but to areas downtown and in Brooklyn where you would not have touched your Manolo Blahnik/Warren Edwards–shod foot to the pavement a mere ten years ago.

Things just weren't going her way. At all. So while Nick might have been getting used to the idea of retirement, she was anything but. She *had* to work and somehow make up her losses. If Nick knew how close they were to bankruptcy, he would die. Her insides quaked at the thought of the truth being discovered. Thankfully she had a loyal client who didn't care if she lived on the moon. Hopefully that client would not abandon her when Olivia gave up physical proximity to her.

So as it got closer to Nick's retirement, she took a deep breath and they put her co-op on the market. They got a buyer who was happy to pay full market value, but they couldn't get board approval. It finally sold but not well. After ten months and no offers, she signed a contract for a pittance. All cash. They would close in ninety days. She began to panic. Moving was no longer a promise but a reality. One last worry? She had made the final decision about which house they bought in South Carolina on her own. She knew the house she chose was far too grand for Nick's taste. But that particular house was what she needed for herself and for the image of her business she hoped to build there.

"This is a disaster," she said, referring to the sale of their co-op. "It's like being robbed. Not to mention, how am I going to unravel years of pack-rat habits in three months?"

"Better days are coming!" said her assistant, Roni Larini. "Besides, I'll help you."

They were sharing a large Greek salad and a liter of sparkling water delivered from Viand Café around the corner, at the tiny but beautiful office she rented in a discreet residential townhouse on East 58th Street.

"Thanks. I know you will. You always do. And I've got the lease on this place until October."

"Maybe you should keep it," Roni said.

"Maybe," Olivia said, but she knew she could not afford to sign another lease. Not without new projects on the books.

Roni could almost read Olivia's mind. She knew Olivia was completely overwhelmed. And it took something as cataclysmic as the nose dive she was experiencing to unravel Olivia.

"I'll check the fine print. Maybe you can sublet."

"There's a thought."

"What's the rent?"

"Four, including maintenance."

"We could get six on a sublet. Easy. Or! How's this? We fix up the back rooms into bedrooms and you'll stay right here when you come to town."

"We'll see."

"You'll be fine, Olivia. We've been to the edge before. Are you getting any sleep?"

"Not much. Nightmares like mad."

"You should start doing yoga again. It makes you put everything into perspective."

Roni often referred to herself as Olivia's *office wife*. She may have only been thirty, but she had made herself indispensable. In truth, Olivia wondered how she would live without her when she moved. But they had sort of a loose but optimistic plan to hold their relationship together by employing the services of frequent emails, FedEx, FaceTime, and Skype. And she would fly to New York twice a month and stay at the Cosmopolitan Club. Lord knows, she'd paid membership dues for years but was always too busy to enjoy the benefits. Or maybe she should give up the Coz Club, put a bed in the storage room as Roni suggested, and save some money. It had been decades since she'd had to reconsider her overhead.

It was true that her expenses would be much lower in South Carolina, which would help their financial constraints. But could she generate enough business from there to get her out of debt? Could she generate any business at all? Would she really be as efficient without Roni by her side in flesh and blood? She had asked Roni to consider moving south with them, but Roni could not. The timing was all wrong. Roni was firmly tied to New York. Her eighty-five-year-old mother was in assisted living, dealing with all the horrors of Alzheimer's. Her two useless siblings and their useless spouses lived in the Midwest in oblivion, pretending no responsibility.

"I know you're right. I should go back to yoga," Olivia said and fished out a large black olive from among the lettuce and tomatoes, popping it into her mouth. "I wish they'd pit these things."

"I wish a lot of things," Roni said.

"Me too."

CHAPTER 1

rats

Their small commercial plane was about twenty minutes north of Charleston, descending through a thick blanket of cumulus clouds to an altitude of ten thousand feet. Once they cleared the clouds, the landscape of the Lowcountry burst into view. Waves of bright-green spartina covered former rice fields and marshlands, their blades standing in sharp contrast against the sparkling blue majestic waters of the Waccamaw River. Olivia was mesmerized. Nick's delight at the scene, and most especially at her reaction, was very nearly a tangible thing.

"Behold paradise!" Nick said dramatically, exhaling a gush of relief. "The sluices of water cutting through the marsh grass in tendrils . . ."

"Just like the ringlets on the back of Miss Scarlett's pretty little head," she said in a terrible southern accent. Then she cut her eye at him and smiled. "I'm sorry. I don't mean to be so cynical."

"You're going to love living here. I swear you will," Nick said, saying a silent prayer that the Lowcountry would work its magic on her. "And your pretty cynicism will roll away on the turn of the next tide."

"I've always enjoyed the time we've spent here," she said.

But it was one thing to stay at the gorgeous Charleston Place Hotel and have room service and quite another to live on the tip of an island in a funky old beach house.

Her eyes were focused on the landscape as it rose to meet them. His eyes were focused on her. (Cue up the theme song from *Out of Africa.*) Her thick blond hair was pulled back in a ponytail that drifted down her back. She was wearing a straw fedora and all white linen, even though it was before Memorial Day. A bona fide New Yorker, Olivia didn't give one tiny damn about when she wore white. She had her own rules.

He loved her in hats. And in white—it reminded him of her tangled in their sheets. Nick was all too aware of her shaky feelings about the move. That's why he went along with the house she chose. To be honest, he was uncertain about which house she actually *did* choose! They had looked at so many he couldn't remember. To be more honest, he didn't care one whit. He was one step closer to coming home, and that was all that mattered to him.

He knew the renovation of any of the old houses would be a huge project, and Olivia loved nothing better than a huge project. Nick thought, if he was right, that the house she did choose was hideous, but she said she saw potential everywhere. Where? He thought. He couldn't see potential in any of them.

The good news was that all the houses were in such disrepair that his relatives, distant as they were, and old friends wouldn't be offended by a vulgar display of wealth. At the heart of it all, he was an island boy, a Geechee boy, a Lowcountry boy. Low-key discretion was the name of the game for his tribe.

Olivia had made at least a half a dozen trips without him back and forth between New York and the island to work on the house, staying in a hotel close by. Surely, just the time spent there on renovations had made her feel some ownership, some affection for the island. Nick felt certain that if he could get her to walk along the ocean with him as the sun was setting, the salt water would exorcise her urban demons, maybe through her feet, pulling them right out to the endless sea like a magnet. Over time her heart would soften. It had to or what?

"Why can I never remember how beautiful this is?" she asked in a whisper.

"Because it changes with the seasons and because it's really just so glorious our brains can't hold the entire memory."

"Maybe."

"You know, when I was a boy someone told me a story about how angels have different jobs. Some watch over drunks and babies, but others paint sunsets and color landscapes. That would be a cool job, wouldn't it?"

"If you believe in that stuff."

"Ah, my lovely, doubting Thomasina!" He took her hand in his and patted the back of it. He meant the gesture to say that here in God's country she would find faith. "In time you will see wondrous things. My daddy called it reading the signs and wonders."

Nick was ready to wax euphoric then. He could have gone on for hours. But the flight attendant picked up the microphone to address the passengers, and although there was an onslaught of static and blank moments of completely missing communication, he knew exactly what she was saying. It was time to close the germ-ridden tray table, press the swarmy, germy button to raise his seat back, and yes, to check the germ-infested-with-something-really-scary buckle on his seat belt to be sure he didn't go flying when the pilot stomped on the brakes as though he was going to slide into the face of the Rocky Mountains at the Telluride Airport, one of the scariest landings he had ever endured. He worried about plane crashes and sometimes obsessed about germs. Okay, he was a germaphobe. Normally he had a pack of sanitary wipes in his pocket. Somehow he had forgotten to bring them. But other than these two minor but troublesome issues, Nicholas Seymour was not neurotic in the least.

The plane landed smoothly and stopped at the gate. Nick smiled with relief as though he had dodged a bullet. Okay. He worried about death too. And he hated to fly. But life wouldn't be so cruel to snuff out the flickering wick of his breath when he was this close to living in the Lowcountry again. Would it? No, he thought, and pushed away a sorrowful and painful mental image of his own wake and funeral. God, how he struggled to disguise his litany of anxieties from Olivia! He knew that she knew all about them, but he pretended she did not. And she did indeed know every single tic of his but overlooked them because she knew that she wasn't perfect either.

They gathered up their things, deplaned, and stood beside the jetway with about fifty other people waiting to reclaim their gate-checked bags. After ten minutes or so, their luggage appeared and they began their way through the terminal toward the rental car counter. The airport was going through a massive renovation, but there were so many people milling around that it seemed Charleston's airport had already seriously outgrown its expansion.

"I remember the day when this airport had only two gates,"

Nick said. "Then it opened a restaurant that merely served fried chicken, deviled crabs, and sweet tea. It was fabulous."

"Airport food? Fabulous?"

"Hard to imagine, but yes."

"Wow. And then they invented air conditioning and the whole world went to hell?"

"Yes, ma'am! The next thing you know we had the pleasure of blue and pink Princess phones and another network on the television."

"Yeah, and right after that Ed Sullivan went off the air and Michael Jackson was performing 'Thriller' on MTV ten times a day."

"You're right! How could you remember that? You could hardly have been born! I recall watching it with some students and wondering how long it took to put that makeup on."

"Yellow eyes. True, I was just a girl of twenty-one, fresh out of school. I always thought he was a fabulous entertainer. Okay, our car rental is at National."

Olivia loved being that much younger than Nick. In an odd way it was nice to be thought of as somebody's pretty young thing. She had been on her own with all the struggles of maintaining her detail-oriented business for such a very long time. The only person she had ever had on whom she could depend was Roni, but she didn't come along until a few years ago.

It was an incredible luxury to believe there was someone in this cold and lonely world who cherished her. Nick's love was the greatest gift she'd ever known. She did her best to reciprocate, but sometimes—well okay, *often*—the stress (and the nut balls who were her clients) of her business got in the way. She could be described as bitchy on occasion. Okay, somewhat often. Actually she was a worrier, and sometimes she may have appeared to be aloof or maybe ill humored when she was just worried. She didn't mean to seem to be the flavor of cranky that gave certain female New Yorkers their reputation. It was really her obsession with self-preservation that meant she came across as buttoned up or frosty in conversation when you first met her. But when she needed to, she could channel Grace Kelly.

The nature of their professional lives was polar opposites, his being far more predictable than hers. He had known different kinds of stresses in academia, to be sure—publishing and all that—but he had been a tenured professor for ages. And as everyone knows, there was no tenure in the world of interior design, no safety net. But on the positive side, as different as their careers were, they still found time for their first passion—travel. They would drive up to Millbrook to shoot birds at Mashomack in the fall. Or hop on the Jitney to visit friends in the Hamptons in the summer. The more spontaneous the decision was, the more they relished it.

"No self-respecting New Yorker spends weekends in the city anyway," she would say.

Nick strongly disagreed but went along with her when she announced upcoming plans. He would've been just as happy to stay at home and read. He hated to admit it, but he especially loved it when her billionaire clients invited them on their drop-dead-gorgeous three-hundred-foot yacht for a sail around some heralded playground of the rich and famous, which happened a couple of times each year. Olivia adored the spectacular thrill of the yacht and all that came with it too. The outrageous behaviors of the yacht's owners and other guests left Nick completely agog and spouting his favorite line: "I should've been a shrink." He would say this and Olivia would respond, "Come on, Nicky. They're my best clients." She always hoped those trips would evolve into more business.

Actually, at the present time the yachtsman and his wife were her only active clients, but the project was winding down soon and there was nothing on the horizon. Obviously, not every getaway was on a private jet or a yacht. So, even though it was on a much less dramatic scale, they were really looking forward to their weekend escape to Charleston. Nick was excited to see the progress on the house and Olivia felt there was finally enough progress to show him.

Nick brought out the best in her, just as a truly great teacher should. She was her most gracious when she was with him. In return, she had introduced him to other worlds that were completely unattainable on a professor's salary. But perhaps most important, she made him feel young again. There was no price tag for rediscovered youth.

They stepped up to the car rental counter and a very cordial man named Ed greeted them. They signed the waiting paperwork, took the keys, and left.

"Boy, that was easy," Olivia said.

"Everything should be so easy," he said.

It was after one o'clock. Outside, the sun was so intense that they stopped midstride on the sidewalk to fish out their sunglasses and quickly put them on. Their sunglasses were in roundish tortoiseshell frames, another preference they shared. Hers were oversize, like Jackie O or Iris Apfel might have worn. His were strictly Ben Silver Charleston gentlemanly style, owlish and the kind a professor would choose. Often, in matters of their own personal taste, they lived up to their stereotypes. One would never mistake her for an academic or him for a designer.

"I'll drive," he said.

"Great! Then I can do my email."

The air was warm. There was a nice breeze and just enough humidity to throw her off balance. Olivia hated humidity. It did grotesque things to her hair and made her perspire in places that should not be discussed in polite company. How she would survive in this climate without a shower four times a day, she didn't know. Nick seemed impervious to sticky jungle weather. In fact, his linen shirt and trousers were barely wrinkled even though he'd been squished into a tiny seat for two hours like a human sardine. She marveled at that because her linen looked like she'd slept in it for a week. At least she thought so.

They found their sporty red SUV, lifted their luggage into the hatchback, cranked up the engine, and backed out of the space.

"You hungry?" Nick said.

"Not especially. Are you?"

"No, but I know from experience that I will be eventually."

Olivia giggled, and she was not a woman given to easy or frequent giggling before she met Nick.

"Well, listen," she said after deleting thirty-something pieces of junk mail and dropping her phone back into her bag, "I'm just a little anxious to see our house. So if your tummy can hang on a little while, let's drop off our stuff and then we can go grab a bite."

"All I want is a plate of fried shrimp at the Long Island Café," Nick said, adding, "But I can wait a bit."

"Okay," she said. "Thank you."

"And a chilly glass of a crisp sauvignon blanc."

"Mmm. That sounds delicious."

"They stop serving lunch at two-thirty."

She looked at her watch. It was already one-forty. She knew he was smiling without even looking at him.

"Well then, sir, we'd better hurry up and get there!"

You see? She wasn't always inflexible.

Soon Nick was opening the restaurant's front door for Olivia and then holding her seat for her at the table. In a matter of minutes, after he inspected and wiped the silverware with his napkin out of habit, they were eating the most perfectly fried shrimp in the entire South and the first tomatoes of the season. The tomatoes were reasonably good even though they were from Florida. An unspoken battle exists among the southern states about who produced the best tomatoes. If you are from Charleston, the richest tomatoes blossomed in the enchanted dirt of Johns Island just like Jack's beanstalk. There was a strong argument to be made for the tomatoes from Estill or Florence, but all these harvests wouldn't come in until the middle of June. This was late April. So until June, the nit-picking South Carolinian tomato aficionado had to step back and make himself happy with the fruits of Florida.

"Just think," Nick said. "Down here we can thrive on the Mediterranean diet and get really healthy. No more soufflés at Le Bernardin or cholesterol killer gargantuan steaks at Del Frisco's! None of those decadent cheese and charcuterie boards at Gramercy Tavern or chocolate death warrants from Daniel! No more, I say! We'll live to be one hundred and one!"

"I'll sort of miss the soufflés," Olivia said in a quiet voice. "And the chocolate."

Nick's enthusiasm evaporated as he realized yet again that Olivia wasn't one hundred percent bought into his monastic vision of their future. He really believed that refined sugar was a killer, but she'd never been particularly grateful for his lectures on topics that were not within the realm of his professional expertise. She should've been, he thought, but she just wasn't.

"Well, we'll just have to scour the town to find the perfect delectables for you! Surely someone in this town can make a soufflé?"

She smiled at him in a weak attempt to restore his mood. "I'm sure there is," she said. "Aren't there, like, three James Beard chefs here?"

"I think you're right!" Nick said, perking up again. "Maybe more. I think I read that somewhere. Don't worry, sweetheart. We'll find the devils and coax all manner of gourmet temptations out of them. I'll make it my personal mission."

"It's not the end of the world," she said.

"Well, if they can't be found, I'll learn to make a soufflé myself!"

"This I have to see," Olivia said and had a quiet chuckle over the mental image of Nick in a toque and a long apron to the floor, whipping egg whites in a copper bowl large enough to double as a baptismal font in a kitchen that looked like a bomb had exploded in it. She dipped the corner of her napkin in her water glass and wiped some tartar sauce away from the front of his shirt. He smiled at her. She smiled back.

"Can I get y'all anything else?" the waiter said, presenting the check. "Dessert? Coffee?"

Nick knew that if they wanted a piece of key lime pie or the bourbon chocolate pecan pie, the waiter would not have denied it to him in a million years, but it was getting on to three o'clock and he knew they had overstayed their welcome. The busy restaurant was empty of patrons except for them. And he was pretty sure the down-home desserts at that restaurant, wonderful as they were, couldn't compete with Daniel

Boulud's or Thomas Keller's sublime confections. It was an apples-to-oranges situation and unfair to compare.

"No, thank you," Nick said, handing him back the bill with his credit card. "But this was delicious. I dream about your shrimp."

"They truly are incredible," Olivia said, smiling honestly.

"Well, thanks! I'll tell the chef and I'll be right back with your receipt."

Nick leaned back in his chair and looked intently into Olivia's brown eyes. While their new locale might have lacked culinary arts to dazzle her Big Apple palate, his Lowcountry offered other, more deeply meaningful experiences. He was holding fast to his conviction that over time she'd understand the wisdom of his decision. And he would investigate the culinary scene. He remembered reading something in *The New York Times* about it not that long ago.

"I'm so crazy about you I don't know what to do with myself," he said.

"I feel the same way, sweetheart. Speaking of crazy, let's go see our crazy new house."

"Let's," he said and got up to pull her chair back. "You know, I didn't even think to ask. Are we going to be able to stay at the house tonight? Or did you make a hotel reservation for us?"

"Thank you, my love," she said and gently hung her handbag over her shoulder. "I have a surprise for you."

"Really? What's that?"

"We're glamping tonight."

"Oh! That sounds like something painful. You haven't been reading that *Fifty Shades* thing, have you?"

Olivia shook her head, smiling. They walked out into the parking lot.

"No, baby boy. It's a combo of glamour and camping. Glamorous camping!"

"Ah! Will your clever ways never cease?"

"I only hope you'll always find them to be clever," she said.

"Me too," he said and put his arm around her waist. "It would be a terrible thing to kick you to the curb and spend the rest of my life alone."

"Hush your mouth, Nicholas Seymour. You'll do no such thing! Tonight we will spend our first night in our new home together!"

"Get in the car, woman, and let's go see what horrors await us."

"Nothing like an old house when you're in search of horrors," Olivia said, shaking her head in agreement. "I just hope we have water and power. Jason promised we would."

"Yes, but let's get our priorities in order. Do we have a bed?"

A few days ago she brought huge shopping bags from Gracious Home into the office. The store was having a one-day sale and Olivia took full advantage of it. She asked Roni to ship the contents to Sullivans Island.

Of course Roni nodded her head and said, "No problem."

And they ordered a king-size mattress and box spring that her contractor promised to set up on a frame.

"What do *you* think? You mean, you don't want to sleep on the floor with me?" Olivia said, smiling.

"I'd sleep on a pile of rocks with you," he replied.

"Precious," she said and ran her perfectly manicured finger along his chin line.

The drive to their new/old house would take them a long ten minutes. They crept through the business district on the Isle of Palms across Breach Inlet, on the lookout for the police, who were infamous for pulling people over if they drove one hair over the speed limit. Sure enough, they spotted a patrol car hidden behind an overgrown oleander.

"Shouldn't they be out solving crimes?" she asked.

"That's the whole problem," Nick said. "They don't have enough crime here."

"Oh, brother!" she said. "Now I've heard it all." That just can't be true, she thought.

Moments later they rolled through the tiny business district of Sullivans Island. A casual observer might have thought the restaurants were giving away free food. Poe's Tavern and Home Team BBQ were filled to capacity with patrons, while scores of other people waited around for a table or crossed Middle Street, paying no mind to the traffic. Maybe they were getting ice cream or a newspaper or perhaps they had a hair appointment at Beauty and the Beach. Or maybe they were just so drunk on carbohydrates they were in a wheat stupor. It didn't matter. People were walking around in the street as though they were in the French Quarter post a Mardi Gras parade in New Orleans, utterly oblivious to cars, bicycles, and golf carts, which crawled, bobbed, and weaved to avoid hitting them. Strangely, no horns blared. People, pedestrians, and those with vehicles merely threw up the wave of a hand to say *Go ahead* or *Thanks.*

"I can remember when people referred to this island as sleepy," Nick said.

"Must've been a long time ago."

"Yeah, I guess it was."

"If this had been Manhattan, EMS would be doing triage."

"Truly. But the crowds are amazing. Did I ever tell you about the brilliant sign my old man made?"

"A sign?"

"Yes, he had a little workshop for himself in the back of the garage. I must've been a teenager because I was old enough to be embarrassed by it. This was when we had that house on Jasper Boulevard, and it was long before they built the connector bridge on the Isle of Palms."

"Nixon was in office?" Olivia wiggled her eyebrows, teasing him.

"No, FDR, thanks. Anyway, on the weekends the beaches on this island and the Isle of Palms were absolutely packed. Around four in the afternoon, traffic would start backing up, and if the Ben Sawyer Bridge opened, it got worse. People would get out of their cars and use your yard as their personal comfort station."

"What? *What* are you telling me?"

"Exactly what you think! These people would go to the beach and drink beer all day. Then they'd get in their car and get stuck in traffic. So when their eyeballs started swimming in their heads, they'd sneak around your oleander bush and, you know, *go*!"

"That's disgusting!"

"No argument there. And it also breaks a whole lot of laws. Never mind. Anyway, after my father catches this guy watering our yard, he got this ingenious idea to paint a sign."

"Which said?"

"It said, *Next Weekend Try Folly Beach!* It was enormous. My mother and I were horrified. Not Rick. He thought Dad was a riot."

"That is very funny," Olivia said. "Your dad must've been a character."

"He sure was. He was a great guy. My brother Rick is a lot like him."

"Isn't it funny how personalities are inherited? How's he doing?"

"No. He and Sheila are in Reno at an RV convention."

"They really love that whole RV thing, don't they?" Olivia said, and thought she'd rather sleep in a ditch than in an RV but she had enough elasticity in her to respect their choices, and some RVs were actually gorgeous.

"Yeah. They go all over the country. They have more friends than anyone I know."

"Probably because of his sense of humor. He's such a character."

"Just like our father was. But the personality thing? Yes. It is funny. Haven't you ever noticed that musicians give birth to musicians and engineers to engineers?"

"And I must come from a long line of pack rats. Whoa, this light is so bright!"

Olivia raised her hand to shield her eyes. Sunglasses alone were not enough to block the merciless glare of the Lowcountry's afternoon sun.

"It's almost summer. We should go into the awning business," Nick said. "We could make a killing."

"Maybe we should," Olivia said. "Awnings would sure make a lot of these houses more energy efficient."

"That's why people build houses with deep porches."

"Oh. But what about the second floors?"

"They need awnings."

They moved past the fire department and another small strip of stores and farther down the island to Fort Moultrie. They passed Stella Maris Church on their right and veered to the left.

"Next driveway," Olivia said.

"So this is it?" Nick said in surprise. "It's huge! I didn't remember it being this big!" What the hell has she done? he thought.

"It's deceiving because it's on stilts," she said, knowing he was right. "You'll see. It shrinks."

"I don't know, Olivia. I thought we agreed on something more modest."

"Listen, Nick, we both know that if I'm to continue to work, we have to have a statement property. I can't live in some ratty old cottage with lopsided floors and warped walls and then tell my clients they shouldn't."

"Right. Right." He knew it was true.

"I have to set a certain tone."

Nick inhaled and exhaled a sigh powerful enough to launch a paper ship across a swimming pool and said, "I suppose."

The yard was filled with trucks. A landscaper was consulting with someone from an irrigation service. Men on ladders were painting the sides of the house while others were walking across the roof. There were still other men throwing old insulation and other debris into a Dumpster and there was an outdoor toilet from Nature's Calling. And, as one would hope, they were all wearing sunglasses.

"Well, one thing's for sure. You know you've arrived when you have your own portable john," Nick said.

"Should have put one in your daddy's yard," Olivia joked.

"Truly," Nick said, "with a coin slot."

When he saw their SUV pull in, a handsome young man began walking toward them. Nick turned off the engine and got out, raising the hatchback with the click of a button. Olivia hopped out and joined him to retrieve her bag.

"Here's Jason," Olivia said. "He's our contractor."

"Really? He seems awfully young to me."

"No, he's not. We're just awfully old."

"Well, I just hate the hell out of that," Nick said.

Nick squinted his eyes in the young man's direction. In her peripheral vision, Olivia noticed Nick sucking in his stomach and standing up a little straighter. She bit the insides of her cheeks to hold back a burst of laughter.

"Let me help you with that, sir," Jason said, taking Nick's suitcase from him. "Ms. Ritchie? Let me take yours too."

"Thanks, Jason," Olivia said and handed over her duffel bag. "Nick? Say hello to Jason Fowler. He and his dad Sam own Sea Island Builders. And they do gorgeous work."

"I sure hope so," Nick said and shook Jason's hand.

Olivia thought, This place is a money pit. It was going to be a while before she would do more to the house than had already been done. How was she going to tell Jason that they had to stop for a while? How embarrassing would that be? It wouldn't be good for her business reputation, that much was certain.

"Nice to meet you, Mr. Ritchie."

"Seymour. My wife is Ritchie. She's liberated."

"Sorry?" Jason said.

"Honey? He's too young to even know what *liberated woman* means. Everybody's liberated these days."

Nick was smiling, but behind that smile Olivia knew Nick was irked. It was bad enough to have his students defer to him. His position and years on the faculty demanded it. But when it happened in his personal life, it startled him, and not in a good way. She began to think that neither one of them would ever adjust to the fact that middle age had arrived, even though on an actuarial table middle age was well behind both of them.

"Well," Jason said, "let's get your stuff inside. I'm anxious for y'all to see all we've done."

"Great," Olivia said.

They climbed the long flight of steps made of handmade bricks. Jason pushed the front door open and stepped aside for them to pass.

"Oh, Jason. The door looks really, really good," Olivia said, smiling and running her hand across the sheen of the varnish.

"Thanks! I had the guys refinish it and put the new/old hardware on it."

The heavy front door was made of oak, with raised panels on the bottom half and a large beveled leaded glass window framed in on the top. The handle was reclaimed, estate-sized, and made of solid brass that had been polished to a worthy shine. They stepped inside.

Olivia gasped and then smiled wide in surprise.

"Wow," she said, walking around the rooms near the entrance, staring from the floors to the ceilings and back to Jason's face. "Wow, Jason, nice work! It's amazing what you can do with a paintbrush, isn't it?"

"And about five hundred gallons of paint," Jason said with a grin.

"It's hard to believe it's the same place," Nick said. "I'm astonished!"

Gone were all the zany colors and dated window treatments that Nick recalled. Everything was painted in parachute white or linen white with warm tone-on-tone accents. The effect was quietly soothing and somehow regal. Yes, the old house that held nearly one hundred and fifty years of secrets, bad decisions, and, one had to assume, moments of great happiness had been coaxed back to life with countless swipes of paintbrushes.

The old dame was issuing a statement that she wasn't done living quite yet.

"It's beautiful, Jason. Simply beautiful! Have you started the bathrooms?"

"Just the one in the hall. What do you want to do with the swan?" Jason said.

"'Leda and the Swan,'" Nick said.

The reference sailed over Jason's head, but Olivia gave Nick a death look.

"I don't know. It's too passé to use, but too campy to just ditch."

"And weird," Jason said. "It's kind of creepy."

"Aha!" Nick said. "You see, Olivia? I told you that thing was, well, a *bothersome* talisman."

Nick loved the naughty implications of Yeats's poem and was always happy to debate whether what went on between Leda and the swan was consensual or rape.

Olivia shot Nick a look as if to say, *Let it go, okay?*

"Why don't we just ask one of the guys to clean it up and store it away. It might be fun to use as a spigot on a footbath or something," she said.

"A footbath?" Nick said.

"Yes, when you come off the beach, you can rinse your feet in a small basin," Olivia said. "Then you don't track sand into the house."

"Lots of people have them these days," Jason said.

"I see," Nick said while wondering, *Whatever happened to using a garden hose? Or a puddle of standing rainwater?* And, he thought, the elegant swan will be reduced to washing feet. A sad fate for Leda's lover indeed.

Olivia rolled her eyes at Nick, then went from room to room, thrilled with the outcome of her choices and Jason's work. Months ago she had asked Nick to choose drawer pulls and knobs for the kitchen and backsplash tiles. He had chosen well. Now, there they were, all in place, including the easy-care antibacterial Silestone quartz countertops that he loved.

"I can't wait to get in here and make a mess," Nick said.

"My sweet husband is the cook in our family," she said. "It's critical for him to love the kitchen. Otherwise we eat my cooking and die."

"I'm thrilled with this kitchen," Nick said. "Are you kidding me? It's gorgeous!"

"Well then, I'm thrilled if you're thrilled," Jason said.

Olivia thanked Jason over and over, and he just beamed with pride and relief. True to his word, there was a mattress and box spring on a metal frame in the bedroom.

"This house has great bones," Jason said.

"I sure couldn't see them," Nick said.

"That's why you have me," Olivia said and blew Nick an air kiss.

At 4:01, pretty much on the nose, the yard was a ghost town. Everyone was gone. They finally had the house to themselves.

"I'm glad you're happy with the house," Olivia said, her eyes sparkling with tiny gold flecks.

"Well, I'm really happy to be here with you." Nick said, thinking, There's no way we need a house this grand.

After a dinner of crudo and tilefish at Coda del Pesce on the Isle of Palms, and a glass of wine on the front porch over the water, counting the stars and watching the moon rise, they drove home, turned off the lights, and went to their new bedroom and almost collapsed in their new bed.

Olivia had dressed the bed as though *Southern Living* magazine was coming in to do a shoot. It was covered in all white Sferra linens, embroidered with French knots and open fretwork on the borders. She'd bought unscented pillar candles, put them on plates, and covered them with hurricane globes. She'd brought in gorgeous white Turkish towels and beautiful hand-milled soaps and bathrobes with their initials on them. It was the last shopping spree she would have for a while, even if these items had been on sale.

"Glamping, you say?" Nick said, buttoning his pajama top.

"Yep," she said and blew out the last candle. "I need to buy lamps."

"I imagine there's a long list of what we'll need." He kissed her forehead and slipped into bed, yawning loudly.

Yes, and I hate to think about what it will cost, she thought.

The moon and the lights from the city across the harbor poured through their windows, making it possible for her to safely navigate the room. She was completely exhausted. Between flying and decisions and wine, she knew she'd be asleep in minutes. Nick was already snoring like a baby panda, emitting small puffs with the tiniest snorts. She climbed in bed and pulled the covers over her shoulders. Just as she was drifting off, she heard a thump and her eyes sprang wide open. She lay as still as she could and listened. There was a scurry and another thump. She gave Nick's shoulder a shake.

"Nick!" she whispered. "Nick! Wake up! There's someone upstairs!"

"What? What the devil?"

Then he was quiet and still and they listened together.

Thump! Rustle! Thump!

"Go on back to sleep, sweetheart. I'll get some traps in the morning," Nick said.

"For what?"

"Rats. Marsh rats. Not Jack the Ripper."

Moments later he was snoozing again, but Olivia's body temperature skyrocketed and she began to perspire. Rats? Rats in the house? More than one? Oh, God! Humidity? Okay. Mosquitoes? Sort of okay. *But rats?* Rats were a DEALBREAKER.

Oh? It's *only* marsh rats? she thought. *Only* marsh rats? Oh, that's good, because for a minute there, I thought it was, like, a serious problem! Exactly what distinguished a marsh rat from other rats? Size? The size of their teeth? Their preference for female human flesh? Face flesh? Her mind was racing and her heart pounding. Had she spent money she didn't have to live in a house infested with Willard's little friends? What had she done? She wanted to weep. Or scream. Or run. Instead, she crept from her bed and stuffed the bottom of the bedroom door with her brand new Yves Delorme towels and pushed their luggage against it. Then she prayed for her life. And of course she said a prayer for Nick too. She wasn't even sure they could afford the bait for the traps.

CHAPTER 2

back in new york

The rat problem had been handled quickly, efficiently, and to everyone's satisfaction.

"You'll never hear another one," Jason said.

"I can't deal with rats, Jason," Olivia said.

"My mom couldn't either," he said.

She wanted to run to Bergdorf's and buy neck creams for thousand-year-old women.

Olivia and Nick were back home in their Manhattan apartment packing the treasures they intended to take to South Carolina. Nick had strong feelings about severely editing their possessions. He wanted to get rid of all their antiques, except for his desk and his favorite pair of chairs. Any rug worth more than a thousand dollars was leaving. All of their paintings, with the exception of two small ones, were to be sold as well. Of the two they were keeping, one was an oil on canvas painted by William Glackens from his flowers-in-a-glass series, and the other was a smallish Guy Wiggins depicting American flags strung along Fifth Avenue on a snowy day. So their precious rock crystal and regency bronze lamps, their Georgian silver serving pieces and flatware, their Persian rugs, their finer ceramics, and all of their skeleton clocks were going to Sotheby's to be featured in a home sale with the remains of another estate. They were de-accessioning—according to Nick, that is.

Olivia had her own plan. She didn't want to part with a safety pin. She fought hard to keep her silver tea service and won that battle. *What will my clients think if I don't have a tea service? Shall I serve tea or coffee in your lovely Channel 13 mugs?* After the dust settled on that front, she pretended to go along with Nick's wishes because she had never seen him take such an authoritative stand on anything. But she had been quietly squirreling things away at her office and storage unit that she had no intention of selling—her fabrics, cloisonné boxes, the puzzle balls, her favorite French clock, and her precious netsukes—all of which would never hear the auctioneer's gavel drop. In Nick's mind, he was practically Moses leading Olivia out of the desert of a soulless Manhattan to the Promised Land, where they needed next to nothing.

"We're moving to the edge of the Atlantic Ocean, Olivia. Right in the middle of hurricane territory. When a storm's coming, you can't start tearing up the house. What are you going to do? Roll up a huge rug and throw it over your shoulder? Or unhang paintings and throw all these ceramics in the trunk of the car? You just can't do that."

"I'm aware, but we don't have to get rid of *everything*. You can't expect me to just turn into a bohemian!"

"Why not? I think you'd make a lovely bohemian!"

"Nicholas!"

Smirking, he was teasing her and was a bit surprised that she put up such a fight. Why couldn't she simply accept his logic and go along with him? God, he loved that hellcat streak of hers. It made his trousers twitch.

"When we get to the island I'm going to start wearing hats and flip-flops!" he said through another smirk, and eyes narrowed, continued: "Yes, and I need a good fishing hat. Wasn't there an L.L.Bean catalog in today's mail?"

"Good Lord! Fishing hats? People will talk about you!"

"I hope they do! *Have you seen old Nick Seymour? He's as peculiar as the day is long!*"

"Good grief!" she said nervously. "Anyway, I've given this whole weather issue a great deal of thought. It's serious, and this is where my pillowcase theory applies, you know."

"You have a pillowcase theory? God, you're so adorable. Okay, let's hear what a pillowcase theory is."

"Well, I will tell you, but if we are to live in such a dangerous place, before we do anything else, I think we have to take some basic precautions."

"Precautions? We're not moving to a third world country, you know," he said, chuckling.

"Please. I know that. But I think we need an SUV, Nick. I really do. I mean, if a bad storm is coming and we have to evacuate, we will need a vehicle with four-wheel drive. Agreed? Charleston can be a bit like Venice, you know."

"Yes, an SUV probably is a good idea. I mean, what with the waters of the Adriatic Sea drowning the pigeons in the Piazza San Marco and flooding Lockwood Boulevard simultaneously."

He snickered and she cut her eyes at him, another habit of hers that excited him. There was a flicker of an amber flame in her eyes. He would have sworn it on a stack of Bibles.

"Right. So, the first things we would need to grab if we have to evacuate are our important papers. Traum Safe is installing a small vault for us in two weeks. It's not the largest one they manufacture, but it's big enough to hold our papers, jewelry, and passports and any cash we might have at home."

"Wait a minute. Darling, we don't have a safe *here*, so why do we need one *there*?"

"For peace of mind, Nicholas. Peace of mind. This safe is waterproof and fireproof, and it will be connected to the police department through our alarm system in case someone breaks in."

She was as dead serious as he was incredulous.

"Olivia? What are you thinking? Crime on Sullivans Island? Blasphemy! It's the safest place in the world. I've told you this over and over. I mean, the only reason we even *have* a police force is to handle the overserved and the occasional speed demon."

"Really? Well then, tell me this. Houses never burn down?"

"Well, yes, especially when careless people fry their own turkeys on Thanksgiving. Now the Sullivans Island fire department will do it for you. Did I tell you that? At no charge! Isn't that, I don't know, *charming*?"

"That's very nice, but, Nick, the house we bought is made of *wood. Old* wood. What if we go off to Asheville or someplace for the weekend and a bunch of kids decide to have a bonfire on the beach in front of our house. The wind changes direction and the fire travels across the dunes and ignites our house? Poof! Gone!"

"I see what you're saying, but that's why we pay insurance premiums," Nick said, and realized right then that Olivia was obviously suffering with some other anxieties he had failed to recognize. "And that's another reason why we don't want to have things at the beach that are irreplaceable."

"Speak for yourself!" She heard the volume of her voice rising, something she detested. *Shrill women should be shot*, she'd been heard to say often. She took a deep breath and spoke again. Calmly. "I just want to protect what we are taking, that's all. Anyway, if there's a storm coming with a name and a category attached to it, I think we ought to be able to place anything of value in a few pillowcases and run if we have to. That's the pillowcase theory." Maybe she had dreamed of such a storm. She wasn't quite sure then.

"I see. But run? Running from a hurricane at the last moment is highly unlikely. We'd have lots of notice. Tell me this. Does this irrational fear of yours have anything to do with living in a freestanding house instead of an apartment building?"

She was wrapping the black and white Staffordshire dogs in Bubble Wrap.

"What do you mean by *that*? I'm going to miss my precious dogs."

She was caught completely off guard by the question, and what did he mean by irrational?

"Yes, but you don't need them. Well, you haven't lived in a freestanding house since you were ten years old."

"What do you mean? We've stayed with friends in houses all over the place."

"Yes, but they were there at the time. A big wide-open house without a boozy doorman and a handyman who doesn't speak English might make you feel vulnerable. Is that possible?"

"What?"

He watched as she considered his words and then as the irritation literally dissolved from her face. Finally she laughed and shook her head. "Nicholas Seymour! You've done it again."

"What did I do?" Peace was apparently restored, and he was uncertain how or why.

"You found the words that perfectly describe this awful dread I'm feeling. It's like I'm short of breath all the time."

Nick put down the small volume of poetry he was wrapping and went over to her. He took her in his arms and hugged her warmly, at last placing a kiss on her forehead.

"My dear Olivia, I love you so much. And if you feel better with a vault in the house, get a vault. In fact, get *two* vaults and *two* SUVs. I only want your happiness!"

"Oh, Nicky! You are such a darling."

"I don't know about all that. My point is, I just don't want to be owned by our possessions anymore. That's all. Living at the beach is supposed to be carefree! Although, I must say, your pillowcase theory is genius."

"You do realize that your newfound '*less is more*' philosophy deeply conflicts with how I make my living? I can't go around like Gandhi in a loincloth with a bowl and stick, you know."

"I wouldn't mind seeing you in a loincloth." He wiggled his eyebrows at her and she suppressed a laugh.

"Nick, I'm serious! When I design a living space, I accessorize it too. You *know* that. If a client visits me and there are no accessories to be seen, how would they think I have the wherewithal to provide them with the atmosphere they want?"

"You have a point. Keep two dogs."

Oh? She thought. Now he's going to kill off my dogs too?

"Olivia. Be honest. This apartment looks like Dickens's *Old Curiosity Shop*! We're drowning in bric-a-brac, knickknacks, and tchotchkes! We need to lighten our load, Olivia. We really do. We need a new equilibrium."

She looked around at the hundreds of stacked art books,

Rigaud candles, needlepointed pillows, Meissen figurines, and Staffordshire dogs of every size and coloration that were strewn about the room, perched on shelves and tucked into end tables, and she had to agree. It *was* too much.

"Okay," she said. "Okay."

He handed her a pack of Post-its and said, "Here. Put one of these on each of the things you can't live without. Then let's see what we've got."

"Good grief. This is exactly what I tell my clients to do!"

The building's internal house phone rang. They had a delivery or a visitor. Nick picked it up.

"Hello," he said.

"Mr. Seymour, Ms. Maritza Vasile to see you and Ms. Ritchie. Sir. Um. Shall I send her up? Up? I said that, didn't I?"

Maritza Vasile the Chatterbox was Olivia's billionaire client with the huge yacht, and their doorman was fully baked at three in the afternoon. What was Nicholas going to say? He had no choice, so he mentally kissed his peaceful afternoon good-bye.

"Of course! Send her right up!" He hung up the house phone and grumbled.

"Who is it, sweetheart? The butcher? I ordered lamb chops from Lobel's for dinner." Like most true New Yorkers they had nearly everything in their lives delivered.

"Wonderful, but no, dear. It's Maritza. I'll be hiding in my study."

"You shouldn't be like that, you know. Where are my shoes?" Her eyes traveled all around the room. Olivia thought it was an unforgivable vulgarity to meet a client in her stocking feet.

"Excuse me, I am a tenth-generation South Carolinian and a bona fide gentleman who never thought it was possible for a woman to be *too southern.* Until I met Maritza. Until *she* appeared . . ."

"Oh, come on now," she said as she located one of her rogue slippers from behind an open box and the other from underneath the skirt of the sofa and slipped them on. "Gosh, this place is a mess! It's not her fault she's so . . ."

"No, I agree. I'm not assigning blame," he said. "A Delta daughter married a Yankee challenge and then gave birth to another challenge, and the trials and chaos force her mind to retreat further and further into the most extreme parlance of the boondocks."

"True. You can take the girl out of Mississippi, but you can't . . . And don't forget she has to deal with Bob's ex-challenges too—that crazy ex-wife of his and that peculiar son. Wait, she has *all* the ex-wives to deal with!"

"True, and I shall pray in earnest for them all. Nonetheless, I'll be in my study. Brooding."

"Fine," she said. "I don't really blame you."

She hurried to the door to open it for Maritza and then hurried back to try to quickly establish order to her living room. That anyone would just drop in without calling ahead would normally provoke a heavy frost from Olivia, but being provoked with the blond bombshell that was Maritza was like getting mad at a puppy. There simply was no point. Puppies could not restrain themselves from wide-eyed, waggy-tail behavior. Maritza had the effervescence of a bounding litter of ten. If you corrected her manners, it would crush her soul. Worse, Maritza might find another decorator.

Olivia stacked some empty boxes and pushed a few others against the wall, ran her fingers through her hair, and spun around toward her foyer just in time to hear her elevator close and to hear Maritza call out, "Hellooooo? Anybody home?"

"In here! In here! What a lovely surprise! How wonderful!"

All one hundred voluptuous pounds of Maritza Vasile seemed to be in perpetual motion as she tottered into Olivia's foyer on spike-heeled gladiator sandals and a bright Pucci print tunic worn over narrow-legged turquoise Capri pants. Her longish blond hair was layered and coaxed into bouncing ringlets and her oversize Gucci sunglasses had a metallic trim that more or less tied into the jangling blaze of gold jewelry she was wearing.

"I was just shopping. I'm so sorry to barge in this way, but . . ."

"No! Please! I'm so happy you did!"

Air kisses ensued. *Muah! Muah!* As she leaned in, Olivia quickly decided Maritza had spent an inordinate amount of time sampling perfumes, probably in the lower level of Bergdorf Goodman. The evidence besides the mushroom cloud of fragrance was the small lavender shopping bag she pushed toward Olivia. In it was another Rigaud candle, exactly like the ones she was about to discard.

"Momma always said, 'Never go calling without a sursy!'" Maritza said, and smiled. "I know you love these."

"Oh! I do! Thank you! How sweet of you!" Olivia opened the box and sniffed, and the strong scent of jasmine immediately made her throat itch. "Delicious!" She lied. She despised jasmine. "Come in. Please, sit. Tell me what's happening."

"You tell me what's happening! All these boxes? You're really moving, aren't you?"

"Yes, we are really moving. But you know that this changes nothing between us."

"Oh, I know that. What other interior designer would I call? I just hate the idea of you not being right across the park, that's all."

"Well, we'll both have to learn to Skype!"

"Skype! Yes! I always forget about that!"

"Anyway," Olivia said in a conspiratorial whisper, "I have to give living in the South a try. Charleston just means the world to Nick."

"The things we do for love," Maritza said.

"Amen. And I'd do anything in the world for Nick."

"He's a precious heart."

"He sure is!" Except when he's counting my Staffordshire dogs.

"I'd love to move back to Mississippi someday, but I can't see Bob chasing flies and skeeters off the screen porch with a swatter."

"Probably not," Olivia said, but thought, How's never?

"I miss my family something awful. You know? I was thinking to myself that there's nothing really stopping me from taking Gladdie down there for a family visit. My momma's got a weak heart and she's living all by her lonesome with her housekeepers. I worry about her."

"Maritza? If she's living in her own home, she's probably stronger than you know."

"Maybe, but not a day goes by that I don't worry about her."

"Well then, go pay her a visit! If she was my mother, I'd go see her."

"You know what? You're right! Maybe I'll go after Memorial Day! But it's just such a royal pain in the derriere because we can't land the jet in Cartaret. So I have to fly to Jackson, get a car, and drive to Momma's. And I can't bring Ellen, so it's just me and Gladdie, and let me tell you, y'all know I love your goddaughter with all my heart and soul, but Lord, she can be so rambunctious!"

This would be the understatement of the day, Olivia thought. "And why can't you bring Ellen to help you?"

"Are you serious? If I go down there with a nanny? By Monday, everybody at the processing plant and Wally World would be running their mouths about it! They'd turn the chickens loose on me and I'd get pecked to death!"

"Good grief," Olivia said and pushed the image of thousands of rabid chickens from her mind.

Cartaret, Mississippi—population under six thousand—held the distinction of being home to the second-largest chicken-processing plant in the world. And a Walmart, which was its saving grace. Of course there was a coffee shop, where Maritza had learned to cook, which by the twists and turns of God's grace led to her position on Bob's yacht and then into his bed.

"Olivia? Y'all got a Co-Cola? I'm 'bout as parched as I can be!"

"You know I do! I keep them just for you!" Olivia held up one finger, meaning she'd pour her a glass of Coke and be right back.

"Oh, gosh! Thanks, Olivia. I'll just make myself at home."

Olivia slipped away to the wet bar in her butler's pantry, leaving Maritza to drape herself across a chaise covered in ice-blue silk twill, which served as the perfect backdrop for the kaleidoscope of her flamboyant tunic.

Olivia snapped the metal cap from the cold bottle and poured it over tiny square ice cubes in a Baccarat tumbler. She put the glass and the bottle on a starched cocktail napkin resting on a small hotel silver tray. It wasn't a question of style so much as she didn't want the icy chill of the glass to loosen the skin on her ivory shagreen end table, and she found coasters to be . . . well, to be honest, never as aesthetically pleasing as linen and silver. She returned to the living room and placed the tray carefully on the table next to Maritza.

"Oh, my! Dahlin'! Thank you! You make me feel so glamorous with all this hullabaloo for a little ol' Coke!"

"It's my pleasure. So tell me, what's new?"

"Well, that's the reason I dropped in, you see. I have the most amazing news, so I wanted to tell you in person!" Maritza picked up her glass and drained it, refilling it with the remainder of the bottle.

"Wonderful! Let's hear!"

"Memorial Day? Y'all are still free, aren't you?"

"Yes, of course! You asked us to save the weekend."

"Well, so . . . drum roll, please! Bob is going to fly all of us to the Caribbean, and he's rented Necker Island! Can you *believe* it?"

"Great heavens! Really? The whole island?"

Necker Island was seventy-four acres of pure hedonistic fantasy located in the British Virgin Islands and just one of many dramatic properties owned by Richard Branson. Olivia was stunned.

"Yes! And hang on to your hat—it comes with a *private submarine*! We can take it out to look at the fish, and then we don't have to snorkel!" Maritza got up, did a little shimmy, and then sat down again. She was very excited. "God, I *hate* snorkeling! I just hate to put my face in the water, don't you? Having our own submarine will just make everything so much easier. Don't you think so?"

"Yes, of course," Olivia said, forcing a tight smile. "Can I get you another Coke?"

"Golly, that would be so nice!"

Olivia returned to the butler's pantry with the empty bottle and glass and thought, With my claustrophobia? Hell would freeze before anyone would convince Olivia Ritchie to climb into a personal submarine. Then she was struck by the bizarre fact that Maritza thought saving her hair and makeup (cost: maybe three hundred) with access to your very own personal submarine (cost: one zillion) was a mere charming convenience when just five years ago she was wearing short shorts and a tight T-shirt, slinging hash below deck for the crew on Bob's yacht.

It dawned on Maritza that her description of the submarine might have sounded obnoxiously entitled, so she followed Olivia and stood leaning against the doorframe and began recounting her day.

"So the very minute he told me, I called Maia K. at Bergdorf's and we spent the whole morning tracking down every caftan in creation. I bought really retro sunglasses like Jane Wyman wore in *A Magnificent Obsession*? Remember her?"

"Of course!"

"And we found these fabulous giant-sized hats for day, which I need because my hair will fry like all get-out. The last thing I need is straw instead of hair. And I bought a pile of fabulous chiffon caftans and open-toed mules for night."

"Sounds very dramatic! I love it!"

"Yeah. I figured I'd be a glamour puss and see if I can't jump-start Bob's, you know, love machine?" She giggled and turned red in the face.

Olivia thought, Oh, boy. This is a lot more than I want to know. She turned to Maritza with another lockjawed smile and a full glass of Coke, and they returned to the living room together.

"You know, when I was a kid, we used to get us these little bottles of Coke and pour a nickel bag of salted peanuts in them and shake it up. They'd bubble up and overflow and then we'd drink it, making a mess, choking on the nuts."

"Why in the world would you do that?"

"You know what? I don't know! 'Cuz kids are stupid, I guess. And back home there wasn't much going on. I guess shaking up a Coke with a pack of peanuts was a big deal."

"Well, kids are silly, which BTW, I think is a good thing. So tell me some more about the trip! I'm so excited!"

"We're gonna have such a great time! I just know it! So if y'all can leave on Thursday . . ."

"We can."

"Great! Then we'll fly out of Teterboro. Bob's bringing *Le Bateau de l'Amour* down in case we don't like the island."

Le Bateau de l'Amour was Bob Vasile's yacht, which was roughly the size of a football field. It had eight staterooms with *en suite* marble bathrooms, two fireplaces, two living rooms, indoor and outdoor dining rooms, an elevator, two hot tubs, a gym, and just about every gorgeous detail that existed for yacht fittings, including a media room, a wine cellar, and a salon. The owners' suite and the library were recently featured in *Yachting Magazine.* His crew of thirty moved it around the world, never touching an American dock so as to avoid paying personal property taxes. It was purchased with the assets of his proverbial fatted calf—a chain of fifty or so steak houses and his vineyards in Napa and a partnership in Burgundy. The vineyards supplied and refurbished the wine cellars and lists of the restaurants. His businesses were a dovetailing moneymaker, to say the least. Recently, Bob bought a vitamin company because after decades of a debauched existence, he now wanted to live forever. And he became vegan, just to see if he could. Being vegan didn't last long.

"I can't imagine we wouldn't like Necker Island, can you?"

"Of course not, but you know my Bob! When he wants to leave, we leave! If he doesn't like something, we get rid of it! So I can promise you on my daddy's grave if Bob doesn't like Necker, we'll be getting on the boat."

Olivia just shook her head. This was a lot to absorb.

"So I shouldn't completely unpack until we know how he's feeling?"

"Honey? Unpack? Don't wreck your nails! There's someone to do that for us!"

"Oh," Olivia said. She was unsure of how to respond. She was always slightly embarrassed that someone was going to unpack her clothes. "You're bringing Gladdie, I hope?"

Gladdie was Maritza's precocious four-year-old daughter, who was conceived as soon as the ink was dry on Bob's divorce papers. Or maybe before, but who was counting? Nick referred to little Gladdie as Maritza's job security. Bob absolutely adored little Gladdie.

"Of course! But how about this? She told me over breakfast that she doesn't want to share her stateroom with Ellen. She wants me to sleep with her and for Ellen to stay with Bob! How crazy is that?"

"Kids," Olivia said, smelling trouble. "Who else is coming?"

Ellen was the nanny. Olivia had known Bob for aeons, having decorated and redecorated different properties for his numerous wives and girlfriends. He definitely, definitely liked the ladies. Before Nick came along, when Bob was almost in between wives again, Bob had put the moves on her too. Olivia had assured him that even as cute as he could be, she'd prefer a friendship and a professional relationship because it could last a lifetime. He had laughed and said that she was right, his lovers did seem to have a short shelf life, and a great friendship was born that still endured.

"You're just like the sister I never had, Olivia," Bob said to her then.

"Oh, Bob! You're going to make me weep with happiness!" Olivia said, pretending to be emotional for about one second, which he knew was a joke.

"You're a shrewd one, Olivia Ritchie," he said.

"Yep, but I'm one hundred percent on your team," she said. "Forever."

"It's okay if I love you a little, isn't it?"

"Yes, but only a little."

And it seemed the ladies kept getting younger, as though a younger woman could keep him from getting older. Oh, Bob, Bob, Bob, Olivia thought.

Maritza continued, "Well, Bob's golf pro and his wife and his friend Buddy the dermatologist and his wife and my shrink Annie and her partner . . ."

"Your shrink? I thought I was your shrink!"

"That's funny! Listen, you know Bob and I have been going through a rough patch since Gladdie was born, and I just want her to see what goes on."

A four-year-long rough patch? "Of course she should come! That's a really brilliant idea, Maritza."

Maritza's face changed, becoming sad, and it suddenly seemed she might burst into tears.

"To be totally honest, Olivia? I'm at the end of my rope. I just feel like everyone hates me."

"Oh, come on, now. You know that's not true."

"Well," Maritza said as one bulbous tear rolled over her bottom eyelid and down her cheek. "You'll see. Pay attention and you'll see. Even half of the *crew* on the boat is hostile to me, like I'm the first woman on the planet to break rank and marry the boss. And his son hates me because he thinks I'm spending his inheritance, and his friends don't like me. Oh, God. I just have all this anxiety in my heart and I just feel like everyone is judging me! And they are!" She sniffed and wiped her face with the back of her hand. But the tears began to fall despite her best efforts to hold them back. She sighed deeply. "Oh, look at me! I'm sorry! I'm such a mess!"

Olivia felt terrible for her. "No, you're not a mess! You're fine! And I'm sure that whatever you're worrying about is probably exaggerated for some other reason. We all get upset sometime."

"No, I just barged in here and I'm so sorry to boohoo like this. But, Olivia, I just can't take it anymore." She took a deep breath and sighed in ragged puffs, struggling to regain her composure. Finally she put her head in her hands and sobbed like a child.

Olivia reached into the drawer of the end table and pulled out a few tissues (kept there because of her dislike of tissue boxes), handing them to her. Then she put her arm around Maritza's shoulders and gave her a squeeze, hoping to comfort her. She spoke to her tenderly as she would have spoken to a daughter if she'd had one.

"Oh, my dear! Please don't fret for one tiny second over dropping by! You didn't barge in, Maritza. You couldn't. My door is *always* open to you! We're friends. Good friends! You can come to me any time of the day or night, and I mean that!"

The poor girl, Olivia thought. She has zero confidence and

probably for good reason. What in the world was Bob up to now? As she thought this, she knew the answer. There were men—not many, but more than a few—who lost interest in women after they had given birth. It was like someone flipped the libido switch in their heads (and elsewhere), and the mothers of their children were damned into eternal sexual exile without so much as an a cappella rendition of "*Thanks for the Memory.*"

Maritza blew her nose loudly and carefully blotted her eyes, which had mink eyelash extensions applied so densely that they resembled tiny dollhouse awnings. Eyelash extensions were among many current trends in the world that were not on Olivia's *must-have* list.

"Everyone hates me, Olivia," Maritza said. "They do. You'll see."

"Well, I sure don't. And neither does Nick," Olivia said, and thought, This poor girl is miserable. She felt very sad for her.

Maritza smiled at Olivia then and said, "Oh, dahlin', you are so gracious. It's like you're almost southern!"

Coming from Maritza, this was high praise. And considering the source, Olivia took it as such.

"If I have any southern in me, I must get it from Nick," she said, smiling because Maritza was smiling again.

"Aren't southern men just irresistible? Your Nick is so dahlin', isn't he?"

"I sure think he is," Olivia said and looked at her wristwatch.

Maritza stood to gather her things and leave. "Well, I've probably overstayed my welcome, but I just have to tell you this one other itty-bitty thing."

Olivia stood, relieved that the visit was coming to an end.

"No such thing!" she said and thought, Mother Machree, please bring this to a close! "Tell me."

"Well, my daddy used to always say that the Lord will provide, and honey, he sure did provide me with the best friend I could ever want on the day I met you."

"Oh, Maritza! You are so sweet!" Olivia said, and hugged her again, feeling even worse for her.

"No, I'm serious! You're the one who saves my sanity. I know you have my back."

"You may depend on it," Olivia said, walking her to the door.

"We have opera tonight," Maritza said. "We're seeing *Rigoletto* for the fifth time. Taking clients out. I'll just be sitting there thinking about shoes."

It did not escape Olivia's notice that Maritza was playing with a glass orb from the entrance-hall table, tossing it from hand to hand. The small but lovely piece was hand blown by the craftsmen of Steuben in the eighties. It rested on a small convex base. Maritza had the poor habit of fiddling with the property of others.

"You're too funny. But truly, how much Verdi can a girl bear?"

"Truly!" Maritza said and replaced the orb on the table.

Then Maritza smiled again, revealing her very sweet nature, which was without guile of any kind. Olivia realized then that despite the widely held opinion that Maritza was a gold-digging whore from nowhere, she truly loved Bob, unlike his previous wives. It was nice that Bob had billions, but he had a big fat problem in the fidelity department, and this poor young woman was struggling to hold her marriage together like any other wife. Well, almost like any other wife. But she was a straight-up nice southern girl, too conventional to accept

Bob's infidelities and too kind to understand his jaded friends. Olivia picked up the orb and its base.

"Here," she said. "I want you to have this."

"Oh! No! I couldn't!"

"Yes. Take it. I want you to put it somewhere in your apartment where you can see it. When you're feeling low, pick it up. Think of it as, I don't know, like I'm there with you. Okay?"

Maritza took it and dropped it into her oversize tote bag.

"Thanks, Olivia. I'll treasure it."

It seemed for a moment that she might start to cry all over again. Olivia was spared any further drama by the ping of the elevator arrival, and she moved quickly to hold the door for Maritza.

"Let's talk tomorrow!" Maritza said with all the brightness she could muster.

Later, when Olivia and Nick were sharing a lump crabmeat cocktail over martinis at Del Frisco's, Olivia told Nick about Maritza's predicament.

"She was completely undone. I'll tell you, she really loves the old son of a gun," she said. "Are you going to eat that olive?"

Nick speared the olive with his toothpick and fed it to her. "If you live long enough, you'll see everything. At least that's what my old man always said. Necker Island, huh?"

"Yep."

"God, I love/hate going on vacation with them," Nick said.

"Oh, suffer. It's necessary for business and besides, I'll make it worth your while," Olivia said.

CHAPTER 3

necker island

It was overcast, drizzling, and actually quite chilly for the end of May. The forecast was not promising for the holiday weekend in the New York area.

"Let's have a moment of silence for all those poor people who spent their last dime to rent a summer house in the Hamptons," Olivia said, grateful they were not among them.

"Boy, I'll say! What does a four-bedroom go for these days?"

"Well, if it has a pool, probably forty thousand or more. That's not even for a house on the water. Rents can still be really obscene."

"And oceanfront?"

"Don't even think about it, baby boy."

They had checked and rechecked the weather for the Virgin Islands, and it was supposed to be perfect—a balmy eighty degrees in the water and on land. Feeling generous, Nick made the chivalrous decision to show some enthusiasm for the trip itself and to be a team player for Olivia's sake. It was the right thing for him to do. He would always balk and complain before they went on one of these trips. Then he would come around. When they finally got to wherever they were going, Nick had a fine time.

"I've looked at Necker Island online, and I must say it does look like paradise itself. It really does."

"I love you for doing this," she said, silently hoping that this trip would somehow produce new business.

"Oh, it's fine really. I mean, you've endured some painfully dry faculty dinners. I owe you."

"Yes, that is true enough, but how terrible could it be to have an entire island to ourselves?"

"Well, speaking as an academic with an interest in anthropology, I will find it interesting to see if the natives go native!"

"I think there will be plenty of shenanigans. We have a possible nanny-gate on the horizon."

"Oh, dear. If it's not the butler, it's the nanny," Nick said.

When Olivia and Nick finally cleared the usual horrific traffic in the Lincoln Tunnel and arrived at the Teterboro Airport, they were met by Maritza, who was pacing the front door area with nervous excitement. Maritza hurried to give them a big hug.

"Hey! Y'all are here! How're y'all doing?" *Muah! Muah!* "I'm so happy y'all made it! Bob's tied up in a meeting, but he'll be here directly. Nick? Do you remember Buddy? And Michelle?" She pointed in their direction. "Can I help you with that, Nick?"

"No, I've got it. Thanks."

Olivia noticed Nick's scowl.

He whispered to Olivia, "Do I appear to be infirm in any way?"

"No, sweetheart," she whispered back.

Part of the group was assembled in the plush waiting area. Bob Vasile's best childhood friend, Buddy Bemis, and his willowy wife, Michelle, were there with Ellen the nanny and Gladdie. Buddy popped up from the deep leather sofa like a man catapulted, which struck Olivia as funny.

"Hey! How are you, Olivia? Nice to see you again, Nick."

"Yes, yes," Nick said, "and you too!"

Michelle looked up from where she sat, curled up like a cat, and gave an anemic roll-of-the-fingers wave to Olivia and Nick. Then she dropped her eyes, returning to flipping the glossy pages of the June issue of *Wine Spectator*. That gesture said it all: if ennui had been a disease, she would've been dead years ago. Michelle's claim to fame was that she produced wine for Bob's restaurants in her family's many vineyards in Burgundy and Saint-Tropez. And Bob owned a small percentage of one of them. Olivia was suspicious that she imbibed slightly too much for the overall good of her health. Nevertheless, Michelle was a woman of her own means to the point that Buddy didn't really have to practice medicine, but how much golf could a man play?

"Michelle?" Nick said and returned a small, unacknowledged wave of equal value to Michelle. He then turned away and discreetly squirted his hands with a pocket-size hand sanitizer.

Olivia shook hands with Buddy, nodded to Michelle, and remembered Michelle's world-weary attitude was one reason Nick did not care to travel with Bob's friends. But Buddy wasn't a total disaster. He was a successful dermatologist, and at least he was reasonably gregarious. How Michelle spent her spare time was anybody's guess. Mostly she appeared to be marinating in a mood.

"Got a very low ceiling out there," Buddy said. "I hope we can get out!"

"Yes, the weather's not ideal," Nick replied.

They all turned at once to look through the large windows, but their focus was shattered by a juvenile screech.

"It's mine!" Gladdie exclaimed loudly. "Gimme it!"

Gladdie jerked an iPad away from Ellen, who was perched with a beauty queen's posture on the edge of the coffee table. Olivia looked at Nick's face, which read, *How many days will we have the pleasure of enduring your godchild?* And when Nick read Olivia's face, it said, *My goddaughter is the poster child for birth control.*

"She sure loves that iPad!" Maritza said. "She's just *crazy* about all these gizmos! Now, let's share, Gladdie. Share!" Maritza repeated the *share* command until it seemed as if Gladdie would drive them all to guzzle liquor straight from a bottle. At last Maritza said, "Why don't you come with me and let's get some popcorn? Doesn't it just smell so *good*? Smell the butter?"

If we continue to reward bad behavior with food, Little Gladdie is going to have a weight problem someday soon, Olivia thought.

Reluctantly, Gladdie handed the iPad over to Ellen and took her mother's hand, stomping off in the direction of the snacks.

Ellen became instantly engrossed in something on the iPad, Michelle was buried in her magazine, so the burden of social interaction was assumed by Buddy.

"So, help me remember, Nick? Do you play golf?"

"Oh, I putz around, but it's not my passion. I like to fish."

Buddy said, "Humph. Well, I think fishing is admirable, but I don't really have the patience it takes. You know, when I was a boy . . ."

Buddy began to ramble about childhood summers in Maine and how his father forced him to learn to cast a line and how miserable he was sitting in the sun waiting for a fish that would never bite. Olivia's mind began to wander. She looked around and thought about the other people coming and going there, and about the benefits of their wealth that they seemingly took completely for granted. A family with two very sullen teenage girls moved past her, and she thought, Wow, how much money would it take to make a teenager appear to enjoy traveling with her family? There is no amount, she thought, and while she sometimes regretted not having children, she thanked her lucky stars for sparing her children like them.

Olivia helped herself to a peppermint Life Saver from the large bowl on the reception desk. Teterboro, like most private airports, offered generous amenities for waiting passengers, like hot popcorn or freshly baked cookies. Naturally there were hot and cold drinks, and on occasion there might be small sandwiches or candy. Passengers were free to avail themselves of any of these in addition to high-definition television viewing, wifi, and piles of current magazines and newspapers to peruse. There was no TSA, no *preapproved known traveler* line to wait in, no unruly bustle as there was at LaGuardia or Kennedy or Newark. When your group was assembled, you simply walked out on the tarmac with a crew member and boarded your plane just like you were taking a taxi, except that your vehicle had a price tag upward of fifty million dollars.

The pile of luggage at their feet was growing. Anne Fritz and her partner Lola had arrived and were chatting with Maritza. They had matching olive-green metallic roll-ons. Olivia was surprised to see that Lola was so young, and she wondered for a moment if Nick would be scandalized by their company. And she kind of secretly hoped they would do something provocative. Poor Nick was bobbing his saintly head, listening to Buddy natter on.

Maritza's various stacked suitcases bore the signature of T. Anthony's leather-trimmed red canvas collection, and Olivia guessed that the well-worn Louis Vuitton duffel bag belonged to Ellen. Olivia had the fleeting thought that Ellen probably planned to spend the holiday in a bikini, parading her lithe assets for Bob's benefit. If she'd had children, Olivia would never have let someone who looked like Ellen even touch her child, much less live in her house. Another mystery. And then there was the Bemises' luggage to consider. Their generic but efficient luggage was two matching black ballistic nylon roll-ons with oversize beige leather ID tags, probably to distinguish their bags from others when they flew commercially. Nick and Olivia's bags were ancient tweed Hartmann pieces that Nick refused to part with because they still worked just fine. The importance of preservation was another quality of Nick's that Olivia admired, but at the same time, she realized that if her clients felt the same way she'd never sell them anything new. Luckily, she was not in the luggage business.

"Okay! Let's load 'em up! Where's Daniel?"

Bob Vasile—the king, the demigod, the alchemist—had arrived, and with him came with all the swagger and booming machismo that one human body could possibly contain without imploding. His sheer presence raised the temperature of the room.

"Dahlin'!" Maritza called out.

Olivia was still standing by the desk watching as at the sight of Bob, Maritza lit up like a miniature version of the Christmas tree at Rockefeller Center. She hurried to his side. Bob assessed her from head to toe, grabbed her, and gave her a fast smooch on her cheek. Then Olivia saw his eyes travel to Ellen, who practically purred under his gaze. Olivia felt a sudden and strong urge to give Ellen a good smack right across her insipid face. Fortunately, Bob's eyes did not linger on Ellen but moved around to welcome his other guests.

"Hey, Buddy! You're looking good for an old dog! Hey, Michelle! We need to talk about our Chablis production! Olivia! Beautiful as ever! How is my mega-talented almost sister? So glad . . . well, hey, Nick! How are you, my learned friend?"

This went on until the last guest had been greeted and told how glad Bob was to see them. Bob's son Daniel and his girlfriend, Kitty, were the last to arrive.

"He's gay," Nick whispered to Olivia.

Olivia gave him a pinch on his arm. "Hush! No, he's not. He's a hopster."

"Hipster. Brooklyn hipster." Michelle said, suppressing a snide laugh, having overheard them. "That's how they all look. Her too."

Daniel was wearing super-tight clothes, and his longish hair and thin beard was unkempt. He had also had no visible means of employment for as long as Olivia had known him. Kitty was a pastry chef, and her body art began with a cupcake parade from her left bicep to her wrist. Her right arm was covered in tattoos of a KitchenAid, mixing spoons, wedding cakes, and an old version of the cookbook *The Joy of Cooking*. At least she had a job. Their look was beyond Nick's comprehension, although he'd taught many students who looked like that at NYU. After all, Nick had carefully studied the Beat Generation, and they dressed like weirdos too. In his opinion.

Bob gave Daniel a dressing down for being late. It didn't bother Bob in the least that everyone heard him.

"Can't you tell time?" Bob growled.

Daniel didn't flinch.

"Sorry, Dad. Traffic."

"Bullshit. Leave earlier," Bob said curtly.

"I thought Sam and Dorothy were coming," Maritza said, looking around as though the couple in question might be hiding behind a potted plant, but the group knew she wanted to lighten the mood.

"They're meeting us there," Bob said. "Sam had a tournament in Miami."

"Oh, okay," Maritza said.

Sam was Bob's golf pro. He and his wife frequently traveled with Bob and Maritza, especially to warm-weather destinations.

"Okay! Here's the deal. We're taking the jet to the Beef Island Airport on Tortola, and then we're going to helicopter over to Necker. Any questions?" There being none, Bob boomed again. "Okay then. Let's get this show on the road!"

Olivia noticed small beads of perspiration as they sprang up on Nick's brow.

"Are you all right?" she whispered, knowing the announcement of helicopters had to have struck terror into her husband's sweet soul.

"Yes! I'm fine. Of course I'm fine." Nick managed a weak smile. "Tell me the truth. Bob doesn't have a death wish. Does he?"

"Seriously? He's about the last person alive with a death wish."

"Okay. Of course."

As though the magical music of the Pied Piper had begun

streaming through the terminal, everyone got up and identified their luggage to the porter, who put it on a trolley and wheeled it out to the plane. They showed their ID to the pilot just to reassure him they did indeed have valid passports and continued to where the gleaming white Gulfstream G650 stood, door open, stairs lowered to meet a small red rug on the tarmac. Above the tail number was painted a small Black Angus steer next to a bottle of red wine, Bob's restaurant logo. Once they boarded Bob's plane, they would be swept into a life few even knew how to imagine.

But there were things the group *did* know, such as not to sit in the first seat on the left facing forward—that was Bob's seat. He would sit there with Maritza in the opposite seat facing him. Who would be asked to take the seats on his left remained to be seen. Ellen and Gladdie? Buddy and Michelle? But certainly not Olivia and Nick or Anne and Lola, and most likely not Daniel and Kitty, who were already headed toward the back row.

"Sit by me, Daniel," Bob said surprising everyone.

"Why? Am I in trouble?" he said.

"Hell, no," Bob said, and slapped Daniel on his back. "I just want to spend some quality time with my son. Is that okay with you? Sorry I barked at you."

"Sure, sure!" Daniel said and took the seat opposite Bob. "It's okay."

"I want to sit with Mommy!" Gladdie cried out. "Mommy! Mommy! Let *go* of me!"

Kitty the Canvas and Ellen the Incumbent stood in the center of the aisle, unsure of what to do, and Olivia had the thought that if her goddaughter was going to screech for the next four hours, she was going to need massive earplugs and a lot of Grey Goose. And Gladdie may have been unconsciously trying to knit the immediate family together in seats that matched their rank, but Bob was calling the shots.

"I'll tell you what, Miss Gladdie, girl of my heart," Bob said, "you sit with Ellen for the takeoff and then you can sit in my lap! How's that?"

"That is just about the sweetest thing I have ever heard," Maritza said.

Hearing this, Ellen rolled her eyes upward and emitted an ungracious sigh.

"Kitty? You sit here opposite Daniel so I can get to know you a little better."

Bob was being very congenial.

"What about the rest of us? I mean, I didn't realize we were going to have seat assignments," Ellen said.

Everyone got quiet for a moment, surprised by her tone. Then Buddy spoke up.

"Yeah, this is Delta Airlines. Can I see your boarding pass? Ha-ha! Funny, right?"

"Sit with us," Michelle said.

That was the end of that. Anne Fritz and Lola had barely said a word, but wasn't Anne's assignment to observe?

Olivia and Nick settled themselves in the very back row where they had sat on prior trips and were relieved not to be in the middle of the brewing fray. There would be plenty of time to make polite chitchat over the next few days. And with any luck an opportunity would arise to casually mention that she had some open time for new projects.

Nick wasn't even particularly frantic about sanitizing his seat-belt buckle, the recliner button, or the burled walnut tray with its gold fittings.

"You have to think that they totally disinfect this plane, don't you?"

"Absolutely."

Nick wasn't even particularly fearful of the flight because it was a known fact that Bob was meticulous about the care and maintenance of his plane. And helicopters. And boats. And well, everything he owned. At least that's what he told himself. Again.

"You okay?" Olivia said.

"I'm absolutely fine," Nick said quietly to Olivia. "Actually, this has all the earmarks of a perfect getaway. But I must say, I'm surprised he doesn't use a hovercraft to get from Tortola to Necker. There has to be less risk."

"Instead of a helicopter?" Olivia said, and Nick nodded. "It's only a thirty-five-minute hop. I'll hold your hand."

"I'm fine. To be honest, I swallowed half a Xanax about an hour ago."

"Well, anxiety is what they're for, sweetheart."

"I brought some bottles for us to taste," Michelle announced. She passed a large canvas tote bag to Bob, who passed it to the steward. "Four reds and four whites."

"That was awfully nice of you, Michelle," Bob said. "Thank you."

"Always thinking of you, darling," Michelle said and—God save the queen—she smiled.

Olivia caught Anne Fritz's eye, and they looked at each other, wondering if Michelle was now or had ever been on the receiving end of Bob's affection. Or was she on the launch pad? One never knew when considering Bob and his personal history. And Michelle's face was inscrutable.

When the plane reached forty-one thousand feet and after

a light meal of various cheeses and charcuterie with fruit, warmed baguettes, and generous pours of wine, they all began to nod off. Bob said there would be a feast for them on the island, so there was no reason to eat very much on the flight. Maritza had a blanket pulled up over her shoulders and Gladdie rested in Bob's arms, fast asleep. As Olivia made her way to the powder room, she had the surprising thought that Gladdie did look angelic, sleeping there on her father's chest, seemingly without a care in the world. She remembered reading somewhere how it was a good thing to give birth to a stubborn child, that such children became leaders, not followers. That was probably true. Maybe she would ask Anne, Maritza's psychiatrist. This would give her something to talk to her about. And she looked at Daniel and Kitty, sleeping soundly with earbuds in their ears, and correctly assumed that Bob had not made small talk with them thus far and probably would not at all.

Olivia resettled herself in her seat, climbing over Nick, who was sleeping as well. As she refastened her seat belt, she thought about how nice it was to see him so relaxed on an airplane, even if it did require medication. Nobody's perfect, she thought, and looked around her, reflecting on the others on the trip and what their relationships were to one another. Some of them seemed to belong together, but other couplings struck her as unsuitable or odd.

Michelle was at least eight if not ten years older than Buddy. Michelle didn't look anywhere near fifty. Olivia had to imagine she was Botoxed and Restylaned within an inch of her life. After all, Buddy was a dermatologist. In fact Olivia thought it would be a miracle if they got through this trip without Buddy's offering her some kind of a shot. Usually after a big meal with a lot of wine, he got to the point of inspecting her face and everyone else's too. Then the offers would follow: he could enhance their appearances, just smooth that stubborn jagged crater between their eyebrows—at no charge, of course. Olivia thought it was the height of all crust to bring along whatever he brought along as though they were going to a Tupperware party. Somehow it took the shine off the moment. For her, anyway.

She reclined her seat to the sleeping position, hoping to get comfortable enough to catch a power nap. Anne and Lola? Well, they were a strange pair, separated by more than a decade too, more like mother and daughter than lovers, but she didn't know them and decided to reserve judgment. After all, wasn't Nick much older than she was?

There was no question in anyone's mind that Maritza and Bob were a god-awful match. But Maritza was determined to please Bob, and he enjoyed the worship even if it turned out to be true that she no longer exclusively held his heart. But who would ever hold the heart of a man like Bob? If a man's not happy with one billion dollars, why would he be happy with one woman? Bob, rare bird that he was, would never tolerate a cage.

Soon the plane began a nearly imperceptible descent, the complete opposite of a commercial jet. There were no hot-dog bankings to the left or right, no ear-popping drops in altitude, and no announcements. Just a quiet landing as though the plane had kitten feet and was coming in on a goose-down duvet.

A customs officer boarded the plane and collected their passports. He left and returned a few minutes later.

"Have a nice stay," he said, and handed all the passports to Bob.

"Tough security here," Bob said, laughing, but only when he was certain the customs officer was out of earshot. After all, he thought, there was no point in getting security people excited.

"Nice landing," they all said to the pilots. "Thanks for a great trip!"

The helicopter's passenger seats were three across, and there were headsets available so that they could talk to each other if they wanted to. Bob, Maritza, Ellen, and Gladdie were the first group to take off.

"I'll hold my princess," Bob said, referring to Gladdie, but he seemed to be smiling at Ellen. It was impossible for Olivia to tell exactly where his eyes were because of the darkness of the lens of his sunglasses. "See you folks with a bottle of cold champagne in just a few minutes!"

Little Gladdie was pretending to be asleep, hanging over Bob's shoulder like a thirty-pound sack of potatoes and making snoring noises. Olivia thought, There is simply no end to this little girl's charms.

The second helicopter's rotors began to turn and Buddy, Michelle, and Daniel's girlfriend, Kitty, climbed on board. When the first helicopter returned, Nick and Olivia boarded for the short hop with Lola, and Daniel would bring up the rear with Anne Fritz and one of the pilots. Odd that Kitty didn't travel with Daniel, and Olivia tucked that piece of info away. Maybe it was to promote camaraderie.

Nick seemed calm enough, Olivia thought, although he kept a tight grip on her hand and inhaled less frequently than she thought was normal. The water below them was sparkling and turquoise. As Necker Island, surrounded by coral reefs, came into view, Nick began to get excited.

He pressed the button on the wire of his headset and said to all ears, "Would you look at that sand? It's as white as the driven snow!"

Everyone nodded, and very soon they were touching down on the helipad. They climbed out, were greeted by a staff member from the resort, who led them to a waiting golf cart that would deliver them up to the Great House to meet Bob and Maritza.

"I rode in a helicopter," Nick said, visibly relieved and smiling widely as they bumped along the path. "And I didn't die."

"Are you afraid to fly?" Lola asked.

"It's been a subject of concern," Nick said.

Olivia kissed his cheek and said, "And I am so grateful that you didn't die! But you have to say, sweetheart, it was an exhilarating ride, wasn't it?"

"A lot of people have phobias," Lola said. "You wouldn't believe some of the crazies I hear about from Anne. People are out of their minds."

"Hello? HIPAA laws?" Olivia said.

Lola rolled her eyes as though the law did not apply to her or to Anne.

"*I'm* not phobic," Nick said, and exhaled with a whoosh. "It *was* exhilarating! In fact, exhilarating is the perfect term for the experience."

Nick said that and then thought, Here I am again, just an old Geechee boy talking about flying in private planes and helicopters. Wow, this is some fast life I'm living.

At the Great House, which was a Balinese-bamboo-and-teak extravaganza, they found Bob on the terrace with Dorothy and Sam Kreyer, discussing their golf opportunities.

"I think the two best courses are Mahogany Run and

Carambola," Sam was saying. "The fellow at Guest Services said he'd be happy . . ."

Bob looked up to see Olivia and Nick arriving, with Lola not far behind.

"That sounds fine. Maybe tomorrow," Bob said to Sam, and then turned his attention to Olivia and Nick. "Here you are! Welcome! Welcome!" He extended his arm to draw their attention to the water and then all across the horizon. "Isn't this something? It's like going to Bali without the jet lag! Let's have a glass of champagne!" The waiter standing by poured two stems of Veuve Clicquot for Olivia and Nick. "Say hello to Sam and Dorothy. You remember Olivia and Nick, right?"

"How nice to see you again," Dorothy said, and offered her skeletal hand to Olivia for a limp shake.

Olivia gave Dorothy's bony hand a perfunctory squeeze of similar import and said, "Thank you. How lovely to see you too!"

Olivia did *not* think it was lovely to see Dorothy. Actually, seeing Dorothy was enough to give you nightmares. Her complexion was geisha pale, and she wore dark vampire-red lipstick. She was so thin it was disturbing to see her in a swimsuit, and when she was dressed, she swaddled herself in fashions so bizarre that she looked like Jane Jetson met Lady Gaga in a dark place. More dark than Jane or Gaga. But the *real* reason she didn't think seeing her was *lovely* was that the first time they were together Dorothy made the statement that she had never used a decorator because they were bloodsucking, unnecessary annoyances posing as style makers. Of course, as soon as Dorothy realized her faux pas, apologies were offered.

"I can't believe my words! I am so *terribly* sorry!" Dorothy had said.

No, she wasn't.

"It's okay," Olivia said, not wanting to make a scene at the time. Olivia held her hand up to dismiss her.

"If I'd known . . ." Dorothy went on.

There was no chance whatsoever that Dorothy the fashionista, who owned a high-concept clothing boutique in the Meatpacking District, had not known Olivia was an interior designer unless she lived under a rock. Anyone who ever read a magazine in New York either knew or knew *of* Olivia Ritchie. So since the day Dorothy sank the gaff between Olivia's eyes, Dorothy and Olivia had had zero love between them. In Dorothy's mind there was room for only one style maker. Dorothy herself. Just to plant the thought firmly so there's no confusing Dorothy with anyone else? Dorothy was the biggest duplicitous bitch in the Milky Way. Her marriage to Sweet Sam was a mystery to all. Nick suspected there was an issue of endowment on both sides, but that was nearly impossible to confirm unless you were his physician or her investment advisor.

Olivia shifted her attention to Bob.

"Bob! This place is gorgeous! How did you ever find it?"

The waiter handed her a glass of champagne, and she nodded her thanks.

"That's my job, Olivia! You know I like to keep life interesting." Bob had genuine affection for Olivia. She knew his life story so well, he almost *had* to be nice to her.

"Well, you surely do that, my friend. Cheers! Where did Maritza go off to?"

"She's checking out our rooms," Bob said and pointed to the top level of the Great House. "Forgive me, but I took the penthouse for us. Cheers!"

"As you bloody well should," Nick said. "Cheers!"

Bob chuckled, picked up a note pad, and said, "And I told the desk to take your things to the Bali Hi cottage, which I think you'll like. Lola, you and Anne are in Bali Lo."

"And we're in . . . ?" Dorothy said.

"Bali Beach," Bob said. "Next door to Olivia and Nick. Anyway, this nice young man will show you where to go, and there's a site map in your room. What do you say we meet back here at seven? We can have a cocktail and then dinner?"

"That sounds like a plan," Sam said.

Seven o'clock arrived and everyone gathered on the deck of the Great House, eager to begin the evening, have an adult beverage, and soak up the breathtaking panoramic views as the sun began to sink into the horizon. They had dropped their urban dress and put on clothes more suited to a chic evening in the Garden of Eden. All the men sported short-sleeve shirts and Bermuda shorts except Nick, who believed it didn't matter when or where you went on the planet, a gentleman wore long pants to dinner.

The women wore sundresses or slacks with breezy tops and flat sandals. But Dorothy's getup was—well, what was it? It was box-shaped dull gray linen that defied description. Was it pants? Was it a skirt? Was it supposed to protrude like that at all those odd angles? Why did it have so many slits and holes? Maybe it was best described as something architectural that represented a post-terrorist attack. The only jewelry she wore was a wide bangle bracelet of hammered silver. And her flat silver sandals had many tiny straps that loosely climbed up her bony legs.

Olivia guessed that her bracelet was probably handmade in some remote village in Mexico by a cottage industry of children or women. It didn't look like the work of Native Americans. And it didn't have the polished look like the work of Elsa Peretti or David Yurman either. Still, the only comment she made to Nick as they saw Dorothy approach the deck was *"What the hell is that?"*

"Caviar?" A waiter offered Olivia and Nick a tray of warm miniature blini with a very generous dollop of caviar topped with a tiny dab of crème fraîche.

"Osetra?" Olivia asked, taking one.

"Yes, ma'am," the waiter said. "And here is the beluga."

"Thank you," she said.

Nick took one and winked at Olivia. Olivia surmised correctly that Nick was not miserable and breathed a sigh of relief.

Next, Maritza appeared with Gladdie and Ellen. Ellen was wearing a gossamer white T-shirt and skintight white jeans. Gladdie had on a baby-blue smocked sundress with a big bow holding up her hair. But Maritza, whose intention was to impress Bob, was a dazzle of brilliant colors in a silk caftan that billowed at one moment and clung at another. It was hot pink and printed with deep blue, red, and yellow tropical birds in palm trees. The plunging V neck, which accentuated her obvious assets, was trimmed with tiny clear jets that would sparkle in the candlelight after dark, as would her oversize earrings and clattering bracelets.

"Maritza! You look spectacular!" Nick said, and gave her a kiss on the back of her hand.

Nodding, Olivia smiled at Maritza, hoping this would give her confidence.

"Oh, please," Dorothy said, giving Maritza's outfit a lot of hairy eyeball. "Make it stop."

"Dorothy!" Sam said.

Dorothy simply shrugged her shoulders, moved to the edge

of the deck away from everyone, and crawled into her own head for a few moments. She thought, Okay, so that sounded a little rude. So what?

Olivia knew that Dorothy thought Maritza was a crass hick. She remembered a drunken remark from their last trip, when she'd heard Dorothy say, *"Who works in a chicken-processing plant and a greasy diner? Please! All she did was screw her way into Bob's wallet."*

Olivia watched as Dorothy saw Sam coming toward her. Dorothy smiled and began walking toward him. Olivia moved in slightly toward the bar, hoping to hear what they said.

"You have to play nice with the others," Sam said, gently chiding Dorothy.

You tell her, Sam, Olivia thought.

"You know, sweetheart, making nice isn't my best asset," she said. "But for you? I'll try."

"He's my boss, Dorothy, and she's our hostess," he said.

"And the thought of them having sex is completely repulsive," Dorothy replied.

"Who thinks about *that*?" Sam said, innocent of the notion that Dorothy might think about it a lot.

"There simply is no justice in this world," Dorothy said. "Do you think I might have another glass of champagne?"

"Fine, but you know, everyone heard what you said about Maritza," Sam said.

"Oh, dear. Well now, that *is* the deepest regret of my life," she said. Her left eyebrow arched.

"Is everything all right?" Olivia asked.

"Oh, please," Dorothy said, rolling back on her heels a little.

Olivia suddenly realized that Dorothy was well lubricated, probably having engaged in some high-octane prehydration prior to the cocktail hour. Olivia and Nick's room had a fully stocked bar, and she assumed that this was true of all of the others as well.

"Oh, please *what*?" Olivia said, ready to tell Dorothy what she thought of her.

"It's too complicated to explain to you. If you really knew me, you'd probably agree with me," Dorothy said, and looked around to see Sam caught up in a conversation with Buddy. "Jesus God, he can't even bring me a glass of champagne?" She brushed her hair away from her face. "Let me ask you something, Olivia. Do you ever feel marginalized? Like you're living on the fringe when you ought to be in the center of things?"

Even if Olivia did feel like that, Dorothy was the last woman on the planet she'd tell.

"You mean like life is passing you by?"

"Yeah, I think I squandered my flowers," Dorothy said. "You know, wrong garden?"

Olivia had a rough idea of what she meant.

"Who's to say?" Olivia said, one of her stock replies she used when responding to the query of a drunk or someone with whom she had no intention of engaging in conversation.

"You're right! Lemme ask you something else."

"Sure!" Olivia couldn't wait for the next nugget, and Dorothy was beginning to slur her words.

"Ya think Bob's dicking the nanny?"

Olivia looked at Dorothy and thought, My God, even if I did know, does she *really* think I'd tell her?

"I haven't the slightest idea, but I think a lot of women would like to trade places with Maritza." Like you, you ugly transparent whore, she thought.

"Well, you probably could've had him too, Olivia, if you didn't go around acting like high-ranking clergy."

"My friends call me the bishop," Olivia said, and thought, Holy hell, she's as drunk as a coot!

"Well, we'll see where his train finally stops, won't we? We'll see."

Bob returned with a flute of champagne and Dorothy took her husband's arm, more to steady herself than for any other reason.

They rejoined the group, Dorothy carefully avoiding eye contact with Maritza.

Olivia watched Dorothy closely. What did she have against Maritza to be so rude to her? Well, now she knew. Dorothy thought that Maritza wasn't worthy of being the wife of a billionaire. Bob's money could take her to every board position in Manhattan she might want. And, under whatever delusion she was suffering from, Dorothy thought she could give Bob some class. Maybe on Halloween, Olivia thought.

Now, Bob might not have all the starch of a waspy Boston Brahmin, and he wasn't a Harvard man bound for a career in international diplomacy, but he didn't need it. And he might not have exemplified the religious virtues of his forefathers. But after Nick, Bob Vasile was the most honest, unpretentious, and least screwed-up man Olivia had ever known—with the exception of his weakness for women. And sometimes Olivia recognized a measure of pretension in Nick's language, but she thought he mostly spoke the way he did to amuse her and others and to make his students pay attention. Nick's pretentious language made Bob roar with laughter.

But Maritza was right. Dorothy didn't like her. And it appeared that Michelle Bemis had no interest in being good company for Maritza or for anyone else. Anne Fritz was keeping to herself and Lola for the moment. Daniel and Kitty were nowhere to be found. This could become a disastrous holiday if things continued as they were.

"So! We're having a beach party tonight!" Bob announced. "Look down there!"

The caviar circulated again and Olivia thought, I could eat my own weight in this stuff.

About fifty yards from where they stood on the deck and not far from the water's edge, there were rugs spread on the sand. Lights were strung between the trees and something fragrant was cooking in a fire pit tended by two men. There was a long, low table set with lanterns and flowers and enormous conch shells resting on white linen. Fat square cushions were placed by the table for seating. It looked like a Polynesian luau on *Fantasy Island*.

"Where's Don Ho when you need him?" Dorothy asked, and she alone laughed at her joke.

"You mean Ricardo Montalbán?" Olivia asked.

"Whoever!" Dorothy said.

"Shall we?" Maritza said.

Ellen rolled her eyes and mumbled, "She says it like she's the queen of England issuing a royal decree. La-di-da."

Gladdie started to giggle. "Hey, Momma! Ellen said you're the queen of England! La-di-da!"

Gladdie broke away from Ellen's hands and began to skip down the sand toward the party, calling out *la-di-da* with every skip.

Maritza's face turned bloodred, and she stopped Ellen, grabbing her arm.

"Don't you like your job?" Maritza said.

Then Ellen's face turned bloodred.

Olivia and Nick, who were right next to her, pretended not to have heard but their ears were perked. Sam was ahead of them with Bob, Buddy, and Michelle, all of them out of earshot, but Dorothy was near them and was sporting a tight grin.

"I didn't mean it like that," Ellen said. "I was just trying to make Gladdie laugh." Embarrassed, she hurried ahead to Gladdie, who was by then way down the beach past the party area, in a flat-out sprint running hell-bent for leather toward her half brother, Daniel, and Kitty.

"Oh. Okay." Maritza said, and turned to Olivia. "You saw that, right? Where's Anne?"

"She's behind us with Lola. Yes, I heard it. That kind of humor isn't funny. It's undermining," Olivia said.

"Young people can be very careless with their words," Nick said. "I'd give her the benefit of the doubt."

"*This* time," Olivia said.

"If y'all think I should, then I will. But she makes me so mad."

"Darling?" Olivia said. "Why don't we simply enjoy this beautiful night? You preside over the evening like the queen and treat Bob like your king and let's see what happens."

"He *has* gone to a lot of effort to give all of us a wonderful holiday," Nick said as though he was Maritza's father.

Maritza's face lit up with the possibilities of a well-executed dose of revenge.

Over a dinner of roasted seafood and tomatoes, onions, and other vegetables, Maritza offered a toast to Bob.

"Here's to my wonderful, gorgeous, brilliant husband who arranged this amazing holiday for us! I love and adore you, Bob. There's not another man in this whole wide world like you! You are my king!"

"Now, that's how a wife should treat a husband!" Sam said. "Here, here!"

Dorothy's eyes were rolled somewhere up in her skull at Sam's remark, and Ellen pretended to gag, but just a slight gag. Gladdie was starting to whine.

"Let's get you to bed, Gladdie," Ellen said. "Bob? Do you want to help me tuck her in?"

If Bob and Ellen tucking Gladdie in was a regular habit at the Vasile home, no one knew except the Vasiles and Ellen, but it seemed highly unorthodox to Olivia.

"No, but I'll be along soon," Bob said, dismissing Ellen. He turned back to Maritza. "So, I'm a king, am I?"

"Yes siree, Bob!" Maritza said, and everyone laughed.

Everyone, that is, except Dorothy and Michelle.

CHAPTER 4

eden and beyond

The last thing the men did that night was agree to a golf outing the next day. The plan was to go island hopping, playing nine holes here and another nine holes there, and to have a lunch of freshly caught grilled fish somewhere. Sam said he knew a place, a rustic backwater joint with sticky floors and no plumbing. It probably violated every health-code regulation under the sun, but the fish they'd eat would've been swimming only hours ago. Maybe even caught to order. Needless to say, the conch chowder was impossible to duplicate. The guys were unanimous—they wanted a macho food adventure just like that one.

"Infectious diseases be damned!" Bob said. "We're not afraid!"

"Hell no!" Buddy chimed in.

"We could never take the girls there!" Sam said.

Olivia giggled herself to sleep over their mousy bravado, which was a first for her—not consideration of their mousiness, but the giggling to sleep part.

So, over a sumptuous breakfast on the Bali Hi terrace amid huge containers of palm trees with pink bougainvillea cascading down the sides, Nick announced he was going golfing too. Olivia was surprised. To begin with, in her mind, golf wasn't really a sport and Nick wasn't exactly a rabid fan.

"Really? Why?" She took a bite of her perfectly prepared egg white omelet with minced *fines herbes* filled with grilled asparagus and Swiss cheese. "You didn't pack your cleats, you know."

"Sam said I could borrow shoes and clubs from the starter. So I'm going for three reasons." He took a forkful of his eggs Benedict, moaning with exaggerated pleasure while he slowly chewed it and swallowed. "My God! This is best hollandaise in the world! Okay, so one, I'll have Sam right there, who might improve my game, which we know needs considerable guidance. Two, I'm not missing that lunch."

"Take Lysol wipes."

"No kidding. And three, they're taking a speedboat there, not a helicopter. So, I thought, why not? And, I understand the boat is an old Hinckley Craft. You know how I love them."

Nick had several big, glossy coffee-table books from Rizzoli on pleasure crafts and to his mind Hinckley Craft boats were the epitome of style and quality. Olivia would agree emphatically that they truly were the diamonds of any marina. A twenty-five-foot launch of mahogany and brass could cost as much as half a million dollars or more. Think Cary Grant circa 1955, zipping through the sparkling water surrounding the Isle of Capri, with Sophia Loren draped over his shoulder. There was no sexier boating experience to be had. To put the value in perspective, Nick's last boat was a twenty-foot Sea Pro that was under twenty thousand dollars including the motor and the trailer. Old Hinckleys were highly coveted and practically unattainable except for a very few of the *one percent.*

"I *know* you do. Take a lot of pictures!" Olivia smiled and took a sip of her mango/guava/papaya juice. She nodded. "Why not, indeed? Gosh, this is good. Don't worry about me. I have a great book to read. After breakfast I'm going to take a nice leisurely walk. Someone said you could walk the whole circumference of the island. It's only three miles. No climbing over rocks or anything."

"Good! Climbing wet rocks is not a good idea, especially if you're walking alone. You could slip and break something, and who would know? You could lie there dead in the surf and wash away with the tide. Swarms of fiddler crabs pecking away at your lifeless body?"

"Good grief, Nick!" Olivia laughed. "Probably wouldn't happen, but I see your point. Anyway, I'll probably walk with one of the girls. Can I refill your coffee?"

"Yes, thank you. Well, just be careful. By the way, we haven't dissected last night. I must say, Olivia, watching Dorothy and, to a lesser degree, Ellen being so insufferably rude to Maritza was appalling."

"They want her life. It's the only justification I can think of."

"They must be insane," Nick said. "I wouldn't want her life for five minutes."

"Me either."

"I mean, Ellen might be Bob's plaything for the moment, but in my opinion, it's never going anywhere. But how awful to have that right in your face."

"I agree. And it's embarrassing. Even worse was Dorothy cavorting around like some kind of femme fatale. Can you even imagine Bob with Dorothy?"

"Not to be crude, my love, but the weenie's in the freezer."

"What a thought! Good grief, Nick!" Then Olivia burst into a deep laugh. "How terrible! You are so naughty."

"Sorry. I only meant to make you laugh. Anyway, today should be a beautiful day."

"I want to find the flamingos," Olivia said. "And don't worry about me. Just go have fun!"

"There are flamingos on this island?"

"Yes, and lemurs! I love those crazy little animals! They're primates, you know."

"No, I did not know that." Nick laughed and shook his head. "They have the strangest beady yellow eyes. Take pictures if you see one! Wait? Lemurs? They aren't indigenous to the Virgin Islands."

"No, they are not. They're from Madagascar, I believe. Branson brought them here to breed because they are an endangered species," Olivia said, taking her last sip of juice. "Or something like that."

"Well, that's not a bad deal for the lemurs, is it? Dragged halfway around the world to a paradise just to, well, procreate?"

"Oh, Nick! You're such a boy!" She shook her head and looked down at her plate, bare except for a sprig of parsley. "This breakfast was as amazing as dinner last night, minus the green-eyed monsters."

"It was," Nick said, wiping his mouth with his napkin and bringing it to rest to the right of his knife. "Jealousy is a terrible thing. Shall we go seize the day?"

"Yes," she said and stood, looking out toward the water. "Poor Maritza. She really loves the old bastard, you know?"

"Yes, it's so obvious. The poor child. She's bound to have her heart broken."

"I think it's certain that she will," Olivia said. "I hate the thought of it."

"What is she? His sixth wife?"

"Fifth. Well, since I've known him."

"We witness the triumph of hope over experience."

"I'll say. Bob's constant changing of the guard is good for business, but I just hate to see this marriage go up in flames. I mean, I think she would've married him even if he had less, don't you?"

"What? One billion instead of twenty?"

"Gosh, honey, do you think we're jaded?" Olivia picked up her tote bag and dropped her novel inside, along with a tube of sun block, a bottle of water, and her cell phone.

"A wee bit. A sad but true story. Let's go."

Everyone had agreed to meet in the large open-air living room space on the main floor of the Great House at ten. After a short walk in the delicious fruit-scented air, with palms swaying, the ocean spraying, and gulls squawking, they arrived and spotted Bob and the other men fidgeting, pretending to putt or drive off an invisible tee. Nick and Olivia could tell that they were beyond ready to leave.

"These fellows are die-hard jocks," Nick said, "I'm just an old duffer."

"I keep telling you, golf is not a real sport," Olivia said. "And I love my duffer, who is not even close to old."

"I love you," Nick said and kissed her cheek.

The ladies were chatting to one another, sort of. At least they were putting out a vibe of amiability for the sake of their husbands and partners. Daniel and Kitty were nowhere to be seen. Olivia imagined they were probably back at Bali-whatever having sex. If she had been that age, that's what she would've been doing. Gladdie was jumping on the sofa with impunity as though it were her very own trampoline. No one said a word to correct her.

"There you are!" Bob said loudly. "Did you get some breakfast, I hope?"

"Oh, yes," Nick said. "I'm raring to go!"

"Then let's get out of here! I hear the call of the links!" Sam said and then added in a falsetto voice, "*Play me! Play me!*"

"Someone needs a caffeine intervention," Olivia whispered to Nick. Nick smiled.

"I have sun block for everyone," Buddy said. "And lip balm. What are you girls going to do today?"

"I'm going for a hike to find the lemurs!" Olivia said.

"That figures." Dorothy said, sighing with deep boredom. "I'm getting a hot stone massage with ancient Vedic oils." She glanced in Bob's direction. "My skin will feel like velvet for days."

In a pig's eye, Olivia thought. It was an expression of Nick's that she loved.

Hearing Dorothy, Ellen frowned. Competition was one hundred percent unwelcome, even from a cadaver. Bob looked straight at Dorothy as though she were crazy. But Maritza was completely composed; either she had not heard or she was ignoring Dorothy's overt invitation to Bob.

"That sounds yummy," Maritza said.

"Interesting word choice," Dorothy said and cut her eyes in Bob's direction again. "It's true. My skin will taste *yummy*."

Dorothy was just too much, even for Bob. He found himself unable to politely overlook her words. "Sam," he said, "please, sir, tell your wife I struggle mightily not to think of my guests as edible."

"Lighten up, Dorothy," Sam said and shook his head with a trace of annoyance.

"Oh, please," Dorothy said. "No one has a sense of humor anymore."

Then Bob laughed like a polar bear and all the other guys except Nick, joined in, guffawing like the pandering frat boys they were. Bob ignored Maritza but wagged his manicured (no polish, thank you) finger at Dorothy on the way out.

"You're a very bad girl," Bob said to Dorothy.

"Thank you," Dorothy said. "I'd like to be."

Olivia and Anne saw the sadness in Maritza's eyes. Lola was engrossed in her phone but looked up to see the tiny drama that had just unfolded. Lola frowned at Anne.

"Jesus Christ," Ellen muttered, but loudly enough for all the women to hear.

Dorothy was pleased with the attention and knew, or at least thought, that the first hook had been sunk into the soft tissue of Bob's curiosity. All men are the same, she thought. He'll be back for more.

Anne Fritz made note of Dorothy's wide grin of satisfaction, wondering what Dorothy was up to. Was she actually making a brazen play for Bob or did she think she was funny? And Ellen? There was no doubt in her mind that Ellen was engaged in some sort of inappropriate behavior with Bob. You would have had to be made of stone not to feel the electrical voltage in the air between them. But since any of them had yet to catch the lovebirds *in flagrante delicto*, she really did not feel it was within her professional boundaries to deliver a judgment call to Maritza. At least not yet. Still, she felt very badly for Maritza. Anne had thought numerous times that Maritza was too sweet for her own good.

When the men were out of earshot, Ellen stood up and said, "I'm taking Gladdie for a swim. Anyone want to come along?"

Gladdie hopped off the sofa and ran to Maritza's side, grabbing her around the legs.

"Come, Mommy! Come with us!"

"Not right now, sweetheart. I think I'd like to take a walk with Olivia and Anne, if y'all want to go? Mommy needs some exercise."

"Bad mommy!" Gladdie said and put a pout on her pudgy pint-size face about the size of China.

Provoked for Maritza's sake, Olivia said, "Gladdie, sweetie, that's not a nice thing to say. Your mother loves you very much and deserves your respect."

"Why?" Gladdie said.

"Because she's your mother," Olivia said. "If you didn't have a mommy, I think you'd be a very sad little girl, wouldn't you?"

Maritza gasped but then started to laugh. Ellen looked at Maritza as though she'd lost her last marble, but then that was how the majority of them looked at Maritza all the time.

"Ellen? You and Gladdie go on for a swim and meet us back here at one thirty, okay? And, Gladdie? Don't even think such things. If you're a good girl, I'll take you for a swim this afternoon. How's that?"

"I don't want to go swimming with you anymore!"

"I'll get you chocolate ice cream?" Maritza said in a singsong voice, reaching out to tickle Gladdie's ribs.

Unfortunately, as Maritza got close to her, Gladdie slapped her hard right across the face. The women fell silent.

Whoo! That kid can pack one helluva wallop for a four-year-old, Olivia thought.

"Somebody needs to show that kid who's boss!" Dorothy whispered.

Michelle's face was expressionless, but her jaw was slack, as was Anne's.

Ellen said, "No comment."

"What happened?" Lola said, looking up from Words with Friends on her iPhone.

For as much as Ellen, probably Michelle, and definitely Dorothy wished Maritza would simply vaporize; and as much as Anne and even Lola just wanted a chance to enjoy a few days in a place like this without a dramatic presentation; and as much as Olivia felt genuine concern for Maritza's emotional and mental health, they all wished Gladdie had not slapped her mother. It was a terrible thing to witness.

Ellen said with exasperation, "She's just disappointed in her mother. Again."

Olivia gasped. How dare Ellen say such a thing? Didn't she realize how impressionable Gladdie was? Or did she?

Dorothy muttered in Michelle's direction, "She's quite the tiny sack of hell, isn't she?"

Michelle said, "Oh, *mon Dieu*!" And she laughed.

Anne Fritz said kindly but authoritatively, "Gladdie? Why did you do that?"

Gladdie looked at Anne and said, "'Cause she made me mad!"

"I see," Anne said.

"That wasn't nice," Olivia said firmly. "You should apologize to your mother at once."

"Sorry, Mommy." Gladdie said. Then, having enough sense to be embarrassed, she began to cry and suck her thumb, burying herself in Ellen's shoulder, kicking Ellen's legs in frustration.

"Poor Gladdie," whispered Dorothy with a large dollop of sarcasm.

"It's okay, baby," Maritza said.

But it wasn't okay and Maritza just wanted peace.

"Poor Gladdie indeed," said Michelle, thinking, Surely there are boarding schools for children of this age? "That child is feral."

"Michelle!" Olivia said, shocked that Michelle would be so cruel, but on second thought, as long as people drank wine, Michelle's business with Bob would remain intact. She had nothing to lose by speaking her mind.

So while precocious Gladdie had no idea what *feral* meant, she knew from Michelle's tone that it was not a good thing to be. She began hollering somewhere up in the diva operatic range that could shatter glass. Ellen clung to Gladdie's twisting and lurching body with a tight grip, then proceeded to give a scathing look to each woman, including Maritza.

"Thanks for stirring the pot, ladies," Ellen said and left, with Gladdie screeching like every demon in hell. "We'll be in the kiddie pool."

"Good Lord," Lola said.

"I know," Maritza said. "Every day I thank God she wasn't twins. She sure can be a handful. Shall we take that walk?"

Handful? Olivia thought.

"Actually?" Dorothy said. "I have a date with that lovely hammock in the shade over there."

Yeah, we wouldn't want to tan that anorexic skin of yours, Olivia thought.

"I thought you were getting a yummy massage with yummy Vedic oils so that you could be yummy," Michelle said and smiled at Dorothy, silently calling her an asshole.

So what do you know? Olivia suppressed a grin and thought, There's life in Michelle after all?

"Ladies!" Anne said to them in a warning tone, hoping to avoid a potential catfight, and then turned to Maritza. "I'll walk with you another time, Olivia. Lola and I wanted to get in a game of tennis before the sun is too high."

"No problem," Maritza said. "Michelle?"

"I have a mountain of email to answer before the close of business in France. But I'll see you at lunch?"

Was Michelle actually being pleasant? Was it a full moon? Was Mercury retrograde?

"That's just fine. You ready, Olivia?"

"Sure! Let's go," Olivia said.

They began their brisk walk, heading out in a southeastern direction, taking the pathway toward the Crocodile Pavilion. They stopped at Lo Road.

"You were right to say what you said to Gladdie. Thank you," Maritza said.

"Well, you're nice to say so. I was just defending you and the institution of motherhood."

"Sometimes it's so hard for me to know what to do and say, you know what I mean?"

"Yes, I do. But I also know that I've never met a single woman who wishes she'd been more permissive with her children."

Olivia watched as Maritza's face went from the depths of insecurity and uncertainty to firm resolve. Then her good nature took over and she began to smile.

"Olivia? You're right! You are so right! Somebody has to be in charge, and it ain't gonna be that child of mine! Or her nanny!"

"That's the spirit!"

"Ha-ha! Now, I studied the map. We can go on down to the water, kick off our sandals, and walk along the ocean. Or we can climb up to the salt pond to see the flamingos." Maritza said. "What do you think?"

"Flamingos!" Olivia said. "Are you kidding? I love them!"

"Me too! Flamingos it is!"

When they reached the edges of the salt pond area, Maritza began to squeal with delight. One hundred or more bright pink flamingos were there, wading in the shallow waters, feeding on the tiny crustaceans that give them their spectacular color.

"Olivia! Look at them! I have to bring Gladdie here! They're moving together like the Rockettes! Have you ever?"

"Esther Williams lives on," Olivia said.

"Who?"

"Esther Williams. She pioneered synchronized swimming about a thousand years before you were born."

"Oh, well. Wow. I've never seen anything so pretty and funny in all my life as these crazy birds. Just look at them! I just can't stop looking at them."

Olivia watched them for a few minutes, smiling because of Maritza's happiness. She had a moment of insight, acknowledging that she rarely ever let herself show Maritza's level of excitement over anything. She admired Maritza then and wanted to do something nice for her.

"If you'd like, we could incorporate these exact flamingos into a fabric."

Maritza became very excited. "We could? Are you serious? You'd do that for me? Oh, Olivia! I'd just about die!"

"Don't die!" Olivia said and smiled. Maritza's innocent charm was growing on her. She snapped a dozen or so pictures with her phone. "We can have it woven into something fabulous for your Time Warner co-op! Like a drill tape border for linen curtains for a guest room? Or if you buy a beach house at some point?"

At that moment, Olivia honestly wasn't trying to hustle business. She was just thinking as a decorator, flexing her creative muscle.

"Oh my! What a great idea! Can't you see it? That mean old Dorothy comes to visit and she says, *What's that?* And I say, *Well, that's the flamingos from Necker Island! My* friend *Olivia had them woven into this here fabric just for me!* She'll be so jealous she'll spit!"

As a general rule, Olivia didn't gossip, except with Nick. Olivia considered gossip to be a vulgar indulgence. But Ellen and Dorothy were both behaving so outrageously and Maritza's marriage was so plainly under siege that she gave herself a dispensation.

"I'd love to see that!" Olivia said. "I shouldn't say this, but wow, that Dorothy is something else, isn't she?"

That was as close as Olivia would allow herself to get to chin-wagging, especially with an important client, albeit her only meaningful one at the moment.

"Honey? Don't get me started! I just can't figure out for the life of me just who the heck she thinks she is."

"Agreed." Olivia said, thinking, Boy, is that ever the truth.

"She wants to trade places with me, but I don't think Bob would touch her with a ten-foot pole. She's too bizarre. Ellen *really* wants to trade places with me and she might be an actual threat. But you know what? They must be cracked! Do they know what it's like being married to Bob? He's like a big pizza and everybody wants a slice! All Ellen and Dorothy see is the money. And poor Sam. He's such a nice guy. He's got to be so embarrassed by Dorothy. I just don't know what to say about Ellen."

"Sam is just a really nice guy. I agree."

"Ellen's a snake," Maritza offered.

Olivia wanted to tell Maritza that everything would be all right. She wanted to make her feel better about her marriage. But she knew Bob's commitment to this marriage or any marriage was always going to be dicey at best.

"True. But in a crazy convoluted way you can't blame them, I suppose. It is a pretty intoxicating life that you and Bob have. It's probably really easy for them to fantasize and get carried away with their blind ambition."

"But you don't act like that."

"I'm not wired like that."

"I guess you're right. I mean, after all, it probably seems to them that I was just some random mistake Bob made. Coming out of nowhere, marrying money. The difference, though, is that I really love Bob."

"I know you do, Maritza."

Maritza's eyes were tearing up and Olivia felt uneasy.

"And we have a baby. It's not nice to try to break up a marriage when there's a baby involved. I mean, it's not nice under any circumstances, but especially with a little girl. She looks just like his momma, you know."

"No, I didn't realize that."

"I'll show you pictures." Maritza sniffed loudly, smiled lopsidedly, and wiped away a tear. "Lord, that man loved his momma like I don't know what!"

"Well, Bob sure adores Gladdie," Olivia said. "And you know what? I don't think Bob's going anywhere. I really don't."

"I'm not so sure. I just wish I could do something to make him love me like he used to."

"Maritza? There's not a woman alive who doesn't feel like that about her husband at some point or another. You need a tissue?"

"Really? Huh. No, I'm okay. I'm going to think of something to win back Bob's heart. Something huge."

"Of course you will! That's the spirit!"

"He just ignores me. All the time! He needs a wake-up call or something."

"You just keep letting him know you love him, sweetheart. He'll come around."

"Do you think so? I could always fire Ellen," Maritza said, with a trace of wistfulness. "But in a way, I'd rather let it run its course."

That remark startled Olivia. Was Maritza admitting that Bob was fooling around with the nanny?

"Oh!" Olivia blurted.

"Olivia, hon'," Maritza said in a world-weary voice, "I ain't blind, you know."

"Of course not! But don't you think it's just flirtation?"

"What's the difference?"

Olivia and Maritza stared at each other, recognizing a new truth. There was such a thing as harmless flirting, and then there was flirting between two people who may as well have been alone and naked. The latter was the variety in which Ellen and Bob were heavily engaged. Bob's intention was to commit adultery. Ellen's intention was to instigate and carry on an affair, undercut Maritza's marriage, and assume the position of the next Mrs. Robert Vasile. Whether or not they were currently actually having sex was moot. The intention was thriving, and that was enough to constitute adultery. At least in Maritza's mind.

"Now, should we go find those funny little furry dogs?" Maritza said.

"You mean the lemurs?"

"Yes! With the ring tails and freaky tiny hands?"

Maritza, who could change moods in a split second, was becoming excited and happy again. Olivia was very relieved to get off the topic of Maritza's marriage. Maritza pulled the site map from her bag and pointed out the area where the lemurs were.

"It's pretty far from here," she said, showing Olivia the map. "You want to try to walk there or do you want me to call for a golf cart?"

What did she say? Was Maritza *deferring* to her? Was this offer prompted by, pardon the term, her *age?*

What! Olivia thought. Now it's happening to me too!

Seeing the look of horror on Olivia's face, Maritza quickly rescinded the offer.

"Oh! Olivia! You were going to walk the whole island alone! I hope I haven't . . ."

"I think I can manage the walk," Olivia said and swung into a lively stride, leading the way.

The lemurs thoroughly restored their good humor, and over lunch, Olivia and Maritza amused the others with stories about the weirdly funny rascals. They were enjoying beautiful salads of local lettuces and other bright-colored vegetables topped with grilled succulent local prawns and sliced citrus. Gladdie, tuckered out from all the sun and salt, was uncharacteristically quiet, just listening for once in her noisy life.

"They come right up to you and stand on their hind legs. One of them climbed right up Olivia's pant leg!" Maritza said.

"I nearly fainted," Olivia said.

"She did! I liked to have died myself, I was laughing so hard! They're super friendly," Maritza said.

"Really?" Dorothy said, as if she cared.

"He probably thought you had food!" Michelle said.

"Probably. And they have those crazy eyes that could stare holes right through you like you wasn't nothing but a slice of Swiss cheese!" Maritza said.

"Indeed," Dorothy said, arching an eyebrow over Maritza's grammar, which deteriorated when she was enthusiastic about something.

"I like cheese," Gladdie said quietly.

"I know you do, dahlin'!" Maritza said. "Somebody's gonna get themselves a good nap this afternoon."

Everyone smiled at Gladdie then. It was so nice to see her exhausted. It really, really was.

Anne said, "Their name, which comes from the Latin word *lemures,* actually means *ghost* or *spirit.*"

"Did you just *happen* to know that?" Maritza said. "Y'all? Is Anne Fritz, like, the smartest woman who ever lived, or what?"

"By golly, we should put her on *Jeopardy!*" Dorothy said dryly.

Anne laughed, ignoring Dorothy, and said, "No, I'm not. I stumbled on it when I looked up this island on the Internet."

"She's still pretty brilliant," Lola said.

"Ha! She sure is!" Maritza said. "So, who wants to go find the big turtles this afternoon?"

The island was home to several species of giant turtles that were also on the endangered species list.

"I do!" Gladdie said. "But my eyes keep getting shut . . ."

Suddenly she was completely fast asleep, sitting up at the table.

"I'll take her to bed," Ellen said, and started to get up from her chair.

"Nah, I'll do it," Maritza said and stood. "You rest a little bit. She must've tuckered you out too."

Maritza gently and easily lifted Gladdie from her chair and carried her in her arms. It was a poignant moment. The women watched her walk away in that slow but determined gait only a child's own mother can exhibit. Olivia wondered if Ellen was feeling any guilt. Or Dorothy.

If they are, Olivia thought, they ought to play poker for a living.

There was not a glimmer of remorse between them.

They all drifted apart after lunch to read or to rest. Bob's wines and more Veuve Clicquot champagne had been served with their meal, so a pleasant, drowsy feeling settled over them. Michelle was the only one who appeared unaffected by the alcohol, but then, Olivia thought, she's probably half in the bag all day long.

Olivia decided to take a brief siesta in one of the hammocks down by the water. She was unaccustomed to napping, but if ever there was a place conducive to safely closing your eyes in public, this was it. She kicked off her sandals, climbed in, and was not concerned about her purse being snatched, the jewelry she wore being ripped from her body, or being mugged. She swung back and forth for a few minutes until a huge long cloud floated into view. Mentally she visualized herself putting all of her worries on it as though it were a train leaving town forever, and she watched until it floated out of sight, taking all her troubles away. The next train would bring new clients, new projects, and money. Yes, it was good to be debt-free and she loved their new swimming pool. She dove in and swam laps. The sun felt so warm and good. She swam and swam and swam.

She must've fallen asleep, because the next thing she knew, Nick was gently shaking her shoulder. It was late afternoon.

"Olivia, wake up, darling!"

"What? Oh, hi! How was golf?"

"Gorgeous. Listen, Gladdie is missing. Everyone is running all over the place to find her. I can't believe you didn't hear them calling."

Olivia's eyes got wide and she sat up quickly. "Missing? Oh no! What happened?"

Nick offered her a hand to steady herself as she got out of the hammock.

"Apparently, everyone was asleep and she simply wandered off. Or, God forbid, someone took her."

"Kidnapped? Are you kidding?" She looked around for her sandals and quickly slipped them on. "Where is everyone?"

The alarm horn sounded, the signal for everyone to gather in the Great House lobby.

"Well, now everyone's headed to the Great House. No one's saying it yet, but you know it's on everyone's mind."

"How terrible! Let's hurry! Maritza must be going insane!"

They rushed there as quickly as they could to find the entire staff arriving and the others gathered around, all talking at once. Everyone wanted to help.

"Someone must've seen her!" Maritza wailed. She was sobbing. Olivia sat next to her on the arm of her chair and patted her back. "Oh, God!"

"Hush, now. We'll find her!" Bob said, and ran his hand through his hair.

Bob looked over at Ellen, who was in a total state of panic, literally shaking from head to toe, stuttering through her tears trying to explain how this might have happened. She had only nodded off for fifteen minutes. She had not heard a thing. She was honestly devastated. Everyone knew Bob and Maritza blamed her. They all did, and the women were less sympathetic to Ellen's plight because she was such an unapologetic, fresh-mouthed slut. This unspeakable thing had happened on Ellen's watch. And the disappearance of a child is always completely terrifying. The possibility of kidnapping for ransom was always at the forefront of Bob's and Maritza's mind. That was the reality of their lives. There were nefarious people all over the world who viewed their extraordinary wealth as an opportunity for them.

The general manager, Hank Green, had already hatched a plan. He showed them all a large map of the island, and with a felt tip pen he marked off the island into zones and assigned three employees to each zone. They would comb every inch of the island. There were still several hours until the island would fall into darkness, but they were each given a powerful flashlight and a headset. He told them to call out the child's name at regular intervals of fifteen seconds.

"Do not worry, Mrs. Vasile," Hank Green said. "We will find your little girl."

"I just hope that no one . . ."

"Shut up! You hear me? Don't even think it!" Bob said forcefully.

An hour passed after the staff had begun their search. Radio communication through headsets was brisk, a message coming in every minute or so. Mr. Green began crossing off areas as they were searched. Bob stood next to him and asked him to repeat every message.

"I feel like I should be out there with them," he said.

"No, sir. It's better for you to be here to comfort your wife," Mr. Green said. "We've had this kind of thing happen before. My staff knows what to do."

Olivia heard the manager and watched as Bob offered no comfort whatsoever to Maritza. His jaw was clenched and his eyes were narrowed. Bob Vasile was angry. Very angry.

Another hour passed and the sun was below the horizon. The sky would remain light for a while, but time was running out. If they didn't find her very quickly, Gladdie would spend the night all alone in darkness.

And then, as they all hoped, a call came in that Gladdie had been found. She was riding on the back of an old giant Aldabra tortoise. She was just fine. Once the location was given, a golf cart driven by Hank and Bob zoomed down the path. Maritza began to weep with relief.

"I couldn't have lived if anything had happened to her!" she whispered.

Olivia heard her, as did Anne. Both of them hugged her, and Olivia noticed that the prolonged hug Anne gave Maritza irritated Lola.

How stupid you are, Lola, Olivia thought. She thought she might have lost her only child!

Dorothy had already poured herself a third glass of champagne, and Michelle was well into the bottom half of a bottle of Pinot Noir. Olivia, Anne, and Lola were completely sober. Buddy and Sam drank nothing and Nick paced the floor between the men and the cluster of women.

Minutes later, Gladdie ran through the lobby of the Great House and flung herself into Maritza's arms.

"I'll never do it again!" she cried.

"You scared all of us to death! I ought to tan your hide!" Maritza cried.

"You ought to tan mine," Ellen said.

"Oh, honey, you are so fired. Are you kidding?" Maritza said.

"No. She's not fired," Bob said. "No one's firing anybody. This was an honest mistake."

Maritza gasped and said, "Bob Vasile, you make me so mad sometimes, I just feel like taking my child and going home to Momma."

"Don't you even think about taking my daughter anywhere, do you hear me? Ever. Or you'll be very sorry."

The look on Bob's face was pretty terrifying. All Maritza could do was run to her room.

It had been a poor decision on Maritza's part to make that kind of impulsive threat in front of Bob's friends. She pushed him up against a wall. At least that's what Olivia and Nick thought. When Maritza reappeared later at the dinner table, everyone could tell she had been crying. There was no doubt in anyone's mind that they had argued and that Bob had badgered her into coming to dinner.

"It was so awkward to have dinner with Maritza after the terrible things Bob said," Olivia said, "but it probably would've been more awkward if she had not shown up."

"I agree with that."

"Well, darling? What do you think?" she said to Nick as they crawled into bed later on. "I still can't believe he overruled and then threatened Maritza in front of everyone like that. Ellen not only ought to be fired, she ought to be publicly caned!"

"We're not in Singapore, but I agree with you. She should be replaced. Should we close the mosquito netting? I think there's a bug in the room."

"Yes, please. Close it. God, was dinner stiff or what?"

"Even the caviar seemed rank," Nick said.

"And the champagne seemed flat."

They had been served saffron-flavored fish stew over steamed rice in beautiful individual tureens. Dessert was some kind of raspberry confection. They could've been eating drywall. No one really tasted the food or remarked on it. Ellen and Gladdie were absent from the table, which was a relief to everyone. For once, Dorothy was properly subdued, probably snickering to herself over Maritza's being demoralized by Bob, but even she offered a toast of thanksgiving for Gladdie's safe return. Everyone had joined in with a *here, here*, but it didn't do much to pick up Maritza's mood. In the minds of the women at least, what really mattered besides finding Gladdie was that Bob had openly chosen Ellen over his wife.

CHAPTER 5

yellow submarine

There was a knock on Olivia and Nick's door at six-thirty the next morning. She opened one eye and looked at the bedside clock and thought, Wow, it's too early for room service, isn't it? Nick seemed to be sleeping soundly, and even if he was playing possum, he didn't stir. She pulled back the mosquito netting, slipped out to the sitting area, and called out softly so as not to disturb her maybe/maybe not sleeping husband. "Coming!"

She opened the door and there stood Maritza, wearing sunglasses and a white cotton caftan and holding a carafe filled with some kind of fruit juice.

"Morning. I need to talk to you. Well, I need to talk to *somebody*, and I'm scared to death that stinker Lola will stab me to death if I reach out to Anne. Golly! She is so possessive! Can I come in?"

"Of course! Nick's still sleeping, so . . ."

"No, I'm not. I'm awake," he called out from the bedroom. "I'm getting into the shower."

"Sorry, Nick," Maritza called back to him. "Good morning."

"Morning," he called back.

Olivia winced, knowing Nick wasn't happy. Maritza did have an unfortunate knack for dropping in at inopportune moments. And this was really a business trip for Olivia, not a vacation, so Olivia could not object. In her heart, Olivia knew that Maritza had no clue that she was overstepping the professional boundaries.

Olivia went to the bar area and took two glasses from the tray. "Here. Let me take that."

Maritza handed her the container and Olivia wondered what Maritza was doing with a carafe of juice in the first place when the staff-to-guest ratio was easily ten or more to one. Nonetheless, she said nothing about it, because what would that prove? She filled two glasses and gave one to Maritza.

They touched sides of the glasses, as though it was a toast to something, and took a long drink.

"So, what's going on?" Olivia said, taking a further sip. "Everything okay?"

"How could it be? I haven't slept all night."

"Last night was pretty unnerving for everyone," Olivia said. "The main thing is that Gladdie was found unscathed. Come, let's sit outside."

They each settled into an armchair on the terrace and drew in a deep breath of the morning air.

"Of course, but after that, all I can think about is how Bob threatened me. Olivia, my husband threatened me in front of everyone! He acted like a beast! That's no way to treat somebody you're supposed to love!"

"I think that in the heat of a moment people say things they don't really mean," Olivia said. "Don't you? I know I've done it."

"Bob doesn't love me anymore, Olivia. It's as plain as the nose on my face."

Olivia was quiet for a few moments, considering what Maritza said.

"That's not true. I completely disagree. Has Bob been undergoing any kind of unusual stress lately?" Olivia put her glass down on the side table.

"Are you kidding? It's the only kind he has! He's opening restaurants in Napa and Sonoma and one in La Jolla. He's on the phone and emailing around the clock."

"The poor man," Olivia said, wondering why she didn't have the job to design their interiors. But she hadn't done commercial spaces in aeons. Maybe that would have to change.

Maritza removed her sunglasses to reveal red, swollen eyes. "Honey, *poor* is the only thing he isn't. I don't understand him anymore. Tell me what to do, Olivia. You've known Bob since forever. I have to *do* something, Olivia. Or I'm going to lose him. Or maybe I already have lost him."

Olivia got up, grabbed a bar towel, and soaked it in the ice bucket, which was magically always filled. "You haven't lost him, Maritza. Let me tell you a story about Bob that most people don't know. It might help you understand why he is so driven." She twisted the wet towel over the bar sink, folded it, and handed it to Maritza. "It will also help you to forgive him."

"Thanks. I'm all ears," Maritza said, leaning back into the cushions of the chair and covering her eyes with the cold, damp cloth.

"I'm telling you this in the strictest confidence, Maritza. You cannot tell him I told you, okay?"

"Deal! I swear on my daddy's grave!"

"Okay. When Bob was a child, his family was very poor."

"I know all about that," Maritza said. "They immigrated to the United States after World War II."

"Right. But I mean dirt poor. They came to Boston with the clothes on their back and a few hundred dollars. Sometimes they ate onions for a week. Because his mother didn't speak the language, she was reduced to cleaning houses to put food on the table. This was a dignified woman who was a math teacher. His father, who was a pretty talented commissioned muralist, suddenly had to put up plaster walls in the homes of rich people. Then his father fell off a scaffolding, broke his back, and couldn't work for almost a year. They nearly starved except for the generosity of their neighbors. But Bob was just a kid and he didn't have any sense of the reality of their poverty. All he knew was that Christmas was coming and he wanted Santa to bring him a bicycle. All his friends had bikes and he wanted one so he could fly through the streets with the other boys."

"Well, Lord love a duck. He was just a kid."

Olivia did not know what *Lord love a duck* meant or if it had anything to do with anything. Most likely? It was merely an unfamiliar southernism. Olivia continued.

"Exactly. His parents couldn't come up with the money for a new bike, but they found someone who was willing to sell a used one."

"It was probably stolen," Maritza said.

"Who knows? Maybe. Anyway, they got this bicycle, painted it black, and put a bell on the handlebars. On Christmas morning, it appeared by their tiny little tree with a red bow on it."

"So was he thrilled?"

"Yes and no. It was obvious to Bob that it was used. I imagine the paint job might not have been so great and I'm sure

Bob was very astute, even as a youngster. But he knew it wasn't from Santa. Sadly, it was the moment he realized there was no Santa Claus, and he felt guilty over what his parents must have sacrificed to be able to give him even this poor, used bicycle. In any case, he had his bicycle."

"So did he cry or something?"

"Bob? Bob cry? Never! Well, *never*, according to him. He toughened up, hugged his parents, and quickly carried the bike down five flights of stairs to the street. His parents were right behind him, frightened for his safety, begging him to be careful."

"I'm sure!"

"Well, you see, Bob had never been on a bike before, except for riding on the handlebars or a crossbar with one of his friends. But he had such passion for the bicycle that in his mind, he had already traveled every street and alley in the entire city of Boston. He completely understood the concept of directing the bicycle by turning the handlebars, and he knew to rotate the pedals to propel it forward. Never was there a boy more mentally prepared to take on the challenges of a bicycle than young Bob Vasile."

"Well? What happened?"

"He got on the thing and took off like he'd been riding bikes his entire life!"

"Amazing!"

"But he had never given a thought about how to stop."

"Oh, no."

"Exactly. He plowed into a pile of garbage cans, went flying, and had to get ten stitches in his head."

Maritza sat up and removed the wet cloth, refolded it, and said, "Good luck finding a doctor on Christmas morning."

"I'm sure. I don't know the details on that part of the story, except that his father beat the stuffing out of him; you'd have to ask Bob."

"His father spanked him on *Christmas*?"

"Oh, I think his father disciplined him frequently. But soon he was back on his bike with all the other boys and zipping all over the streets of Boston."

Maritza covered an eye with the cold cloth, applying some pressure to relieve the swelling, and looked up at Olivia with the other. "And why is this story going to make me forgive Bob?"

"Because all the other boys knew how to jump their bikes over this particular creek and Bob did not. But rather than be called a sissy or something worse, like getting beaten up, Bob gave it a try. Well, the creek was wider than he thought, and the water was colder and deeper. He lost his bike and nearly drowned in the process of trying to find it."

"How terrible! Didn't the boys help him?"

"No. They left him. So Bob had to go home, freezing and soaking wet in the middle of March, and confess what happened to his parents."

"And his daddy was mad?"

"Furious! I'm pretty sure he got a whipping that day too. I know his father called him some pretty terrible names for years, like *stunade*, which I think means *idiot*. Anyway, after his mother dried him off and got him into clean clothes, he and his father went back to the creek with a rake they borrowed from someone to try and fish the bicycle out."

"What happened?"

"They pulled out six bicycles!"

"Oh! How wonderful!" Maritza laughed.

"Yep. So, Bob and his father fixed them all up and sold them."

"No *wonder* Bob is like he is. The entrepreneur."

"Yes. Even then. He learned all about disappointment, tenacity, and ingenuity at a very young age. And that you shouldn't ever have to depend on anyone."

"And not to get caught doing something stupid."

"Exactly."

"How did you hear this story?"

"Well, when Nick and I were dating and Bob was single we used to have dinner now and then. One night he drank three martinis and told us all these wild colorful stories about growing up on the other side of the tracks. If he knew that I told you this story, you'd have to find another decorator."

"Why?"

"I guess because he doesn't want anyone to know how humble his beginnings were. We were sworn to secrecy."

"Pride. Pride is a sin."

"Personally? I think it's so interesting how we are all shaped by our childhoods. Listen, Bob can be completely charming, and you know it."

"When he wants to be."

"Maritza, men like Bob just want to feel like big shots. They want to win every game and take home the biggest fish. They want you to think they're truly awesome and they are, but they want your complete adoration. What Bob has accomplished in his life all on his own is absolutely incredible. But deep inside him there's still that little boy who found out the truth about Santa on Christmas Day, who had to be fed by neighbors because he was too small and skinny, whose father whipped him with a belt when he felt like it, and who lost his beloved bike in a creek."

"So he's permanently screwed up?"

Sometimes Olivia wondered about the actual size and functioning capabilities of Maritza's brain.

"No, sweetheart. He's permanently insecure and cannot bear the thought of other people having power over him, and he's terrified of failure. He would not make a good loser in any situation. And this includes losing you and Gladdie. Poverty can be mortifying, you know."

"So what are you telling me, Olivia?" Maritza put the cold cloth on the side table.

"Bob loves you and he loves Gladdie. But on some days and in certain situations, it might seem like he loves himself a bit more, especially when his insecurities jump into the forefront of his mind without warning. It's how alpha men are, Maritza. They can't help it. They see the world only through their own eyes. And men are always going to do just what they want to do. But in my heart I really believe Bob loves you."

"So I should just sit back and smile and pretend he's not screwing the nanny?"

"No. You should remain focused on your relationship with him, not his with her."

"Can you say that again?"

"Treat him like a king, Maritza. Treat him like a king. And to the extent you can, pretend Ellen doesn't exist."

"And what should I do about Dorothy?"

"Oh, dear. What to do about Dorothy? Well, first, she's really Sam's problem. Isn't she? And other than that, I guess I'd try to see the humor in it. Bob's not interested in her."

"She's gross."

Olivia said nothing. She simply stood, her polite way of letting Maritza know that this session was ending. She could hear Nick rustling around in the bedroom. He was out of the shower and dressed for the day.

"I'd like to have breakfast," he said, coming into the sitting room. He cleared his throat, which he always did when he was annoyed. "Shall I wait for you or should I go on ahead?"

Maritza stood as well. She walked over to the bar and inspected her eyes in the mirror. "The swelling's going down. I've got to get moving too."

"I'll be along in ten minutes," Olivia said.

Nick arched his eyebrows, cocked his head to one side, and gave her a look of suspicion and doubt.

"No! I will! Maritza is just leaving!"

"Okay, ladies. I'll see you in the Great House."

Nick left and Maritza turned to Olivia.

"Thanks, Olivia. You're like a walk on the beach."

"You're welcome, but for what? And pray tell, how am I like a walk on the beach?"

"I feel better. You know, my problem isn't solved, but I feel better! So thank you." Maritza gave her a hug and left. "See you later!"

Olivia stood in her doorway and watched Maritza make her way down the path toward the Great House. She wouldn't have wanted to go through what Maritza was dealing with for all the money in the world. But there was no real advice to give a woman whose husband was and had always been a philanderer. From Bob's point of view, he probably figured he was giving Maritza a lifestyle she would never have otherwise, his name, and a baby, and what else in this world could she possibly want? But Maritza wasn't sophisticated or cynical enough to say that gargantuan net worth was all she needed. She was innocent enough to expect love and naïve enough to expect fidelity. In a normal marriage those things would not be too much to expect.

But Olivia had never seen Bob really love anyone or anything except his businesses and the bottom line, except a rare bone-in rib eye and an old Bordeaux. And Gladdie. That child brought out something in him that bordered on obsession. Over the years she had observed again and again that he didn't seem to care so much about how much money he made as he did about the win. Bob was a natural predator with a superspeed, calculating, and very sharp mind he used as a weapon.

After almost tripping over two small turtles on the pathway, Olivia found Nick alone in the Great House lobby with a silver pot of coffee and a downloaded copy of *The New York Times*. He stood as soon as he saw her and pulled out her chair for her to sit.

"Thank you, my love!"

"My pleasure," Nick said and took his seat, diving back into the newspaper.

"I nearly squashed some baby turtles on the way over here."

"I saw them too. You really do have to watch where you step."

They were alone in the cool morning air. The incoming tide was washing the shore with a predictable rhythm of low and gentle music. A beautiful blue-and-gold macaw sat on a branch in a nearby tree screeching *Where's my food?* while someone from the kitchen approached him with a small plastic tub filled with a few ripe mangoes and bananas. The bird hopped down, peered in, and devoured it all.

"This place really *is* a bit of a zoo!" Olivia said. "Did you order breakfast?"

"Not yet. I was waiting for you." The macaw began screeching again. "That's my friend Mac," Nick said. "He wants seconds, and he thinks the breakfast service is too slow."

"Well, he's wrong. He shouldn't complain. He's lucky to be here. Like us."

Olivia filled herself a cup, added cream, and gave it a stir. Nick continued to read.

"So, with all the hullabaloo last night, you never told me about the Hinckley or your golf game. How was it?"

"Fabulous," he said, and didn't look up from the newspaper.

"Nick?"

"Hmmm," he said.

"What has you so riveted? Did the world blow up?" She took a sip and waited.

"No, I . . . Sorry, dear. I was reading this article about a dispute over the borders of New Jersey and New York, which, as you know, has been a bone of contention since the American Revolution. It seems they've discovered a map that might settle it for once and for all."

"Well, it's about time. So, are you fellas playing golf today?"

Nick folded his paper and put it on an empty spot on the table. "I don't think so. Listen, I want to talk to you about Maritza and Bob before anyone else appears." Nick said.

"What is there to say? He treated her very poorly last night."

"Yes, he certainly did. But I had a thought that you might want to consider adding to your files."

"What's that?"

"What really shook Bob up last night was the thought of losing Gladdie."

"Well, of course! We were all upset. Where are you going with this?" Olivia asked.

"I think he has a highly developed idea of what's his and what he's willing to share. That's all."

"Hmmm. So you're saying he views Gladdie as his possession only."

"Something along those lines. Maritza said something about taking Gladdie and going home to her mother, which to *my* mind is just a general metaphor for female frustration. But that was when Bob blew his top. Remember?" Nick said.

"Yes, of course. I actually had a similar thought."

"Well, she just needs to consider the fact that if she wants out, he *will* fight her for custody. And somehow, even if it isn't in the best interest of the child, I believe he will win."

"Well, that's stupid," Olivia said. "It really is."

"I agree. Anyway, as to today's agenda? I heard some talk last night about taking the submarine for a spin."

"Oh! I had almost forgotten about that crazy thing! Maritza was very excited about it. To be honest, I pushed it out of my mind."

"It's supposed to be able to descend to some amazing depth."

"No thank you. Too claustrophobic for me. Besides, who knows if it's safe?"

"Well, *I'd* be curious to see what's down there. You know how I hate scuba diving or snorkeling. I mean, if a school of fish touched me, I'd have a heart attack. But this would be an absolutely antiseptic way to go have a look."

"Okay. You have fun with that! You'll let me know what you find, I hope?"

Nick laughed and said, "Let's see just how scary this thing is before we say yes or no."

"No, no. You're so much more brave . . ."

"I don't know about that."

A waiter appeared to take their orders.

Olivia asked for a poached egg on a dry English muffin with a fruit plate.

Nick said, "I know I shouldn't do this, but I'm going to have the eggs Benedict again. And may I have some extra hollandaise on the side?"

"Of course, sir," the waiter said, smiling.

"You know, Nick, you may think I'm a stinker to say this, but for someone who's swearing he wants to live without all the trappings of a foodie life, you're sure rocking the hollandaise."

"Rocking the hollandaise?"

"It's what the young people say."

"Ah, well. Life is filled with contradictions, my dear." He wiggled his eyebrows at her. "What can I say?"

Soon everyone in their group was there except Bob and Maritza. Buddy and Michelle and Anne and Lola had already had breakfast in their room. Gladdie was sitting with Ellen at a distance from the group, eating blueberry pancakes. Was Ellen avoiding everyone? Dorothy was cooing over Sam, who had probably read her the riot act. Anne and Lola were dressed in tennis whites. Daniel and Kitty made an appearance at last. He was wearing super tight jeans and a T-shirt with flip-flops, and she was wearing some kind of loose retro baggy dress and rubber sandals. They looked pale and exhausted, asked for a plate of *anything* or dairy-free green smoothies and some gluten-free toast, just nothing with a face—no bacon, sausage, eggs, or fish.

How much sex can you have? Olivia thought.

Nick, who knew exactly what she was thinking, replied, "Evidently, a lot."

Olivia gave him a teasing pinch on his arm. He read her mind on occasion and her face often, and it always surprised her. Or maybe he was just thinking the same thing. Neither of them remarked on the request for gluten-free toast. They merely exchanged knowing looks. Did the entire human race suddenly develop celiac disease? I mean, did they? Please.

Bob waltzed in, but his cell phone rang and he waltzed out again to take the call, giving them a wave. Maritza appeared, dressed in a colorful print top over a swimsuit with sandals. Olivia thought she looked great. Dorothy eyeballed Maritza and sucked her teeth in disapproval. Everyone ignored Dorothy. In addition to her top, which was probably designed by Pucci, Maritza wore a very large-brimmed straw hat and sunglasses with lenses tinted light enough to be worn indoors. People who wore dark sunglasses indoors got on Olivia's nerves. What are they hiding? A drug habit? A black eye?

"Y'all? Please listen up for a minute."

Everyone got quiet.

"I just want to say something before the day gets away from us. I am truly sorry about my hysterical behavior last night. I was so frightened over Gladdie that I said some things I really didn't mean. And I don't want to ruin this wonderful holiday because of my nerves, which seem to get a teensy bit out of control without my permission. So please forgive me. And let's go back to just having fun? Please?"

"That's sure okay with me," Michelle said, showing no emotion one way or the other. "I hate drama."

"There's nothing to forgive, Maritza!" Buddy said.

Olivia thought Michelle's breath carried a curious trace of alcohol, curious only because of the hour. She wrote it off to mouthwash. Frankly, if Michelle wanted to drink herself into the grave, it was of no concern to Olivia. After all, the reason she was in their midst was purely and only business.

"Maritza?" Anne said. "You don't have to worry about what you said or about ruining our good time! Any one of us would've been completely unhinged if our child had gone missing."

"Thank you, Anne." Maritza said with a very theatrical show of relief. "I appreciate your kindness so much, you just don't know."

"Jesus," Lola said, with a look of disgust. "Gag."

"Lola!" Anne said and whispered, "Hush."

"Oh, brother," Dorothy muttered loud enough that everyone heard.

"Shut up, Dorothy," Sam said quietly and then spoke up. "Maritza? No one blames you for anything. Kids are just kids and they do these things! It's all okay."

"Thank you, Sam. You sure are a sweetheart."

Sam walked over and gave Maritza a kiss on the cheek. "Don't mind Dorothy," he whispered to her.

"Ignore her," Buddy said. Buddy gave Maritza a hug, and even Michelle smiled.

Michelle would have agreed—if anyone had asked her, which they did not—that Maritza might be a ditz, but she also thought that Maritza had taken an unfair amount of undeserved grief from Bob the prior night and from almost everyone else in general. I mean, even if you don't care for dogs (which is legitimate), that doesn't mean you like to see them abused. This is approximately the level of concern Michelle held for Maritza, which was ten times the amount Dorothy had and untold multiples of what Ellen felt. Anne and Olivia were on the payroll, and therefore any sentiment flowing from them would always seem disingenuous and misplaced. And Lola, Daniel and Kitty had other priorities.

"Support for Maritza's plight appears to be building," Nick said quietly.

"Yes, one teensy grain of salt at a time," Olivia said.

"Hmmm," Nick said. "Hardly enough to sustain her."

"Or anyone," Olivia said.

Hank, the general manager, appeared for a group chat to pique their interest in other daily activities, including the submarine. "How is everyone this morning?" he asked.

"Fine as wine in the summertime!" Maritza said, which of course caused eyes to roll. There would be zero tolerance for homespun anything. When she realized she sounded like Minnie Pearl from the Grand Ole Opry, she added, "Thank you for asking! Isn't this a beautiful day?"

Who could argue with that?

"Yes it is! Now, ladies and gentlemen, besides windsurfing, waterskiing, aerobics, yoga, tennis, and swimming, I want to tell y'all about our submarines. I think we are the only resort in North America that offers them. Ours is a top-of-the-line Triton, an eight-ton fully submersible vessel that descends to a depth of thirty-three hundred feet, going down a few hundred feet per minute. It takes a pilot plus two other guests, and if you'd like, our pilot can show you how to operate it on your own. It uses just a simple joy stick, so easy a child could maneuver it, although I'm not trying to give our young Miss Gladdie any ideas!"

"I wanna subbereen!" Gladdie said, loudly enough to rankle the collective nervous system.

"She doesn't even know what it is, but she wants one," Maritza said. "That's my girl!"

Great, Olivia thought, and when she made eye contact with Michelle, it was plain to see that Michelle agreed.

Everyone turned their eyes to the tiny imp with the milk mustache and laughed. She was full of beans again and ready to raise hell nonstop for the next twelve hours.

"I hope you slept well," Maritza said to Ellen, and winked at Olivia.

Olivia thought it was good to see that Maritza wasn't kowtowing to Ellen.

Hank continued. "So, what's particularly exciting about this submarine is the depth to which it can go. The island is surrounded by reefs, and while I'm a big fan of scuba diving, it can take you down only so far. And once you pass three hundred feet, there is a whole other world to be explored. You'll see barrel sponges and all sorts of luminescent creatures, massive six-gill sharks and other kinds of deepwater fish. Just a couple of years ago the Triton was used to film the first giant squid ever seen in its own habitat. It's very exciting, and we are super excited to share it with you."

"Is it dangerous?" Sam asked.

"Not at all. The Triton has a perfect safety record. One hundred percent safe. One hundred percent dry. Triton subs take over twelve million people a year on trips and they've never had a problem."

Bob had returned and got in on the tail end of the conservation.

"Sam, why don't you and Buddy take the first ride and then I'll go on a ride with Nick. I've got to make a call."

"Sure!" Sam said. "Buddy? You in?"

"Yes, sir!"

Everyone wanted to see what a personal submarine looked like, so they gathered up their things and all of them, including Ellen and Gladdie, followed Hank down to the marina, where a sixty-five-foot-long catamaran waited with five handsome, suntanned young men on its deck. Well, at least they seemed young to Olivia, and she knew she should be ashamed of her initial thoughts about them. She looked around, and sure enough, Dorothy and that slut Ellen were licking their lips. Wouldn't it be great if Bob and Sam could catch these two in the sack with a couple of deckhands? She smiled at the thought of it.

Of the crew of five, four were on hand to operate the catamaran and the sub and the other fellow was the pilot for the sub.

"Morning! Welcome aboard!" the captain said.

"Mel! Say hello to Bob Vasile and his guests!" Hank said.

Bob and Mel shook hands, and then Mel shook hands with everyone else as they were introduced.

Sam and Buddy climbed onto the catamaran with Bob, Nick, and Hank. The ladies waited on the dock.

"What a beautiful boat!" Bob said.

"Thank you, sir," Mel said. "We're very proud of her."

"How fast can she travel?" Bob asked.

"Up to twenty knots. You could never launch and recover a Triton with any other boat as easily as we can with this cat."

"She sure is yar!" Maritza said, and the women looked at her as if she were a raving lunatic. "Excuse me, all you pickle pusses! Katharine Hepburn? *The Philadelphia Story?* The boat *True Love*?"

There was no name or term recognition to be found among the younger ones.

"I think I remember hearing about Katharine Hepburn from my grandmother," Kitty said.

"Me too," Lola said. "Didn't Katharine Hepburn cross-dress?"

"Not any more than Lauren Bacall," Olivia said.

"Who?" Kitty said.

"My grandmother talked about her too," Ellen said. "Isn't she dead?"

Olivia, Dorothy, Anne, Michelle, and Maritza finally found that they had something in common—contempt for the unforgivably young and uncultured.

Ignoring the women, Bob said to Mel, "Take my two pals out first and I'll go later with Nick. I just want to have a look at the lift."

"Well, you ought to watch *The Philadelphia Story* sometime," Olivia said to the younger women. "It's a classic."

"I'm afraid the issues of propriety might go straight over their heads," Michelle said.

"It's an informative movie about being classy," Dorothy said, directing her remark to Ellen. "It wouldn't hurt *you* to watch it."

Ellen gasped and for once was speechless.

"Like you know the difference," Lola said, in defense of Ellen.

"Stop it!" Anne said.

"Ladies!" Maritza said.

Good grief! Olivia thought but did not say.

Silence hung in the air, and the good-natured feelings of the morning sank to the bottom of the sea.

Maritza said, "I'm going on board. I'm dying to go on the sub! How about y'all?"

"Not me," Olivia said. "No desire. I'll watch the movie, though."

"Me either," Dorothy said.

Anne just stood there, jaw clenched.

"You don't want to go?" Lola said to Anne.

"Not at all," Anne replied. Anne was miffed because Lola took Ellen's side.

Women, Olivia thought.

"You go down three thousand feet and tell us how it is," Michelle said to Maritza.

"Well then, I will!" Maritza said.

Bob, who had ears like NASA and the SETI Project rolled into one, turned back to Maritza and said, "You don't have to do this, Maritza. It's really a guy thing."

"Really?" She was about to argue and then remembered what Olivia told her about treating Bob like royalty. "Well, dahlin', you know best. But do you think I could just look at it? Just a peek?"

Bob melted from Maritza's obsequious response. If there was anything he caved in to, it was a good bootlick. Yeah, boy, a genuflect to his almighty power did him right in.

"Sure, sweetheart. Here, take my hand." Bob reached out to help Maritza board the catamaran. "Watch your step now."

Maritza turned around and winked at Olivia. "I'll be right back, y'all!"

Olivia relayed this anecdote to Nick later on during the cocktail hour on the terrace of the Great House. There was a new mountain of caviar on the cocktail buffet and plenty of smoked fish with assorted breads. Bottles of vodka stood in blocks of ice stuffed with herbs and the champagne bucket was filled with two bottles. Olivia wondered if Bob owned stock in Veuve Clicquot.

"So, Maritza actually wound up piloting the submarine with Bob as her passenger," Olivia said. "He's definitely a catch-more-flies-with-honey kind of man."

"Most men are."

"But I have to tell you, I'm exhausted from these women."

"Boy, that's completely understandable. They make you wonder, don't they?"

"What drives them to be so bitter?"

"Yes. And what else do they want that they don't already have? You know, I've always believed you have to get up grateful. Do you understand?"

"I think so, but tell me just what you're thinking."

"Well, if I wake up and my knees hurt, as you know they often do, I ask the Good Lord to know I'm grateful for everything else. Like just the simple fact of being here another day so that I can love you and love the world. Now, sometimes I might throw out a question about how my aching knees are a part of His eternal plan, but I don't ever really expect to get an answer."

"The minute you think you're in direct conversation with God, I want to know, okay?"

Nick laughed and said, "Sure. I'll do that."

Two chefs were nearby, slowly poaching shelled Guinea chick lobsters and prawns in clarified butter in copper pots over an open fire. Dinner was set up on the terrace of the Great House. Again, it was beautiful enough to have been the scene of a small wedding.

"My mouth is actually watering," Nick said.

"Baby boy, lobster poached in butter isn't exactly on the Mediterranean diet!"

"This is a special occasion," he said. "So, tell me again about the women?"

He listened to her with one ear, and at every pause in their conversation he raved about the submarine ride again, about which he was more excited than anything else, except speed-boating around the Caribbean in the Hinckley Craft. Oh, and the jet that brought them here. And their Balinese bungalow. And the food. Did he mention the helicopter?

"Nick?"

"Yes, my turtledove?"

"How are you ever going to adjust to the simple life on Sullivans Island?"

"I'm an easy man, Olivia. Don't you worry about me. By the way, did I tell you what my friend Bob told me about a new hotel in Fiji that's being built? He wants to go and take all of us!"

"Your *friend* Bob? No. Do tell," Olivia said, almost smelling the special fragrance of sulfur that comes only with spiritual corruption. Nick was on the threshold of the dark side.

"Ah, Olivia. Come on. He's a good guy to his friends. Right? Anyway, it's called the Poseidon Undersea Resorts. It's actually underwater. The *entire* hotel is under bloody water!"

"That's what I'd be afraid of."

"No, no! It's safe! You can lie in your bed and watch dolphins and every kind of fish swim right by the glass walls! It has a hundred-seat restaurant and a bar and everything you can think of. Isn't that amazing?"

"Amazing. I *hope* it's fabulous, because it needs to be to get me to travel with these women again. I'm telling you, I can't wait to get away from them. Too negative. Day three and I'm completely worn out. I can have a business lunch with Maritza five days a week if I need to, you know? Much easier and same mission accomplished. I mean, it's not like any of the others would give me any business."

"I hadn't thought much about the other women, other than

the obvious. You're right. Rough crowd. I'm sure they're not much company for you. They can't be. The women on Sullivans Island are a lot nicer."

"We'll see about that. And Maritza is a sweet girl, but I'm old enough to be her mother! I mean, I don't mind her confiding in me, but gosh, this is hardly a vacation."

"Well, I'm sorry to know that." Nick looked down and then back up at Olivia's face. "I hope you don't mind that I'm having—actually, I'm surprised to admit this—the time of my life. This is so much better than the trip we took with them to the Amalfi Coast." Nick noticed that Olivia's goblet was bone dry. "May I get you something stronger? A vodka martini?"

"Yes, please. At least one of us *should* be having a *grand* time. This is just too much work."

"Well, when we get home, let's head straight to Charleston. Say! Isn't that Bob's boat in the harbor?"

Sure enough, *Le Bateau de l'Amour* was at anchor about five hundred yards from the beach.

"Yes. Yes, it is! I wonder if we are leaving?" she said, and hoped it was a sign that they were.

"I have no idea," Nick said.

"Well, a trip to Charleston sounds wonderful."

Over dinner Bob announced he felt the need for change in atmosphere. They didn't know and would not find out if it was because of the issues between Maritza and Ellen or what. But they would be leaving in the morning.

CHAPTER 6

after he's seen paree

Back in Manhattan after a brief cruise around the Caribbean, Olivia and Nick stood on the curb outside their apartment building and watched the moving van pull away. Their remaining possessions were on their way to Sullivans Island, South Carolina. After they finally agreed on what to keep or sell, their rugs, ceramics, and paintings found their way to a storage facility of Sotheby's. All of it was appraised, photographed for the Sotheby's catalog, and stored in anticipation of an August estate sale. Some other items—personal possessions and winter clothes mostly—were sent to her office on East 58th Street, where Roni and Olivia spent much of the last week in a whirlwind hurrying to finish the conversion of the two small rooms that were being used for mountains of samples and office supplies into an acceptable bedroom and sitting room.

"This is truly bittersweet," Nick said as they watched the van make a right turn onto Second Avenue. "Okay! That's it! It's all gone!" Nick turned to Olivia and found the same quizzical sadness in her expression that he was feeling. "Gosh, I feel so weird about this all of a sudden."

"Me too. I have a sinking feeling. Well, we have our pied-à-terre, thank goodness, or I think I'd weep."

"Amen. Olivia? I think the pied-à-terre was a good idea."

"I know you had your doubts."

"Not any longer. I realize I need to be weaned from Manhattan. If I just jumped on a plane to Charleston, never to return, I think I'd feel like I was missing a limb."

"Well, that's the thing, isn't it? You love this city, you hate this city. When the cab's right there or you can get that eight o'clock table at La Bernardin or can snap up those two tickets in the orchestra to *La Traviata* at the last minute, you wouldn't want to live anywhere else on earth."

"Yes, that's true. And heaven forbid some terrible disease gets you, the best medical care in the world is at your fingertips."

"But!" Olivia was about to launch into a litany of complaints against New York City.

Insane cost of living. Fierce winters. Gridlock. Tourists. Terrorism. Crimes of every kind. Overcrowding. Potholes. Pollution. Competition at every turn, whether it was for a promotion at work you landed over your best friend or successfully grabbing that last Hass avocado at Citarella. People have been killed for less in New York. It was a coldhearted jungle.

"Yes, indeed. I know those *buts* all too well! Well, for a time we'll have the best of both worlds."

"I'm actually looking forward to this new chapter in our lives." Olivia said. "It's going to be very interesting to see how we settle into Dixieland."

"Dixiela . . . *Olivia!* Okay, darling girl, you know how I adore you, so I'm going to tell you this *because* I adore you . . ."

"What?"

"In its best interpretation *Dixieland* is a reference to a particular kind of New Orleans jazz music. In its worst, it's pejorative, referencing the South during slavery. Mammy and pappy standing by?"

"Oh no! I did not know that! I'll never say it again!"

"And we are moving to the *Lowcountry*. A very different animal."

"Center of the universe. Got it."

"Exactly!"

"Would you like to get a bite to eat? And then we can check out the apartment?"

"Sure! Let's walk over to Magnolia's."

Over a BLT and a western omelet that bore no resemblance to the tender omelet she had enjoyed on Necker Island, they struggled to define their feelings. There was no question about it. Olivia was feeling morose, but so was Nick, and *that* was surprising to both of them.

"I have a theory about this," Olivia said. "Would you like a french fry?"

Nick reached across the table and took two enormous french fries from Olivia's platter.

"I don't know why I always say no when the waiter wants to know if I'd like to have fries on the side. Maybe it makes me feel virtuous."

"Please," Olivia said and grinned. "Then you wind up eating mine!" She pushed the ketchup toward him.

"Well, this way we both indulge somewhat less. So? Your theory? Does it involve pillowcases?"

"No, Dr. Smarty Pants. It's relative to the concept of retirement."

"I think I see where you're headed. This stage of life means there's a lot more road in our rearview mirror than there is through the windshield."

"Mortality. I hate to even think about it."

"Yes. I thought I would be—I don't know—thrilled about retirement and relocating. I thought I'd feel like doing cartwheels! And while I'm profoundly happy to return to the island of my youth, I'm somehow sad too."

"We have to find something for you to do. Besides cartwheels. You'll break a hip, and then what?"

"Funny. Well, I actually rang up the South Carolina Historical Society and had quite a nice chat with the executive director, a lovely woman named Faye. Jenson is her last name, I think. I offered to, you know, volunteer—cataloging or whatever they needed. She suggested that I come in first and see what they have in the collection, spend a few afternoons reading. So that's what I'm going to do."

"Nick! That is an ingenious idea!"

He brightened up then.

"Yes. I think it is too. I mean, I've spent decades teaching history, and I'd bet you money that there are all sorts of stories in South Carolina's history I've never heard about. I'll bet they have old Civil War diaries and maybe even Revolutionary War correspondence. Who *knows* what all they've got?"

"Well, if I know you, you'll get in there and find the scandals and the secrets," Olivia said, and saw the sparkle she loved return to Nick's beautiful eyes. "And then we'll have things to talk about at every dinner party in Charleston! We'll be the new darlings in town."

"I certainly hope so! And maybe I'll write a book about my discoveries and become famous in my . . ." Nick was loath to use the words *old age* in reference to himself.

"How about sabbatical years?"

"Yes, I like the sound of that much better."

The waiter unceremoniously slapped the check on their table.

"Nick?"

"Hmmm?" Nick was checking the math and calculating the tip.

"Everything is going to be all right."

"Yes. I know. It's a new chapter, not the final chapter." Nick slipped a five and a one-dollar bill under the saltshaker. "This omelet and sandwich just cost us thirty-six dollars. Including the tip. I won't miss that!"

"You and me, Nick, just we two. I love you so."

Nick looked up and smiled so warmly at Olivia that she felt the warmth inside her heart.

"I love you too," he said. "Olivia?"

They had probably professed their love for each other thousands of times over the years, but neither one of them ever tired of hearing it said.

"Yes?"

"I miss the submarine."

"Oh, my dear sweet man. You can't say I didn't warn you. Their life is very addictive."

"You know the whole *Gatsby 'the rich are different'* thing?"

"Of course!"

"Well, they are. And Bob is a handful. But it's not necessarily a bad thing all the time."

"Well, the nice part is that Bob is fiercely loyal to his friends and colleagues. From where I sit, I don't particularly care if he's arrogant or bombastic. I'm not his wife. I'm his interior designer."

"That's right, missy. Let there be no confusion about that!"

"Very funny. I've had clients who were just as arrogant and

bombastic and they didn't pay their bills or they reneged on their contracts. Bob pays his bills." Her stomach began to hurt.

"An important feature in the relationship."

"You have no idea."

They paid their check and decided to walk down Park Avenue toward the office just to see the flowers. The medians were planted with thousands of pink begonias at their peak. The air was warm but surprisingly pleasant for a June day that could have been sweltering. They held hands and crossed the side streets. A breeze laced with the sweet smell of summer greens mixed with a trace of something more elemental drifted from east to west in a whoosh the whole way across the island.

"I'll miss this," Nick said, taking a deep breath and sighing. "I'll wake up in the night longing for this!"

"What? The look of Park Avenue in bloom or the smell of fuel emissions?" Olivia said.

"Is *that* what I've smelled all these years? Dear Lord!"

They reached the office and Roni was there waiting for them.

"Welcome to Le Petit Château! I had a set of keys made for you, Nick," she said, tossing them in his direction.

He caught them and said, "Thanks! I hadn't even thought of that yet."

"That's why I'm here!"

"Come see what Roni and I have done," Olivia said.

"I haven't been over here in ages!" Nick said. "It's smaller than I remember."

They were standing in the living room that served as Olivia's showroom/office. There was a love seat with an armchair by the window. Two glass desks on chrome bases with matching white leather desk chairs stood on opposite walls. A small round conference table with four chairs that would now double as a dining table. Roni had put a bunch of flowers in a vase in the center. There was also a lovely bottle of champagne chilling in an ice bucket with two tall stems.

How thoughtful, Olivia thought, and Nick nodded to her in agreement, another small example of their synchronistic thoughts.

"Well, you needed something to mark the moment!" Roni said. "It's a big day for you two!"

"Roni Larini? You are the sweetest woman alive!" Olivia said.

"Get a third glass and share it with us!" Nick said.

"Oh, no, no. But thanks. I have to get going in a few minutes."

Nick took a peek at the kitchen, which was a small galley tucked away. Olivia had furnished it with extra pots, pans, glasses, and dishes from their co-op so that now it was fully functioning. He smiled, thinking that he could easily prepare a simple meal in there.

The bedroom had a new queen-size bed with a tailored upholstered headboard and was made up with white linens trimmed in a Wedgwood-blue Greek-key design. Olivia loved white linens. Two end tables veneered in a blond wood stood on either side of the bed, and a chest of drawers of a similar finish stood against the wall, with a rectangular beveled mirror suspended above it. The end-table lamps resembled tiny chandeliers. The walls had been painted a pale smoky blue-gray color.

"It's amazing what paint can do," Olivia said. "This room is transformed."

"I know," Roni said. "It's like a miracle."

The other bedroom, painted a similar transforming hue,

held a tan linen sofa and a large television on the opposite wall atop a low-slung entertainment center, another chest of drawers, a small narrow coffee table, and two floor lamps. Framed *New Yorker* covers hung above the sofa. There was a walnut and wrought-iron industrial-looking bookcase that held some of Olivia's favorite reference books, a few personal photographs, and stacks of architecture and design magazines. It was cramped and Spartan at the same time, Olivia thought, but it would have to do. Some of the things that Nick thought went to auction—the netsukes, the puzzle balls, her tiny French clock—all those treasures Olivia refused to part with, she and Roni wrapped, placed in boxes, and tucked under the bed. She would reintroduce them into their lives in South Carolina one at a time and Nick would never know the difference. She hoped.

"Where'd you find the bookcase?" Olivia asked. "It's wonderful!"

"Crate & Barrel—fifty percent off because it has a ding on the back you can't even see." Roni said. "Hey, Nick? When I get to Charleston, are you going to give me the grand tour?"

Nick flipped on the bathroom light, scanned the room, and flipped it off.

"You bet!" Nick said. "I'll take you all around and turn you into a belle!"

"Ha! Roni's driving our silver and jewelry down and the skeleton clock."

"Yes, I don't trust movers with things like that glass dome. Never mind sterling silver. Besides, I can help you get unpacked and organized," Roni said.

Olivia and Nick were flying to Charleston the following day. Roni would arrive Tuesday with their car, the day the movers were scheduled to arrive.

"I see," said Nick. "Well, that's awfully nice."

"Thank goodness! I'm going to need help. So what do you think of the apartment, Nick?"

"I think this will be just fine!" he said. "It reminds me of my old bachelor pad in the Village, which wasn't much more than a monk's cell. This is very charming."

Olivia smiled and remembered sleeping there with him in his tiny bed and falling out, hitting the floor in the middle of the night. The floor, she recalled, was a commercial grade of tile glued to cement, hard and cold. A bruising and memorable detail.

"It kind of reminds me of that place too. Roni? Where are all the samples and swatches?"

"In the closet in the second bedroom and in the closet by the front door. Don't open the door too quickly!"

"Say, by the way, how's your mother getting along?" Nick asked.

"Well, she's about the same as she was last year, only crankier. Thanks for asking," Roni said and sighed heavily. "She'll probably outlive us all. I'll only be gone for a few days, and the nurses have promised to take extra special care of her. And they have my contact information if they need me."

"Yes," Olivia said. "It's getting harder and harder to be unavailable these days."

"Isn't that the truth? Well, I'll leave you two kids now. Behave yourselves!" Roni said, and gave Olivia a hug. Then she hugged Nick. "Okay then! I'll see you in Charleston."

"Watch out for the eighteen-wheelers on I-95!" Nick said.

"Yes! Be careful!" Olivia said.

Roni left, and Olivia turned to Nick and said, "If she doesn't move to South Carolina with me, I'm going to die."

Nick had popped the cork and poured for them. He handed Olivia a glass.

"No, you won't, but she is really wonderful. Cheers!"

Over steaks and salad in a favorite neighborhood haunt later that night, they went over their plan for the next day. Of course Nick was nervous about flying.

"I have a car picking us up at eight in the morning. We're flying JetBlue out of Kennedy at noon. I got a fabulous price on the tickets."

"Great! But do we need to leave so early?" Nick said.

"Yes, sir. Rush-hour traffic."

"Oh, right. Okay. Are you packed?"

"Yep, and so are you. I shipped most of our clothes with the movers. We just have one bag each. Don't worry, babe. I've got this one handled. And I've got the flight for Roni's return too."

There was a bit of decent news. Roni and Olivia were advised that the entire move was tax deductible because technically she was relocating her business. It wasn't much, but she'd take it.

Olivia had a difficult time sleeping that night. The lights of the city somehow made their way into the bedroom, casting just enough brightness into the room to make it feel like dusk. She could see the windows of the apartments across the way. People were still awake and moving around. Typical, she thought. It seemed to her that every time she had to get up very early the next day, she would toss and turn the night before. Besides, they were using a new mattress and in a new location. Nick, however, slept like a great redwood, falling into the forest of dreams.

Olivia left the bed to get a drink of water and looked at the neon face of their alarm clock. Four-twenty. If she could get back to sleep, she could still get another two hours. She needed it. Money worries were really getting to her. Nothing had come from the Necker Island trip except flamingo-trimmed curtains. Right now, she had about ten thousand dollars in their personal checking account and another thirty in their money market. She used half the money from the sale of their co-op to reduce the mortgage payment on their beach house and most of the balance in renovations. She had a couple of very small jobs going besides the work she was doing for Maritza and Bob, but barely enough was coming in to maintain their lifestyle. The business account was almost empty. Besides the mortgage, insurance, taxes, and monthly maintenance on the beach house, she still had the rent and utilities on the New York apartment to cover and Roni's salary. Nick's retirement was not a lot of help in the big picture, but it covered their day-to-day expenses. Something had to give in the next six weeks or she would have to start soliciting business, something no one in the field at her level would ever do without suffering a tidal wave of snickering and elevator whispers. She might as well put up a notice on the bulletin board in the lobby of the D&D Building that she was dead broke and desperate.

How ridiculous! she thought, and punched her pillow into submission. If the world thinks you're in trouble, they avoid you like a leper. If they think you're too busy, they beat down your door.

It was critical to keep the mythical beast fed.

Nick turned over, forcing Olivia to move toward the edge of the bed. Suddenly she heard the chime of her French clock from under the bed. Had she wound it by accident? Oh no.

"What's that?" Nick said in a sleepy voice.

Olivia panicked. "It's the apartment next door, sweetheart. Go back to sleep."

He threw his arm over her side and pulled her close to him. "Nope," he said. "It's your clock. It's okay."

In the complete darkness of that tiny bedroom, she smiled and snuggled up against him. He knew her that well and he loved her still. She guessed he had some understanding of their financial situation as well. In a way she hoped he did. It would mitigate her guilt and fear. The facts weren't exactly buried. He could've picked up a bank statement from her desk any time over the past six months and given it a look. Had he done so? She could not presume to know the answer to that or anything else at four-thirty in the morning. It didn't matter so much then. His muscular arm around her torso and his gentle regular snoring took her away into a peaceful sleep.

The flight to Charleston was quiet and smooth, except that the seats were oversold and there was a lengthy struggle to coerce two passengers to give up their places in return for a travel voucher. The value of the travel voucher increased every ten minutes until the pot was sweet enough for two folks to relent.

Their flight was on a somewhat larger plane and Nick seemed slightly less nervous than usual. But it also seemed as if every single passenger had brought more on board than they were allowed. Every seat and overhead compartment and the space under every seat was jammed to capacity.

"How are you doing?" Olivia asked.

"I flew in a helicopter, you know. This is nothing."

"Right," she said and smiled.

Although he did wipe down his seat-belt buckle, his reclining button, and his entire tray table with a Purell wipe. So did she.

"I saw something on television—Channel Seven, I think—that said this was a good idea."

"I believe you," Olivia said. "It can't hurt."

"I'm telling you, this is where germs are. When is the last time I got a cold or the flu? Tell me that."

"It's been a very long time," she said, smirking as discreetly as one could when confined to what seemed like a tuna can, seated next to the smirkee.

"And this is why," he said, holding up a wipe like *Exhibit A*. "Are you smirking at me?"

"Please! I would never! I think you're precious. That's all."

They landed in Charleston, retrieved their luggage, picked up the car keys from Ed at National, got in a brand-new white Ford Escape, and exited the airport. The day was very warm, and if you stood in direct sun for even a short period of time you would definitely get sunburned.

"It's hot," Nick said.

"Yes. I'll tell you what," Olivia said, blasting the air conditioner. "Flying on JetBlue between New York and Charleston is a breeze. I mean, I think it's as good as a commercial flight can be."

"Hmmm." Nick was quiet for a moment. "I'm listening to you, agreeing, and then my conscience gives me a kick in the head for even knowing the difference between what it's like to fly commercial versus private. Furthermore, my conscience thinks we sound obnoxious, especially when there are people starving in the world."

"Oh, God! Oh, God! You can't be serious!"

"I'm dead serious. What about Darfur? The Lost Boys?"

"Oh my God, Nick! Suddenly, you're like who? Francis of Assisi? I'm not *complaining* about flying on a commercial airline. And flying private is not how I would spend *my* money. I fly private for business and only on occasion. When I do, and you come, you are the beneficiary of that as well!"

They were waiting to merge onto I-526 East to take them to the islands. Traffic was heavy.

"Boy! You're in some mood today! What's the matter?"

"Where in the world did all these cars come from? Well, herein lies the problem. It's just way too easy to step into Bob and Maritza's life and think of it as *our* life, that's all."

"It's true. Maritza never goes to TripAdvisor to shop for bargain fares like we do."

"That's right. I just think we're awfully lucky . . . no, *extremely* lucky to have such fabulous vacations as someone's guest, and we should be grateful, not guilty."

"My mother was a Catholic."

"Oh, please. You're the one who ordered the extra hollandaise!"

"Oh, remind me of my wretched excess."

"I'm only teasing. Do you want to grab lunch at the Long Island Café?"

"I think they'll be closed by the time we get there. We could get burgers at Dunleavy's."

"Burgers it is."

They rode around the block three times before finding a parking spot.

"The traffic on this island is getting ridiculous!" Nick said.

"No argument from me!" she said.

After a lunch of superb hamburgers with cheese, sautéed onions, and bacon and on the way to their new/old house, Nick said, "So, are we going to have our first dinner in our new home tonight?"

"Well, sure!" Olivia started to laugh. "Except, no dishes or pots and pans. Remember?"

"Right. And the movers are coming when?"

"Tomorrow. Before ten."

"Well, good! So, I say let's put our things away and see what we can do to get ready for them."

"I'm sure the house is covered in dust. But Jason and his crew are supposed to be there wiping down every surface. We'll see."

"And maybe, at some point, we can have a nice walk on the beach?"

"You bet."

They turned into their driveway, stopped the car, and got out. The portable john was gone. The Dumpsters were gone. Holding their carry-on bags, they stood in the yard and looked up at the enormous white elephant they were about to call home.

"Sure is big," Nick said.

"It will shrink. Watch." What have I done? Olivia thought.

When the movers arrived, Olivia was ready for them. She directed the men with a roughly sketched floor plan of where she wanted furniture placed. By noon, it was starting to come together. Sort of. To Olivia it seemed sparse, without her familiar belongings.

Maybe they won't make the minimums at auction and we'll get our things back! she thought.

"Did you say something?" Nick said, hearing her thoughts in the ethers.

"No. But I was just thinking that this place looks bare."

"Well, let's get everything all unpacked and then we can see what we have."

"I'm pretty sure it's going to look really naked, but big bowls of flowers and plants in all the rooms will help."

"I'd like to see you really naked," he said and wiggled his eyebrows at her.

"Oh, Nick. You're such a teenage boy. You know, babe, this house is a lot bigger than our apartment was. We don't have nearly enough accessories to make this place look like home." And I can't afford to buy a doormat yet, she thought.

"Maybe I'll take up painting again and cover the walls with marsh scenes and egrets and magnolias."

What? Olivia thought and said tentatively, "Maybe. I didn't know you could paint!"

"Didn't I ever entice you with my etchings back in the day?"

"No, darling. Not me. That must've been some other googly-eyed girl."

"Oh. Sorry, dear. You know, there were legions of women before you. I practically had to beat them off with my umbrella!"

"I'm sure," Olivia said, and laughed.

Roni rolled in around one in the afternoon. Olivia went to the front door to greet her.

"You're here safe and sound! How was the drive?"

"Epic," Roni said. "I spent the night in Virginia Beach last night."

"You know, that's where Edgar Cayce spent the last part of his life. The Sleeping Prophet?"

Roni stepped over the threshold and into the foyer. Then she turned and saw the view of the water and Charleston harbor.

"Never heard of him. Holy cow. Well, now I know why you bought this place. This view is a killer."

"Thanks. I know. The house, however, is a bit of a disaster."

"Really? Well, at some point, you'll get it all fixed. It's a pretty big house."

"Not really. It's deceiving because it's elevated. You have to deal with floodplain FEMA maps down here."

"Right. So, after you survive this audit, you can renovate bit by bit."

"What audit?"

"The State of New York and the IRS would like to have a word with you," Roni said, reaching into her tote bag and pulling out two very serious-looking envelopes.

Olivia felt the blood drain from her face and thought she might faint.

"Oh, great. This is just what I need."

CHAPTER 7

olé!

A mountainous range of boxes were piled up in the kitchen all the way to the ceiling. Olivia sighed.

Roni said, "I got this."

Unpacking and organizing Nick and Olivia's kitchen consumed the remainder of the afternoon and would take at least one more day to complete. To Olivia's way of thinking, setting up the kitchen was the most heinous part of moving because the kitchen just wasn't a part of her soul. Olivia was good at laying out a space, but Roni was a natural at organizing anything. Olivia was whirling from room to room, adjusting the distance between chairs and sofas, collecting boxes and packing paper to discard. The number of boxes was overwhelming.

"So, I started to tell you that Maritza called," Roni said to Olivia.

"Why didn't she call me? She has my cell," Olivia said.

"She said that she tried, but she couldn't get though. So did I, by the way."

"That would explain why my cell phone hasn't rung since I got here. This could be a major problem."

"No kidding. You might have to put a booster on your router, whatever that means."

"I'll get right on that," Olivia said, thinking, If cell phone reception is a problem for us, other people must have the same problem. I'll ask the neighbors who to call.

"Right. Anyway, two big things. One, she's looking at a possible house to buy on Nantucket, a big old monster. She wants to know if you'll fly up to meet her next week. You'll fly to Newark or LaGuardia and their plane will take you to Nantucket. It's just a consultation fee, though."

If she was hired to do the job, the consultation fee was deducted from her other additional charges. It was something she had to do or clients thought they could do the job on their own after watching the *Property Brothers* a couple of times. They would download software and give a plan to a construction company and act as their own general contractor.

"Well, I think, *hell yes!* I'm repacking as I'm unpacking!" Olivia said, thinking, Yes, thank you, this could save my life for a while.

Olivia was still reeling from the news about the audit, reeling to the point that she had yet to open the envelopes and read the letters. Most likely, she'd give them a glance and hand them back to Roni to send to their accountant and lawyer.

"And two, she wants to know if you and Nick want to go to Spain over the Fourth of July and sail around the Balearic Islands. Bob's son is getting married on board the yacht."

"How could we say no to that? A family wedding? Of course we'll be there."

"Anyway, you need to call her. She's hysterical."

"Why? What's wrong?"

"Colette, Bob's ex-wife, Daniel's mother, is going to be on the yacht as well."

"No! Oh, dear. Colette can be difficult. And Maritza didn't take the news well?"

"Are you serious? I got such an earful! Bob said to her something like how can we not invite her? She's his mother? Even so, I don't know if *I* could deal . . ."

"The only thing they have in common is that they call each other *that bitch*."

"Well," Roni said, "given the facts, who could blame them?"

"True," Olivia said. "I'm going back to work on the closets. And I'm going to throw in a load of wash."

Jason, true to his word, had installed the washer and dryer. She stood before the shiny new appliances, her left arm clamped around a load of bath towels on her hip, completely mystified by the numerous control knobs and LCD display.

Now, how does this thing work? There's no coin slot, she thought. "*Roni?*"

"Coming!"

After Roni showed her how to get the washer going, she returned to the kitchen and Olivia made her way back to the bedroom closets, passing Nick in the room that would be his study. He was sitting on the floor; there was a lot of muttering and frustration coming from his direction. He was attempting to hook up the stereo and trying to ensure their computers could respond to their shared printer. For the moment, a shared printer was the most economical decision. Then there was the matter of the stereo, the fax machine, and their landlines, which had to be made to work. The wires looped around his arms and stretched across the floor would surely give him nightmares about being strangled by spaghetti.

"Maybe you should help Roni," Olivia said. "After all, you're the cook."

"I think you might be right," Nick said, looking very relieved. He got up from the floor, ran his hand through his hair, and wiped the dust from his khaki trousers. "I'll just wash my hands."

"Yes, you don't need to bother yourself with this technical nonsense. It's not the best use of your time. I'll ask Jason to help with the television and all this other stuff. Those young guys could rewire a whole house in their sleep."

"Well, aren't they smart? Let them!"

He didn't exactly stomp off to the bathroom because Nick was not the kind of man who stomped off to anywhere. But Olivia knew by his exasperated expression that if not in the physical sense, mentally he was stomping off. And although he didn't say "the young upstarts," she could practically hear him thinking it.

By five o'clock that afternoon, everyone needed a break. The heat of the day was broken and the sun had traveled to the western sky, throwing off vibrant flashes of rose and purple. The sunset would be beautiful.

Roni and Nick appeared at her side with glasses of iced water.

"Why, thanks!" Olivia said, helping herself. She had just finished unpacking the third wardrobe box of their clothes and shoes and hanging them in the closet. "I might sound like Joan Crawford from *Mommie Dearest*, but I'm so glad I went to Bed Bath & Beyond yesterday. I hate wire hangers."

"Me too," Roni said. "The closet looks so much nicer when

clothes are sorted by color and hung in one direction on the same kind of hangers."

"But we're a bit anal," Olivia said. "I got Joy's hangers."

"I have her mop too," Roni said. "Nick, your stuff looks brand new!"

"We know my closet won't stay like this for long," Nick said. "I mean, let's face it. Right?"

"It's okay, baby boy," Olivia said. "You have other redeeming qualities."

"You know what?" Nick said. "Olivia and I have yet to put one foot on the beach. It's low tide now. So why don't we all take a ten-minute walk to stretch our dogs?"

Olivia drained her glass and considered the idea. It was a beautiful time of day, the sun not nearly as vicious as it had been when she ran out to pick up sandwiches for their lunch. But she definitely wasn't wearing the right outfit for the beach. She'd have to roll up the legs of her pants or put on a pair of Bermuda shorts, which she despised but accepted as a necessary evil in her new life. Let's face it, she thought, the back of my thighs have seen better days.

"Can we have a wardrobe consultation? Shorts? Sundress?" Olivia said, thinking that at some point she was going to have to cross the threshold of a Talbots and acquiesce in dressing like the natives.

"I don't own shorts," Roni said. "Or flip-flops."

"Should I cover my hair with a hat?" Olivia said. "I just had my color done and I feel like it will oxidize in five minutes."

"You're probably right," Roni said. "The sun is still very intense. What about jewelry?"

"Let's put our jewelry in the vault," Olivia said. "And our wallets. Or I can just lock the house. Should I turn on the alarm?"

"Olivia! Stop! Ladies? This poor orange is not worthy of your pulverizing squeeze. Let's simply leave our shoes on the sand dunes, roll up our cuffs, and walk. Hmmm?"

"Do you think it's safe?" Roni asked. "To just walk out like that?"

"Yes," Nick said. "I do. This is not Mumbai or Jakarta, or some place teeming with drug lords and disenfranchised desperadoes."

"He's probably right," Roni said.

Roni and Olivia exchanged skeptical expressions, and finally Olivia said, "Let's throw caution to the wind. We're only talking about ten minutes." She picked up her sunglasses from the side table.

"Really. What's the matter with us? Let's go," Roni said, taking her sunglasses from her purse. "We sound like old ladies in a Woody Allen movie."

"A bit," Nick said, smiling as he exchanged his regular eyeglasses for his prescription sunglasses. He held the door open for them to pass.

They stood on the porch for a moment and then descended the steps to the front yard on the ocean side of the house. It took a few moments for them to adapt to the salt and humidity and for their eyes to adjust as well. Nick opened the gate to the beach and they followed him.

"Just leave your shoes right here on the sand," he said. "It's what everyone does."

"And no one steals your shoes?" Roni said.

"I've never heard of a single case of shoe theft," Nick said, and laughed.

When they kicked off their sandals, they were surprised by the coolness of the sand. Then they rolled up the cuffs of their pants and began to walk close enough to the last ripple of the waves so that the water just barely washed over their feet. At first the ocean was chilly enough to startle them, but after a few more minutes it seemed warm enough to be a soothing bathtub.

"Good grief!" Olivia said, walking on ahead. "If this was Southampton, my feet would be purple with hypothermia. This water is perfect!"

A dozen or so sea gulls were waddling around the water's edge. The birds scattered into low flight as they approached, only to land twenty or so feet away. Other tiny birds, sandpipers mostly, darted around and continued to peck away at the mud, finding some kind of treat below tiny bubbles in the surface.

"Would you look at these little birds?" Olivia said.

"They're adorable," Roni said.

They smiled at each other. It was uplifting to see nature in action, and the warmth of the air and water were so soothing.

"Look at what we've been missing!" Olivia said.

"Boy, no kidding!" Roni said.

"I checked this morning and the ocean temperature is around eighty-three degrees. Perfect for a swim," Nick said. "Did you happen to run across our swimsuits yet?"

"I surely did," Olivia said. "They're already folded away in the chest of drawers, just waiting for us!"

"Maybe we can take a dip later on," Roni said. "Mine's in the car. I didn't even check into my hotel yet. This *is* pretty wonderful!"

"Oh no! You mean, you haven't had a chance to hang up your toothbrush and we've had you working like a dog all day?" Nick said.

"It's very sad, the way I'm treated and all that. It's medieval, in fact." Roni laughed.

"Oh, here we go. Where are you staying?" Olivia said.

"I found a beautiful B&B on the Internet. It's downtown."

She told them the name of it and Nick whistled.

"No bargain," he said.

"Gosh, it might've been a better deal for me to buy another mattress and box spring than for you to stay there," Olivia said. "We have three empty bedrooms that need to be furnished anyway."

"Well, neither one of us thought that part through, but it's not a big deal. I want to see the historic district anyway. The next time I'd love to stay here if you'll have me," Roni said. "But right now, I'm thinking I'd like to be in this gorgeous water up to my neck!"

"Well, ladies? It appears that we have two choices. Either we can go downtown and have a delightful meal and see the sights. Or we can go for a swim now, which I recommend. And then have dinner at someplace casual east of the Cooper," Nick said.

"What does 'east of the Cooper' mean?" Roni said.

Nick said, "Ah! It's secret code. It's where we are until you reach and cross the Cooper River. Remember that big bridge you drove over that takes you from Charleston to Mount Pleasant? The one with the port and all the container ships under it? It's over there!"

Nick turned and pointed to the Ravenel Bridge on the horizon.

"Yes! Of course," Roni said.

"That is the Cooper River. We are east of it. Now, if you went to the other side of the peninsula, there's another river.

The Ashley. If you cross the Ashley River Bridge, you are west of the Ashley."

"Now I understand! All these years I could never quite get the distinction," Olivia said.

"Well now! She's got it! So, again, either you are east of the Cooper, on the peninsula, or west of the Ashley. And then there's south of Broad, of course."

"What, pray tell, is south of Broad?" Roni asked.

"It's the oldest and some would argue most historic part of Charleston," Nick said. "Not that there aren't other important historic areas *north* of Broad Street."

"Ah! So Broad is a street and not a river!" Roni said.

"Correct," Nick said. "So what will it be, ladies?"

"I'm thinking I'd like a swim," Olivia said. "Well, maybe a wade in the water."

"Don't make me sing," Nick said. Nick was referring to the old spiritual "*Wade in the Water*," but Olivia, unfamiliar with the genre, didn't get the connection.

Neither did Roni.

"You mean Kristen Wiig? That *SNL* sketch?" Roni said. "Funniest thing I ever saw! Ha! *Oh! Don't make me sing!*" Roni began to laugh and laugh and couldn't stop. Every time she tried to collect herself, she'd look at Nick and crack up all over again. "Remember the cats? They were out there on the balcony rail just howling?"

Nick had no clue what *SNL* stood for. Olivia had no idea what she was talking about either. They just looked on, mystified, as Roni cackled.

"Don't you watch *Saturday Night Live?*" Roni said, trying to help them understand.

"I haven't watched *Saturday Night Live* since Dan Aykroyd

called Jane Curtin an ignorant slut," Olivia said. "I can't stay up that late anymore."

"*Ignorant slut!*" Roni broke into laughter again. "Remember them? Oh, God, they were hilarious! And Bill Murray was that dweeb Todd giving noogies to Gilda Radner? Oh! They were so ridiculous!"

"Oh!" Nick said, finally figuring out what *SNL* meant. Jesus, he thought, I'm older than Adam's house cat! "And just who is this Kristen Wiig?"

Roni explained, but it still meant nothing to Nick, who honestly preferred Ken Burns's documentaries or Book TV for television entertainment.

Nick said, "Okay, so let's go for a swim now and I'll take you crazy girls out to dinner afterward. How does that sound?"

"Oh, God!" Roni said, finally regaining her composure. "I haven't laughed that hard in ages! Remember the *Coneheads*?"

"Yes. They were great. Anyway, good idea, Nick." Olivia said to Roni, "Come on, you lunatic! Get a grip."

"Right!" Roni said. "Sorry."

They walked back to the house, quickly changed into their swimsuits, grabbed towels, and hurried back to the beach. Nick dropped his towel and sunglasses on the sand and ran into the water with abandon, diving under a wave.

"He looks like a kid!" Roni said, wading into the water over her knees.

"That's my nature boy. I don't think I've never seen him so happy!" Olivia said, laughing, following Roni and going in farther until the water covered their waists. "Should I get my hair wet?"

"Who cares?" Roni said. "I'm getting mine wet." She dove under the water, coming up ten feet away from her.

Nick swam toward them. "Come on! Jump in!"

"Are there fish in here?" Olivia said, concerned because the water was opaque and she couldn't see her feet as she could in the waters of the Caribbean. In Necker Island she could go in the water up to her chin and look down to see if her nail polish was chipped on her little toe.

Nick started laughing, "Oh, no! There are no fish in this part of the ocean! They're all out there!" He pointed in the direction of Johns Island. "No fish at all!"

Roni laughed and Olivia laughed then too.

"They're shy," Roni said.

"Oh, screw both of you and my hair too," Olivia said and swam out a distance. Then she threw herself on her back to float. Olivia was a strong if infrequent swimmer, but floating just seemed to be a better idea.

If Nick and Roni were still teasing her, she couldn't hear them because the water covering her ears created a vacuum, a lovely silent vacuum. She was suspended by salt, floating along for the longest time, looking up at the clouds moving overhead. And she felt good, really good. It didn't matter then that the IRS and the State of New York were interested in her. Who cared about money? Well, she did, because they needed it sort of desperately. But maybe Maritza was going to save them with another house to decorate. This was the ultimate state of blissful therapy. Yes! When she was worried, she thought, I'll just come down to this beach and float right here in the water! What could be more relaxing? Maybe this was what Maritza meant when she compared a visit with her to a walk on the beach. She felt better too! She marveled at how absolutely wonderful it was, so she just continued to drift, ignoring the world. All she could hear was the low rumble of an engine in the distance. Then, out of nowhere, she felt something nudge her. Was it a *shark?* She jumped, frightened only to realize that the water she was in was way over her head. To her complete horror, she was in the channel! Panic set in. She began to spin around frantically, looking around for Nick and Roni. They were on the beach, tiny dots in the distance, waving to her. Something nudged her again and Nick jumped in the water and began swimming toward her. Then he stopped and went back. She was too far out. Then there was the deafening blast of a horn, a foghorn. But there was no fog. But there *was* a container ship rounding the bend and entering the channel. It would run her over if she couldn't get away fast enough. The undertow was increasing and Olivia was being dragged farther out by it. Something nudged her again, and it kept coming back and pushing her toward the shore. But it was still a long way to safety. The ship was coming toward her, moving at a brisk clip, and the weight of it naturally caused a powerful dispersal of the water. If Olivia couldn't manage to get back to the shallows, she was in real danger. She knew this instinctively and something—she didn't know what—kept pushing her, giving her a boost, propelling her ahead, yards at a time. Maybe she was having surges of adrenaline. She swam on, fighting the undertow. The ship grew closer. Finally, just as she was so exhausted and almost ready to accept the fact that she might not make it, she felt something huge, a body underneath her and she grabbed it, throwing her arms around it. It might have been a shark. She didn't know or care. All she knew was that it was taking her toward Nick *and* it was her only chance to make it. Her face was in the water and it seemed then as though she was swallowing the ocean through her nose and mouth. Was she drowning? Suddenly this thing, this beast she had her arms around, began to roll its body in the surf, trying to shake her off.

"Let go!"

She heard this again and again and wasn't sure if the words were meant for her or not. Who was calling her?

"Let go!" She recognized Nick and Roni's voices, pleading with her. *"Olivia! Let go!"*

She let go, and whatever it was that had brought her to safety swam away. She tried to stand but collapsed in water that was less than three feet deep.

The next thing she remembered, something was pushing on her chest hard enough to crack her ribs and she expelled salt water in a great gush.

"Ms. Ritchie? Ms. Ritchie?" The voice, a pleasant male voice, seemed to be coming from very far away.

"Ms. Ritchie? Come on, now. Open your eyes. You're all right."

She looked up into the eyes of a young off-duty paramedic who just happened to be there on the beach, line fishing. He had seen the whole episode unfold and jumped in to help. She began to cough and cough, and to her embarrassment, her chest convulsed again and she heaved even more water onto the beach. She continued to cough.

"Thank God! Thank you, sir!" Nick said. "How can we ever repay you?"

"Oh, God! Thank God!" Roni said. "Olivia, let me help you sit up."

The paramedic said, "No need. I was glad to help. You folks ought to try swimming away from the channel, down in that direction. You'll live longer."

"Thank you. We will."

The man walked away from them and back to his fishing lines, which were planted in the hard-packed wet sand.

"You scared the hell out of us, Olivia!" Roni said, and burst into tears.

"What are you crying about?" Olivia's voice was raspy and hoarse. "I'm the one who almost drowned." She coughed a few more times and then took a deep breath.

"Oh, my darling girl!" Nick knelt in the sand and put his arms around her. "If I had lost you, I don't know, I couldn't have lived."

"Yeah, and I'd spend the rest of my life making tuna sandwiches at Smilers Delicatessen on Third Avenue!"

This was a very dramatic statement from Nick and a typical piece of sass from Roni, but even in her present mental state, returning to life from an actual near death experience, Olivia rolled her eyes.

"Oh, for God's sake, Nick. Yes, you would. You'd live. I'm just fine," Olivia said adding, "Help me stand up, please. And, Roni? You can't work at Smilers. You're Italian American." Nick pulled her to a standing position and she ran her hand through her hair, which at this point resembled dreadlocks. "I must look like holy hell."

Nick handed Olivia his shirt and she wiped her face with it.

"Actually, for a girl saved by dolphins, you look pretty good!" Roni said.

"What do you mean?" Olivia said.

"Look!" Roni said.

Olivia turned to face the ocean and the area where Roni pointed. A pod of bottlenose dolphins, probably eight or ten of them, were rising up and diving back under the sea in their traditional arcs, but they seemed to be unusually close to shore. And maybe it was their collective imagination, but Nick, Roni, and even Olivia would've sworn in a court of law that the dolphins were doing everything they could to capture their attention. Olivia stepped closer to the edge of the water and waved at them. One of them breached into midair, looked at her, and made a repetitive thrilling chirp. Then he swam backward on his tail, staring at her.

"That dolphin is looking straight at me. Am I supposed to answer this fellow?" Olivia said.

"I would. He might be the very one who saved you." Nick called out and waved to the dolphin. "Thank you! Thank you very much!"

"It's just plain bad manners not to say thank you to the dolphin," Roni said. "Wait, I can't believe I just said that."

"Sweet Baby Jesus, I'm here for twenty-four hours and I'm talking to the animals!"

"Dr. Dolittle, I presume?" Roni said, and giggled. "Unbelievable."

"Signs and wonders, sweetheart," Nick said. "What did I tell you?"

Olivia looked at Nick. He wasn't kidding. Then she looked back out to where the dolphins were still horsing around, seemingly waiting for some recognition from her. It was surreal, but maybe there was some actual bona fide magic in the Lowcountry. And *something had* brought her close to the shore. That part was absolutely true. *Strange* but true. She admitted that much to herself.

"You can't make this stuff up," Nick said.

"Thank you!" she called out, waving her arms, and thought, Boy, am I glad they weren't sharks. "Thank you!"

There was a lot of chirping and calling from the dolphins. Then they dove under the waves and swam out of sight.

Nick, Roni, and Olivia stood at the edge of the tide's high-water mark for what seemed like a really long time. Each of them was lost in thought, trying to rationally process what had just happened. They looked around for the fisherman. He was nowhere to be seen.

"That fisherman saved my life too!" Olivia said.

"You and about a billion other Christians," Nick said.

"Oh, come on, Nick! You don't really believe . . ."

"Do you?" Roni said.

"I've told you this so many times," he said solemnly. "This island and the whole Lowcountry is a place unto itself."

"Oh, come on, Nick," Roni said. "What in the world are you talking about?"

"Only that you'll notice things that happen here that are otherwise completely inexplicable. Even irrational. Now, maybe these phenomena happen everywhere, and maybe you just notice them *here*. I don't know."

"You mean like that invisible hand that pulls you back when you're about to step off a curb and get hit by a bus?" Roni said. "I've heard stories like that."

"Exactly! It's not your time to go," Nick said to Olivia and pointed at Roni. "That's *exactly* what I mean."

"I don't even know what to say except that I am one grateful woman to be alive."

"Do you really feel all right?" Roni asked.

"Perfectly fine, except for the part where I had an actual conversation with a dolphin, which I did. And the other part where I bodysurfed almost to the beach on the back of one. And, by the way, there's a lot of power in their snouts. I'll bet I'm going to bruise like a peach from where I got pushed along."

"We can ice the spots. My mother put ice on everything. And in everything. Especially vodka."

"Hmmm. Speaking of adult beverages," Nick said, "I think a good Cab and a thick steak might help us put this situation in perspective. Anyone care to go to dinner? Let's go somewhere special."

"I agree. It's not every day that . . . well, you know," Roni said.

"My hair may never be the same," Olivia said and added, "And I won't either. Who would believe this?"

"I'm going to google dolphin rescues," Roni said.

They went back up to the house, had their showers, and started getting dressed. She studied her body in front of the full-length mirror. There were deep red blotches on her hips and ribs but no bruises so far. Olivia slipped on a long linen sundress and sandals and simply braided her long wet hair.

"I'll find a salon tomorrow," she said to Nick. "I'm not going to let something insignificant like my hair stand in the way of our cocktail hour. It takes forever to dry it, as you know."

Truly, Olivia did have enough hair for two women.

"You look beautiful," Nick said.

"Thanks, sweetheart. And you smell delicious. Let's find Roni and get out of here."

Soon they were in Olivia and Nick's rental car and headed to Halls Chophouse downtown. They put Roni's luggage in the back.

"So, you can use this while you're here," Olivia said. "It's fun to drive."

"Thanks!" Roni said.

"We can Uber home," Nick said. "Then we don't have to take two cars."

"Uber is a verb now," Roni said, and smiled.

"And then we can have two martinis," Olivia said. "I think we earned them."

"You can have mine," Roni said. "Two martinis would send me to Betty Ford."

"I always forget you're a cheap date," Olivia said.

"You don't drink at all?" Nick said. Nick was suspicious of total sobriety.

"My mother drank enough for both of us. Maybe I'll sip on a glass of champagne."

"You mean, you have no indulgences?" Nick said.

"Ice cream and gelato," Roni said.

"Well, thank goodness! I feel much better," Nick said. "There's a parking spot!"

Parking was at a premium downtown because there were roughly ten times more people than there were places to leave your car. Once inside the restaurant, they were led to a table upstairs.

"I'd like to see the wine list," Nick said.

They ordered vodka martinis and champagne and were perusing the ten-pound leather menu.

"Very good, sir," the waiter said. He stepped away and returned with a ten-pound wine list.

"Good thing I got some cardio this afternoon," Nick mumbled, hoisting the leather-bound list to a level where he could read it.

Of course, after the drama of the day, no one could make a decision about what to order until a sizzling bone-in rib eye steak with onion rings passed their table.

"That's what I'm having," Olivia said, and her eyes grew large. "I know it's a mortal sin on a plate, but it smells so darn good."

"Yes, it does," Nick said. "I'll have the same thing."

"I don't want to be odd person out, so I'll have the same thing too."

The waiter took their orders and Nick chose a 2009 Beringer Vineyards Cabernet Sauvignon to drink with their meals and asked for another glass of champagne for Roni.

Scarcely three minutes passed until the waiter returned with their cocktails while they recounted the afternoon.

"Cheers!" Nick said. "To our health!"

"Cheers!" Roni said, lifting her flute. "To life!"

"And longevity! And by the way, folks, I can never eat fish again," Olivia said, taking a sip.

"My heavens, Olivia, you can't say that!" Nick said, fishing out an olive. "Fresh fish and shellfish are the backbone and pride of Lowcountry cuisine!"

"I know how she feels, Nick. How can she be sure she's not eating one of Danny's friends?" Roni said.

"Danny?" Nick said.

"Danny the Dolphin," Roni said. "I named him."

"I see," Nick said. "Well, in this culture we don't eat dolphins, and they only hang out with each other."

"Oh," Roni said.

"Like, birds of a feather . . . ?" Olivia said.

"Yes." Nick stared at Roni and was quiet for a moment. "You know, Roni, there is a world of research that's being done trying to measure the aptitude of dolphins and to decode their language and so forth. They are highly intelligent, as we have known for some time. And there is no doubt in my mind that a dolphin saved Olivia's life this afternoon. I feel like maybe we should do something to honor that."

"Like what?" Olivia said.

"Maybe we should eat what they eat. I happen to know they eat fish and shellfish. They have teeth, you know," Nick said. "They belong to the same family as the pilot whales and the orcas."

"How do you know this stuff?" Roni said. "I thought you taught history."

"I did. But I looked it up on my smartphone while you ladies were getting dressed tonight." Nick said. "What a world we live in today! Anyway, if they eat fish, we can eat fish without an ounce of guilt. Besides, our Lord caught fish."

"Okay," Olivia said. "I'll eat seafood, but not tonight, and it might be a while before I go swimming again."

"Nonsense. We can and will go swimming where that nice young man recommended." Nick said. "Was it luck that put a CPR worker on the beach fifty feet from us?"

"Nick? That's two references to religion in one day. Where are we going with this?"

"Nowhere, really. I just think that what happened today is too coincidental to be called coincidental. Call it God or whatever you want, but that was the *unseen hand* in action."

"Maybe," Olivia said, "but the question is why?"

"Yes, my love. *Unseen hand* is the answer, but *why* is the question."

CHAPTER 8

jump!

After a simple breakfast of yogurt, fruit, and toast, Olivia and Nick began cleaning up the kitchen. As they were putting their bowls in the dishwasher, Roni arrived. It was just a few minutes shy of nine o'clock.

"Good morning! I bought you some supplies," Roni said, dropping several bags from Whole Foods on the kitchen island. "Nick? Thanks again for dinner last night. It was delicious!"

"You're welcome! It was a pleasure to be out on the town with not one but two glorious females! Would you care for coffee?" Nick said.

"Sure! Thanks!" Roni said. "Olivia? Have you seen Danny this morning?"

Roni giggled and Olivia shrugged her shoulders. Nick poured Roni a mug and handed it to her.

"You mean, did I see Danny my dolphin friend? Um, no," Olivia said. "You've been shopping at this hour? This is when I remember how much younger you are than me. Thanks! Just give me the receipt."

Roni pulled a long roll of paper from her purse and handed it to Olivia.

"I love to go to grocery stores in new places and see what they've got. The Whole Foods in Mount Pleasant is a treasure!"

"Good to know." Olivia said. "What did you buy?"

"The basic stuff you need—sugar, flour, salt, plastic wrap, aluminum foil, garbage bags, Ziplocs in two sizes, sponges, dishwashing liquid, and—jeez, just take a look!"

Olivia began emptying the paper bags and she had to agree. They needed every thing that Roni bought. But she wished Roni had shopped at the BI-LO. Nick picked up the receipt, looked at it, and covered his mouth with his hand in shock.

"Outrageous! I can't believe," he said, "that you spent this much money and there's nothing to eat in all of these bags!"

"Actually," Roni said, "somewhere in one of these bags are a dozen eggs, coffee, a pound of bacon, a pound of butter, and a loaf of bread. Oh! And half-and-half."

"You're a sweetheart to do this, Roni. Thanks!"

"It was on the way, so I just pulled over. No biggie. So did you call Maritza yet?"

"Not yet. I was just going to refill my mug, go out on the porch and do just that!"

"Well, tell her I said hi."

"I will!"

Olivia added a bit of half-and-half to her coffee and left them to continue setting up the kitchen. Once outside, she saw a huge container ship entering the harbor. She stood there for a moment, awestruck by its massive size, and she gained a new appreciation for the power of its weight. She began counting its freight. This gigantic vessel held eight containers across the width of its deck and fifteen of them in length. Each stack was six or eight containers high. There was probably a fleet of eighteen-wheelers waiting near the docks to take them all, one by one, to their final destinations.

The container ship passed their property. It was the same kind of ship that had nearly killed her. She knew she'd never look at them quite the same way again. The gargantuan size of the container ships was like the star-filled night sky over the dark ocean—both reminded her that she was a mere speck in the scheme of things. And the ships and the dolphins would be a permanent reminder that she had survived for a reason. She had been there in that deep water at that moment for some kind of cosmic reason. Absolutely. There was a lesson to be learned from her harrowing experience, but she still had no idea what it was.

She shook her head and pressed Maritza's number into the keypad of her phone. A shrimp trawler came into view. Its nets were down and a flock of hungry sea gulls followed it closely. It was a beautiful sight: the boat and the gulls and the sparkling endless water.

"Maritza? Good morning! It's Olivia. Roni said I should call?"

"Oh! Olivia! I *cain't* begin to tell you how happy I am to hear your voice!"

"Well, wonderful! I'm glad to hear yours too! Roni is down here with us in South Carolina, and she said . . ."

"Oh! That's right! Y'all moved! I keep thinking you're still around the corner and across the park! How did it go?"

Olivia had the thought, Dammit, Maritza! Are you really this much of a ditz? Yes. She was. Out of sight, out of mind.

"Well, it was bedlam at first, but I think we're finally beginning to get our arms around it all."

"I keep forgetting that I've got to send y'all a little something for a housewarming. How does y'all's stuff look in the new house?"

"Not quite right yet, but it will."

"What I'm really asking is, is there something that y'all need?"

Olivia started to laugh because only Maritza would ask such a question and in that way.

"Oh! Goodness! You don't have to buy us a single thing!" Olivia considered how sweet that was and said in an unusually familiar way, "But I'll tell you this much: I'm truly glad I can get fabric at a discount because there's a lot of reupholstering to be done. The light's different here, you know?"

"What? Y'all got a different sun down there?" Maritza laughed.

"You'd think so. Everything takes on a sort of gray-blue hue in the morning and an odd yellow cast in the afternoon. There's a tremendous amount of glare from the water, and even the smallest aspect of a pattern pops out in bold detail like it never did in New York. Never mind the wear and tear I never noticed. Now that shows in a *whole* new way! It's all about the light."

The truth was that Olivia felt disoriented. There were no rugs to anchor the rooms. The beautiful floors were heart pine and rich with the patina of over a hundred years. But still. And she missed their clocks, ceramics, and paintings, the things that would make anyplace feel like home. The house looked as if it was putting itself on display but was only half dressed. And the crazy light's changing all the time was very distracting.

"I'll bet that's true! That's exactly why I want you to come to Nantucket with me. Only you would think of what color the light is. You and Monet, that is."

"Monet? The French Impressionist?"

"Yep. I went to this show at the Met with Bob, and I read on one of the little signs they put on the walls next to the paintings that he painted the light of the landscape, not the actual landscape."

"I've never heard that."

"Yep, well, that's what it said. That's why he's an Impressionist. Anyhow, y'all have an eye for that sort of thing. You and old Claude!" Maritza giggled.

Just when I think she's a complete screwball, she starts quoting the curatorial department from a show at the Metropolitan Museum of Art, Olivia thought.

"Just me and Claude Monet."

"That's right! So Bob and I are looking at buying this big old house and I'd just like to have your opinion of it before we sign on the dotted line, you know what I mean?"

"Maritza, I would be thrilled to help and I'm honored to be asked. May I bring Nick with me? He loves Nantucket."

"Of course, bring Nick! I'll get it all organized and email you the details."

"That sounds perfect. Thanks."

"Is tomorrow too soon?"

As a general rule, when Maritza called, Olivia dropped everything. She did this not only because it was what Maritza had come to expect or because she was her only living, breathing client of any heft. She did this because it was what *all* her clients expected. Otherwise they'd simply call someone else. Well, not Maritza so much, but most of her other clients felt no loyalty at all. They wanted what they wanted when they wanted it. Period.

"Actually, if we could have one more day . . ." Olivia held her breath.

"Of course! I know you're trying to get settled. And did Roni tell you about Spain?"

Olivia sighed in relief.

"Thank you! Yes! Oh, my goodness! How fabulous! We can't wait. And she told me that Daniel is getting married. Wow! Is Bob thrilled?"

Bob has to be aghast, Olivia thought. A young man with Daniel's résumé (read: trust fund of untold wealth) could have anyone he wanted.

"Dahlin'? The question ought to be, am *I* happy about Bob's ex-wife Colette coming on the boat with us for the wedding? And she's spending the night."

"Oh, dear." Olivia was unsure of what to say. "Well, thank heavens it's a big boat."

"Honey, Noah's Ark would be too small for me and that bitch."

"I'm sure. This is going to require some incredible resolve, Maritza, but my money's on you."

"Olivia, you know how hard I try to make Bob happy. I feel like he's just doing this to make me even more insecure than I already am. Things between us aren't any better than they were on Necker. He and Ellen are always whispering when I come into a room, and then they get all quiet. They must think I'm stupid. She's such a tramp."

Olivia never would've pointed out to her that only a few years ago Maritza was the tramp. So she said, "I'm sorry, Maritza." What else was there to say?

"And now he's throwing his ex-wife in my face."

"Well, let's be honest. It's not so unusual for the ex-wife to want to be present at the marriage of her child, is it?"

"No, but it's awkward. Can't she just leave after they cut the cake? She has to stay over as our guest? And between us? This girl Daniel is marrying? She doesn't have a daddy to give her away. Not a pot to pee in or a window to throw it out of."

What an image! Olivia thought.

"The poor child. That has to be a real heartbreak for her."

"Who knows? I'm gonna ask her if she wants to go shopping for a dress, something to hide her tattoos. She'll probably say no, but I'll ask her."

That girl has no problem showing her tats, Olivia thought.

"Who knows what young people want these days? I don't think brides blush anymore."

"Truly. All I know is Bob is gone more and more. Maybe that's why he wants this house on Nantucket—one more place to escape."

"Let's have a look at it together before we jump to conclusions."

"Oh, Olivia! What am I going to do?"

"Well, if the Nantucket house is as amazing as I'm guessing it is, you're going to buy it and we're going to decorate it to a fare-thee-well so that Bob swoons over it! He will see how talented you are and fall in love with you all over again!" This was the moment to be assertive and Olivia knew it. She *needed* the job.

"Do you really think that will work?"

"I think it's worth a try, don't you?"

"Anything is worth a try. The only good thing that's happened to me since I saw you the last time is that Bob took me to Naples for a quick trip."

"Italy?" A two-day trip to Italy would not have surprised Olivia at all.

The tour boat that left from the Charleston Marina was

making the turn right in front of their house. Olivia watched the passengers as they stared at her house and took pictures.

"No, Florida. But I hardly saw him the whole time. He's looking to open two more restaurants there, so he was in meetings all day and night. At least we stayed at the Ritz-Carlton, so it wasn't torture."

"The Ritz-Carlton there is beautiful. I did some work for a client in Naples a few years ago and I stayed there a lot."

"Hey! Remember that guy Mel from Necker Island? The submarine captain?"

"Vaguely."

"Well, by coincidence he was in Naples too, and he gave me another lesson on how to use the Triton! He was there at the marina doing demos."

"And you loved it?"

"I adored it! I can't tell Bob, though. You know, he thinks they're only for dumb ol' men."

"Well, I sure don't agree with that."

"Oh, Olivia, I don't care. I just want Bob to be happy. I think I might buy him one for his birthday. The one I want to get him is only around a million three. Those things can get very expensive, and of course, you have to ask yourself, how much is he really going to use it?"

Olivia wondered if Bob had so much money that Maritza could spend that kind of sum unnoticed.

"It's always important to consider the practical side of things," Olivia said, thinking, You've got to be kidding me.

"Well, we'll see. Mel said he'd look into it for me. I think it would be a fabulous surprise, don't you? Anyway, let me stop running my mouth and go get Nantucket organized for us. Watch your email!"

"I will!"

Jason came through the door with two young guys. When he saw her on the phone, he mouthed *Hello!*

"In there," Olivia whispered and pointed to Nick's study.

Jason and his men went back inside toward the room with the small mountain of unattached wires.

"Thanks for everything, Olivia. I feel like there's hope when I talk to you!"

"Maritza? There's *always* hope!"

Olivia pushed the *End* button on her phone and went into the kitchen for a bottle of water.

Roni was measuring shelf paper and laying it down inside the cabinets.

"How's Maritza?"

"Understandably annoyed. I'm going up to Nantucket with her the day after tomorrow."

"Good! I'll have contracts ready."

"Good idea! How's it going in here?" Olivia asked.

"You have more teaspoons than anyone on earth," Roni said. "And commemorative mugs."

"My sweet husband has a soft spot for mugs. He buys one every place we go."

Nick came into the room carrying a box of dishes. "I most certainly do not!" Nick said.

"Yes, you do. Okay, he didn't buy one on Necker because it had no gift shop and neither does Bob's boat."

"That's not a boat. It's a ship!" Nick said.

Jason stepped into the kitchen to say something to Olivia, but he saw Roni first, because Olivia was digging around in the pantry.

"Hi there!" he said. "I'm Jason Fowler."

"You are?" Roni all but squealed.

"Morning, Jason," Nick said.

"G'morning, sir," Jason said.

Nick harrumphed. Olivia heard this unfamiliar tone in Roni's voice and looked up to see what was going on. Nick looked from face to face. Roni's face was bloodred. Olivia and Nick were beyond the age of sensing pheromones in the air, but had they been able to, they would've noticed that the room was swarming with them. Perhaps the entire house was suddenly flooded with them. It was as though they all were trapped in a snow globe full of raging, sexy, twerking pheromones. Even the normally supercomposed, all-business Jason Fowler was way off kilter and grinning like an idiotic schoolboy. Nick cleared his throat and left the room.

"Excuse me," Nick said.

Olivia made a mental note—Nick was jealous.

"Jason? Say hello to Roni Larini. Roni helps me run my business in New York. Roni? Jason is our general contractor."

"Cool," they both said.

"How's the technology battle going?" Olivia asked.

"I've got to put a booster on your router," Jason said.

"That's *exactly* what I *told* her she needed!" Roni said.

"Awesome. How long are you in town?" Jason asked.

"One more day," Roni said.

"Would you like to have dinner tonight?" Jason said. "Oh! You probably have plans."

"No, actually, I don't and I'd love to have dinner," Roni said.

They exchanged cell phone numbers. Roni told him where she was staying and Jason said he'd see her later. He was off in search of a router booster. Moments later, Nick reappeared in long khaki trousers and a starched blue shirt neatly tucked in. He had his navy blazer slung over his shoulder and he was wearing his best Top-Siders.

"Where're you headed, looking so fine?" Roni said. Her complexion had lost its flush and returned to normal.

"I'll be back in a few hours," Nick said, kissing Olivia on the cheek. "Going downtown to read. I'll call you before I cross the causeway to see if I can bring you anything."

"You are the sweetest man alive!" Olivia said, as she always did.

"There's too much commotion here for me," he said.

"I understand," Olivia said.

A moment or two later they heard the front door shut. Nick was gone.

"Did I really say I'd have dinner with Jason? Am I crazy?"

"Maybe," Olivia said, smiling. "But you have a date. I was a witness."

"Okay, I'm losing it," Roni said. "Gimme the poop on Jason. Single? Never been married? Divorced? Kids with three baby mamas?"

"I know he had a pretty serious girlfriend from South Dakota or someplace out there in the wilds of the heartland, whatever that is. See if he's on Facebook."

"Excellent idea!" Roni said and pressed the *F* icon on her smartphone. She pressed in his name in the search bar and waited while the cog spun, searching for answers. "No. He's not. But his business is here." She pressed the *Like* button. "Now he knows I like his page."

"How utterly romantic," Olivia said.

"You're such an old biddy sometimes," Roni said.

The day passed quickly, and the number of boxes left to open began to dwindle. Jason and his crew were able to connect the phones, computers, stereo, and turntable. By two o'clock a classic recording of Miles Davis was playing all over the house. As soon as it started playing, Roni and Olivia went to find Jason to congratulate him.

"That sounds so great!" Roni said.

"I like vinyl a lot better than CDs," Jason said.

"Nick does too. He says the sound is richer," Olivia said.

As promised, Nick called around three o'clock. He sounded happier.

"I stopped at Whole Foods to see this place for myself, and I must say, it's like Giants Stadium!"

"Really?"

"Yes, well, not really. But when you're used to shopping at the Whole Foods in Manhattan and barely having room to think, you find all the space stunning! The butcher department is amazing. They have everything, including suet. The produce is gorgeous. Never mind the bakery. So what can I bring home for us for dinner?"

Bring *home.*

The word stung. Was this her *home*? Yes, it was. Somehow Olivia had been telling herself that this was her *second* home. But the facts were that this was now their primary residence. They banked here, they would pay taxes here, and their driver's licenses would be issued by the South Carolina Department of Motor Vehicles.

"Olivia? Are you there?"

"Yes! Sorry! My mind wandered off for a moment. Um, just bring whatever looks good! You know I love everything you cook."

"And I love you!" Nick said.

"I love you too! Did you have a good time at the historical society?"

"It was absolutely incredible. I'll tell you all about it over cocktails!"

Around four o'clock, Roni announced that she was leaving for the day. "You're pretty sure this guy isn't an ax murderer?"

"I'm reasonably sure," Olivia said. "Just go have a good time."

"I'll give you a full report in the morning," Roni said on her way out the front door.

Olivia was alone in the house then. She had spent the better part of the day accessorizing the living room and their bedroom. The space that would be her office had no furniture at all. She simply dropped files and her address book and her laptop there and measured for a desk and chairs. She walked from room to room, trying to decide what else the house would need to make it feel like home. Basically, they had moved Nick's office intact. It was going to be so ridiculously easy for him to settle in. Somehow she had allowed herself to be stripped of her possessions, and now it made her angry. Nick could just go in his study and there was hardly a perceptible difference between his new space and his old one. He had his desk and his favorite chairs, his maps and books. All of his model soldiers were already in place, except for the glass that would seal them off from dust. Jason's glass contact person was coming to measure. Nick's life was in fine shape.

She felt sick inside, and for the first time she recognized that her Manhattan life was behind her. She couldn't hop over to Saks to check the shoe sales or stop by the Chanel cosmetic counter in Bergdorf's and have Preston give her face an update. There was no Lobel's in Charleston to deliver dinner, and on top of everything else, she had no housekeeper. She had no business contacts or clients in Charleston. She didn't have doctors or lawyers or anyone to do her hair.

"What the hell have I done?" And she asked herself why, for the love of God and everything holy in this world, had she not anticipated her *own* needs? It's what I do for a living! She blamed herself. She'd been playing the Denial Game. Denial was stupid. Her life was now in Charleston unless she decided she wasn't going to spend it with Nick. The thought of her life without him was unfathomable.

She heard the front door open and close. Nick was back. She hurried to meet him in the kitchen, hoping that seeing him would shake off her state of mind.

I just have a lot of work to do, she thought, giving herself a pep talk. And I'm up to the task. It just *seems* overwhelming, but it really isn't.

"Hi!" she sang out as though all was right in her world. "Can I help you with anything?"

Nick was in the kitchen unpacking four bags of groceries. "Yes! Give me a kiss!"

Olivia kissed his cheek and then threw her arms around him, leaning into him and hugging him tightly as though she would never let him go.

"What's all this about?" Nick said, hugging her back. "Are you all right? Did you hear a rat upstairs?"

"No! Thank heavens!"

"Coyotes in the yard?"

"Good heavens, no!" Were there *coyotes* on the island? Oh, dear God!

"Well then, tell me what's wrong."

"I don't know, I just . . ."

Nick ran his hand down the back of her head, smoothing her hair, and gently he kissed the crown of her head.

"It's going to be okay, Olivia. I know, this is an enormous change for you . . ."

"It changes everything," she said in almost a whisper.

"Well, Dr. Nick has the cure for what ails you."

"You do?"

"Yes. What you need is a glass of wine and a roll in bed with honey." He wiggled his eyebrows suggestively.

Olivia couldn't help but smile, and she felt better just to know that Nick understood her.

"It's not even dark yet! But I'll admit, that always cures anything!"

"I know!"

"But I want dinner first," she said.

"Supper," he said.

"What?"

"Down here in the Lowcountry, dinner is called supper, especially when you eat at home. Well? Maybe not. Let me think. Technically, you go out for *dinner*; but you could also say that you're going out for *supper*. Maybe supper implies something more casual these days, like *going over to somebody's house for supper*. Although Sunday dinner is usually served at around three in the afternoon."

"On Sunday?"

"I know. It can be a bit bewildering."

"You're never going to make a Lowcountry girl out of me."

"I might die trying, but I will never surrender the cause!"

"Did I tell you that Roni has a date with Jason?"

"No kidding!"

"They're having supper," Olivia said, and winked at Nick.

"Oh, you little minx!"

"By the way, we're going to Nantucket the day after tomorrow."

"I believe I heard that rumor this morning."

"Unless you prefer to stay here?"

She gave him the details and he could only smile and shake his head.

"Of course I'll come. There's a museum there I want to visit. You know? I love your business. But tell me this. If they asked you to jump through flaming hoops of fire, I imagine you'd have to do it?"

"It pays the bills, Nick. It pays the bills."

"Hmmm. It's time to pull a cork," he said and lifted a chilly bottle of Chablis from the shopping bag. "And I have a piece of cheese in the bags somewhere. And some water crackers."

"I'll find them," Olivia said, and with that, the third evening in their new home was under way.

She fixed a plate of cheese and crackers and they walked outside with their glasses of wine to watch the sunset, hoping they'd catch a glimpse of the dolphins. Olivia put the food on a table between the rocking chairs and stood against the railing with Nick.

Down on the beach, there were couples walking arm in arm along the water and others with their dogs, chasing balls and catching Frisbees in midair. Overhead the pelicans flew in formation, their wings casting long shadows across their front yard. And fat black-and-white sea gulls were everywhere, walking all over the beach like they owned it.

They watched as four beautiful sailboats went out to sea and then as several fishing boats made their way toward Shem Creek, finished for the day.

The air was deliciously drenched with salt and moisture. Olivia's hair, which she had twisted up into a knot, began to loosen and curl, creating tendrils all around her face. She kept peeling them off her cheeks and tucking them behind her ears, but the breeze would loosen them again.

"Don't bother with your hair," Nick said. "Those lovely curlicues make you look like Botticelli's *Venus*!"

"Are you telling me I'm half baked on a clamshell?"

"Not a bit, my darling girl, and you know it. Cheers!"

"Cheers!" They took a sip and Olivia said, "So, tell me what happened at the historical society today. I'm dying to hear!"

"It's just absolutely astounding. You know, there's so much to learn about this world and all the many diverse and fascinating people who inhabit it, never mind the ones from long ago."

Nick's eyes had that same irresistible dancing twinkle that stole Olivia's heart when they first met. The recognition of it ignited a quiver through her whole body and her arms got goose bumps. It was a mighty powerful twinkle.

"So who'd you dig up, Nicholas Seymour with the crazy eyes? It's a good one, right?"

The repetitive sounds of the ocean washing the shore were calming, the perfect background music for a good story. And the sun was slowly inching toward the horizon.

"Dave the Slave."

"Who?"

He turned to face her. "David Drake, also known as Dave the Potter or Dave the Slave. He was born into slavery in 1801, up in Edgefield County. He made some of the most remarkable earthenware pots ever built."

"Earthenware pots."

"Yes. You know, before indoor plumbing you had to bring your water to the house from the well. These pots and jugs were a critical part of life. Earthenware was more desirable because it was impervious to water and didn't break as easily."

"I don't know how people endured that kind of life," Olivia said, and cut a piece of Gruyère. She fed it to Nick.

"Thank you. Neither do I. But there are several supremely interesting things about this fellow. First of all, he had only one leg. The legend around him suggests that he lost it in a train accident. To my way of thinking, losing a leg was one way to avoid working in the fields, which was backbreaking labor."

"Good grief! Do you think he laid himself across a railroad track? He could've died!"

"Easily! I don't know. That would require more research, and one still might not reach a definitive conclusion. Details of slave life are spotty. Cut me another piece of cheese, will you, my pet?"

"Of course!" Olivia cut several cubes and balanced the plate on the rail.

"But anyway, unusual fact number two: he was literate! Teaching a slave to read and write the language was illegal because it was thought literacy would lead to unrest and uprisings."

"How stupid." Olivia helped herself to a bite of cheese. "This is so good."

"Agreed, but as an historian, I seek the facts and try to weigh those facts in the context of their time. No judgment."

"I *know* that, but that whole period in time is mortifying." She fed Nick another bite and half a cracker. "God, I love cheese!"

"I love *you!* Well, it was an unenlightened era, to say the least. Nonetheless, his first owner, a staunchly religious fellow, was named Henry Drake. He owned a large plantation in Pottersville. Drake felt that the teachings of the Bible would have a positive effect on his slaves, so he taught them to read."

"*That* was nice of him. All you open-minded southerners."

She meant it just as a joke, but there was some truth in that some of her friends growing up in New York assumed the entire South was populated with narrow-minded, Bible-verse-spouting, patriarchal, misogynistic, judgmental bigots, whose ancestors probably owned slaves or condoned the institution. And they all owned trucks for no apparent reason.

"Good grief, Olivia! I know you hate slavery. We all hate slavery. It's an abomination before God Almighty. But *I* didn't invent it and none of my ancestors *ever* participated in it or thought it was right. Just because I'm a son of the Lowcountry, it doesn't mean I approve of any part of slavery in any culture one iota."

"I'm sorry. I'm being rude. Please finish your story."

"It's hard to talk about anything related to slavery without your going on a rant. I agree. But anyway, there happened to be another slave on the same plantation with no arms. Henry was his name."

"Seriously? What are the odds on that?"

"I don't know. Not high. But if he was born on the plantation, he probably stayed there all his life."

"I'm sure. Where else was he going?"

"Exactly. So Dave decides he wants to be an artist and make pots, but he can't turn the wheel with one leg. But Henry can turn the wheel just fine. So Henry turned the wheel and Dave applied the clay and together they built thousands of pots and jars. Like forty thousand. Now, here's why they were so unique."

"Tell me, sweetheart," she said in her best *come hither* voice, teasing him.

Nick was very excited to tell Olivia this quirky story, and Olivia was excited by Nick's enthusiasm. Nick laughed and used his Boris voice from *Rocky and Bullwinkle.*

"Ah, Natasha, my temptress! Your moment will arrive later this evening, when I will treat you to a night of magic in the boudoir!"

"I can't wait for zee darkness."

"Okay. Okay. So, anyway, Dave was a poet! He wrote short poems on his pots! How do you like that?"

"Such as?"

"Well, one of them was something like *Sure must be the fourth of July, fifes play and flags fly.* Then he signed them *Dave* and dated them. And they're gorgeous things, beautiful glazes and ingenious design. There are a dozen or so on display at the Charleston Museum."

"It might be fun to try and buy one," Olivia said.

"The last one that sold at auction went for over one hundred and thirty thousand dollars."

Olivia coughed. *"What?"* She whistled, but no sound came from her lips. "For a clay pot from Pottersville, South Carolina. You're lying to me!"

Nick laughed and Olivia did too.

"No, ma'am! It's a documented fact."

"Maybe we'll find one for Bob instead!"

CHAPTER 9

fishin'

The next morning, after a slow start due to some earnest pyrotechnic gymnastics the prior evening, Nick went downtown to go read at the historical society.

"I want to read the papers of Laura Bragg," he said.

"Who's she?"

"Very interesting character. She was the first female director of a scientific museum in the United States. And she was allegedly very controversial."

"What did she do?"

"I'll let you know."

He kissed her cheek and left.

Olivia set up shop on their dining room table, which would be her workspace until she bought a desk. She began making lists of what she had to do. She needed to find a local upholsterer for starters. She made a note to ask Jason to recommend a good local landscaper and tree-trimming service, a pest-control company, and a housekeeping service. Maybe he might know a good used-car dealer?

Around eleven, Roni came strolling in with coffee from Starbucks.

"Morning! A skinny latte macchiato for you and a Tazo chai for me."

"Thanks! How was last night?"

Roni plopped herself in the dining room chair opposite Olivia and sighed.

"It was the perfect date, probably only because I'm leaving town. You always want what you can't have."

"You just don't know how true that is."

"Jason is a blast and funny as a rip! And he has *such* nice manners! Ah, southern men!"

"You don't have to tell me!" Olivia said, removing the top on her cup and inhaling deeply. "Wouldn't it be wonderful if coffee tasted as good as it smells?"

"Yeah, it would. Well, you sort of wrote the book on the charms of southern men. We stayed downtown and went to someplace called *Fish.* Awesome! Just awesome. When we were across the table from each other, he acted like I was the only other person in the room. Olivia? Did you ever meet someone and it's like you've known them all your life?"

Roni had that wistful look, the one Olivia knew from experience had the launching power to send a girl over the moon.

"Yes. Only one. Nick." Olivia handed the audit notices from the IRS and State of New York to Roni. "Southern men aren't always scanning the room to see who else came to the party."

"Hmmm. The last guy I dated in New York hardly knew I was there. Ah well, it's too bad Mr. Fowler lives in South Carolina. He's gonna cry for me something terrible. That poor man! Breaks my heart to think about it. What do you want me to do with these?"

Olivia smiled. Roni clearly liked Jason very much. Olivia hoped she liked him enough to find excuses to return to South Carolina as soon as possible and frequently and that Jason would remain available. It was a lot to hope for.

"I looked at both of them. They just want records. Keep copies for us and send the originals over to our accountants. Tell the accountants to give them whatever information they want. We don't have anything to hide."

"Right. I know we don't. It's just unnerving. And it generates expenses we don't need."

"That's the real issue. And it makes me nervous. Anyway, this is the first time I've ever shown a loss."

"Yeah, well, you know I always say better days are coming."

"They'd better get here soon."

"Do you want me to call all our vendors to send swatches and samples here?"

"Yes, I don't know why I didn't think of that before now."

"Because your head is still in Manhattan. "

"What's the matter with you and Nick? Don't you know it's rude to read other people's minds?"

"Whatever. I'll send you a duplicate of your portfolio too. In fact, I'll send it in PowerPoint as well."

Her book was all she really needed to acquire projects. Once a prospective client saw the before-and-after photographs of other living spaces she had renovated or redesigned, she was always given the job. Unless money was an issue.

"I think I'm going to try to rustle up a few new clients around here. We need a safety net. I mean, heaven forbid Maritza gets hit by a truck. We'd be out of business. What time is your flight?"

"Two this afternoon."

It was getting on to noon.

"You'd better get going. The rental car contract is in the glove compartment."

"Got it!" Roni said. She took the last sip of her tea and stood.

"Roni? I really appreciate you driving the car down to us and all. Well, thanks for everything."

"It was actually fun and I'm glad I could help! Heck! You can't do anything without me."

"That's exactly what I'm worried about. That and the IRS."

"And money. Good thing I keep our invoice template on my laptop. I printed up a basic contract this morning. At least it's something to start with." Roni handed Olivia a manila envelope. "Just fill it out."

"Well, it's on my laptop too, should I need it."

"I know it's there. Who do you think put it on there? Ha!"

Olivia wished Roni a safe trip and stood at the top of her steps, watching Roni drive out of the yard and through the gate. She knew it was selfish and immature to feel petulant and abandoned, but she couldn't help it. Then she wondered for the hundredth time how long it was going to take to get used to her new life.

That afternoon, after a lonely egg salad sandwich and a glass of iced tea, Olivia went back to work on her lists and made some phone calls. Nick came home and changed his clothes to go surf fishing.

"How was the historical society?"

"I'm just going to quickly change because the tide is just right for the old man and the sea. I'll tell you all about it when I get back."

"Of course!"

A few minutes passed and Nick came to the dining room to let Olivia know he was off.

"I've dreamed about doing just this over and over. I mean literal dreams. Did I tell you I had a dream I was fishing right out there with my father? We were so happy, just casting and reeling in nothing and casting again."

Olivia looked up from her laptop and burst into a huge grin. "Well! Look at you!" Olivia said. "That's some getup, bubba!"

"Whom may I ask are you addressing as *bubba*?"

"Isn't that a term of endearment?"

"It *can* be," Nick said.

"Well, I *meant* it to be," Olivia said, realizing she was once again on the receiving end of another lesson in southernisms and their correct usage.

"Then it *is* one. This is not the correct hat," he said. "There should be a brim all around to protect my neck from the sun. We talked about me investing in a fishing hat, didn't we?"

Nick was dressed in wrinkled khaki cargo shorts, a T-shirt commemorating the 2011 New York Marathon, an old chambray shirt, surf shoes, and a baseball hat. He was Oscar Madison in full bloom, practically bubbling with anticipation.

"Yes, but you look adorable just like this!" Olivia would investigate and ask who sold proper fishing hats in the area. Then she would surprise Nick with the nicest one she could find.

Nick smiled like a young man would. "I'll bring us home a nice fat fish for dinner!"

"And if you don't catch anything?"

Nick whispered behind his hand. "I'll buy one over at Mount Pleasant Seafood, but don't tell anybody."

"Well, *use the Force*, Nick! Go get us a fish! And say hello to Danny for me."

Nick laughed and kissed her on the cheek.

"I will. God! I feel like a boy again!" he said, and all but ran down the steps toward the beach.

Olivia watched him zip down the walkway and through the gate and was heartened to think that just throwing a hook in the water could bring Nick so much joy. And he had dreamed about fishing in this very part of the beach, not once but many times. How passionate was his yearning to come home to Sullivans Island? How much had he missed this place? Olivia missed New York, but thus far she had truly missed only the conveniences of it. Nick's heartbeat was synchronized with the Lowcountry in a way she had never felt attached to any particular geography.

She suspected that her upbringing was the culprit. Her parents, long gone, were serious people who rarely showed affection for her or for each other. They were atheists. Her father was a high school chemistry teacher and her mother was a part-time bookkeeper. They lived in a brownstone in Chelsea, quietly and unassumingly, reading nineteenth-century literature, watching the thermostat like hawks in the winter, piggybacking slivers of soap onto new bars and pressure cooking with onions whatever was on its last leg and discounted at the grocery store. They were peevish people and accused her of being impractical, of always having her head in the clouds. They never understood Olivia's desire for what was to them an ostentatious life. In fact they were embarrassed by her flashy success and never forgave her for it.

What they didn't realize was that she romanticized their excessive deprivation. As a young girl she would pretend to be a Russian peasant teenager, freezing on the tundra gathering sticks for the fire, living on cold soup, with holes in her shoes. At the same time, she absorbed every beautiful thing she saw in all the museums in New York from the illuminated manuscripts at the Morgan Library to the great works and artifacts at the Metropolitan Museum of Art. Her parents took her to Carnegie Hall concerts and occasionally to the ballet, but never to Rumplemeyer's for ice cream, as the parents of her school friends did. In spite of them, she came away from her childhood with a keen eye for excellence and a great appreciation of how art and music and literature reflected not only history but the human condition of longing for truth and beauty. The city gave her what her parents could not. A big city could enrich the life of an impressionable little girl.

Nick's parents also lived a modest island life, but they gave him a world of things to feel passionate about and to love. Passion and love were highly encouraged. His mother took her sons to church every Sunday and injected the fear of God into the marrow of their bones. She made lovely dinners, cooking with abundance, and set a table where anyone who was hungry was welcome. Nick or his brother was always being told to go find another chair for the unexpected guest. She taught both boys beautiful manners: how to be kind and forgiving and why they should not judge others. His father brought home dogs, cats, and all manner of pets to delight Nick and his brother and teach them to be responsible. He taught both sons to fish, to love women, to always be loyal to each other, to love the island itself, and to be proud of our nation's history. Perhaps most important, both of his parents showed Nick how valuable and useful a good sense of humor could be. His childhood home could barely contain the copious laughter and warmth.

Olivia's parents gave her none of those values. She never even had a guppy to call her own. It was no wonder that Nicholas Seymour swept her right off her feet. In his soul was the endless banquet she was starving for, and she didn't even know how hungry she was until the day they met.

From the very start he was fascinated by her meticulous and feverish need to be creative and how she hung on to things. And she was beautiful to him. That a young woman so smart, so talented, and so beautiful would love a crusty old professor like him nearly brought him to tears.

She watched Nick until he passed the bend of the beach and was out of her line of sight.

No surprise I adore him, she thought. He's more alive than ten men. His heart is filled with so much love, enough to go around.

Nick had come back to the Lowcountry and slipped right back into his boyhood life, never missing a beat. Olivia, on the other hand, was adapting slowly, and her heart carried some gloom she was desperately trying to squelch. In any case, she came with him to live on the island because she loved him so very much. She was determined to rise above the feeling that she was the proverbial fish out of water.

She needed to cheer herself up. She decided she'd make a salad to go with the catch that Nick hoped to land and maybe they'd share a baguette and some fruit for dessert. When Nick got back they'd go to the store. That sounded like a good idea, so she made a short list of the things they would need—lettuce, obviously, a lemon or two, some fresh thyme. They could decide together on the fruit. She put that list to the side. Then she gasped.

"Oh, no!" she said to the empty room. "We're about to become one of those old couples that grocery-shops together. He pushes the cart and they argue over the cost of Honey-crisp apples and what the doctor said they shouldn't have. And what's healthy and what isn't! I can't let this happen. Coupons. We're going to start using *coupons*."

She was just slightly north of fifty, but she got a good glimpse of where life could lead if she wasn't diligent. Depends, Metamucil, and bickering over who brought the coupons or left them on the kitchen counter. Then she laughed.

"Nonsense," she said to the empty house.

Just for the heck of it, Olivia went online to Overstock.com, looking for office furniture at a good price. She had not bought office furniture for herself in ages, but she seemed to remember that Overstock had great values. So did Ikea, but she and Nick were not about to buy anything that had to be assembled. And, when she bought office furniture for her clients, she usually went to Kentshire looking for nineteenth-century English partner's desks. But for herself? She only wanted a *look* at a *price*.

Her prospective office was actually half the size of Nick's study, but she felt like he deserved the better room because he would spend untold hours there reading and futzing around. If she got terribly busy, she could rent an office somewhere. Although her space had water views, between two to four in the afternoon the direct sun heated the room like a kiln, raising the temperature so much that she would leave the old Venetian blinds in place until she could make the time to replace them. Window coverings were not high on her list of priorities.

After much surfing back and forth between Jonathan Adler's website and Overstock, she finally ordered a desk and a credenza finished in white laminate, thinking she'd have an all-white office to blend with the rest of the house. And she ordered two chairs in white leather and chrome, two chrome lamps, and a heavy acrylic wastebasket. She used a twenty percent off coupon that popped up in the margin of a website and she beamed, knowing Roni would applaud her thrift. You see? she thought. I'm not completely coupon-averse!

She decided she'd keep all the office supplies out of the direct sun for obvious reasons and in the bedroom closet adjacent to her workspace. Where was she going to find clients? she thought. Where, indeed? Maritza's current job offering, in Nantucket, if it panned out, would be over in six months. They would need a new source of cash flow after that.

The thought of this brought about another great sigh. She was resigned to her fate, but moving here meant she was back at square one and starting all over again. Her old clients were not going to call her. They probably thought she retired if they thought about her at all. Except Maritza. At some point she would send out a mailing, adding her new address to her old one. But just like every mailing she had ever received from anyone else, the subliminal message would still read *out of the game.*

She knew she would have to find new clients the same way she always had—word of mouth. She would join something: the Gibbes Museum of Art, the Charleston Symphony, Spoleto Festival, the Charleston Library Society. She was sure there were many others in a city like Charleston. How much would that cost? She visited their websites, making notes of membership fees and volunteer opportunities.

All of those organizations had boards, and those board members were her target audience. Boards of trustees existed because they were able to offer the organization oversight, social and professional connections, and yes, money. Usually board members were people of a certain means. People of a certain means used interior designers. And if joining a few nonprofits at an upper level of membership didn't bring her a few clients, she would hire a public relations firm, one who would see to it that she attended the right benefit galas, who would be sure she was photographed for the right newspapers, and who would perhaps help her place a feature article in the right magazines—like *Charleston Home + Design*, *Coastal Living*, or *Garden & Gun*. She wasn't in the kind of business where she could open a storefront and hang out a shingle. Although there was always the pipe dream that a retail business that sold her private label of home furnishings might be fun. Whenever she toyed with the idea, Roni would immediately talk her out of it.

"Really? You want to stand on your feet ten hours a day and fight with little old ladies over how long your candles retain the scent? You want to deal with shoplifters and credit card companies? And inventory? You want to work on weekends and holidays?"

Olivia laughed then to think of Roni and how she expunged any poetic notion Olivia may have had about working retail right out of her head. It was another reason Roni was so important to her. She kept Olivia's chickens in the vicinity of the coop.

It was nearly five o'clock when Nick returned. Actually, Olivia heard water running, and unsure of what this sound meant, she followed the sound to its source outside. When she leaned over the porch railing, there was Nick rinsing his feet with a hose. He was sunburned and as salty as any sailor could be.

"Somebody left us a hose!"

"Well, good! How was the fishing?" she asked and wondered, Are we going to start bathing in the yard? This was exactly why we need a footbath, she thought.

"Come down here, woman, and look in the bucket! Look in the bucket!"

Olivia descended the steps, excited to find out what her Nick had captured from the sea. In the bottom of what would become known as Nick's Fishing Bucket, were two small fish, flopping around in the muddy salt water, begging for mercy. They could not have fed supper to a medium-sized housecat.

"Is this dinner, sweetheart? Or supper?"

Nick began to laugh and laugh. His belly was bouncing slightly and his eyes were tearing.

"Oh my God in His beautiful heavens! No! It's *bait!* Real sportsmen catch their own bait."

"Oh!"

"I'm just going to cut them up and throw them in the freezer. If we weren't going to Nantucket tomorrow, I'd go back out there and use these little babies to get my big fish. How was your afternoon?"

"Well, I think it was productive." More productive than yours, she thought but did not say.

As long as he came home happy, she didn't care if he caught anything at all.

"Good!"

He rinsed his hands, dried them with the hem of his very stinky shirt, and pulled her to him. He smelled like man sweat and the ocean. She was unaccustomed to the odor and resisted his embrace like the damsel fights the evil duke's advances in a bodice-ripping novel.

"Nick! Jeez!"

"Too manly for you?"

"Wasn't last night enough?"

"It's never enough!"

She broke free and shuddered from head to toe. "Baby boy? You need a shower!"

Nick gave a rowdy laugh and Olivia hurried back inside, hoping he'd take her out to dinner. She didn't feel like shopping, then cooking, and then cleaning up when they had to pack for Nantucket as well. And they had to get up in the morning at an ungodly hour.

"I'm just warning you, sweetheart," Olivia said later, taking a bite of her crab cake at the Long Island Café. "Maritza is obsessively fretting over Colette coming to the wedding. You're going to get an earful."

"If she torments me with her incessant nattering, I shall break into the conversation and give her a lecture on the most obscure battles of the Civil War."

"That should take care of the problem."

Armed with a plan of resistance, they flew to Newark the next morning on the six A.M. flight. Nick wiped down the germy spots around his seat, buckled his seat belt, and promptly went to sleep. Olivia realized then that they should always fly at the crack of dawn because Nick wasn't alert enough at that hour to get nervous. She dozed off and on, and when she heard the pilot announce their beginning descent she gently nudged Nick.

"Wake up, sweetheart," she said softly.

"What?"

"We're landing," she said.

When they touched down, Olivia texted Maritza.

Landed! On our way to Teterboro. Can't wait to see you!

A moment or two later, Olivia's cell phone pinged.

Can't wait to see y'all too! I'm here waiting! Maritza pinged back.

"I'm exhausted," Nick said in the taxi. "I got too much sun yesterday."

"Yes, your face is really red. Be sure to drink a lot of water today. You can snooze on the plane, but I'm working. Unfortunately I'm on the job."

"You don't think it might be rude if I go back to sleep?"

"At this hour? No, sir, I do not. She's not sensitive about things like that. Besides, she's going to want to harangue about Ellen and Colette. If you're sleeping, she'll feel freer to speak."

"Where are we staying?"

"The White Elephant."

"I've stayed there before, but it was years ago."

"Oh, really? With whom?"

"Oh, some little tart with big breasts. I can't recall her name. Long time ago."

Nick was looking out the window, but Olivia could tell by the back of his ears and his jaw that he was stifling a laugh.

"You know what, Nicholas Seymour?"

"Yes, my precious pet?"

"You're lucky that I'm the kind of girl I am."

"Yes, I am."

"Another kind of woman would've shot you in the face for a whole lot less."

"I count my blessings every day. And I love that hellcat streak of yours."

He reached over and took her hand in his; then he leaned back against the probably germ-infested seat back, smiled, and closed his eyes. Olivia looked over at him, and in the brutally unforgiving early morning light of New Jersey, she saw all the wrinkles around his eyes and she loved every single one of them. Every single one.

They arrived at Teterboro and Maritza was standing by the check-in counter talking to a woman at the desk. When she saw Olivia and Nick, she stopped and hurried to greet them.

"Oh, hey! I'm so glad y'all made it!" She hugged Olivia and gave her two air kisses.

Muah! Muah!

"Good morning!" Olivia said, hugging her back.

"Wow! Somebody sure forgot their gosh darn sunscreen!" She said to Nick.

"Yes, thank you. Someone certainly did," Nick replied.

He was smiling, but inside he was slightly annoyed. These kinds of remarks irritated Nick, and especially that morning, when Nick was clearly feeling the effects of too much sun. It wasn't that Maritza was the kind of woman who took some schadenfreude in the suffering of others. She wasn't like that at all. But there appeared to be no filter between her brain and tongue. Nick had a dull headache and felt slightly nauseated.

"Do we have any aspirin?" Nick asked.

"Of course!" Maritza said. "In one of the galley drawers on the plane."

"Great," Nick said. "Thank you."

"Darling? Are you feeling ill?" Olivia said.

"I'm okay," Nick said. "Two aspirins and a nap and I'm sure I'll be fine."

"Well, the pilots are already on board if y'all are ready?" Maritza said.

And as they had when they went to Necker Island, they boarded Bob's gorgeous G650 and left the normal world behind.

There were two large vases of peonies on the end tables, and the plane smelled wonderful.

"Oh! What beautiful flowers!" Olivia said.

"Thank you! I just decided that when I'm not flying with Bob, I'd order flowers. Flowers make me happy," Maritza said.

"They make me happy too!" Olivia said, wondering if they'd go flying through the air when the plane took off.

Nick took the aspirin from Maritza and headed for the back of the plane with a bottle of water.

"I'm just going to shut my eyes for twenty minutes," Nick said. He settled himself in his seat, reclined the chair, and checked out.

"I love how men say *I'm going to go to sleep now* and ten seconds later they're asleep. How does that work?" Maritza said, sitting in Bob's designated seat.

"I don't know, but it's another one of those truisms about men that seem a little unfair to our gender," Olivia said, taking the seat to Maritza's left. "I can't fall asleep until I've ticked off a mental checklist for what I need to do the next day."

"Please! I haven't slept through the night since Gladdie was born!"

"I'll bet," Olivia said.

They were quiet for a moment because bringing up Gladdie dredged up thoughts of Ellen, which naturally led to thoughts about Bob's infidelity. As a result, a small dark cloud seeped in through the oval-shaped windows and throughout the cabin.

"I am very excited to see the house," Olivia said to lighten the mood.

It worked. Maritza perked right up and became the epitome of the happy housewife, leaving Olivia to wonder about the contents of Maritza's medicine cabinet.

"Oh!" she said brightly. "I think you'll love it. The question is, will it be too much work to bring it back to its glory days?"

"I love old houses. What year was it built?"

"1900. Would you like coffee? After takeoff I can make us cappuccinos. We finally got the coffee maker installed."

"Sure! I'd love to see how it works."

Olivia thought, Wait a minute. Bob spent sixty-four and a half million dollars on his plane and his coffeepot was on back order? Priceless!

One of the pilots came out of the cockpit to move the flowers to a secure spot and to make sure they were buckled up. He said, "Flying time is about an hour and five minutes. There's a squall around the Boston area, so we'll divert easterly and take her up to forty-three thousand feet. You shouldn't feel a thing."

"Great!" Maritza said casually as though she'd been flying on private jets her entire life.

In minutes they were airborne. Olivia looked back at Nick. He was sawing logs. As soon as they reached cruising altitude she got up and went to the back of the plane. She carefully covered him with a light blanket because she knew sunstroke caused chills. She kissed his forehead and he didn't flinch.

"Oh, dear! Is Nick's snoring going to bother you? I can tell him to roll over on his side." Olivia said.

"Heavens no! Let the man be! Bob snores so god-awful bad I make him sleep in another bedroom." She was quiet for a moment. "That probably wasn't the smartest idea I ever had."

"Well? Who's to say?" Olivia wasn't picking up the thread on that topic. "All men snore, especially if they drink wine and eat red meat."

"Well, now you're talking about Bob's religion!"

"Exactly! Tell me some more about the house," Olivia said.

"I saw it with the broker and Bob last week. It's pretty fabulous. There are eight bedrooms and eight full baths. I think it's about ten thousand square feet. And there's a guest cottage. But no swimming pool."

"Really? No pool? How odd. When's the last time it was renovated?"

"Not since 1991. So the kitchen is a disaster and the bathrooms aren't great. But here's the thing. It's the view! It's right on the harbor and it has a dock. That's why Bob wants it."

"He'd have a place to park his submarine!" Olivia said, knowing that this absurd conversation could start a civil war in some cultures.

"Right? And the location is perfect. It's right at Brant Point. You'll see."

"Location is always the most important factor to consider. How big is the property?"

"Oh, heck. I don't know. Maybe an acre or so."

"So it's manageable."

"Yeah. If everything goes to hell in a handbasket, Bob could cut the grass."

"Let's hope we never see the day!" Olivia said, and laughed with her. "Let's make some coffee."

"Sure."

They were about half an hour into the flight. They enjoyed their cappuccinos, and the aroma of the brewing coffee beans brought Nick back to the land of the living.

"What's that wonderful smell?" he said.

"We have a cup for you, darling! How're you feeling?"

Nick stood and stretched, ran his hand through his hair, and said, "I feel perfectly well, thank you. And if I may say, I think a cup of whatever you ladies are savoring would make me feel even better."

"Let me get it for you, Nick," Maritza said. "Sometimes caffeine can be a miracle drug."

"I heartily agree, Maritza," Nick said and smiled, thinking, She's pleasantly tolerable some of the time.

Maritza handed Nick his coffee and said, "So, Nick, you know you're welcome to come with us to look at the house."

"Well, thank you. I think, however, that I'd like to pay a visit to the Nantucket Shipwreck and Lifesaving Museum. Every time I've been to Nantucket the time gets away from me and then I don't go. I've wanted to see it for some time. Nantucket has a fascinating maritime history, as I'm sure you know."

"I do know that. I used to go there when I was just a little girl."

"How nice! And of course, I'd like to drop into the Whaling Museum, if time permits." He took a sip. "This is delicious! I already feel better!"

"You're welcome! I have a car and a driver who can take you there. It's off the beaten path."

"And that is precisely why I never got there! Anyway, you ladies don't have to worry about me. I know how to amuse myself."

"Well, you can have the car all afternoon."

"Why, thank you. I won't be gone too long," Nick said.

"Olivia and I can walk to the house I want her to see from the hotel. In fact our hotel is so close, it's like my daddy used to say, you could spit on it in a good wind!"

"What a thought!" Olivia said. Spit? Not again! Olivia thought. Really?

"I know! Y'all, it looks like we're going to be landing in a few minutes. We'd better buckle up!" Maritza said.

They all took the rules seriously, so they buckled their seat belts and raised the seat backs.

"So the plan is to check in, have lunch, go see the house, and go shopping. Drinks are at six at our hotel and dinner is at CRU at eight o'clock. How does that sound?"

"It sounds perfect!" Olivia said.

The plane landed so softly that Nick didn't even realize they were on the ground. Olivia could tell he was dumbfounded by the look on his face.

And Maritza, who knew that Nick was a nervous flier, smiled and said, "Featherlight landings are a point of pride for our pilots. They know I really don't like getting the fillings jiggled out of my teeth."

"Well," Nick said, "I used to think I was going to die in a plane crash, but now that I've flown in a helicopter and actually skippered a submarine, I'm no longer terrified."

"Honey? When your number's up, it's up," Maritza said, "and the chances of you crashing in our plane are zero."

"Intellectually I understand, but you know these fears are never grounded in rational thought," Nick said. "But I feel perfectly at ease on your plane. In fact I may have been cured!"

Headline in the *New York Post*: PHOBIA CURED BY A G650! Olivia could see it in print. Maybe we should line up all the worrywarts and take them for a ride on Bob's jet, Olivia thought.

They went through the tiny terminal with a snack bar and a gift shop and Maritza said, "Y'all remember that TV show called *Wings*?" She pointed to a picture of the cast of *Wings* hanging on the wall.

"I remember that show," Olivia said. "I used to watch it late at night."

"Well, they used the outside of this airport terminal as theirs. But they shot the interior shots out in Hollywood. Isn't that fabulous?"

"No kidding," Olivia said.

Nick said nothing, but Olivia could smell his wood burning.

When they had checked into their hotel room, she said, "So, I take it that you're not impressed that *Wings* was partially shot here?"

"Most definitely not," Nick said. "This island used to be the whaling capital of the world."

"I think I knew that. This is a nice room, don't you think? Look, we have a water view!"

Nick stepped over to the window and looked. Then he grunted. "It's beautiful. And did you know the first American female astronomer, Maria Mitchell, was born here and discovered a comet when she was only fifteen years old?"

"No, I did not. Just fifteen?"

"Yes, it's a fact. And in 1820, Herman Melville was inspired to write *Moby-Dick* because of what happened to the whaleship *Essex* and her crew."

"No kidding. Well, that's impressive."

"Yes, ma'am. I think so too. And in 1841, Frederick Douglass made his first antislavery speech right here on this island. *Those* stories ought to be on the walls of the terminal. *Wings*. Please."

"You need to eat something. You're cranky. Maybe there's a Snickers in the minibar. Do you want me to look?"

"No, but I am starving. All I'm saying is please, let's not trivialize this island. Give her her well-earned dignity."

"You might need a Bloody Mary too."

"I just might."

Soon they were seated on the covered terrace reading over the menus, drinking their water, and picking at the breadbasket. The waiter placed a Bloody Mary in front of Nick, and Olivia and Maritza raised their mimosas in a toast. Nick lifted his glass.

"Mr. Seymour is about to become very agreeable. Cheers!"

"Cheers!" Maritza and Olivia said.

"What did that mean, Nick? Are you feeling disagreeable?" Maritza said.

"My sweet husband thinks pop culture is ruining the world."

"Well, it is, to some degree anyway," Maritza said.

"How do you see that happening?" Nick said.

Olivia got nervous and hoped that Nick wasn't setting Maritza up to expose the fact that she didn't understand what the term *pop culture* even meant.

"Well, all you have to do is turn on the television. The programs are all copies of each other. If *Cheers* worked, then why not try *Friends*? One took place in a bar and the other one had a coffee shop. And who cares anyway? And all this reality stuff? If *The Real Housewives of New Jersey* did well, why not have *The Real Housewives of Beverly Hills* and *The Real Housewives of Atlanta*? Those are some awful people just acting trashy. There's hardly anything original, and what is original is garbage. Anyway, television's terrible. It's all stupid. Pretty much. I think I want the lobster salad. How about y'all?"

"I'm going to try a lobster roll," Olivia said. "I like *Downton Abbey*."

"*Downton Abbey* doesn't count. That's sacred." Maritza said.

"And I'm going to have the fish tacos." Nick took another sip of his Bloody Mary and looked at Maritza. "Even *I* like *Downton Abbey*. And I liked the first few seasons of *Mad Men*. But I agree with you. By and large, television serves a segment of this population with whom I do not identify, except for PBS and sometimes some other channels like National Geographic. And of course, we need CNN."

"I like to watch the Olympics, especially the winter games,"

Maritza said. "Anyway, who cares about pop culture? I can't wait to show you the house, Olivia. If you love it half as much as I do, I'm going to ask Bob to buy it."

Everyone around them was getting their food.

"Nick? Please tell our waiter we have an appointment."

"Yes, dear," Nick said and looked around for any of the waitstaff, who at that moment were not to be found. "Typical," he said and stood. "I'll be right back."

Lunch was wrapped up within the next forty-five minutes, and Olivia and Maritza were soon saying good-bye to Nick.

"Have fun!" Olivia said and blew him a kiss.

Nick drove away with the driver and Maritza said, "Let's go! It's just right up the street."

They walked the short distance to Easton Street, where the broker waited.

"This is one magnificent house, Maritza." Olivia said.

It was a sprawling Nantucket shingled house with fully matured landscaping of deep blue and purple hydrangeas. The whole place—with its towering chimneys and covered porches and the sheer mass of it—screamed old Yankee wealth and New England tradition, but in an appropriately muffled voice.

"I know! Wait till you see the inside! Hey, Nicole!"

"Hi!" the broker called out. "Nice to see you again! Hi! I'm Nicole Bousquet," she said, and shook hands with Olivia.

"Olivia Ritchie. Nice to meet you."

Olivia wondered if Nicole would be earning the customary six percent.

"Well, let's go inside," Nicole said.

From the minute they stepped over the threshold, Olivia was transported. They were right on the water and there were water views from almost every single room. The was a beautiful graceful staircase, hand-painted floors in the foyer, and an enormous family room with French doors along an entire wall that opened to a deep and wide deck, which led to a rolling lawn down to the dock in the harbor. The floor plan was wonderful, so the rooms flowed easily. There was plenty of storage and plenty of space for a large family or an even larger party.

"You could have dinner for two hundred people here. No problem," Olivia said.

"The owners have done that more than once," Nicole said.

Avoiding the vulgar question about price, Olivia asked Nicole for a brochure, which would list the cost in addition to a lot of other information. She handed it to her. Twenty-six million. Olivia staggered for a moment. What made this old funky house worth so much money? In the city, that much could buy you a fabulous penthouse. Granted, there were some Manhattan properties listed for over a hundred million that were being snatched up by Russian oligarchs. But twenty-six million for a Nantucket cottage? She needed a moment to digest it.

They went through the kitchen and all over upstairs. Then they visited the guest cottage last. Olivia hated to admit it, but she was charmed to pieces.

"What do you think?" Maritza asked later over a glass of wine in the lobby while they waited for Nick.

"I think I'd like to see it again tomorrow morning if we have time."

"I'm sure we can arrange that. But you know, your opinion is the one I value the most. Do you think Bob and I should buy it?"

Olivia was quiet for a moment and then said, "Listen, in a normal situation, you'd ask yourself certain questions, like: How much are you going to use it? How much is it worth to you to own it? But you and Bob are in a position in which very few people find themselves. I didn't realize you had such a fondness for Nantucket."

"Well, there's so little humidity," Maritza said and laughed.

Now, there's a good reason to let go of twenty-six million of your favorite dollars, Olivia thought. But she was right about the humidity. Her hair *was* behaving, for once.

"Yes, you're right," Olivia said.

Maritza sensed a trace of disapproval in Olivia's response, so she came clean.

"To tell you the truth, I have fallen in love with this island because it feels like home. When I was a little girl, I had an aunt who had a cottage here, and I would come and spend part of the summer with her."

"Yes, I heard you mention that on the plane."

"Yep. So I have wonderful memories of this place. And I think Gladdie would be safe here. Nantucket is a wonderful traditional place for families, and Bob needs to be reminded that we're a family. And once you gut it and make it look like it should, I think it would become Bob's favorite place to be."

Money aside, those are pretty solid reasons, Olivia thought.

Olivia just didn't want to be self-serving and take an insecure woman like Maritza and push her toward something for her own gain. Olivia wasn't that hardened.

"Maritza? If you buy the place, you and I will make it a paradise."

CHAPTER 10

nantucket looms

After a delicious seafood dinner and highly animated conversation in the back room behind the bar at CRU, they agreed to meet for breakfast in the dining area the next morning at eight. Nick had spent the better part of the dinner entertaining Maritza with the history of Nantucket from the tales of Tom Nevers and the Nantucket Indians to the stories of the treacherous Rose and Crown Shoal, Walter Chase and his heroic rescues with the surf boat, the *Coskata.* She was a rapt student, absorbing every word and asking lots of questions.

"Walter Chase said to his men, '*You have to go out, but you don't have to come back!*' Can you imagine saying such a thing in today's world?"

"No. I haven't heard these stories since I was knee-high to a grasshopper! And I've *never* heard of Tom Nevers. I thought it was just a neighborhood. All this information is so good to have because I can tell it all to Gladdie and make her the smartest girl in school!"

Olivia thought, Did that mean Gladdie might receive her formal education on the island?

"Well, and remember, history teaches much more than just a list of dates and facts. It teaches us how to be. What kind of people do we want to *be*? The men who walked these beaches during terrible storms swinging their lanterns and peering though spyglasses, watching the turbulent waters, searching for ships in trouble?"

"They were a bunch of nuts," Maritza said.

"Maybe. But those men were also selfless and brave. Let's not forget that they endured every kind of inclement weather to help save lives. It was below *zero* when Chase's soaking wet and near-exhausted men saved the crew of the *Kirkham*. And save lives they did."

Nick was on a lecturing roll, becoming as boisterous as a revival preacher in a tent. Olivia put her hand on his to calm him down.

Nick took a breath and exhaled. "Thank you, sweetheart. I was about to break the sound barrier, wasn't I?"

"It's okay," Olivia said, thinking that his enthusiasm was part of what made him such a beloved professor.

"It sure gives you a lot to think about," Maritza said. "I mean, they risked their lives for strangers. I don't know if I'd do that, do you?"

"Well, our armed forces do it every day, as do our police officers and firemen and all sorts of first responders. Sadly, that kind of work is not in my nature. Thank God there are people who can do it," Nick said. "I'm more of a diplomatic peacemaking sort of fellow."

"You would've made a wonderful ambassador," Maritza said.

All Nick heard was *would have.*

Olivia, always sensitive to Nick's feelings said, "Game's not over! The White House might still call."

So morning found Nick and Maritza chatting away while they dressed and packed, expecting to leave the island that day.

"Maritza loved all the stories you told last night," Olivia said.

"You know, her desperation is pitiable," Nick said. "She's in deep trouble with her marriage if she thinks that a renovated old house and an arsenal of facts about a new locale might recapture the heart of her husband."

"You're right."

"The poor girl. She's really hanging on to a dream made from gossamer threads."

"Yes, she is. The tragedy here, as you know, is that she really loves Bob. She would do anything in this world to have his heart."

"That's so sad. And you don't think he loves her at all?"

"No. I've known him a long time. This might sound terrible, but I think he is deeply *amused* by her affection and he sort of revels in the adoration. But sadly, I don't think Bob ever learned the value in really loving someone else besides his children. He wouldn't recognize love if it bit him on his nose. I think he's immune."

"That's a helluva statement. It's probably a trust thing. Well, we'd better get moving. It wouldn't be nice to keep Maritza waiting."

"I've *been* ready! Who spent over half an hour with his morning toilette?"

"I admit it, but my nose is already peeling. I just wanted to be my most presentable self."

"Oh, good grief," Olivia said and laughed. "Let's leave our bags with the bell captain."

"Why not?" Nick said, and the door whooshed to a close behind them.

They dropped off their bags, went to the dining room's unmanned hostess desk, and scanned the room for Maritza. They spotted her and made their way to her table.

"Good morning!" Olivia said.

"Morning! Well, the deal's under way!" Maritza said, sipping her iced coffee. "Bob put an offer in for twenty-two, so we'll see what happens. There are no contingencies and the offer's all cash, so I've got my fingers crossed."

"I think I need waffles this morning," Nick said. "Spending money calls for carbohydrates."

Olivia laughed and agreed. "I'll split them with you?"

"That's a deal!" Nick said.

"Then you're only half bad," Maritza said and giggled. "I'm having French toast and I don't care!"

"I'll help you with that," Olivia said.

Nick bobbed his head in somber agreement. "It's what friends are for."

"And sausage! So. Right after breakfast we're supposed to meet Nicole, and then I thought we should go shopping! I want to show y'all Petticoat Row. How does that sound?"

They ordered their breakfast and their waiter filled their cups with coffee.

"I'd like to see the house," Nick said, "but then I'm supposed to meet an old friend for a bowl of chowder. You ladies can boost the local economy without me tagging along."

"Bob doesn't like to shop either," Maritza said.

"Really? Who are you meeting?" Olivia said, suspecting a blonde from his past.

"Nathaniel Philbrick. He's an author and historian who lectured for one of my classes about ten years ago. He's written some very good stuff like *Mayflower* and *In the Heart of the Sea.* I'll pick up copies for Bob and ask Nat to sign them. I think he'd enjoy them and he'd learn a lot about the island, not to mention the tenacious nature of the whalers."

"Bob understands tenacious just fine," Olivia said.

"That's so nice!" Maritza said. "Thanks!"

"What's Petticoat Row?" Olivia asked.

"It's just a part of the shopping area on Centre Street between Main and Broad," Maritza said. "They call it that because a long time ago when the island was crawling with whalers, they went out to sea for years at a time and their wives watched the stores."

"Wait a minute," Nick said. "You know *this*, but you'd never heard of Tom Nevers until last night?"

"Did Tom Nevers ever own a women's clothing store? I don't think so," Maritza said and rolled her eyes.

Nick looked at Olivia. "I give up."

Their food arrived quickly and disappeared under a flurry of forks and hands passing across the table.

"Gosh!" Maritza said, deeply exhaling. "That was so good it was a sin!"

"Yes," Olivia and Nick said.

They paid the bill and walked over to the house on Easton Street. Nicole was there waiting, and she introduced herself to Nick.

"This is a *very* special property," Nicole said, with a trace of awe in her voice.

"Yes, it is," Nick said in agreement and whispered to Olivia, "It bloody well *ought* to be!"

"Shhh!" she whispered back.

"Nicole? Is there any word on our offer?"

"Not yet," she said. "As soon as I hear anything, you'll know within the same minute. I promise!"

No kidding, Olivia thought, exchanging knowing looks with Nick. This very nice lady will be able to take the rest of the year off and the next one too. Even if they reduce the commission to one percent!

They went inside, walked slowly from room to room, and Olivia took dozens of pictures. Nick couldn't keep his eyes from the water.

"Lovely views, don't you think?" Nicole said to him.

"It's astonishing," Nick said. "Almost as astonishing as Sullivans Island."

"Where is that?" Nicole said innocently.

"Um. If you dropped a pin on the center of the universe," Olivia said, "it would . . ."

"Land on Sullivan's Island!" Nick said and laughed.

"I see," Nicole said.

"So what do *you* think?" Maritza asked Nick.

"I'm wondering if a place like this needs an historian in residence? It's very beautiful."

"The guest house will have your name on the door!" Maritza said.

By the time they met back at the hotel, Maritza had cut a swath through the shopping areas, her credit card a powerful machete. She struggled under the bulk and weight of shopping bags from Milly & Grace, Vis-A-Vis, Nantucket Looms, and Smiling Button. Olivia and Maritza ordered hats from Peter Beaton, and Olivia found a painted cast-iron antique doorstop that represented a fisherman standing in a small boat. Her purchases were insignificant next to Maritza's.

"Maritza?" Nick said. "The island of Nantucket is going to dim the lights in your honor when we leave. This is an awesome haul!"

"I know!" Maritza said. "We had such a good time!"

"We surely did. How was your friend?" Olivia asked.

"Charming and brilliant. Did y'all have lunch?" Nick asked, still incredulous, staring at their bounty.

"Yep. We had fabulous crab cakes at the Club Car and put the hurt on more than a few shops. Didn't we, Olivia?"

"I'll say we did!" Olivia said. "We found some wonderful things for Maritza and Bob's new house too! Really beautiful alpaca throws at Nantucket Looms. I got one for us too."

"Thank goodness. I was worried for a moment," Nick said. "I've been dying for an alpaca throw."

"Laugh now, but come winter, you will cocoon yourself in it," Olivia said, and smiled.

"It's a good thing they're just three of us on the plane!" Maritza said. "And by the way, kids, I'm going to have the plane take y'all to Charleston. Give me your tickets and I'll have Bob's secretary get them refunded."

"Oh, Maritza! That's incredibly generous!" Olivia said.

"Look, I yanked y'all out of your house on one day's notice when you're trying to get your new place organized, so I'm figuring y'all must be as tired as I am, right?"

"Uncle," Nick said and kissed Maritza's cheek.

"I don't want you to hate me. I want you to come back."

"We'll see you in just ten days. Olé!" Olivia said.

"And here are the books I got for Bob," Nick said.

"He's going to love them!" Maritza said

It was six-thirty with plenty of light left to the day when Nick and Olivia turned the key in their front door on Sullivans Island. Had they flown commercial, it would have been ten-thirty. The house felt welcoming then, as though it was a living, breathing thing, happy to have them back.

"It smells good in here," Nick said, carrying their duffel bags into the bedroom.

"My potpourri and candles are finally starting to talk to each other," Olivia said. "You hungry?"

"Always. Shall I whip up a couple of omelets, or do you feel like going down the island for some barbecue?"

"Barbecue. Hmmm. I'm too pooped to go anywhere. But if you went to Home Team and brought back a pulled pork sandwich, I'd eat it without a single complaint."

"Hmmm."

"And I'd kiss your face," Olivia said, and he looked at her through squinted eyes. "Big-time. Okay. All over!"

"I'll be right back. Hold that thought!"

When they had a hankering for it, there was nothing on earth that tasted better to them than pulled pork on a bun with the sweet red barbecue sauce from Home Team BBQ. Barbecue, a treasure Olivia was almost unfamiliar with until recently, was fast becoming her guiltiest pleasure. And Nick's.

They ate together on the porch, smelling the salt and listening to the waves washing against the shore. It was too late in the day for dolphin sightings by the time they sat down. Even the birds had returned to their rookeries and roosts for the night. The sun was already below the horizon, but the sky was putting on a stunning show of almost indescribable colors. Clouds were underlit in endless fields of purple and red. Wide radiant gold streams of fan-shaped light broke through those same clouds here and there, melting into the mango horizon. That night's sunset was worthy of royalty and the miraculous.

"What a sky we have tonight!" Nick said. "I wonder which angel painted it."

"It's unbelievable. Probably the spirit of Michelangelo," Olivia said, taking another bite. "This is delicious. I love it."

Their humble sandwiches were wrapped in aluminum foil, and the rocking chairs in which they sat cost less than dinner in Manhattan. Still, they were almost breathless from the great beauty that surrounded them and the deep haunting flavors of the slowly roasted and smoked pork.

"And I love you."

"I love you too, Nick. So much."

There was a sense of complete serenity all around them. Their simple supper may have seemed pitiful given the spectacular ever-changing sky as night drew close, but they felt profound gratitude just to witness such splendor for the few moments it would last.

In the morning, Nick announced he was returning to the sea to find and conquer the biggest fish in the surrounding waters. Olivia was already on the phone with Jason.

"I'll call you back in five minutes," she said and hung up. "Nick! Don't go anywhere yet!"

She rushed to the bedroom and hurried back with a shopping bag from Nobby Clothes Shop on Nantucket.

"Here! I know this isn't exactly what you're looking for, but it's what all the men on Nantucket wear when they go fishing. So I'm told, anyway. Until we find the right one, this might do."

"Why, thank you, sweetheart!"

Nick opened the bag and pulled out a baseball hat with an extra long bill. He held it in his hand and looked at it. Then he put it on his head and went to the hall to have a look in the mirror.

"I look like a duck," he said and burst out laughing.

"Oh, my god! You do! You look like a duck!" Olivia was horrified.

"I look like a bloody fool!" Nick said, still laughing. "Who wears these hats?"

"I'm going to guess men who are terribly secure?"

"Am I really going to wear this?"

"You most certainly are not! Give it to me. I'm sending it back."

He kissed her cheek and handed her the hat. "Thank you for the thought. I'll be home for lunch."

"Sunscreen!"

"Got it! Just rubbed a forty-five SPF all over my baby face and neck."

She watched him swagger down the path with his fishing bucket until he was out of sight. For all sorts of reasons she couldn't stop smiling.

She called Jason back and he answered immediately.

"So, you didn't tell me. How was your trip to Nantucket?"

"Incredible. You wouldn't happen to know a good contractor up there, would you?"

"Yes, actually, I do. I went to school with a guy whose family lives there, and his dad owns a pretty big construction firm. I could call him for you. What do you have?"

"A very special client who's about to buy a twenty-six-million-dollar house that hasn't been renovated since you were in knickers."

"Knickers?"

"It's an old saying. Anyway, it's a big job. And I need a local architect or I might use someone from New York. I don't know yet."

"Well, there are three I work with here. Christopher Rose, Steve Herlong, and Beau Clowney."

"Hold on, I need to write all this down. And what's the name of your friend in Nantucket?"

"Martin McKerrow. His family's been on Nantucket since the *Mayflower* dropped off his ancestors."

"Wow. He must be from some powerful DNA. Nantucket's got one heck of a winter climate."

"I've never met another family like his. And he might be the smartest guy I've ever known."

"Would you give him a call and tell him to expect a call from me?"

"Of course. Anything else?"

"As a matter of fact, yes."

Olivia gave him a list of all the contacts she needed for the house and for their personal lives.

Jason said, "I'll have to ask my parents about some of these. My mom is very particular about her doctors and well, everything. I can tell you, whoever she uses are the best."

"That's why she's so radiant!" Olivia said. "Would you ask Elaine to call me?"

"Sure!"

The big fat fish continued to elude Nick for the next few days. Nick would come in the house announcing that he had returned from battle.

Olivia would say, "Great! What did you catch?"

And after a sorrowful pause, Nick would call back, "More bait."

This went on for a few more days until he finally took himself to Haddrell's in Mount Pleasant and bought more respectable gear, sand spikes, and a cooler on wheels, which to him was a great personal indulgence. While he was going to hell with himself, he bought a Tilley T3 fishing hat. Parting with seventy-five dollars for a fishing hat was like twisting a knife in his heart, but dinner at Le Bernardin in New York was often several hundred dollars. Le Bernardin was strictly a restaurant for very special occasions. But no matter how deliciously unique the offerings were from their brilliant kitchen, they couldn't compete with the uniqueness of a fish on the plate that was caught that morning. Well, he wanted to believe that.

Then he made another decision. He decided to fish very early in the day at Breach Inlet instead of Station Nine. Breach Inlet was really a fish funnel taking fish from the ocean over to the Intracostal Waterway. It was hardly a man-against-nature venture, but he was frustrated and demoralized by his empty bucket.

He cast out into the middle of the waterway. Then he anchored each of his four lines in sand spikes, sat down in his new nylon-webbed aluminum folding chair (ten dollars at Harris Teeter), and waited for a strike. Within two hours he landed three good-sized spottail bass, two whiting, and a three-pound flounder, the biggest one he'd ever reeled in. He pulled the hooks out with his new pliers and rebaited two of them with half of a small blue crab. He was hoping to catch some mullets. Red mullets adored blue crab. He did manage to get four mullets, and to his surprise he got a pompano on the hook of the rod baited with sand fleas.

"You're not supposed to be in this water!" he said to the fish, pulling the hook from its cheek and dropping it in the cooler to thrash around with the others.

Nick realized then that he needed a fishing buddy because someone had to explain to him how a pompano wound up in

Breach Inlet. And his sanity might be called into question if anyone noticed he was talking to the fish.

"My manly pride has been restored!" he announced as he came through the door before noon. "Tonight we will feast on the finest fish ever to cross your persnickety Manhattan palate! May I have a roll of paper towels and a soup pot?"

"*Persnickety?* Who are you calling persnickety?" Olivia reached into a cabinet and produced a pot. "Paper towels are in the laundry room."

"You, my turtledove. And me too." Nick stepped into the laundry room and took a roll from the shelf. "Come see the catch of the day!"

"You're getting as brown as can be, except for the areas covered by your sunglasses."

"Ha-ha! An occupational hazard shared by true sportsmen all over the world! A badge of honor! Now, come and see."

Olivia followed him outside. Nick had discovered an old oyster table under the house and positioned it near the hose in a shady spot. He had his fish laid across the table by size and species, ready to clean and gut them with his newly acquired shiny serrated fishing knife.

"Wow!" Olivia said. "That's a lot of fish for two people! If you keep doing this, I'm going to have to find us some friends!"

Olivia made a mental note to visit her neighbors to introduce herself to the neighborhood, although she had been expecting them to knock on her door. Wasn't that how it went in the South? She'd have to ask Nick.

"True enough. I thought I'd roast the flounder and the pompano and make a fish stew with the rest, except for that whiting, which to my mind is too puny to be anything but bait."

"And how are you going to cook the larger fish?"

"Over a wood fire with olive oil, lemon juice, and thyme. Maybe a handful of rosemary. And salt and pepper, of course. Just like the fish we had in Santorini."

"And where exactly are you going to build that fire?" Olivia said, smiling.

"Oh. Right! I've put the cart before the horse. We don't have a grill yet. Back to Haddrell's! More money out the door!"

"We have some money for a grill. I just got a consultation check from Maritza."

How much could a grill cost? she thought.

"Good. Maybe there's a sale going on, with the Fourth of July being so close."

"We really ought to be careful for a while, at least until Maritza and Bob close on the house and until I know what my audit is about."

"What audit?"

"I didn't tell you? I got some fan mail from the IRS and the State of New York. No biggie."

"Bastards! Terrorizing a woman! Would you like me to give them a shellacking?"

Olivia smiled. "I don't think they're gender sensitive, baby boy. You clean your fish. I'm going to work on my presentation for Maritza and Bob for the Nantucket house."

"I'm happy they're buying it. I love you having rich clients."

"Like Maritza would say, *They ain't rich. They're stinking filthy rich!* You want lunch? I got some Johns Island tomatoes this morning from the Co-Op."

"You're reading *my* mind now! I was just dreaming about a tomato sandwich on Wonder Bread with Duke's Real Mayonnaise and a glass of iced tea!"

This kind of meal was something well within the range of her limited culinary skills.

"Done! I'll call you when it's ready. But I must say, it's a peculiar combination."

"Food of the Gods. I give you my most solemn word."

Olivia, hoping to make the lunch slightly more genteel than a sandwich slapped together and cut in half on a platter, neatly trimmed the crust from the white bread and applied a thin layer of mayonnaise to two slices for him. Then she spread a thinner coating of butter on hers. Next she sliced the tomatoes so thinly one might read the *New York Times* op-ed page through them and placed a layer of tomatoes on their bread. Finally she sprinkled the tiniest amount of salt over the tomatoes and cut the sandwiches into triangular fourths. She minced parsley and basil together, applied the smallest layer of mayonnaise to the edges of the crusts, and dipped them in the tiny herbs, creating a green crust. She placed them one on the other in a row on sandwich-sized plates and poured tea. She put the plates on the kitchen breakfast bar with napkins and lemon wedges in a small dish. She'd seen this done on a YouTube video, entitled something like "*Elevating the Mundane to the Sublime.*"

This looks *so* pretty! she thought, feeling a bit of pride, and called Nick to come and eat.

Nick, like men are wont to do, was taking his sweet time getting to the table. She called him again.

"Darling! The sandwiches are getting soggy!"

She leaned over the porch rail and there he was, trimming away the inedible and truly disgusting parts of the fish's digestive system. He threw the last cleaned fish in his pot and wiped the fish entrails into a bucket. She gagged and then congratulated herself for slicing the tomatoes so thin because they would *not* make the sandwiches soggy.

"Sorry!" He rinsed his hands with the hose, hurrying up the steps past her and into the kitchen.

He must be hungry, she thought.

She was right on his heels. "Wash your hands with soap." There were stains of unknown origin on his shirt, and she wasn't asking him to explain them. "Maybe you want to change your shirt?"

"Why?" He looked down and saw the spots. "After I clean up the table. It needs a good hosing down or we'll have every cat on the island coming around howling. What's this?" he said, laughing and pointing to their lunch. "Are we having a ladies' tea party?"

"What do you mean?"

Nick scooped Olivia into his arms and kissed her squarely on her pouting lips.

"Augh! You're all fishy!"

"Sorry. Let me show you something, sweetheart." He released her and put one of the dainty triangles into his mouth and ate it. "Not bad! But different."

"You're welcome."

"Okay. Watch your ever-loving husband show you how this is done."

He took a huge tomato from the vegetable basket and rinsed it. Then he set it on a paper towel. He pulled the cutting board from the dish rack and wiped it dry. He laid out four slices of white bread and smothered them with thick smears of mayonnaise. Then he salted and peppered the mayonnaise on the bread.

"Now, some folks skin the tomato and others don't. Me, I like the skin. So here we go. We're going to treat this tomato like a filet mignon." Nick cut the bottom and the top from the tomato and sliced the tomato itself into four thick rounds.

Then he cut the rounds in half. He arranged them on two slices of the bread so that the bread was entirely covered. He topped the tomatoes with the remaining slices of bread and cut the sandwiches in half.

"There are probably nine hundred calories of mayonnaise in there," Olivia said.

"No, there aren't. Take a bite," he said, handing one to her. "Okay. Maybe two hundred."

Because she was the obedient wife and because she wanted to please him, she complied, taking a large bite. Then she moaned with surprise and pleasure as she chewed. *"Mmmmm!"*

"I love to make you moan," he said.

"Nick! This is ecstasy!" She wiped traces of mayonnaise from her mouth with a napkin.

"I know," he said, smiling at her and very pleased with himself. "You're welcome."

"Thank you. Oh, I have so much work to do," she said and sighed, taking another bite.

"The Nantucket house?"

"Uh-huh." After she swallowed she said, "Yes. I think I'm going to take a quick trip up there to meet this contractor before we go to Spain. I might even take Jason."

"How come?"

"Another set of ears. I need someone on site all the time. And I want to get a clear sense of what restrictions we might be working with. You know, Nantucket has all sorts of rules and regulations, and I just want to be sure we do everything by the book and as expeditiously as possible. For Maritza's and Bob's sake." And for the sake of our own bank accounts. "You want to come?"

"I'll go next time. You might want to bring Roni along too."

Olivia thought about it for a moment and realized Nick was one step ahead of her on fertilizing the budding romance.

"God, I love you so much, you are the smartest man in the universe."

"Well, I don't know if I'd go *that* far . . ."

"You're so adorable. And you know what else?"

"What?" Nick had already consumed his sandwich and the ones that Olivia made. "Split another one with me?"

"Yes. Definitely. We have to get Daniel and Kitty a wedding gift. What in the world should *that* be?"

"Something they can exchange." Nick was well into making another sandwich. "Those two aren't going to like anything you like."

"You are right about that. Tiffany's all-purpose wineglasses. And maybe a muzzle for Gladdie."

"You're terrible. Good plan. Maybe a bushel of Johns Island tomatoes."

"I am forever converted. I want more for supper. Why can't we grow them here?"

Nick arched an eyebrow and smiled over her unconscious usage of *supper*. He said nothing.

"It's all about the dirt. We'd have to sneak over to Johns Island and steal some dirt."

"Maybe we can buy tomato plants over there already planted in the largest possible clay pots? You know, legitimately buy the dirt?"

"Witness the creative mind at work!" Nick said. "I would never have thought of that. It's too obvious! I'll make some phone calls. But after I find a woodburning grill."

Nick left and Olivia decided to call Maritza to put together the meeting in Nantucket.

"Hi! Maritza! It's Olivia. How are you?"

"Oh, Olivia! I'm just so sad. I've been crying for two whole days."

"What's happened?"

"We lost the Nantucket house. Now I have to start all over!"

Olivia's heart sank.

"What do you mean? Bob was outbid?" Bob never lost a game of ticktacktoe, much less a bidding war.

"No, the sellers decided not to sell. They got all sentimental and just said they couldn't do it. I'm so mad I could . . ."

"Spit?" Olivia said and thought, Well, so could I.

CHAPTER 11

island drumbeat

Every time Nick drove away with the car, Olivia was stranded. She was reconciled to that because she was delaying buying that second car until their finances were more predictable. But now that she didn't have the Nantucket job, she had no finances to predict. She downloaded Uber and decided a walk on the beach might be a good idea to calm her nerves.

"I'm not trapped," she said to the empty house. "I've got Uber and I'm going to find work."

She wished she could Uber the whole way back to the early nineties, when she had more business than she could handle. It was hellishly hot that afternoon and the world was still. It was almost four o'clock, dead low tide, and not a breath of air was coming off the water. She grabbed a hat, her cell phone, and her sunglasses. And for the first time, she left the house unlocked and empty.

How absolutely weird it is, she thought, to leave your doors unlocked. The whole concept of unlocked houses was without question counterintuitive to a native New Yorker. In Manhattan, there were doors and doormen and more doors through which one must pass to gain entrance. And you had to have your own set of keys, because there was not just one lock but always a dead bolt and yet another key that would give you access with a click and a twist of the doorknob. And then there was always the conundrum of whether to trust the superintendent with the dead bolt key as well as the other? But here, doors were unlocked everywhere, at least on the beach side of the homes. Was there that much less crime on the island, or were the people more honest? Olivia didn't know, but it was an interesting thought to ponder.

As before, she slipped off her sandals and left them in the white sand above the waterline. Then she had the thought, Who'd want my beat-up old shoes anyway? If someone was that desperate, they could have them.

She began to walk toward the lighthouse, and as she did most days, she wondered when, if ever, she would stop feeling so foreign. And what was it that made *anyone* feel like she belonged somewhere? Growing up in one place, to be sure, would give you that sense of ownership of a town or a neighborhood or a particular house. People in all the boroughs of the city talked about going back to the old neighborhood to see if it had changed and *how* it changed, and if it had changed at *all,* they said it broke their hearts. They'd stand around and reminisce about the old corner candy store or about a bar they sneaked into for an underage beer or the playground where they got their first kiss. Those people had a sense of place like Nick did. But what about all the millions of people in the country who grew up and moved all the time? Especially military families. How good were they at adapting? Pretty darn good at it, she guessed. She needed to sharpen up her acclimating skills.

Olivia looked out across the water and spotted the dorsal fin of a dolphin. She stopped and watched. She had not been swimming in deep water since her near drowning, venturing in only up to her thighs, just to cool off on extremely hot days.

The dolphins came around in the early morning and late afternoon, and she loved to watch them, feeling an odd kinship. Suddenly there were two, then three, arcing above the water, and then they spun around and started to chirp. Oh, how she loved their song! She waved at them and laughed, wondering if they were from the same pod that saved her life.

Three teenage boys jogged past her and one said, "You waving at the dolphins?"

She was about to give him a dose of New York with a *You got a problem with that?* Instead she laughed and said, "Yes! That's my old pal Danny."

At that point the young man was jogging backward and said, "Really?"

She looked at the dolphin and back at the jogger and said, "Maybe! Who's to say?"

She watched the kids jog off into the distance and waited and waved at the dolphins until they swam away. She decided it was time to call Roni and give her the lowdown.

Roni answered and Olivia said, "Bad news."

She told her the story and Roni said, "Something else will come along. Or maybe they'll buy *another* house."

"Maybe Nantucket is loaded with those kinds of houses. I should go online and look, but don't you think her broker already has?"

"*I* would, but who knows? Olivia? What does a twenty-six-million-dollar house on Nantucket look like?"

"I'm going to guess it looks about like a seven- or eight-million-dollar house down here on Kiawah Island but with a deep-water dock."

She walked until she felt her anxiety fading away, and then she turned to return to their house. She'd had problems in business before, but never like this. For the very first time, she couldn't see the future because she'd always gone from one job to the next and often handled many jobs simultaneously. Maybe it had been a mistake to take control of their finances when they got married, because now she had huge problems *and* huge secrets. She had played it cool long enough. It was time to level with Nick. She gave the ocean one last look, and sure enough, a dolphin breached the water. When it came back up for up for air, it chirped at her.

"Send me some clients!" she called out and thought, Well, now I'm officially losing my mind.

When she reached home, Nick was in the front yard with two men and a delivery truck directing them to where to put the grill. It was the biggest grill she had ever seen, except for the ones she designed into the homes of the mega-rich. It was all stainless steel, with side extensions, a backsplash, and storage underneath. There was no way Nick could have handled this behemoth himself. It took two burly men and a dolly on wheels to move it.

"Let's just bring it around to the other side of the house," Nick said.

"Hi, honey," Olivia said. "Wow! That is some grill!"

"Yeah, I got a great deal on it."

"Really? How much did it cost?" Olivia asked.

"Yes, just set her down over there. Yes, in the shade, right on the brick patio under the magnolia." Nick said. "It's going to need to be leveled."

"We've got some shims on the truck," one of the men said. "I'll grab them.

Olivia could see that Nick was very excited, like a boy finally getting that elusive pony. She lifted the hood and peered inside, and having no idea what she was really looking at, she closed it with a thud.

"This good, Mr. Seymour?" the man said, standing back and appraising its steadiness.

"That's perfect! Thank you!" Nick shook hands with both men and gave them twenty dollars each. The men walked away and Nick turned to Olivia. "Isn't it beautiful?"

"I imagine it is, as grills go, I mean. So, how much?"

"Well, it was a floor model, so I got it at a tremendous discount."

"And? Come on, tell me."

"Four thousand, but that includes a two-year warranty on all parts and labor."

"*Four thousand dollars for a grill?* Are you *kidding* me? That's *insane!*"

Nick was stunned and sharply offended by her reaction. Was she questioning his judgment? Since when?

He said, "It *was* eight thousand! Olivia, grills can cost up to fifty thousand dollars for some of them."

"I'm aware of that. I purchase them from time to time."

"This is a nice one, but it's not exactly the Madonna of all grills!"

"Okay. Nick? I think it's time we had a talk." She was feeling short of breath.

"About what?"

"Money. Let's go inside."

Olivia knew that he had charged it on a credit card, and that when the bill came in, she would not be writing a check for the amount of the bill in full. For the first time in her adult life she would be making a minimum monthly payment and being charged interest. It gave her the shakes to think about it.

They reached the kitchen and he took a bottle of wine from the refrigerator. Nick knew he was about to hear something unpleasant and thought it wise to fortify himself.

"It's after five. May I pour you a glass?" he asked and poured one for himself.

"No, not quite yet. I think I want to be as clearheaded as possible for this conversation."

"Olivia? What has happened?" He leaned back against the gleaming center island and looked at her. "Tell me."

The story began to pour out of her, one miserable client at a time, and then she broke down and wept with shame and embarrassment because she had not confided in him all along. And because her business, the most important thing that defined her as an individual, was failing.

"Look," he said, "this isn't great news, but it's not like inoperable stage four cancer. What I don't like here is that you didn't tell me sooner. I would've bought a simple Weber grill. Here." He offered her his linen handkerchief.

She took it, blotting her eyes and sniffing loudly. "I couldn't tell you. I just couldn't."

"You can blow your nose in it."

"No, I can't! Then I'd have to wash and iron it! We don't even have a housekeeper!"

She reached for a paper towel and blew her nose into that.

"Olivia? Why didn't you tell me the truth?"

"Because the Nantucket job was so huge, it would've made us whole again. And now it's lost. It's all lost."

"And there's nothing new coming up?"

"No. Nothing."

He ran his hand through his hair. "Okay. How long are we good for?"

"Sixty days, maybe ninety." Olivia was staring at the floor.

"Well, we've got the Sotheby's sale in August. That should generate something. What about the contents of your warehouse in Secaucus?"

"There are a few things there that might be salable."

"What can we do to cut expenses?"

"Nick? For the kind of business I have? My expenses aren't that high. What I need is a job."

"My intuition tells me that you'd be better off with lots of small or medium-sized clients you could rely on than one big one. But let's think this through. And there's something else we need to address, Olivia."

For the first time in their marriage she saw that Nick was very unhappy with her.

"What?"

"You know what you've done here, don't you? You've jeopardized our stability by not telling me what was going on. And I have an absolute right to know how sound our finances are, just as well as you do."

He was now beginning to smolder, but he carefully modulated his voice to remain civil.

"What are you saying, Nick?"

"I'm saying that if I'd had the facts, I never would've allowed you to buy a house like this."

"*Allowed* me?"

"Yes! And I'm saying that because you hid the truth from me, you've compromised my trust in you. This is not a good thing, Olivia."

"I'm sorry, Nick. I never had this kind of catastrophe happen in over twenty years. Not even close."

"It's not just happening to you, Olivia. It's happening to us."

"I think I'd like that glass of wine now. Please."

He opened the cabinet, took out a goblet, and poured her half a glass.

"We'll get through this, Olivia, but from now on? No more secrets. Agreed?"

"Yes. Agreed."

"Tomorrow I want you to lay everything out for me so I can better understand our position."

"I will. First thing."

"I want you to know this. I'm not blaming you for the downturn. You've made it clear how it happened. I'm just wondering how quickly we can recover. We need a plan."

They had dinner that night and the fish was truly marvelous, but a pall had been cast and it seemed to be almost impenetrable.

"Nick, look," she said as they sat down to eat, "I've been uprooted, relieved of my accoutrements, and dropped into unfamiliar territory like a droid delivery from Amazon."

"Well, not to stand on ceremony, but this was always our agreement."

"I know. I don't know where new business is going to come from, but I know it's going to take some time to get back on steady ground. And I also know it would be a lot easier for me to regroup if I was in New York."

"What are you saying? That you want to leave me?"

"Nick! Not for all the money in this world!"

"Well, it sure sounds like you resent the Sotheby's sale."

"That should be another discussion."

"Okay."

"But I'm thinking that if I can get Roni to rustle up a few new clients, and I'll make calls as well, I can fly to New York, make the presentations, order goods, arrange a work schedule, and fly back here to you. Roni can oversee deliveries and installations like she always has."

"How long would you be gone?"

"I'd prefer to look at it as commuting, and I guess I'd be doing it until we're out of the hole."

"Have you thought to ask Jason about sending clients your way?"

"No, but that's not a bad idea either."

After fourteen years of bliss, the honeymoon was officially over. Olivia's secrecy wasn't fatal, but it created an ugly undercurrent of mistrust. Nick was left to wonder: if she had hidden something so critical to their security, what else might she be hiding?

And Olivia went to bed that night, resentful and thinking it was unfair for him to retire and place the burden of being their principal source of income on her. How long did he expect her to work? Would she ever be able to afford to retire? Did he get himself a nurse and a purse when he married her? Had it been a mistake to marry a man so much older? Was he just going to fill the freezer with fish while she schlepped the hard concrete sidewalks of New York? What the hell had she done? For once, she fell into a dreamless sleep.

First thing in the morning, she showed him all of their accounts and her business bank statements.

"It's a good thing we have my retirement money, Medicare, and a Social Security check, meager as it is."

"Yes, it is. A good thing, I mean."

Nick left to go downtown to the historical society to read. He wasn't chilly to her, but his demeanor was decidedly different. He sighed a lot over breakfast, and when he left, he said, "I'll check in with you before I cross the causeway."

"Thanks, sweetheart."

She called Roni.

"Listen, we've got to find some business fast or we're cooked," Olivia said.

"I'm aware. Hey, remember I joined the Young Fellows at the Frick? Well, I got invited to a dinner party by this woman I met at a gallery talk. She just bought a co-op in the East Sixties. She wants my opinion. Apparently you decorated her mother's house in Southampton years ago."

Thank you! It's a start, she thought.

"Maybe her mother needs new curtains by now. Who is she?"

"The daughter's married and took her husband's name, so I'll have to ask."

"When's the dinner?"

"This Thursday."

"What kind of taste does she have?"

"French mid-century."

"Oh, for the love of St. Pete! When is this mid-century horror show ever going to be over? Take her down to all those shops around Howard Kaplan."

Howard Kaplan Design was actually a specialist in country French furniture, some mid-century, and other household accessories, but the neighborhood around it was jammed with shops containing mid-twentieth-century everything from cookie jars to chandeliers.

"I'll do it. So what else can we do?"

"I think we start combing the records going back, say, seven years or more and see who might be ready to freshen up their homes. Then we have to come up with a suitable excuse to contact them, one that doesn't scream desperation."

"When do you leave for Spain?"

"Next week."

"That doesn't give me much time. How about this? Why don't I set up a few appointments with old clients if I can and you fly up and have lunch or drinks or dinner somewhere cool and see what comes out of it?"

"I think it's the only way. Meanwhile, that five hundred dollars we spent for you to join the Frick may have been the best money we've spent in a while. Who knows where it might lead?"

"You're right. There's a lot of new money in the city now. They need our tasteful direction." Roni laughed.

Roni arranged three days of lunches, cocktails, and dinners for Olivia. Nick wasn't thrilled about her going away, but Olivia left for New York on Sunday. Olivia felt like a few days apart might soothe his grumpiness.

"I'll meet you at Teterboro on Thursday," she said. "The information for your flight is on your desk."

"Okay," Nick said. "Thanks."

"What's wrong? You've got funny look on your face."

"I don't know. It's just, well, does Maritza have any idea how canceling the job with you impacts us?"

"Not a clue. She's only upset about losing the house for herself."

"Of course."

"That's just how it is. Interior design is a tough business. I'll call you when I land."

Olivia's delight to be back in Manhattan far outweighed the

success of her meetings, which ranged from lukewarm to just fair. Her old clients for the most part agreed to a meal or a drink just to see what was going on with her or to tell her what was going on with them. Two seemed to have some potential, and she promised to follow up with them when she returned from Spain. Thursday morning she went to Tiffany's and bought a crystal bowl for Daniel and Kitty's wedding gift and took a cab to Teterboro. She hated leaving the city.

The three nights she spent alone in her office on East 58th Street were fraught with worry—worry about Nick and how disappointed he seemed to be in her and worry about acquiring new work. Somewhere along the line, her worry about Nick turned into annoyance. Where was *his* commitment to solving this financial black hole? Did he offer to go back to work? No, he didn't, did he? Maybe if he put down his fishing rod for a while, he could ask the College of Charleston or the Citadel for some part-time work. Why not? She was certainly doing her part. Had she not humiliated herself enough by resurrecting her old clients and hinting around as subtly as she could that she had some time on her hands? But then, she thought, maybe this was what happened when you were too arrogant, too proud. Maybe the universe was trying to teach her the lesson that she never should have taken her success for granted for a single minute. Maybe moving out of New York was the gigantic mistake she thought it would be. And—Nick had said it, really—maybe she should never have had all of her proverbial eggs in one basket. It made her so mad that he was so right. And now they were to spend the next five days with Maritza and Bob and conduct themselves as though everything was all right between them.

Her taxi pulled into the entrance area in front of the terminal at Teterboro Airport. She paid the driver and got out. Nick was standing right inside the glass vestibule, waiting for her. When she looked at him and saw the loving expression on his face, her anger toward him melted. He opened the door for her to enter.

"Hey, gorgeous. I missed you."

"Oh, Nick!" She threw her arms around him and kissed him all over his face. "I missed you too, baby. I'm so sorry."

"Me too, sweetheart. Let's go have some fun in Spain, and to the devil with our worries for a few days."

"You're right. Our worries will be there waiting for us when we come home."

They greeted everyone, and it was almost a repeat performance of their last initial greeting except that Anne Fritz and Lola were absent. In their place to even out the dirty dozen were Kitty's mother Betty, a retiring stocky woman of obviously humble means, and her uncle Ernest, wearing a clerical collar and a thin black suit, an ordained minister who was along to witness and conduct the ceremony. Their discomfort and suspicion of everyone and everything were clear.

Of course, Buddy and Sam were discussing golf with each other, Dorothy and Michelle were ignoring everyone, Gladdie was tearing around the waiting area, and Ellen was posing, giving coy looks in Bob's direction whenever she thought he was looking. Daniel and Kitty were off to one side, quietly talking to each other, smiling and holding hands.

"Welcome!" Maritza said. "I'm so glad y'all are here!"

"So are we! Where're Anne and Lola?" Olivia asked Maritza.

Bob answered, "Look, Olivia. You know me for how long? I don't mind taking all my friends on a little getaway now and then. In fact, I *love* to share what I have. But that dumb bitch?

She treated me like a bug under glass when she was a *guest* at my party on Necker, and then she sent me a bill for eighteen thousand dollars!"

"Good *grief!* That's *terrible!*" Olivia said.

"Outrageous," Nick said. "Hourly rate times hours spent with us. Unreal."

"She wasn't that helpful anyway," Maritza said. "So we decided it was time to go our separate ways."

"Separate *ways?* I *fired* her *myself* and it felt good!" Bob said.

"Well, at least you got *some* satisfaction out of it," Olivia said with a big smile.

"Ha-ha! See? Olivia knows me! Every now and then it feels good to take a little bite out of somebody," Bob said. "Just a little chomp!"

"Please. Robert Vasile," Olivia said, "in all these years, the only time I've ever seen you bite someone is when they're taking advantage of you."

"I wish you did my PR," Bob said to her, and then he spoke to everyone else, "Okay, folks, we've got wheels-up in ten minutes! Let's look alive!"

"What's in all those boxes?" Olivia asked Maritza.

There was a tower of pink boxes waiting by the massive pile of luggage and golf clubs. They were labeled *Fragile!* on all sides.

"Oh, honey, that's Kitty's wedding cake. She's going to put it together on the boat."

"Oh, right! She's a pastry chef."

"Yep, and she brought her flowers too!"

"Well, that's nice. When's the ceremony?"

"The night after we arrive. God, don't you just love weddings? You know, I did ask her if she wanted to go get a dress with me. I would've bought it for her."

"Well, what did she say?"

"Well, believe it or not, she's wearing her momma's wedding dress."

"You know what? I think that's very sweet! Makes you look at her in a whole new light, doesn't it?"

"Maybe for you," Maritza said. "But she's still an odd duck to me."

The seven-hour flight to Palma was completely serene, the best kind of flight to have. This time Bob shuffled the seating arrangement. Bob placed Kitty's mother and uncle across the aisle from him and Maritza. Olivia had to say that Bob and Maritza were doing everything they could to put the prospective in-laws at ease. Having them along minimized the usual bawdy and catty chitchat, and it caused extraordinary fits of eye rolling from Ellen, from Michelle, and heaven knows, from Dorothy whenever Betty or Ernest spoke.

After considering the demeanor of Kitty's mother and uncle, it did not seem to Olivia or to Nick that this was a particularly good match—Kitty and Daniel, that is—if Kitty's ultraconservative background would play a big role in their future. Or maybe it was an excellent match, and that conservatism would bring reality to Daniel for the first time in his life. In their back-row seats they whispered to each other.

"Not to be catty, she's like Aunt Bee from Mayberry," Nick said.

"Shhh!" Olivia said. "I loved Aunt Bee. She's probably in shock, bless her heart."

"That's a southern expression used exclusively by belles, you know."

"Oh," Olivia said. "Well, excuuuuuse me!" And she laughed, so happy that Nick wasn't provoked with her any longer.

What would've been the point of staying angry? If he wanted transparency in their marriage, she would give it to him. They were in the hole together and would get out of the hole together. And after a lot of thought, she had to say she would not have liked it if he had withheld a truth of that magnitude from her.

After they were airborne, Maritza began passing a tray and Betty helped her. Olivia thought, Well, that's nice. Maritza had arranged for platters of sandwiches, baguettes, and individual chef salads to be brought on board for all of them to share. Michelle brought some bottles of wine. In honor of the bride and groom, a nice bottle of champagne—Veuve Clicquot, of course—was opened and consumed along with small tributes for their happy life together. As comfortable as it was on Bob's jet, when all twelve seats were filled, it wasn't so easy to navigate the aisle and it didn't feel as spacious. The tight quarters made for some ironic first-world rich-people remarks. *When is the last time you played Twister while you were drinking champagne at forty-one thousand feet? Excuse me, I'm just trying to reach the beluga!* Eventually they had eaten enough, drunk enough, and twisted around one another enough and everyone finally wanted a nap, even Gladdie, who was the first to succumb on Bob's lap.

It was another remarkable landing, this time in Palma on Majorca, coming in almost silently, and they could barely feel the wheels touch down. It was very early in the morning. This time they had to go through actual customs in the TAG terminal, which was basically two men in military-looking uniforms who glanced at their passports as they walked through a metal detector single file. Betty and Ernest's passports were brand-new, leading Olivia to suspect they had never been out of the country. She was developing a soft spot for them.

All of their luggage was brought around to a waiting van and loaded while they climbed onto a small bus. The minibus would take them to the port, where they would be met by the launch that would take them to *Le Bateau de l'Amour.* All these transfers were completed in the time it usually took most people to drive to the nearest Starbucks. Everything Bob did went off without a hiccup, like a well-oiled machine.

When Betty and Uncle Ernest saw *Le Bateau de l'Amour* floating in the harbor and realized that was where they were headed, they actually gasped.

Maritza heard them and saw their shock and said, "It looks big from here, but once you're on board it starts to shrink."

Nick laughed and said, "That's exactly what Olivia tells me about our new house!"

"Because it's true," Olivia said.

"Can you believe those awful people decided not to sell us their house on Nantucket? I'm still so mad!" Maritza said, ignoring the fact then that Betty and Ernest were practically catatonic.

Bob turned to face Olivia to hear her response.

"It came as a surprise to me too," Olivia said.

Bob paused and then said, "And I imagine you had cleared the decks to take this on. Am I right, Olivia?"

"Yes, but it's not a problem," Olivia said.

It was really hard for Olivia not to show any emotion and she tried to appear unruffled. Yet she knew her disappointment was plain to see, even from behind her sunglasses.

Bob reached over and patted the back of her hand. Olivia took the gesture to mean something like *Hang in there*, which was nice but wouldn't pay the mortgage. She swallowed hard. Her reality was so far removed from Bob's reality that she was certain he had no idea how much trouble she was in, but she would never let him hear it from her lips. She still had her pride, and she still believed that you never let anyone see you sweat.

Somewhat sleep deprived, the group motored out to the enormous yacht in a state of respectful awe, saving their energy for what might happen next. Pretty much the same thoughts were rolling around in all their minds, and if they could've issued a collective opinion of the moment in one word, they would've said, "Cool."

Getting off the launch posed a challenge as the water was extremely choppy and it was windy. But there were a half-dozen or so of Bob's crew waiting, so as the boat bobbed down, Olivia prepared herself. As the boat bobbed up, the two men took her by her upper arms and swung her onto Bob's yacht, which was as steady as though it rested in dry dock. Bob, needing no help, simply stepped off the launch, as did Maritza, Ellen, and Gladdie.

"Let's go watch *Cinderella*! I wanna watch *Cinderella*! Come on, Ellen!"

Ellen was immediately whisked away to the viewing room belowdecks that had thousands of movies on demand.

"I'll see you later!" Ellen called over her shoulder to Bob.

"You guys are just a pack of old sea dogs!" Sam said, wobbling as he tried to balance himself on the deck.

Buddy grabbed his arm to help him. "Whoa there, pal! Hang on!"

"I've got this," Dorothy said, her wide-legged gauze pants whipping all around her like Old Glory on a flagpole.

"Thanks!" said Michelle. She stepped off the ladder and Buddy held her arm firmly.

Betty was next. "Oh, my goodness!" she said, laughing and smoothing her sensible dress, as she found her footing in her sensible shoes. "They should see this back in Omaha! Who'd believe it? Come on, Ernest! You can do it!"

Ernest was hanging back, the last one to leave the launch. He seemed very uncertain as to how he would get off the smaller boat gracefully and maintain his dignity. He was a long drink of water, weighing in at under a hundred and fifty pounds, all angles and knobs. In addition, Uncle Ernest looked green around the gills.

"Hold this, young man! Thank you!"

One of the crew took Ernest's well-worn Bible and two of the sturdiest-looking male crew members stepped forward and hopped on the boat to lift him up onto the deck of Bob's yacht. Ernest continued to hang on to the ladder with clenched fists.

"Betty? Remember when I told you I was a landlubber? I wasn't kidding!"

"Come on, Uncle Ern! You've made it this far!" Kitty said. "I can't get married without you!"

"Just close your eyes and let go of the ladder, Reverend!" Bob said. "Come on, now . . ."

"One, two, three! *Oh, God save me!*"

The reverend was lifted into the air by the crew on the bobbing launch, handed right into the arms of two others, and placed squarely on his feet. He opened his eyes.

"Praise God!" he said and began to laugh.

Everyone laughed with him, even Dorothy and Michelle.

They ascended the long, wide stairwell, and at the top was a scene from a modern-day nautical episode of *Upstairs*

Downstairs. The majority of the crew was assembled to welcome them. Two female shipmates offered them rolled wet towels from a silver platter garnished with an orchid to wipe the salt spray from their hands, and two others offered small glasses of a mixed fruit drink.

"Welcome aboard!" they said and, "Welcome back!"

"Is there any alcohol in this?" Betty asked.

"No, ma'am, just ginger ale and guava juice."

Betty nodded her head and said, "Guava juice? My word! This is a beautiful boat, Bob! Don't you think so, Ernest?"

"Thank you," Bob said. "Whenever you're ready, we'd be happy to give you a tour, if you'd like."

"This is like something right out of a Hollywood movie!" Ernest said, draining his glass. "I believe I'll have another, if you have it to spare."

"Ernest?" Maritza said. "Welcome to the land of plenty! We've got all the guava you want!"

"Isn't that something?" Ernest said.

"My word!" Betty said again and shook her head in disbelief.

The deck on which they stood had a large round teak dining table bolted to the floor.

"Watch this, Ernest! You'll love it," Bob said. "Hand me the remote, Sam."

Sam removed a remote control wand from a drawer in the buffet and handed it to Bob.

"Okay, everyone stand back a bit," Bob said. "I love doing this!"

Bob pressed a button and the top of the table lifted up, separated into wedges like the slices of a pie, and turned to the left; other wedges were raised from beneath them and turned to fit into the gaps like puzzle pieces; and then it was all lowered into place. It went from being a table for six or eight to a table that could easily seat twelve or fourteen people. The new leaves were of a different color, stained to resemble burled walnut and mahogany, and when they were settled into place, they created a radiant star in the center of the table.

"Well, how do you like that?" Ernest said. "I am amazed! Where in the world did you find something like this?"

"Ask her," Bob said and pointed to Olivia. "Olivia is the official decorator of my personal life."

Olivia was remembering going to David Fletcher's studio and talking about the origins of this kind of table from the nineteenth century and a furniture designer named Robert Jupe.

"Oh! Well, uh, this is a capstan table, custom designed for this boat and made by a designer in northern England. Kendal is the town. David Fletcher is the name of the furniture maker. Anyway, I've been following his work for years and I think he's just brilliant."

"You don't worry about leaving it out here in the elements?" Ernest said.

"Well, that's a really good question. We gave it a UV resistant finish and it's constructed of teak, custom painted to look like walnut and mahogany. It's been in place for ten years, and I think it still looks great."

"I've never seen anything like that in my whole life!" Betty said.

"Take me now, Lord! I've seen it all!" Ernest said. "Say, Bob? I'll bet that set you back a pretty penny."

"I knew I liked you, Ernest! A man of the cloth who recognizes the beauty of pennies!"

Ernest chuckled and Bob continued.

"Yeah," Bob said, "we had this guy Fletcher on the boat for a week while he put it together. Nice guy."

"This is really something else!" Betty said.

"Come on," Bob said. "Let's get you to your stateroom."

"Stateroom? Oh my!" Betty's eyes were as big as saucers.

Maritza said, "Yep, you're bunking with Kitty and Ernest is in with Daniel. We can't have any moofky-poofky until these two tie the knot!"

"You're a fine woman, Mrs. Vasile," Ernest said.

"Tell that to him," she said and hooked her thumb in Bob's direction.

CHAPTER 12

i do! i don't!

Their first night passed quietly. It was true that everyone was somewhat fatigued from the trip, but it was quiet because half of the passengers had almost no interest in Betty or Ernest. In fact, when Olivia thought about it, it seemed odd that Bob didn't fill the staterooms with Kitty's and Daniel's friends instead of his own. As a result, there was no traditional bachelor party. No hoopla at all. There was only Bob at the helm of the dinner table telling stories about himself and the few things that he could remember about Daniel's childhood to try and entertain Kitty's family.

"I was working and traveling a lot during those years," Bob offered as an excuse.

Betty, on the other hand, regaled them with nearly every moment of Kitty's formative years. "She could twirl a fire baton like nobody's business!"

"I'd be afraid to catch my hair!" Maritza said.

"So would I!" Olivia said. "You're very brave, Kitty."

Kitty grinned and shook her head. "Mom? People don't want to know all this stupid stuff."

"Yes, we do!" Maritza said. "I couldn't twirl a baton to save my soul, much less one on fire!"

Betty laughed and continued. "I know now that I'm here that this might seem like a silly thing, but I brought you two jars of strawberry rhubarb preserves." Betty said. "I put up ten gallons in quart jars every summer and I just thought you might enjoy them. They're in my cabin."

"Stateroom," Dorothy said, correcting her, adding. "Rhubarb. How quaint." She reached for the bottle of wine and filled her glass to the brim, even though dinner had been cleared from the table. Betty's affectionate manner toward Maritza irritated the hell out of her.

"Stateroom! It just sounds so *grand*," Betty said.

"Well, that's 'cause it *is* grand," Dorothy said. "Where's Toto? Hello! We're not in Mississippi anymore." She alone laughed at her joke.

"We're actually from Nebraska," Ernest said.

She's looped, Olivia thought, and looked at Nick, who smirked in agreement. He reached out and took Olivia's hand in his, kissing the back of it.

Betty did her best to ignore Dorothy, who was obviously swimming the River Vino. "Anyway, Maritza, tell me about your folks. Are they still in Mississippi? I had a cousin there. I haven't spoken to her in years."

"Well, my momma is in Cartaret, which is out of the way, but it's so pretty. She's a very serious gardener, and you should see her yard when all the azaleas are in bloom. It's just gorgeous."

"Is that where ya learned 'bout tha birds an' tha bees, Marizza?" Dorothy said, slurring her words enough to cause Buddy and Michelle and Olivia and Nick to lean in and finally stare at her.

Dorothy just cackled, as though she was Amy Schumer and Tina Fey rolled into one. Sam ignored her. Kitty and Daniel snickered. Dorothy drained her goblet just as the waitstaff was putting down dessert, cherries jubilee flambé.

Olivia thought, Uh-oh, somewhere in between Necker Island and tonight Dorothy developed an unquenchable thirst.

"Oh! How beautiful!" Maritza said.

"I thought we needed something celebratory in honor of the wedding," Bob said.

Olivia said to herself, That's some bull. He has it every chance he can. She looked at Nick, who smiled in agreement.

"Looks great!" Kitty said. "I'll make this for you, Daniel."

"Sweet," Daniel said.

Dorothy looked at her plate, frowned, and said, "Do you thin' I mi' have another glass of wine? I'm so bored I cou' scream."

"Have whatever you want," Sam said.

"Then I think I'll have a lil' nap." Dorothy pushed her cherries jubilee to the center of the table, folded her arms on the table, put her head down on her arms, and passed out cold.

Sam ignored her, still talking to Buddy about whatever their sidebar discussion was about—golf, Olivia guessed—and seemed to have no intention of removing her from the scene. There had to be some trouble in their paradise, Olivia surmised.

As soon as she could, Michelle sneaked away, saying that she was very tired. Ellen was the next to fold on the excuse of getting Gladdie to sleep.

Maritza hated herself—but not really—for enjoying seeing Dorothy make a complete fool of herself. Olivia and Nick hated to admit it, but later on admit it they did in pillow-talk whispers. In fact, they snorted with stifled laughter.

But dinner was not over quite yet. The rest of them sat

around the expanded marvel of the remote-controlled dining table, trying to pretend there wasn't an unconscious woman in their midst.

Olivia looked at Kitty. She had pale skin and short-cropped black hair. She could be quite pretty with some cosmetics. Maybe. And her tattoos were worrisome, because what if she decided to change careers and she was stuck with small appliances and cupcakes? And worst of all, how would they look at seventy? The poor child. She's actually sweet and shy.

"Tell us about your cake, Kitty," Olivia said, trying to let Kitty take the lead. "I understand that you baked it yourself and that you're putting it together tomorrow?"

"Kitty started baking when she was just a little bitty thing," Betty said, as though Kitty had severe laryngitis.

"Mom! I can answer for myself!"

"Made my birthday cake when she was just ten years old!" Ernest said.

"Arg. Never mind."

"That's so sweet!" Maritza said. "So tell us, Kitty!"

After expelling a portion of foul humors with a guttural sigh, she said, "Okay. Two layers are hazelnut because it's my favorite; two are German chocolate because that's Daniel's favorite; and the icing is classic vanilla-bean buttercream with marzipan flowers. The surprise is all in the decoration. It's not going to be like a cake with some stupid bride and groom on the top."

"Kitty was on *Cake Wars*," Daniel said. "She won ten thousand dollars."

Olivia had the uncharitable thought that Kitty's winnings were roughly ten thousand times more than what Daniel had ever earned in his entire life.

"That's my baby!" Betty said. "I have it all on a DVD."

"What's *Cake Wars*?" Bob asked.

"Oh, honey!" Maritza said. "Food Network! I love that show! What did you bake?"

But on considering the real world of the ninety-nine percent and the world of his son's in-laws, Bob said, "Actually, that's a lot of money for a cake."

"Well, I can't wait to taste your wedding cake," Nick said. "I love all cake."

"For *Cake Wars* I made a cake that had an aquarium theme. There was a giant shark coming out of the top of it, teeth and all. He had a bloody fish dangling from one of his teeth. And baby orcas swimming around the bottom devouring other fish that devoured smaller ones. It had a kind of food-chain border."

"That sounds really scary!" Maritza said.

"You're scared of a cake? Really? God, that's so lame," Daniel said.

Maritza turned red, but because of the hour few could tell.

"I know you're getting married tomorrow, son," Bob said, "but don't be snide to Maritza."

"He's just nervous," Betty said. "Aren't you, son?"

"No. Not *really*," Daniel said and looked at Kitty. The bride and groom rolled their eyes.

This trip was like the Olympics of eye rolling, Olivia thought. And then she said to herself, Bob defended Maritza? Bull. Olivia knew him well enough to know that he defended Maritza to look good in the eyes of Betty and Ernest. If they had not been there, Daniel's remark would've flown right into Bob's left ear and out of his right without so much as a sneeze-inducing tickle. These were decent, wholesome midwestern people, with the kind of reputation for being straight shooters that Bob couldn't buy. And Bob always wanted what he didn't have.

"Whatever," Daniel said.

"Excuse me," Maritza said, having had enough sarcasm for one evening, and left the table. "I'm going to say good night now." She went around the table and gave Betty a hug. "We're so happy y'all are here."

"Thank you, Maritza," Betty said. "This had been the most amazing day!"

"Kitty, if you need a hand with your cake I'd be glad to help you," Maritza said.

"No, thanks." Kitty said. One more eye roll.

"Yeah, she used to cook belowdecks for the crew," Daniel said.

"Yeah, I know she did," Kitty said.

"*She* is the cat's mother," Betty said automatically, because she had drilled it into Kitty that it was impolite to refer to another person who was actually present in the room as *he* or *she.* But Betty's hand flew to her mouth because it was also impolite for her to reprimand Daniel.

"My mother used to say that!" Olivia said, coming to Betty's defense with a laugh. "She said it all the time. I'm afraid that *too* many linguistic niceties have been tossed aside in today's world."

Nick said, "I used to see it all the time in the classroom, people coming in and saying *Yo, dude!* Just where is *Yo, dude!* going to take you in this world? Wall Street? A boardroom? An operating room? I think not."

"Yo! Mr. Seymour!" Daniel said and thought he was a Rhodes scholar for the moment.

"That's funny, Daniel." Nick smiled at him because a young

person never learns anything from being demoralized. "A good command of the language is a powerful tool. People forget about the great beauty of words, but words strung together well endure through the ages. Look at our Constitution and think about how important it was to be concise. Or a Shakespearean play."

"Or the Bible," Ernest said.

"Touché!" Olivia said. "Good one!" Olivia stood and gave Maritza a hug. "Sleep well."

"Thanks," Maritza said quietly and headed inside.

No one else acknowledged her departure except Nick and then Ernest, who stood up halfway from their chairs and then resumed their seats a moment later.

"Hey, Dad? When is Mom coming? I miss her *so* much."

Olivia could see Maritza bristle even though she was walking away from them. She pushed up the sleeves of her silk caftan and shrugged her shoulders

"Tomorrow afternoon. She's in Palma, shopping."

"My word," Betty said.

Olivia noted the look of concern on Betty's face as if she was wondering for the first time about the maturity and suitability of Daniel to be her son-in-law and very likely the father of her only grandchildren. And what kind of a father-in-law would Bob be? Betty sighed deeply as the realization set in that it was too late in the game to do anything about it. Her only child, who'd been raised to love God, her family, and the American way—was she marrying for money?

Olivia could see straight into Betty's heart and felt bad for her. As much as she, on that rare occasion, ached for a child of her own, she was once again keenly aware that children also bring heartbreak, disappointment, and problems that can't be solved. Young Daniel's character may have been beyond salvage.

The hour was late and *Le Bateau de l'Amour* was under way but moving at a lazy pace until the captain felt certain that all the passengers were safely in their beds. Then he would open up the engines to a faster clip. Their course was set to head toward Ibiza and the other Balearic Islands.

Ernest and Betty said good night, followed by Bob, Buddy, and Sam. Sam, of course, was burdened with the unconscious body of his wife. It was one of the few times he was glad she weighed so little.

Bob said, "Let me hold the door for you, Sam."

"Poor girl," Buddy said.

The almost newlyweds decided to take a stroll on the top deck and maybe have a soak in the hot tub. Once the yacht moved away from the lights of Majorca, thousands of stars appeared in the deep cobalt sky. Nick and Olivia decided to have a look at them from the vantage point of two recliners that were forward on the third deck.

"Isn't it funny how it doesn't seem to get quite as dark here as it does in New York?"

"We're closer to the equator here." Once they were settled, Nick exhaled and said, "Boy, this is the life, isn't it?"

"Yes, but speaking as a close observer for the last twenty-five years, all this glitter isn't quite what it's cracked up to be. I mean, not just Bob, but the majority of my clients, they have all this money and all their *stuff*, but where's their joy?"

"And where's the love?" Nick said. "Do you see any real affection between our bride and groom?"

"Well, I think there's a lot of heat. But neither one of them seem to have much in the way of manners."

"Yes. Sadly, it's true. Well, my precious love, let us lie here together for a moment or two in pleasant repose and take in the awesomeness of the Milky Way, which is truly awesome."

Olivia giggled at Nick's words. "Awesome. Let's do."

The first glimmer of daybreak found them before they found their rooms. They had fallen asleep on the deck, lulled to sleep by the gentle rocking motion of the yacht. And *Le Bateau de l'Amour* was at anchor, within viewing distance of a charming-looking port town whose harbor was filled with dozens of small boats, bobbing in the water like won tons in a bowl of soup.

Olivia was surprised. She sat up and stretched her arms over her head. "Wow. Nick? Wake up, sweetheart! It's morning." She shook his shoulder gently. His eyes popped open.

"What? What the devil! Oh, my! I haven't . . . I haven't done this in years!"

She helped him to his feet and they made their way to their room. He seemed unsteady to her. When they stepped over the watertight tall lip of the outside door that led into a living room, Nick tripped because he didn't lift his foot high enough to clear it. The riser of the door was designed thus so in heavy turbulence the closed door provided a solid seal and seawater wouldn't find its way into the interior rooms. Between that and holding open the heavy door when he tripped, they both nearly fell.

"Whoa! Are you all right?"

"Yes, yes. Just the insult of osteoarthritis. I'm a bit stiff from all that fresh air. I'll take a pill and I'll be fine."

"We almost hit the literal deck! Why don't I ask for some coffee? And a glass of juice?'

"Good idea. In the parlance of the young people, getting old sucks."

"I'll decide when you're old," she said.

Nick had a long hot shower, a cup of cappuccino, and an anti-inflammatory gel cap and declared himself cured. "I'm ready to greet the world!"

"Go ahead to breakfast. I'll be along in a few minutes."

He kissed her cheek. "I'm ravenous. You're sure you don't mind?"

"Not a single bit! Save me a seat."

He left, the door whooshing to a solid close behind him.

Breakfast was a casual affair on Bob's yacht, and Olivia could see it all from memory. There would be a buffet of cereals, fruit, cheeses, smoked fish, and charcuterie. If anyone wanted rye toast, an omelet or waffles or a two-minute egg, all they had to do was ask. There were usually a few different blends of smoothies on the buffet in addition to croissants with an assortment of jams and jellies. The expanded table was set with beautiful Limoges china, Italian hand-embroidered linens, and Christofle silver flatware. Each place setting had its own salt and pepper cellars, and blocks of butter filled several silver butter crocks. There was a beautiful centerpiece of flowers and fruit that would change with every meal. What made this breakfast casual was not the food or the service but the dress code. Bob's hospitality was boundless.

With the exception of Betty and Ernest and of course Nick and Olivia, everyone would appear at the table in a robe over a swimsuit or work-out clothes, having just finished their cardio or weight training in the gym. Dorothy would have on a full face of makeup with a swimsuit and hopefully a robe, hung over and in a foul mood.

Olivia thought, I can definitely wait a while before seeing her.

Michelle would arrive in yoga clothes and have nothing to say to anyone. Maritza would be wearing something Dorothy despised, a catalyst to start the eye rolling and teeth sucking. She was in no rush to see that either. Betty and Ernest would be slipping deeper into a state of worry for Kitty's future and a general state of malaise. If dosed with truth serum, Olivia would've sided with them in their opinions, and that would be fatal for her professional relationship with Bob. It was best to delay the advent of her appearance.

Kitty would most likely already be working on her cake. She had stated plainly that she wanted no help. Daniel would be somewhere eating granola and yogurt and gluten-free toast, earbuds in, listening to his music, wishing there was just one person on board whose company he enjoyed besides Kitty. Ellen would be cajoling Gladdie to drink her juice while playing footsie with Bob if she was within range of him. Maritza would be brooding until she snapped out of it or maybe not. Maybe she was getting into the swing of things for the wedding.

So Olivia encouraged Nick to go to breakfast without her so that she could dress for the day in peace. She wanted to dress in something worthy of greeting Colette, who would undoubtedly arrive early with dogged determination to ruin the day for Maritza.

Olivia had worked with Colette on several residences she shared with Bob in their halcyon days—a condo in Aspen that looked like a Ralph Lauren Home ad; their apartment near Lincoln Center, which was all chrome, white, and modern; and *Le Bateau de l'Amour*, which was very traditional with some nod to marine accessories. Bob was the one with all the taste. Colette was just a hanger. A former Ford runway model, everything she put on hung on her as though it was custom designed just for her.

Colette's marriage to Bob went the longest distance of them all, but they were disastrously matched to begin with. Colette was a fling Bob had while married to Elaine, but then when he discovered Colette was in the family way and carrying a son, Bob left Elaine and married her. Like Henry VIII, Bob wanted a male heir, an aspiration he had no doubt rethought from time to time.

Olivia had told Bob on more than one occasion that it was unnecessary to marry everyone he slept with. Bob would admit that so many ex-wives did make things more complicated. And Colette was an especially tough customer. She made sweet Sam's wife Dorothy look like Mary Tyler Moore. After a decade or so of being thoroughly henpecked by Colette, Bob began to cat around in search of kinder arms. And what do you know? He found them right under his nose belowdecks in the galley. *Le Bateau de l'Amour* finally earned its name.

By the time Olivia did appear for breakfast, the Bemises and the Kreyers had already taken the launch to shore on the excuse of finding a gift for the bride and groom. Olivia was happy not to have to deal with them. Maritza was working with someone from the crew to lay out the area where the ceremony would be performed.

"Good morning!" Olivia said. "How are the plans coming along?"

"Oh! Hey!" Maritza was really happy to see Olivia. "Did you eat?"

"No, I'm actually going to grab something now. Come sit with me."

"Okay, sure!" She turned to the crewman and said, "You don't need me, do you?"

"No, ma'am," Anton said. "I'm pretty sure I have the gist of how you want it laid out. And they're working on flowers in the pantry, if you want to see them."

"Just surprise us. How's that? Let's go, Olivia. After the way Daniel spoke to me last night, he ought to be glad I didn't make him walk the plank."

"Yes. He seems more surly than usual. What's going on?" Olivia said.

They stepped out onto the deck, where Nick sat with Betty and Ernest, chatting away. Ellen and Gladdie were just leaving.

"He's just an entitled little monster," Maritza whispered. "It's that simple."

Olivia nodded in agreement and then caught Nick's eye. "Hi, sweetie! Can I get you something since I'm up? Good morning, Betty, Ernest. I hope you both rested well?"

"Slept like a baby," Betty said cheerily. "I was just saying to Nick that this place is so picturesque!"

"Yes, it is," Olivia said and turned to the crew member who had appeared to take her order. "I'll just have a cappuccino and whatever's on the buffet." She put some slices of smoked salmon on a plate with a wedge of Brie and a handful of grapes.

"Very good, Ms. Ritchie."

Maritza took a seat next to Betty.

"Mommy! Come watch *Cinderella* with me and Ellen!"

"Not now, sweetie," Maritza said.

Gladdie frowned, crossed her arms, and stamped her tiny feet at Maritza.

"Mommy's tired, sweetie. I'll watch it with you tomorrow. We have a wedding today."

"And I'm the flower girl!"

"Come on, Gladdie," Ellen said. "She's too busy for you now."

Sullen Gladdie and smug Ellen left them then, and Betty and Ernest were slack-jawed.

"I think I'd like a Coke with ice," Maritza said to Jessica, the crew member who was one of four waiting the table for that meal. "Just ignore my nanny, Betty. She's got an agenda."

"Sure thing, Maritza," Jessica said. "I mean, Mrs. Vasile."

"Stop! You'd better not get all weird with me, girl!" Maritza said and laughed.

Jessica giggled and walked away.

"Isn't it strange for the help to call you by your first name?" Betty said and added, "Oh, I'm sorry! That's none of my beeswax."

"No, no! It's okay. Jessica used to be my bunkmate. "

"Oh," Betty said, again unsure of how things worked in Maritza, Bob, and Daniel's world. "Well, she looks enough like you to be your twin."

They began to talk about the ceremony, which would take place at six that evening against the backdrop of the setting sun. A special dinner would follow a champagne and caviar reception, the menu of course designed by Maritza. A local trio was coming on board to play for a few hours. After that, Kitty and Daniel were taking the jet to Saint-Tropez, where they would spend a week on Bob's other large boat, a gorgeous schooner-rigged sailing yacht that measured one hundred and eighty feet in length. It had a crew of ten.

"Boy oh boy!" Betty said. "I'm waiting for that fellow Robin Leach to jump out from behind the curtains!"

They all laughed.

"Remember him? Whatever became of him?" Maritza said.

"Hopefully," Olivia said, "he's living his caviar dreams."

"I always liked him," Betty said. "Well, it's getting on to ten o'clock. I should go see if I can help the bride."

Maritza said, "Betty? If you'd like to have your hair done this afternoon, we have a stylist on board."

"You do?" Betty said. "Why, that would be so nice! Thank you!"

"The salon is on the same deck as your stateroom. Would you like to say three o'clock?"

"That sounds just fine. Thank you so much!"

Olivia said, "I've got to give them my dress to steam out. It looks like an accordion."

Just as Olivia stood to leave the table, she saw *Le Bateau de l'Amour's* launch approaching them. and on that launch was Bob's ex-wife, Daniel's mother, and Maritza's archenemy—Colette.

Colette Vasile had arrived, resplendent in a most dramatic haute couture ensemble.

"Sweet baby Jesus!" Maritza said in horror. "She's gonna spend the whole day *and* the whole night?"

Ernest and Betty were aghast at Maritza's profanity and turned to see who was docking at the stern. Even Nick's interest was piqued. As discreetly as they could, they all moved to the rail to watch the tall, willowy, glamorous Colette ascend the stairs and be greeted a little too warmly by Bob. She was wearing white crepe wide-legged pants and a navy-and-white-striped boat-neck silk sweater. Her purse was a large red patent leather Valentino tote bag. She wore an oversize and very dramatic red straw hat with a Hermès scarf tied around its crown and cat-eye designer white sunglasses. The launch's captain handed Colette's Bottega Veneta duffel bag to a member of the crew.

"Red lips at this hour?" Maritza said. "I always said she was tacky."

Olivia put her arm around Maritza and said, "It's going to be okay."

"Oh dear," said Betty, finally getting the picture.

"I need to go fix my face," Maritza said.

"This is getting interesting," Nick whispered to Olivia. "I think I'll go get my book and sit out here for while." He thought, The last time I saw Colette, she was married to Bob. The big cats are going to have a face off. Nick was titillated.

"I'll see y'all in a little bit!" Maritza said and turned to escape to her room.

"Yes. Suddenly I feel like I need a makeover," Olivia said. "Maritza! Wait! I'm coming with you. Don't you know she's been planning her arrival since she got word of the wedding? Show me what you're wearing for the ceremony."

"Okay. Did you see Bob kiss her?" Maritza said.

"That doesn't mean anything and you know it. It's just Bob being continental."

"I don't think he had to hold her so close, do you?"

"Listen to me, Maritza." Olivia stopped her right in the middle of the living room. "You've got to tell yourself that Colette is here because *you* understand that she *should* be here and you have *no* objection to it. If she sees that you're uncomfortable with her presence, it sends her a message that is better left unsent. Do you know what I'm telling you?"

"Yes. Bob is my husband now. Not hers. And this is my yacht, not hers."

"I sincerely hope you don't have to remind her of that, but yes, that's the general story. Always deal from strength, not weakness. Got it?"

"Got it," Maritza said and her bottom lip quivered.

"None of that, Maritza! Pretend you're Meryl Streep and give that mean old bitch an Oscar-winning performance." There! Olivia finally called the situation what it was. "When she's gone tomorrow, I'll sit on the deck with you and we can call her every name in the book."

"I'll try," Maritza said.

Olivia had her own serious doubts about Maritza's ability to rise above the utter nonsense she was about to be forced to endure.

Somehow Olivia helped Maritza completely avoid Colette until lunch. Olivia sat with her while she had her hair and makeup done, and they went over her outfit for the evening, considering all her options several times. Her hair was put up into an elegant twist and her makeup was soft and dewy—very natural, except for the eyelash extensions.

"I think I'm going to wear the pale blue dress. I love the sparkles."

"You're going to be stunning!" Olivia said.

By one the whole gang convened on the main deck where the table was set for thirteen. Everyone was milling around, waiting to be told where to sit. Ellen and Gladdie were having pizza in the media room, watching *Cinderella*. Again.

"You'll know where to find me, Bob," Ellen said to him in her sultry voice.

Betty, Ernest, Olivia, and Colette heard her as plain as day, and Ellen's demeanor was not lost on any of them.

"Y'all just sit wherever you want," Maritza said. "I'll be right back."

Maritza went inside for a tissue.

"What the hell is going on around here, Olivia?" Colette said. "By the way, it's nice to see you again." Colette was as phony as could be, but she hoped there was some vestige of congeniality between her and Olivia. After all, she needed *someone* to talk to.

"Hmmm. It's nice to see you too and I wouldn't know what's going on. I'm just the decorator. You should ask Bob."

"Oh, right. I'll do that. Thanks."

Olivia looked at her with a completely blank expression and shrugged her shoulders. She wasn't getting involved in the Ellen/Bob quagmire.

"I think all these nannies can be moody." Olivia gave her that much to chew on, which was basically nothing. "They're so young. And truly, who does that work?" At least Olivia wasn't being a bitch.

"Uh-huh. Overly ambitious young women with no prospects, that's who," Colette said. "You still in the city?"

"I'm commuting. Nick retired so we have a place on Sullivans Island, right outside of . . ."

"Charleston! What a coincidence! How about this? I just bought a huge house on Tradd Street! It needs to be gutted back to the bricks! Want the job?"

"You bet I do," Olivia said. "Thank you." My God, Olivia thought, is this wretched woman going to follow me into eternity? And she quickly told herself she wasn't betraying Maritza. This was just business. "I'd be honored and thrilled to do the job. We can start as soon as this trip ends. How's that? I'll put together some storyboards. Historic Charleston colors?"

"Perfect. It's kismet, that's what it is! Just send all the bills to Bob. I'll have keys made for you."

"Good. Of course," Olivia said with relief, knowing she'd get paid at least. She felt better for the first time in weeks. And she hoped Maritza wouldn't object. Why would she really? "We'll talk later."

"It will be like old times," Colette said. "With this one, I think I want the house to look like my family has lived there for a few hundred years but updated for the times."

"I know *exactly* what you want," Olivia said.

"I know! You always get it!" Colette said.

The menu was wonderful. They were offered several choices of entrées. Roasted calamari served with linguine garnished with olive oil, lemon zest, shaved fennel, black olives, and scallions. Grilled prawns with chopped tomatoes, red onions, and cilantro with a lime vinaigrette over Boston lettuce. Or a simple fish, Nick's favorite, just grilled with lemon and olive oil and fresh herbs. There was a platter of grilled vegetables for those who ate nothing with a face and a wide selection of sorbets and gluten-free biscotti (in consideration of the bride and groom) to finish the meal. Corks were pulled, champagne and white wines were poured, and everyone's spirits were high.

Maritza returned smiling and didn't say a word when Colette took a seat next to Bob. Maybe Maritza had reached into her medicine cabinet for a few milligrams of something. Everyone was talking at once.

Because it was the first time Colette had met Kitty's mother, she took a special interest in her for all of about twenty seconds when Betty said something like how happy she was to have Daniel in her family. If there had been a digital readout going across Colette's forehead it would've read: *What? Are you kidding me? Please tell me why my pain-in-the-ass son should make you happy? Is this just some bullshit platitude, make nice, chitchat?* Colette didn't know the meaning of "make nice." Olivia made note of the instantaneous change in Colette's attitude, thinking, Working with Colette again is going to be just awful.

Maritza looked beautiful, relaxed, and serene, but it didn't take long for Colette to take a jab at her.

"So, Maritza, you do know that Bob and I are walking Daniel up the aisle, don't you?"

"There is no aisle, Colette."

This brought a smile to Michelle's face and Olivia's.

One point for the current wife.

"I see," Colette said and withered on the vine. "Well, Bob is sitting next to me."

"That's how I planned the seating. I'll be on his other side."

Two points for the home team.

It was a terribly awkward moment, so much so that the second bitch at large made an attempt to clear the air.

"We bought a little something in town for the happy couple," Dorothy said to Daniel, after consuming one prawn cut into bites the size of garden peas. She passed a shopping bag around to Kitty.

Kitty opened the bag, pulling out a scandalous amount of tissue paper and disrobing the gift as though she were conducting a striptease. Finally she lifted out a large wooden salad bowl with a very irregular shape.

"Thank you," Kitty said and actually smiled. "It's beautiful. Look, Daniel."

"Very nice. Thanks," Daniel said.

"It's made of hand-carved olive wood, which of course is local. And there are tongs somewhere in there too."

Olivia knew that salad bowl didn't cost a dime over twenty

dollars, if that. She pinched Nick and gave him some wide eyes, but Nick didn't understand what she meant. What Olivia was trying to tell him telepathically was: *Here's Bob taking Dorothy's drunk ass on a hundred-thousand-dollar vacation, and the best she can do for his son's wedding gift is a salad bowl with tongs? Their businesses must be on the skids.*

Michelle and Buddy then produced a box tied elaborately with a multitude of ribbons, curled grosgrain and streaming satin of every color and width Olivia could name. It was simply a beautiful package.

"Save the ribbons for Gladdie!" Maritza said. "We can use them for her hair!"

"Oh, *now* you're saving money?" Daniel said.

"Sure," Kitty said and gave Daniel a naughty-boy slap on the hand. "Bad boy." Suddenly the nice side of Kitty, the girl Betty raised on corn and red meat, began to emerge. "This was so nice of you, Mr. and Mrs. Bemis. Thank you."

Inside the box was a beautiful tall and heavy hand-blown clear glass vase. It had a wide bottom and a narrow neck, the kind of vase that would stop hearts with one perfect long-stemmed calla lily placed in it at an angle on a table in a foyer.

"How dramatic!" Kitty said. "It's a treasure! I love it. Don't you love it Daniel?"

"Um, I guess so," he said. "Thanks!" he said to the Bemises.

"Now, you have to write down who gave you what so that when you get back from your honeymoon you can write proper thank-you notes," Betty said.

"Oh, Mom! You are just priceless."

Everyone had a chuckle at Betty's remark.

"What did I say?"

"Nothing," Bob said. "You're just adorable!"

"I am? Well! That's a first for me!" Betty said.

"Come on, Betty," Ernest said. "Let's go get ourselves ready."

They all left the lunch table, intending to give Olivia, Maritza, and Kitty some time for last-minute details, but as Colette passed Maritza, she sniffed loudly as though she smelled something rank.

Kitty waited until Colette was far enough away and said quietly, "If that's the best she's got, it ain't much."

Maritza smiled and so did Olivia. It was the first bit of daylight Kitty had shown Maritza, who in just a very few hours would be her stepmother-in-law. She was trying to be nice, no doubt as a result of a severe talking-to from her mother.

The musicians arrived at four-thirty in their own launch. The photographer arrived by water taxi at five and began taking pictures. The ladies had long disappeared to dress. At five-thirty, the crew carefully moved the wedding cake to its own small table on deck where the reception would be. It was a crazy-looking thing but a beautiful one. The top layer, a five-inch round that was five inches tall, was covered in buttercream frosting and had marzipan hydrangeas on its top. It was leaning thirty degrees portside. The second layer was an eight-inch round that was five inches tall; it was covered in marzipan roses and other small flowers that cascaded down the sides of that tier. It leaned thirty degrees starboard. On it went, layers headed port or starboard until you reached the bottom layer, which was the square cake on which the whole fantastic production rested in a garden of exquisite flowers. There would be plenty of cake for the guests and the crew, a thoughtful gesture.

"What does it mean, all cockamamie like that?" Maritza asked Olivia when she came on deck for the ceremony. Maritza was a sparkling vision of the Balearic Sea in an aqua chiffon tight-fitting dress trimmed with silver sequins. She was wearing a pair of diamond earrings that looked like chandeliers. They were large enough to cause cataracts if worn on a sunny day.

"She said it's an interpretation of that song 'Sailing, Sailing,'" Olivia said. "You know, 'Sailing, sailing, over the bounding main, many a stormy wind shall blow, ere Jack comes home again?'" Olivia was wearing her favorite black summer crepe dress with flat sandals, pearls, and her diamond studs.

"So it's a ship in stormy waters! How smart is she?" Maritza said.

"I suspect, very," Olivia said and thought, That cake might be the perfect metaphor for a lot of things.

Now, Olivia might have added that Maritza's earrings were sure to stop Colette's heart but for two things. One, Olivia wasn't certain Colette had a heart, and two, she would be working for her again. Can't dis the boss and expect a good outcome. Fortunately, Olivia thought again, Maritza didn't realize Olivia was playing both sides of the fence. Yet.

Soon they were all gathered and of course Colette, who intended to show up Maritza, wore a very slinky gown that glittered in gold, with canary diamond earrings that were large enough and spectacular enough that Dorothy, who'd been wearing sunglasses all day, began to shake. And Dorothy's ensemble defied description except to say it was red and weird.

Colette's earrings had to have been a guilt gift from Bob; at least they looked like something he might have brought home after he did something completely unforgivable. Olivia had the funny thought that great sex doesn't last, but diamonds are forever.

Bob and the other men were sporting white dinner jackets with black tuxedo trousers, one more handsome than the other. And they all smelled good; even Ernest was—as Olivia would say—rocking some Old Spice. Suddenly the evening began shaping up and looking like a swanky soiree from a James Bond movie.

Promptly at six o'clock, the entire crew gathered and stood as a group in the background. The pianist began to play and Gladdie came tiptoeing through the door in a baby-blue dress with cap sleeves and a full skirt of tulle shot with glitter that just dusted the tops of her Mary Jane silver shoes, which glittered as well. She had a basket of rose petals. She dropped the petals gingerly as she walked slowly until she got to the place where Kitty's uncle stood with Daniel.

Then she shouted loudly enough for all of Spain to hear, "I'm Cinderella!"

There was much muffled laughter.

Ellen, dressed in a clinging wrap dress, slipped into the group and found a chair.

Next Kitty appeared in the doorway, smiling and even trembling, adding to the charm of the occasion. Her mother's dress was so stunning that all the women gasped. Had stocky Betty really ever been that tiny? The dress had a sweetheart neck encrusted with pearls and little glass diamonds, long lace sleeves that nicely covered her tattoos. The cut of the dress accentuated her narrow waist, which was cinched with a cummerbund. The ball gown skirt was made of duchess satin, with inverted pleats and tiny covered satin buttons climbed all the way up the back. Her short hair was gelled up, curled with a curling iron, and decorated with flowers pinned inside of curls. As it turned out, Kitty had a beautiful figure hiding under all those baggy clothes. And as she had been made up by one of the crew, they all discovered she had a lovely face. She carried a beautiful bouquet of flowers, brought in from Nebraska.

"Holy crap!" Sam said. "She's a babe!"

"Shut up!" Dorothy said. "You're such an idiot."

"She's beautiful," Buddy said.

"Who knew?" Michelle said. "You're an idiot too."

Kitty smiled and walked slowly toward Daniel. Daniel was transfixed, as though he'd never really seen Kitty before.

The vows were mercifully short, were spoken clearly, and went off without a hitch.

"Do you, Kathleen Elizabeth, take this man, Daniel Robert . . ."

"I do," she said.

Minutes later, her uncle Ernest was encouraging Daniel to kiss his bride and shouts of joy went up all over the boat. One of the crew fired *Le Bateau de l'Amour*'s saluting cannon and the celebration began. Horns blew from every corner of the harbor. The musicians stepped up their tempo, playing "Danke Schoën." Needless to say, the crew was opening magnums of Veuve Clicquot, whose corks were popping and filling flutes. Most of the crew had the night off in honor of the wedding.

On the buffet table of hors d'oeuvres, under a profusion of fragrant roses and lilies, there was a mountain of beluga and Osetra caviar from Petrossian ready to be dolloped on the tiniest warm blinis and finished with a dab of crème fraîche. One of the chefs stood by carving nearly transparent slices from a leg of Iberian ham, which comes from precious pigs raised on acorns, a Spanish delectable banned in the United States. There was foie gras on toast points from a goose probably raised on Mozart, tender abalone flown in from San Francisco that garnished a special ceviche of fluke and Prince Edward

Island oysters. In time they would sit down to a dinner of lobster from Maine and prime rib from Nebraska, and if they didn't eat themselves into complete oblivion there would be hand-churned gelato served with Kitty's very clever cake.

Amid all the talking and laughter and the devouring of the extravagant buffet, Bob finally offered a charming toast.

"Friends? Tonight is a very special night. My only son, Daniel, has brought this beautiful and talented young woman into our family, and I want to thank him for that. Marriage is a very special commitment. I should know . . ."

Everyone laughed at that, including the crew.

"Well, what I mean to say is that in this unconventional world of anything goes where everyone seems to be rewriting the rules of society to please themselves and to justify their bizarre behavior, you two, Kitty and Daniel have chosen to do the traditional thing, which is to marry. I am proud of that, Daniel, and I am proud of you. And, Kitty? I can't wait to know you better and to see more of your amazing cakes. Anyway, I want to thank you all for being here tonight and for being a witness to a very important day in my family's history. And to the newlyweds, my wish for you both is perfect health, prosperity, endless love, and many babies! Congratulations!"

Everyone said, *Here, here!* It was almost time for dinner.

Colette approached Maritza and Olivia, who were chatting with Kitty.

"I'm so happy to be working with you again, Olivia," Colette said and turned to Maritza. "I just bought an old house in Charleston, minutes away from where Nick and Olivia moved. Isn't it a small world?"

"*No*, she *didn't* tell me," Maritza said and looked at Olivia in horror. "Is this true?"

"Yes," Olivia said and died inside. "You see, I *was*—I mean, I have *time* now that . . ."

Maritza cut her off.

"I see." Then Maritza said to Kitty, "So, Mrs. Vasile? How does it feel?"

Her remark was directed to Kitty just because she wanted to be the first person to address her as such. But Colette answered instead.

"What, Maritza? How does what feel?"

"I wasn't talking to you, Colette. I was speaking to Kitty."

"Oh, that's right! She's Mrs. Vasile now! Now there are two of us, right, Mrs. Vasile?"

Kitty, sensing trouble, said, "Uh . . ."

"Excuse me, Colette, there are three of us," Maritza said.

"But only two that really matter," Colette said.

"I'm not going there with you, Colette."

Maritza stepped away and Colette put her foot down firmly on the hem of Maritza's gown. As Maritza stepped forward, the gown ripped, exposing Maritza's bare backside.

Oh boy, Olivia thought, here we go.

With that, the cats got in the bag and had some choice words for each other before they even sat down for dinner.

You're nothing but a whore!

Who's the whore calling me a whore? You're the whore!

He married you only because you were pregnant!

At least I gave him a son! You gave him a brat!

Don't you dare call my child a brat!

As soon as he knocks up the nanny, he's going to dump you!

He will not! We're a family!

No! You stole my husband and you're a home-wrecking cow!

"Ladies! Ladies! Please!"

"Mom! Stop!"

Bob rushed over and grabbed Maritza's arms from behind, concealing her nakedness. Daniel rushed over and grabbed Colette, holding her back. Bob's footing was unsteady as he held a wildly gyrating Maritza away from his ex-wife. She tried with all her might to break Bob's hold. All she wanted to do was punch Colette in the face.

"Now, let's calm down, ladies. This is a wedding, not a gutter . . ."

The word *gutter* so infuriated Maritza that she broke free, fell backward, and toppled the table with the cake and fell into it. Everyone froze. The music stopped.

"Oh my God!" Kitty screamed. "Oh my God! You wrecked my fucking wedding cake!"

"Yeah! You crazy bitch! And you attacked my mother!" Daniel said.

Kitty's uncle Ernest stared as if he had never heard that kind of language until then. He stumbled over to a chair, clutching his chest, and collapsed. Betty hurried over and fanned him with the handkerchief tucked in the bosom of her dress.

The crew scrambled to clean up the cake. Bob struggled to help Maritza up and save her dignity at the same time. She pulled her dress around her to cover that which was hanging out that the sun seldom sees. Her entire body, including her hair, was splotched with cake and icing.

"It's okay," Betty said in between reviving her brother and wiping her own brow. "Kitty! It's okay. It's just a cake. It's just a cake." Boy, these rich people are truly not like us, she thought.

Kitty inhaled and exhaled quickly, starting to hyperventilate, and then she centered herself and found a moment of Zen that calmed her right down. She resumed normal breathing and looked at her mother.

"You're right, Mom. It's just a cake. And guess what? I have extra layers in the kitchen and more buttercream too. Maybe someone could frost them?"

"Of course! Right away!" The chef who was slicing the ham dropped his knife and sprinted toward the kitchen.

"That's my girl!" Betty said. "Ernest? Ernest? Shall I get a doctor?"

"I'm okay," he mumbled and seemed to come around. "Maybe a little shot of O Be Joyful might bring me to my senses."

"Get the music going!" Bob said.

The musicians began to play again.

Olivia and Nick finally made it to Maritza's side and said, "Are you okay?"

"I'm very disappointed in you, Maritza," Bob said. "Very."

"She started it," Maritza said and began to cry.

"Oh God. Here come the famous waterworks!" Bob said and walked away.

Maritza looked around to see if the world was staring at her. They were not. The others had turned away as if her distress was not important, except for Colette, who stood there smirking.

"You're a nothing," Colette said. "Bob regrets the day he met you."

"Excuse me," Maritza said. "I'm going to change."

Olivia said, touching her shoulder, "I'll come with you."

"I'm fine," Maritza said, pushing her hand away and left.

Olivia froze. Her instincts were correct.

She went to Nick and said, "Maritza's upset that I'm working on Colette's new house."

"Come on, now. That's ridiculous. It's just business. Besides, Maritza loves you to pieces."

"Yes, but I think she sees this as fraternizing with the enemy."

"Let's not worry about that now. And if you need me to talk to her, you know I will."

"Oh, Nick. Thank you," she said, thinking, No man is getting into my business. Not even Nick. "You are so wonderful. Do you know that?"

"That's true," he said and kissed her hand.

"I'm worried. We need the business, Nick. You know we do."

"Olivia, my precious pet, if I walked away from a university every time I was made to work on a committee with a disagreeable, jealous, or politically competitive colleague, I could not have kept a position for more than a year. She's not walking away from you."

"But women think differently," Olivia said. "Decorating your home is so personal."

"I imagine there is a strong element of that in your work, but still, I wouldn't panic quite yet. Let's not let a little spat ruin the night for us! Come dance with me. They're playing our song!"

"What song is that?" Olivia didn't recognize the melody.

"The one they're playing." Nick laughed at pulled her into him. "All the music is ours."

"You are an incurable romantic."

"Guilty. God, you smell good!"

Everyone went back to dancing and eating, and the new cake was brought up frosted and ready to cut. Daniel and Kitty took the first slice and fed each other. The photographer took some shots and everyone applauded. Minutes later, the crew was passing trays of cake and forks.

"She might look like a freak, but she can sure make a cake," Dorothy said.

"Yes, she can," Sam said.

"I don't think she looks like a freak," Olivia said. "Her mother's gown is retro Grace Kelly's wedding in Monaco."

"Oh, now you're a fashion maven too?" Dorothy arched an eyebrow and had another bite of cake.

"I watched that wedding a hundred times," Olivia said.

"I'm sure," Dorothy said.

Later as the party continued, Olivia and Nick began to realize they had not seen Maritza in quite a long while. Dorothy said she saw her come back on deck in another gown. Sam was less sure about that. Colette claimed complete ignorance. No one seemed to know anything for sure.

The crew, even those on duty, enjoying champagne along with the wedding party made for a crowded deck, and with all the alcohol that was consumed, everyone seemed hard pressed to be certain of anything. By midnight the newlyweds said good night and Betty was going to bunk with her brother in the stateroom that (of course) had twin beds. The musicians and the photographer were long gone.

At first there was no sense of alarm or serious concern but as the night grew later, Bob finally checked their room. Nick and Olivia went with him. There was no sign of Maritza, only the frosted remains of her Bob Mackie gown on the bathroom floor. This was not a good omen.

"How could this be?" Nick said.

"I feel terrible!" Olivia said.

Bob called the captain, who got the crew going on a search. Nick and Olivia looked everywhere too. Two hours later, after every square inch of the yacht had been thoroughly gone over, it was decided that Maritza had somehow simply vanished.

"She'll turn up," Bob said. "She's just being dramatic."

"She's probably hiding in the crew quarters," Michelle said.

"Why would she do that?" Buddy asked.

"Because that's where she came from and that's where she belongs," Colette said. "Only on someone else's husband's yacht."

CHAPTER 13

gone

Bob walked the circumference of his yacht with Captain Jack, as did other crew members, shining hurricane-strength flashlights into the water, slowly and painstakingly looking for any kind of clue, any trace of clothing, anything. Nothing.

"I can't believe she jumped ship," Bob said. "Why would she *do* that? It doesn't make any sense!"

"I don't know, sir. It seems very out of character for Mrs. Vasile."

The night was as still as death itself. The only sound was the gentle lapping of the water against the hull. It was around two in the morning, and those not dead asleep in their beds were suddenly very sobered by the terrible news. They were anchored at a place in the harbor where the water was quite deep. It was too far to swim to shore unless you were a gold-medal-winning Olympian. If Maritza had jumped overboard, she could never have made it to dry land.

Some of Bob's family and guests had gone to bed before it was generally understood that Maritza was actually missing.

Betty and Ernest would have recoiled in horror, thinking that she was captured by pirates or that she'd jumped in despair, given what happened with the cake and her dress and the terrible things Colette said. And if Maritza didn't turn up, Ellen would be delighted to hear the news in the morning. Michelle and Colette announced that there was nothing they could do, so they might as well turn in. Colette was so smug, Olivia wanted to give her the good noisy smack she deserved.

Finally, after all the walking and peering into the water produced nothing but a fear of the worst, the chef made a pot of strong coffee and the remaining guests gathered in the living room, including Olivia, who was pacing the floors, blaming herself for a least a part of what could have put Maritza into a state of mind to do something rash.

"Okay, okay. Let's think this through," Bob said. "Someone said they say her on deck in a different gown."

"Dorothy. She *thinks* she did, but lemme tell ya, she also drank enough champagne to float this boat," Sam said. "And she *told* me I saw her too, but I don't really remember seeing her for sure. But let's be honest, she's always telling me what to think. I couldn't swear I did see Maritza, at least not with any certainty."

Bob said, "Do you remember what time that might have been?"

"No. I'm sorry. Maybe ten o'clock? Ten-thirty?"

"I *never* saw her come back," Olivia said. "But then, I didn't expect to see her again last night."

"Why not?" Bob said.

"Good grief! Bob! You're not serious, are you?"

"Yes, I am," Bob said. "Do you think she was so embarrassed she would just chuck the wedding and stay in her room?"

"I would have!" Olivia said. "I wouldn't have trusted myself not to give Colette a good slap!"

"No, you wouldn't. Besides, she had plenty of other clothes to wear. About what time was it when the band stopped playing?" Bob asked.

"Midnight, I think," Nick said. "I remember looking at my watch."

"Captain Jack? Did you or any of the crew see any other boats approach besides the ones bringing the musicians and the photographer?"

"No, sir. I can tell you absolutely no other boats came within twenty meters of us. We were on alert for paparazzi with those horrible long-lens cameras they all have these days. And I ordered our own launch and the Zodiac to patrol the area all night, just for that reason."

"That's just what you want, a tabloid wedding," Olivia said.

The chef passed a tray of steaming mugs and everyone took one, hoping the caffeine might jar a memory.

"Thanks," Buddy said.

"And you searched every hold on the boat? Every closet? Anywhere that she might have been able to hide in?" Bob said.

This remark was so ludicrous it sent Nick up the wall. He could stay quiet no longer. "Bob? Sit down." Bob did as he was told. A first.

"Why would Maritza hide herself? She's not a child," Nick said quietly. "Unless, God forbid, she came to some great personal harm."

"She is as healthy as a horse, so even if some maniac from the band attacked her, she could defend herself. Besides, there's no sign of a struggle anywhere," Bob said, throwing any notion of foul play out of the window. "I could never believe someone would actually hurt her."

Olivia could think of *more* than one person who would've liked Maritza gone. Why wasn't Bob asking *that* question? And Olivia was racked with guilt. And feeling terrible. After all, she considered Maritza to be more than a client—the daughter she'd never had. If she had done anything that would contribute to Maritza's doing something rash, she would never be able to forgive herself.

The conversation went on for another hour, and every plausible explanation for where Maritza might be found led to a dead end.

"Jack? At daylight send a couple of our guys ashore with pictures of Maritza to ask around if anyone saw a woman who looks like her getting off a boat between ten-thirty and midnight. Let's try to keep this quiet, okay?"

"Sure thing," Jack said.

"This is a little bit unbelievable," Buddy said. "I mean, I keep asking myself if wrecking a cake and a catfight with an ex-wife is enough to make somebody commit suicide, and I just don't think it is."

"Yeah, but we're men, and if we knocked over a cake we'd say we were sorry and that would be the end of it. I mean, ruining someone's wedding cake is pretty awful, but it's not the end of the world," Sam said. "Maybe she slipped?"

"That's not exactly what happened," Olivia said. "I was standing right there."

"So," Bob said, "walk us through it."

"Okay. So, Colette walked up to Maritza and Kitty and me and made the announcement that I was going to totally renovate an historic home in Charleston that she just bought."

"I didn't even know she had one," Bob said.

"That doesn't surprise me," Sam said. "Why would you know?"

"Yeah, you've got a few things going on in your life," Buddy said.

"Anyway, I think that upset Maritza."

"Why would that upset her?" Bob said. "Why should she care?"

"To be honest?" Olivia said. "Maritza is a very sensitive woman, and perhaps she thought I was betraying her in some way."

"Why would she think that?" Bob said. "You're the Vasile interior designer for all my wives! Always were and always will be. The bills all come to me anyway!"

"That may be true, but Colette was pretty aggressive. She tried to engage her in an argument by stating that she and Kitty were the only Mrs. Vasiles who mattered."

"Aw, come on! That's some high school horseshit," Bob said. "And Maritza got her *feelings* hurt?"

"It was very rude, Bob." Olivia said. "You have to give her that."

"Okay, but she *knows* how Colette feels about her." Bob said.

"Bob, just because she knows doesn't mean it's okay for Colette to tell her she was worthless and that you regretted the day you met her," Olivia said. "I mean, I'm sorry to say all this, but you want the truth, so here it is."

"God, she's awful. Colette, I mean. How did her dress get torn?" Bob said.

"Colette stepped on the hem. *I* saw that much," Nick said.

"She's a crazy bitch. She always was," Bob said.

"No comment," Sam said.

"Nothing from me either," Buddy said.

Olivia added, "And then you and Daniel stepped in and actually, Bob, it was you who lost your balance, throwing her off balance. You were able to recover, but Maritza was wearing very high heels, and then she got tangled up in her gown, so down she went."

"That's not how I remember the moment, but you might be right," Bob said.

"There have been more than a few studies done on the difference in how things are perceived and how they are remembered," Nick said. "If ten people had witnessed what happened between Maritza and Colette, you might get ten different responses."

"I know that's true, Nick, but Colette really *is* the meanest woman I ever married. Everyone would agree to that," Bob said with a straight face. "Lucky I got out of that one."

"Well, I don't want to bite the hand that feeds me," Olivia said. "And maybe you weren't aware of this either, but Maritza and I achieved a level of friendship that I never enjoyed with your other wives, which is why I think she was probably upset that Colette could be so rude to her and then I'd go to work for Colette."

"Maybe, but that's so silly, Olivia," Bob said. "You shouldn't feel any guilt. You've got bills to pay like everyone else in the world."

"True story," Olivia said. "I sure do."

Bob gave Olivia a glance, reminding himself that she lost a chance to renovate and redesign a twenty-six-million-dollar house on Nantucket. How many jobs had she passed on to make herself available for Bob? He would be extra generous with Colette, even though she was insufferably evil, and tell her to give Olivia a free hand to buy whatever she thought would dignify the house.

"So the question still remains, Where is Maritza?" Nick said. "What happened and where did she go? And why? Maybe she just couldn't take it anymore."

Bob dismissed that idea, looked at his watch, and said, "Well, I don't know. But I do know we're not going to solve this tonight. We need some answers. Maybe someone saw her. Maybe she's just over on Ibiza in some hotel, cooling off. I certainly do not believe she attempted to commit suicide. I mean, I can understand why she might not want to deal with *Colette* anymore. She's so vile she even gives *me* the willies. Anyway, my prediction is Maritza will turn up. Let's try to get some sleep. There's nothing more to be done for now."

With that Bob got up and left the room.

When Olivia and Nick turned out the light in bed, Nick rolled over to Olivia and said, "Well, I have a theory."

"Let's hear."

"Like you, I think Maritza has just plain had it with this entire cast of characters, including her obnoxious daughter," Nick said.

"Well, you see that's the thing that's troubling me. Even though Gladdie is very overly indulged, Maritza really loves her. I don't see her abandoning her only child. Can you?"

"No, on second thought, I think you're definitely right about that."

She rolled over toward Nick to see his face and he was already asleep, blowing little puffs of air through his lips.

How do men do that? she thought. They just lie down and go to sleep. Amazing.

They slept until eight o'clock and Olivia woke up, remembering what had happened the night before. She and Nick hurried to dress for breakfast and wanted nothing more than to go to the table to see that Maritza was there, safe and sound.

It was not to be.

Bob was there reading the news on his iPad. Ellen was seated to his right and Gladdie was in between them, eating pancakes with her fingers. Colette was on his left, smiling and pretending to be the hostess, chatting up Dorothy and Michelle. Knowing that Colette was at the root of all the hullabaloo, which he deemed to be totally juvenile and unnecessary, Bob turned his chair away from her to better ignore her.

By the clench of Ellen's jaw, Olivia surmised that Ellen was not happy with Colette's presumption to the throne.

The bride and groom had already left for Saint-Tropez. Bob had been there to see them off, but he did not think it was a good idea to throw a shadow on their honeymoon with the story about Maritza. It wasn't necessary.

Everyone else was in various stages of arriving and leaving the breakfast table and perhaps they were somewhat subdued, but the mood was almost like it was business as usual.

"Good morning, Bob," Olivia said. "Any news?"

"Cappuccino?" a crew member asked her.

"Yes, two, please, and grapefruit juice? Thanks."

"Good morning," Bob said. "No, not yet. But I'm sure she's fine. She'll turn up."

"You seem awfully sure about that," Nick said. "Um, I'd like a Swiss cheese and mushroom omelet."

The crew member looked at Olivia with a questioning expression. Their boss's wife may have been missing, but people still had to eat.

"I'll just find something on the buffet," Olivia said, adding, "Thanks."

"Well, Jack has his ear glued to the harbor news station and nothing has washed up on shore," Bob said as though he was casually looking for a lost large rubber duck. "And he's got a half-dozen men onshore asking around. I'm sure she'll turn up before lunch."

"This is simply terrible," Betty said. "Ernest is inside on his knees just praying as hard as he can for her safe return."

"Well, that's awfully nice," Bob said. "But make sure he gets something to eat."

Michelle was less interested in the blather coming from Colette, and she strained to hear what Bob was saying.

"Bob," Michelle said, "I'm a whole lot less sanguine than you about this. I think that if we don't know any more by lunch, we should plan to contact the authorities. Does anyone agree with me?"

Buddy said, "Shhh! Don't intrude, honey. And you don't want to frighten little ears." He motioned toward Gladdie.

"Agreed, Buddy. I told Dorothy to MYOB too," Sam said.

Dorothy was emotionally incapable of minding her own business, but the arrival of Colette had trimmed her sails. The line to ensconce oneself in Bob's sheets had grown overnight. Olivia couldn't help but wonder if Bob slept alone last night or not. It really would be the height of all bad taste to bonk the nanny or the ex-wife while your present wife was MIA and before you knew whether or not it was *you* who drove her to throw herself in the Balearic Sea.

"I suggest we all busy ourselves this morning with a good book or a movie until after lunch. The plan is to set a northeast course to see the eastern side of Majorca and drop anchor on the tip of Majorca and take the launch over to Cala Ratjada. There are some amazing caves there and a castle on top of the hill that has a clear view of Menorca."

"Excuse me, Bob," Betty said. "But we're not going to leave without your wife, are we?"

"Betty? She's a big girl. She knows where to find us," Bob said. "This is the biggest boat in the harbor. All she has to do is call a water taxi."

Betty had a look on her face that hung somewhere in between revulsion and incredulousness. That was the moment the thrill over Kitty's becoming a part of Bob's family was gone.

"Where's Mommy?" Gladdie said, looking around.

Bob, who always had an answer for everything, stumbled around for the right words and finally said, "Uh, she went to town to go shopping. She'll be back for lunch. Don't worry."

Gladdie sensed that he was lying and she didn't know what to say, so she started to cry, not like a spoiled brat, but like a frightened little girl. Bob's heart melted.

"Come on now," Bob said and Gladdie climbed on his lap. "There's my girl. Let's dry your eyes now, okay? Your mommy wouldn't leave you! She loves you!"

"I think I might spend the day, Bob," Colette said. "I haven't seen the Caves of Drach in ages!"

Ellen made some kind of guttural sound that bordered on a growl. Not loudly, but it was pronounced enough for Colette to hear.

Colette swung around to Ellen and said, "Oh, I'm sorry. Does the help have an objection?"

Everyone at the table was instantly riveted.

"Of course not," Ellen said.

"Of course not *who*?" Colette stared at her. "Answer me, Ellen. Whom are you addressing?"

Ellen stared back at her defiantly.

Colette smiled delivered a classic Colette response. "I'm Mrs. Vasile, Ellen, and *you're* the hired help."

"Whoo!" Dorothy said and shook her head.

"Colette? Ellen? That's enough out of both of you." Bob said. "Ellen? Why don't you take my precious child to watch *Frozen*?"

"You're the *ex*-wife," Ellen said, lifting Gladdie into her arms. She walked slowly and finally went inside.

Michelle smirked and said, "Pass the butter, please?"

Olivia looked around the table to see that Betty was completely horrified and nervously wrapping a muffin in a napkin for Ernest. She couldn't get away from them and back to Ernest fast enough.

"Well, thank you for breakfast, Bob," Betty said. "If there's any word on Maritza, please let us know."

"Of course! Don't worry about her! She's fine."

Olivia and Nick were not going to discuss their doubts about Maritza's welfare or whereabouts with any of the others, but after breakfast they went forward to the deck chairs on the bow and had plenty to say to each other. There was a delicious salty breeze and the sun was climbing to the top of the sky. They sat and were alone together, stealing a moment of privacy to share their thoughts.

"Well, we've got ourselves a helluva situation here," Nick said. "What if the poor girl did fall off the boat or what if she got pushed? There were a few people last night who could've had motive."

"I think so too. But who are you thinking? Colette? Dorothy?"

"Maybe. And even Daniel. I've heard him make plenty of catty remarks about Maritza. Isn't it always the classic problem with divorce that the children want their parents to stay together at any cost? He could've done it for Colette's sake. And I'm sure he thought Maritza was spending his inheritance every time she opened her wallet."

"Do you think Daniel was so stupid that he didn't notice Bob's involvement with Ellen? A dead Maritza wouldn't bring Bob back to Colette."

"True. That's true. I guess we can rule out the likelihood of Daniel pushing her. But what about the others?"

"I think they're total bitches but not murderers. Can you see Colette or Dorothy wearing orange for ten to twenty? They'd die."

"So, okay. Let's take murder off the table for the moment. Do you think she might have jumped?"

"No."

"Kidnapped?"

"I can't see it. I think Bob humiliated her one too many times. I think Maritza has plain had it. And remember he said how disappointed he was in her?"

"I surely do. It was awful."

"Bob doesn't realize he makes *himself* look bad when he says things like that. And you want to know something that contradicts everything we're saying?"

"What?"

"In his heart? Bob is a really sweet man; I mean he's a pussycat. He's generous, he's smart. There are so many good things about him. He's a true visionary in so many ways. He can be so thoughtful and on and on the list goes. He just has this one fatal flaw."

"Which is?"

"He doesn't understand love, with the exception of the affection he feels for Gladdie."

"Well, you've known him long enough to know how he ticks. Do you think it's too early for a beer? The combination of warm weather and salt water makes me crave beer."

Olivia looked at her watch. It was after eleven-thirty.

"We're on vacation. I'll go get you one. You just stay right there."

"Thanks, my love. I'm too tired to get up."

"Me too. Too much excitement."

Olivia felt so good then, luxuriating in the warmth of the sun. In that moment she felt she could've lived out the rest of her days in that very deck chair, but her own heart ached with Maritza's pain. She prayed Maritza was safe and that she would return or be returned as soon as humanly possible. Olivia got up to find a crew member and ask for a beer for Bob.

By lunchtime there was still no sign of Maritza. They all gathered at the table hoping Bob had some news to share, except for Gladdie and Ellen, who was cleverly avoiding Colette.

"Okay, folks. Here's the latest. I found her cell phone and her passport," Bob said in a somber voice.

"Oh God! Bob! No!" Olivia burst into tears.

"This is not good news," Nick said and handed Olivia his handkerchief with a compassionate look that said *Compose yourself.*

"Who leaves home without their passport and cell phone?" Michelle said. "Right?"

"Right," Buddy said.

"What does that mean?" Dorothy said.

"Well, it greatly lessens the likelihood that she left voluntarily or that she planned to leave," Sam said.

"Hey, Bob?" Buddy said.

"Yeah, I know. It's time to call the police."

Olivia felt ill and she looked up to see Betty's face. Betty was completely aghast and gripping Ernest's arm so firmly he was grimacing in pain. Dorothy was baffled. Michelle poured herself and Dorothy a large glass of wine. Michelle looked bewildered, which would explain her uncustomary hospitality toward Dorothy. To no one's surprise, Colette was amused.

"I just asked Jack to call them. But let's eat quickly, because once the police get here, we're not going to have a moment's peace for who knows how long?"

"What's going to happen?" Ernest said.

"We're probably going to file a missing persons report and ask the police to help us find her," Bob said. "They're probably going to search the ship looking for clues. I can't get into the vault to see if anything's missing because Maritza changed the code and I don't know the new one. So I asked Jack to get one of the guys to drill it open, but Jack said, and he's probably right, we should wait and do that with the police present."

"Absolutely! This could be an active crime scene for all we know!" Colette said. "Watch your fingerprints, ladies!"

Colette laughed. Everyone, even Dorothy, was shocked by her callousness.

Within the hour there were a dozen or more Spanish policemen on the *Le Bateau de l'Amour*. Most of them had never been on such a glamorous ship, and they could barely contain their awe. A few policemen even snapped selfies with their phones. Bob was in the main living room with the head police officer answering questions.

Olivia and Nick discreetly watched them from the table on deck through the glass doors and windows. After about thirty minutes Bob, Jack, and two officers went with a technician from the engine room and drilled open the vault.

"The vault's empty," Bob said to the group, who had all remained at the dining table drinking coffee and iced tea. "All of her jewelry is gone."

"Oh, dear heavenly Father! Do you think . . . ?" Ernest said. He couldn't bring himself to say the words.

But that's why Colette was there—to say the unsayable.

"Robbed and kidnapped?" Colette said. "Looks like it."

"Sweet Jesus, Colette, you'd just love that, wouldn't you?" Bob said. "You are so easy to dislike."

Everyone drew in a collective gasp. It was the first time Bob had really taken Colette on.

"Maybe, but it's a distinct possibility, isn't it?" Colette said with a completely unflappable attitude.

"Just shut up, Colette. So the police want to interview everyone," Bob said. "And Colette, I'd strongly advise you to be extremely civil and courteous. Spanish jails are notoriously dark and dank."

Colette cocked her head to one side and gave Bob the evil eye.

"I can't stand to think of Maritza in a dangerous situation like that," Olivia said.

"Well, what else is there to think?" Dorothy said.

"Who wants to go first?" Bob said.

Betty and Ernest jumped to their feet.

"I stand ready to clear my good name!" Ernest said.

"This is a terrible business," Betty said. "I'll be glad to sleep in my own bed again."

Olivia and Nick shared a psychic moment in each other's

eyes. For as terrible as the situation was, Betty and Ernest were the only ones keeping it real.

The police left before dark after all the questioning of the captain, crew, and passengers. Jack vouched for his crew in a sworn affidavit. The police took some DNA samples from Maritza's hairbrush, razor, and toothbrush and asked everyone to remain in the vicinity for the following seventy-two hours or until they were notified. They took the names of the musicians and the photographer from the wedding and said they would be brought in immediately for interrogation. And the highest-ranking police officer, who spoke English, promised Bob he would stay in touch, and if he learned something of value, he would contact him right away. Bob promised the same.

In the evening, things were very quiet. Out of respect for Bob and Maritza, the partying was over. Even Colette retracted her talons. After a simple dinner of roasted fish, everyone began to drift back to their cabins to let Bob have the deck to himself. He seemed to be very unhappy. He should be, Olivia thought.

Olivia and Nick remained there at the table with him. He seemed to want to talk.

"I just don't understand it," Bob said. "How could she slip through my fingers like this? The police officer said that if it was a kidnapping, we'd probably be contacted soon about ransom. Ransom! I just pray to God that whoever has her doesn't hurt her. I couldn't stand it."

"Look, Bob, maybe there's another explanation," Olivia said, hoping there was one.

"Yeah, she might've jumped, but I don't think so because of the robbery. I haven't been the ideal husband. I mean, you know that. I've made my life so complicated. But I do care about her. A lot."

"We know you care, Bob. Maritza is a sweetheart," Olivia said. "She's the kindest woman you ever married."

"Yes," Bob said.

"Maybe the robbery and Maritza's disappearance are unrelated," Nick said.

"That would be too coincidental," Bob said. "I just feel like this is my fault! I wish I knew what to do. I feel so awful! You know, Maritza would cook for me. I never had a wife who could cook. She makes me a cake on my birthday. No one ever made me a cake besides my own mother. She sewed buttons back on my shirts for me. She just did all these wonderful things for me. Sounds silly, I guess."

"The woman really loves you, Bob. The most precious gift someone can give you is their heart," Nick said.

"Yes, I can see now that it is. And I blew it. I made so light of her affection that either she jumped or she let herself get into a precarious situation that led her into grave danger. And I failed to protect her. This is my fault. I'd give anything I own to see her face right now."

CHAPTER 14

bob's side

It was Saturday, the Fourth of July, right before eight in the morning, when the police boat pulled up beside *Le Bateau de l'Amour*. Captain Jack hurried down to meet it and he sent one of the crew to find Bob. Bob was on the treadmill and quickly got off, grabbed a towel to wipe away his sweat, and hurried to the main deck, taking the steps instead of the elevator.

"Good morning, Officer!" Bob said, shaking his hand. "Would you like coffee?"

It was the same policeman Bob had spent time with the day before.

"*Gracias.* Thank you. Coffee would be *muy bueno.*"

Bob nodded to a crew member, who would have the coffee order out in a flash.

"Please. Come and sit. Tell me what you have learned."

"*Gracias*, thank you. Well, we have something, *pero* it's not much and it may turn out to be nothing, but it is something to start with."

"Tell me. Please."

"*Sí, sí.* As soon as I returned to *la estación* yesterday, I called the musicians and the photographer. The musicians, all three of them, came down to the station right away. They were shocked and surprised to hear this terrible news. And they said, and all of them were questioned separately, that they had never had trouble in their lives beyond traffic violations. We checked, and *es verdad.* These are all honest men who have never been arrested for anything. *Nada.*"

"That's it?"

The coffee arrived and was placed before them. Bob watched as the police officer put four sugars in his cup and stirred.

"No, there is *una cosa más.* So we said we would like to let our forensics team search their boat and they said it was no problem for them. Absolutely no *problemo.* And so we went down to the marina and my team went over their boat with a fine-tooth comb. That's the expression, *sí?* Fine-tooth comb?"

"Yes." This bastard is sure taking his sweet time getting to the point, Bob thought. "And?"

"And? There were some long blond hairs in the bow, under a tarp where they keep the life preservers and oars. I can't tell you that they match your wife's DNA until they come back from the lab."

"You think my wife was on their boat?"

"*No sé.* I do not know yet. But the space was big enough for a small woman to crawl in and conceal herself."

Bob's mind was spinning.

"And the photographer?"

"I know the photographer. He is my wife's fourth cousin and he's an idiot. *Muy estúpida.* Ibiza is a small island, really. Families have been marrying each other for centuries. He is a bad result of a small gene pool. Anyway, when I put two and two together, I knew it could not be possible that it was him. He is not worth the telephone call." The police officer finished his cup of coffee and smiled.

"Do me a favor," Bob said. "Humor me. Call the idiot. Maybe he saw something."

"Of course. I will do it then. Well, that's it for now."

"How long will it take to get the DNA information?" Bob asked, wondering how many other things there were that the police would not think was worthy of the follow-up time.

"We should know by Monday. Oh, and Mr. Vasile, we have been policing the shores of all the Balearic Islands and nothing, *gracias a Dios*, has washed up of any consequence."

Bob swallowed hard and stood up from the table. "Thank you, sir, and thank you for coming to tell me this in person."

"*De nada.* You're welcome. I will be in touch. And you're certain that there was not another man in her life?"

"Not a chance. Maritza adores me."

"I see. You know, Señor Vasile, women leave their husbands every day. They get, well, I'm sure you know how women can get."

"Better than most men do, I think. Yes, women walk away from their families every day but not like this," Bob said. "They don't disappear into thin air in a foreign country without taking their cell phone and passport unless something very bad has happened. And there's the better part of a million dollars worth of jewelry gone too. If she was leaving me, I would've heard from a lawyer by now."

"A *million* dollars? *What? Señor* Vasile! You did *not* tell me her jewelry was worth so much! I have to turn this over to the *FBI!* Or maybe I misunderstood!"

"That is an excellent idea," Bob said. "Please do it right away!"

"*Sí, sí.* Yes. I think you're right." They shook hands. "*Lo siento mucho.* I'm very sorry."

This police officer is such a dummy, it's unbelievable.

The main deck filled up quickly with crew who had been behind the scenes waiting for the police officer to leave. They began setting up the breakfast buffet in one well-orchestrated swoop.

Ellen and Gladdie were having breakfast in their room, as Ellen was still seething over Colette's insults, or what she perceived to be Colette's insults. Bob had tried to explain to Ellen that technically, Colette was right. However it wasn't Colette's *place* to correct Ellen because Colette did not sign her paycheck, but she was correct in that it wasn't *Ellen's* place to voice her displeasure over her employer's guest list. Perhaps, Bob suggested as diplomatically as he could, she should not make her feelings or the nature of their personal relationship so obvious. This infuriated Ellen to new heights because she saw it as rejection from Bob, and it pushed her another rung down the ladder, further away from her goal. So the last twenty-four hours had taken a painful toll on her affair with Bob, and as a result Ellen and Bob were barely speaking.

Frankly, Bob felt a measure of relief, given the real-life disaster he had on his hands.

God, he thought, sometimes women just aren't worth it. All that bitching and whining for a piece of ass? The price was just too high.

And, speaking of bitching, he calculated how much longer he had to tolerate Colette. Forty-eight hours! He might have to wring her neck if she pushed him too hard. He had never touched a woman in anger in all his days, but Colette was enough to drive the Dalai Lama to do real physical harm.

Bob was in a sour mood and very worried for Maritza's safety. And he missed her. He admitted that to himself. He missed her. She was such a cheerful girl and always flitting and fluttering around, trying to do things to make him happy. Out of habit, he fixed himself breakfast from the buffet—a plate of toast, cheese, and a handful of red grapes. Maybe pancakes might make him feel better. No, he decided, too many carbs. He looked at his plate and thought, Well, toast has carbs. Grapes have carbs. Maybe they just seem more harmless.

So there sat Bob staring at the untouched plate and the coffee dregs in his cup when Buddy and Michelle arrived for breakfast at about roughly the same time as Colette, Dorothy and Sam, and Olivia and Nick.

Colette looked around at the group and said, "Oh dear. Have Betty and Ernest lost interest in us?"

"Good morning, Colette," Bob said. "I'm pretty sure they are so horrified by us they can't wait to get off this boat and put us in their rearview mirror."

"They're a humorless pair," Colette said and sat down next to him.

"Morning, Bob! Did I see a police boat pulling away?" Buddy said.

"Yes, I had a visit from our police officer about half an hour ago."

"Did he have any news?" Sam asked.

"Not really. They found a few long blond hairs in the bow . . ." Bob brought everyone up to date. "And he decided to call the FBI."

"It's time for them to get involved," Sam said as though he had been involved with law enforcement all his life.

They all began to fills their plates and eat.

"I think," Nick said, "we need our *own* plan to find Maritza. There have been no calls for ransom money, correct?"

"Correct," Bob said, and pushed his plate away. "Not yet."

"What about a press conference?" Olivia said. "You have to eat, Bob."

"I hate the press," Bob said. "I don't have much of an appetite."

"Who doesn't hate the press?" Dorothy said thinking of some negative write-ups her boutique had suffered in the Style section of *The New York Times.*

"I agree," Michelle said thinking of how *Wine Spectator* magazine had killed her 2003 Chardonnays by rating them at an all-time low of ninety-two.

"Well, the press can be useful, especially at a time like this, you know, to flush out the bushes? If someone out there is holding Maritza against her will, a press conference might give them an impetus to cut a deal sooner than later," Olivia said, having had her fair share of good and bad press over the course of her career. "You just have to manage the PR yourself."

"Well, if anyone cares what I think, I'd say she's been gone too long if she's just having a temper tantrum," Dorothy said. "Sadly, I just don't get a sense of her spirit being nearby."

"What are you? A psychic now?" Colette said. "Spare us, okay?"

"Good grief, Dorothy," Sam said. "Don't start going all New Age on us."

Dorothy frowned. She just wanted a voice at the table, but ever since the advent of Colette, she couldn't get a word in edgewise.

Bob completely ignored her and Colette.

"I should probably discuss a press conference with the

police first," Bob said. "I had another thought that maybe I should contact the American embassy in Majorca and they could tell me how to proceed. I thought by now these local police would've run her passport number against U.S. Customs and Border Patrol, but I don't think it has even occurred to them yet. In fact, this idiot police officer asked me if I thought Maritza was having an affair!"

"That's ludicrous," Olivia said. "And you know what, Bob? I'd call the embassy right now and ask them to call the FBI just to be sure it happens."

"That's what I told him. And, you're right, Olivia. I'm going to."

"No kidding, and on the cover of every supermarket tabloid," Dorothy said. "*Wife of Billionaire Missing in Mallorca!* I can see it now."

"Oh, God," Bob said.

"What about the airlines?" Sam said. "Do you think she might try to get on a commercial flight?"

"Where would she go?" Bob said.

"Commercial? Please. I'm getting a rash!" Colette said.

"Colette? Don't be such a snob, okay?" Bob said, thinking he had been way too generous to his ex-wives, giving them shares in NetJets. "Should I tell them all how I met you thirty years ago?"

"Oh, I think we all remember that Colette was Elaine's masseuse," Dorothy said.

"Oh! That's right," Michelle said, with a very wide grin. "I don't know why I kept thinking she was a manicurist."

Olivia had had it with political correctness and the simultaneous lack of it. These women never gave her ten cents worth of business anyway, except Colette, who had just given her a job, and she was the one who needed the biggest smack. She said, "Listen, we need a plan. I want us to get Maritza back today! We just can't sit back and let the authorities handle this."

"I think we all agree on that," Nick said.

"Who made you the queen of the world, Olivia?" Colette said.

"Olivia happens to be a dear family friend as well as a well-respected businesswoman *and* Gladdie's godmother, so knock it off," Bob said. "What are you thinking, Olivia?"

"Same as you. That this police department is thinking locally. Have they checked all the hotels to see if anyone like Maritza has checked in?"

"I'm gonna guess not," Bob said.

"Shouldn't they be doing that?" Buddy asked.

"You'd think so," Sam said.

"It's time or past time to open this thing up globally," Olivia said. "Bob? I would call the embassy this instant, tell them everything you know, and give them the police officer's contact information. I'd give them Maritza's passport number and her cell phone to check her calls in and out and then I'd think up a statement. Word it carefully and get on television and beg whoever has Maritza to let her go. Or if she's not being held, I would just beg her to come back or to at least let us know that she's all right!"

"You know something else you might do is to send some crew members over to the island—as many as you can spare—to check hotels, restaurants, bars, even the hospital and the jail," Michelle said. "I mean, she has to be *somewhere*! Check public parks and hiking trails? After all, when Gladdie went missing on Necker, they had a plan to cover every square inch of the island."

"Thank you, Michelle. I knew you were a team player," Bob said. "You know, I still can't believe this happened."

"It's a bitter pill," Nick said. "And deeply troubling. If anything like this ever happened to Olivia I'd lose my mind." Then Nick reached over to Olivia and squeezed her hand.

"Yes, but these are good ideas. I've just been numb with shock. But that's over now. It's time to act," Bob said, and one of the crew refilled his cup with hot coffee. He looked at her and said, "Ask the captain to see me right away, and please bring me a pad and pencil, okay?"

"Yes, sir," she said and hurried away.

Once Jack got to the table, he sat with Bob and Olivia and they began to make a list. Within the hour a dozen members of the crew were on the launch headed to the island with local maps and a plan to search specific areas. The embassy had been called, the local police pledged their full cooperation with the investigation, and the information was on its way to U.S. Customs, the FBI, and every major airline, including ones that flew to the Middle East, South America, China, and smaller domestic Spanish commuter airlines. Once all that information was released, Bob's phone began to explode with calls from the media. *The New York Times*, the London *Times*, *USA Today*, *El País*, *El Mundo*, and others. Next to call were CNN, ABC, NBC, CBS, and the BBC. Olivia took down all their numbers and promised to call them back with the details of the arrangements for the press conference.

They wanted a statement, a picture of Maritza, an interview with Bob, so many questions . . . had they ruled out pirates? Suicide? Abandonment?

Olivia asked the manager of the Hotel Torre del Mar to give Bob usage of their largest meeting room to have his press conference. They graciously complied. By two-thirty that afternoon, Bob was on the launch with Olivia, Nick, Sam, Dorothy, Michelle, and Buddy. He told Jack that if he heard anything from the crew to let him know at once. Right before they boarded the boat, Betty and Ernest finally emerged from their rooms and asked for an update. Bob told them everything that he knew and invited them to come to the conference if they wanted to.

"Oh, my!" Betty said. "I think it's best for me to stay put right here."

"Me too. I can't really help anyway. All I can do is pray," Ernest said.

"Ernest, I know that you and Betty think we are all a bunch of screwballs, and we might be, but we are doing everything in our power to find my wife. Anyway, help from a higher power would be wonderful, and believe me, your prayers are deeply appreciated."

"You believe in the power of prayer?" Betty said.

"Yes, but more than that, I believe in the power of God. I love my wife and I need her in my life. Now more than ever."

It was decided to take the press conference out of the realm of the yacht so that if she had been kidnapped, the kidnappers would not ask an exorbitant price for Maritza's freedom and return. It was just a practical consideration that did not work.

Pictures of Bob's yacht wound up in the news anyway, and by nightfall, Bob's face was on every news channel around the world. The world of the ninety-nine percent watched in amazement as Bob Vasile wept like a baby while professing his love for his wife. Before they went back to the boat, they all had a drink at the hotel's bar.

Bob and Michelle read the wine list and debated the merits of a Corton-Charlemagne versus a French Sancerre.

"I'm getting tired of white burgundy," Michelle said.

"We'll have a bottle of the Sancerre," Bob said to the bartender. "Maritza loved Sancerres."

"Please don't speak of her in the past tense," Olivia said.

"You really love her, don't you, Bob?" Sam said.

"Yeah, I never saw you cry, man," Buddy said. "You must be really hurting!"

"It was a bit much for me to endure," Colette said. "I mean, honestly!"

Bob stared at Colette and choked up again. "You know what? We're a bunch of hard-core cynical bastards, all of us—except Nick and Olivia."

"Olivia is less cynical than I am," Nick said.

"We're not so perfect," Olivia said. "I have my cynical moments."

"I didn't say you were perfect," Bob said. "I just said you weren't hard core."

"Oh, I feel much better." Olivia smiled.

"I have to explain this to you guys and I'm having a hard time because it's something I just realized I felt! Here's this beautiful young girl, Maritza, who tells me she loves me . . ."

"She was a dirty nasty gold-digging whore, if anybody wants the truth here," Colette said. "I'm glad I don't have to look at her stupid face anymore."

"Jesus, Colette. How can you *say* things like that?" Olivia said. "What on God's earth has made you so evil? I can't stand another minute of this. You need to shut your mouth right now!"

"I don't take orders from you, Olivia."

Olivia said, "I'm saying *no one* is well served with this kind of indecent talk."

"Oh, bug off, Olivia. This has nothing to do with you. Besides, aren't you the one who's out of line to speak to me this way?"

"Find yourself another decorator, Colette. I quit."

"You can't quit! You're fired!" she said.

"Go shove it, Colette!" Olivia said, and it was on the loud side.

Nick stepped over to Olivia's side and put his arm around her shoulder, giving her a squeeze.

Bob lost his cool, but he didn't raise his voice.

"You know what, Colette? I don't know when you got so bitter and mean, but you're just awful. You're horrible. I want you to go over to the police station and tell them that you're leaving town. Then I want you to take the launch, get your stuff, and get the hell off my boat. I hope to God I never have to be in the same room with you again for the rest of my life."

She stood and stared at him, just seething with anger.

"I ought to tell the press what you're *really* like."

"I ought to tell the police you had plenty of *motive*."

Colette took a step back in shock and struggled to speak. "Go to hell, Bob. You broke my heart and ruined my life."

"I didn't ruin your life, sweetheart. You ruined it yourself."

With that, she finally turned on her heel and began to leave the bar.

Bob called after her. "And after today your NetJets shares are canceled!"

Bob laughed and Olivia laughed with him.

"NetJets shares? Oh, Lord, Bob! Now, there's a *real* knife in her heart. I'd applaud, but it's probably in the worst possible taste," Olivia said.

"No, it isn't," Bob said. "Go right ahead."

There was light applause from the gang and Bob took a bow. Then Olivia took a slight bow and they applauded again.

"I'll always have work for you, Olivia," Bob said.

"Thank you," Olivia said.

"Anyway, I started to say earlier, before I dealt with my charming ex-wife, is that along came Maritza, beautiful, smiling Maritza, and all she wanted to do was make me happy. And now I've lost her. She was the one person in my entire life who really loved me for myself. She was kind and sweet and just so damn nice. Every day. And I love her. I just realized it today when I faced all those cameras. They told me to just speak from my heart. I realized that I love her and I don't want to live without her. And even if she doesn't love me anymore because I've been an asshole to her, which I have been, I'm going to make her love me again. So how's that? At long last Bob Vasile is really dead in love. But if she's found dead, I don't know what I'll do."

"Oh, Bob! Don't think that! We're going to find her!" Olivia said, wiping away her tears with the back of her hand.

Nick, of course, smiled and produced a perfectly pressed handkerchief. He offered it to Olivia.

"Yes, she has to be alive," said Michelle, wiping away a tear. "Bob? That's the most beautiful thing I think I've ever heard you say." Buddy put his arm around her shoulder and gave her a squeeze.

Dorothy just sighed deeply and looked at Bob with moon eyes. Sam looked at her and shook his head. Dorothy was just a disaster of a wife.

"You should start hearing more about her whereabouts soon," Sam said. "CNN is all over the world and never mind all the others. It's out on the wires now."

"Well, any tips are supposed to go to local authorities, right?" Buddy said.

"Yes," Bob said, "that's right."

"Phones are no doubt ringing off the hook." Sam said.

When they got to the marina and saw the launch there waiting, Bob realized the time had come to tell Gladdie something about the truth.

"You have to tell her something," Olivia said on the ride back. "Tell her the truth, but just tell her gently and in general terms. You know say something like, 'I know you know that Mommy isn't here, but I want you to know that I am doing everything I can to bring her home as soon as possible.'"

"I don't know. You're probably right. Maybe I should ask Betty what to say. She's a kinder, gentler soul than either one of us. She'll give us a good answer," Bob said.

"That's an excellent idea," Nick said.

Betty was in the living room, reading a book. When Bob approached her she said, "I hope you don't mind that I borrowed this novel. I finished the one I brought with me. I love a good book."

"No, of course not. You can help yourself to anything you need," Bob said. "Betty? May I ask your advice about something?"

"*My* advice?" Betty was instantly flustered. "Well, of course!"

Bob sat on the edge of the coffee table and looked at her. "You're a mentally healthy woman," he said.

"Well, thank you!" She laughed and closed her book. "I sure hope so!"

"Yes, and you see the thing is, I haven't said anything to Gladdie about where her mom is, and I think it's time to say something. This is going to be the third night without her.

And even though Gladdie's just a little girl, she's still entitled to some kind of explanation. Do you agree?"

"Of course!"

"The question is, How much truth does she need to hear?"

"That's an excellent question. I think you tell her very sweetly that there's a problem, that her mother has gone away and you're not sure why, but that you're doing everything you can to find her and bring her home."

"Yes. That's almost exactly what Olivia said. That's about as simply as I could put it. Thank you, Betty." He stood to leave.

"Bob?"

"Yes?"

"Ernest and I don't think you're all a bunch of screwballs. Your lives are just the opposite of ours, that's all. I mean, my brother and I have an old rowboat we like to paddle around at our lake house up in Tekamah. And we travel like most folks do—by car or sometimes we fly someplace. We went on a cruise one time to the Bahamas and I liked that. But we live quietly and modestly."

"There's nothing wrong with a quiet life. Or a modest life. I think my life and all of this . . ." Bob stopped and waved his arms around. "All of this doesn't really make me happy. But being rich and unhappy is a lot better than being *broke* and unhappy. I'm not gonna lie."

Betty laughed then and Bob laughed with her.

"Ernest said to me earlier that rich people put on their pants one leg at a time just like poor people do."

"Ernest is right."

"Everyone has their problems in life. It just seems like yours happen in Technicolor."

"It sure does seem that way, today especially."

"Well, it's interesting for someone like me to see all of this, you know, grand living. I'm just a retired high school librarian. I have to wonder how my girl is going to fare as your daughter-in-law? And as Daniel's wife?"

"I don't know, but Kitty has a good head on her shoulders. And most important, she comes from a nice family."

Betty smiled, and for the first time all week, she felt comfortable with Bob.

"Thank you," she said. "And, Bob?"

Bob stood. It was time to go talk to Gladdie.

"Yes?"

"I hope you find Maritza very soon."

"Thank you. I do too."

Bob knocked on Ellen and Gladdie's door. There was no answer. He went down to the media room and found them there eating popcorn and watching *Frozen* again. He flipped on the overhead lights. Ellen refused to meet his eyes and Gladdie complained.

"Turn off the lights, Daddy! We're watching a movie!"

Bob flipped the switch and the room went dark, illuminated only by the large screen.

"Okay, well, when it's over, I need to talk to you about something."

"Tell me now," Gladdie said.

"It can wait." Bob closed the door and waited outside. He knew his daughter well.

"Pause it!" Gladdie barked to Ellen.

The movie went on pause and the lights were turned on. Gladdie ran to her father's arms and he swung her high in the air, landing her on his hip. If Maritza had heard Gladdie so rudely giving Ellen orders, she would've said something.

"If you get any bigger I'm not going to be able to do this!" he said.

"Do you need me for anything?" Ellen said.

"No, I just want to have a word with my girl about her mother. Why don't you give us a few minutes alone?"

Ellen shrugged her shoulders and rolled her eyes at him.

"Take all the time in the world," she said, walking past him and heading toward the stairs.

Bob watched her walk away. It was over between them. He'd give her a big fat check and a letter of recommendation. He couldn't wait to have her gone. Then he had a brief thought that Maritza knew about the two of them. Of course Maritza knew. She was a lot of things, but stupid wasn't one of them.

"You want to walk?" he asked Gladdie.

"Yes."

Bob put her feet on the ground and took her hand. Her hand was so tiny in his, and it was such a pretty little hand, her fingers shaped exactly like Maritza's. He tried to remember if his father had ever held his hand. As he searched his mind he realized he had no memory of any tender moments with his father at all. His mother, though, had held his hand countless times. She ruffled his hair, kissed his head, and tucked him in with a beautiful Italian lullaby that her mother used to sing to her when she was a child. He remembered then that he had heard Maritza singing to Gladdie too. What was the song she sang? Wasn't it "Moonlight in Vermont"? Or was it a Beatles song? The memory was a fragmented one. He hated that he couldn't recall the title.

"Let's go to my room," he said.

"Okay," she said.

When they got there, two of the crew members were pressing his sheets on the bed, wrinkled from the previous night's tossing and turning.

"Oh! Sorry! We thought you were ashore!" one of them said.

"We'll get out of your way!" the other one said.

They were pretty young girls from England. Pretty young girls from England made up about half of his crew. The other half were male. England seemed to have an endless supply of young people who wanted to sail the world. Captain Jack made sure the male/female ratio was well balanced to keep life happy belowdecks. They hurried past him with their irons and quietly closed the door.

Bob turned to Gladdie. "Let's sit on the sofa, okay?"

"Okay," she parroted.

She climbed on the sofa without his help, and for the first time in a while, he noticed what a tiny thing she was. She was too small for her legs to hang over the cushions when she sat back.

"So, what's up, Daddy?" She said it like a much older child, and it surprised him.

"Well, Gladdie, we have a problem. It's about your mom."

"Is Mommy gone forever?"

"No! Heavens no! But she *is* gone. We just don't know *where* quite yet."

"Do you want me to help you look for her?"

"Oh, sweetie, Daddy is turning the whole world upside down looking for her. And I'm going to find her and bring her back to us."

"You hurt her feelings, you know."

"What do you mean?"

"When Mommy fell in the cake, you said you were disappointed in her. I remember because you told the same thing to me when I was riding the big turtle."

He wondered then who was it that said little pitchers have big ears?

"Well, sometimes grown-ups get excited and say things they don't really mean. I love your mother. And I'm going to find her. Do you understand what I'm telling you?"

"Yes. I love you, Daddy. Can I go now?"

"Yes. You can go, and Gladdie?"

"Yes?"

"I love you too! Come give your daddy a hug!"

She threw her skinny arms around his neck and hugged him for all she was worth. He could feel his heartbeat against hers and he knew that wherever Maritza was, she had to be plenty miserable without the hugs of her only child. Bob vowed to himself again that he would find Maritza if it was the last thing he ever did. And then he realized he had been so focused on himself that he had not notified Maritza's mother. If she saw it on CNN before he called her, Maritza would *never* come back to him.

CHAPTER 15

lost and found

Bob appeared on the deck where everyone was gathered for cocktails, including Betty and Ernest, who sprang themselves from solitary confinement on deciding that Bob was not the prince of darkness. The table was opened to its fullest diameter and set for dinner with yet another pattern of china, crystal, and flatware. Beautiful flowers graced the center of the table and were surrounded by tiny tea candles nestled in scallop shells.

"You all are not going to believe what I did!" he said.

"You got rid of Colette, which was real progress in my book," Sam said.

"I can't believe you were ever married to that dreadful woman," Michelle said.

"She makes me look like a cupcake," Dorothy said and smirked.

Bob said, "I never should have let her attend Daniel's wedding. I should've Skyped her in. Or at least had her stay in a hotel on shore."

"True, but what? You were going to tell us something?" Olivia said.

"Well, I'm cooked, that's for sure. I forgot to call Maritza's mother to tell her what was going on. Can you believe that? Like, where is my brain? If she turns on her television, I'm a dead man," Bob said. "I just came out here to tell all of you to go on and have dinner and I'll join you as soon as I can."

"Wait!" Olivia said. "I know her mother. Remember? I spent all that time with her at the wedding. Can I help you make the call?"

"Absolutely! Come to my office with me. What time is it? Okay, it's noon there."

"Go!" Nick said.

A crew member was behind the bar pouring wine and champagne for everyone.

"I'd like a very generous pour of Grey Goose on the rocks, and please bring it to my office as fast as you can," Bob said.

"Yes, sir!"

"And bring the bottle," Olivia said, knowing Bob well enough to know if he was drinking vodka to deal with his mother-in-law, he was going to need additional reinforcement.

As quickly as it was humanly possible, Bob looked up Maritza's mother's phone number and dialed it from his satellite phone, because it gave him a superior and clearer connection than his smartphone. He put the call on speakerphone so that Olivia could help if needed.

"Hello?"

"Martha Ann? It's your son-in-law, Bob. I'm here with Olivia Ritchie."

"Bob Vasile. Well, what do you all know? Oh, hello, Olivia! I hope you're well?"

"I'm okay, all things considered. You?"

"I'm fine, thank you."

Bob was getting antsy and said, "Martha Ann? Do you have a moment?"

"Bob? Should I try and take a wild guess why you're calling me? I've got a kitchen full of casseroles and every woman I know in this town is in my living room. Do you think we don't watch the news down here in Mississippi? I almost had a heart attack! I turned on Anderson Cooper and there you were running your mouth like a teenage boy!"

"I'm so sorry I didn't call you first, Martha Ann. Please accept my deepest apology."

"Your deepest apology ain't worth diddly-squat to me. The one you owe the apologies to is Maritza! Tell *her*!"

"Believe me! That's exactly what I want to do!"

"How's my granddaughter, Bob?"

"She's fine, but she really misses her mother. I've been such a fool!"

"Hmmm. Yes, you certainly are! About the biggest fool I ever met in all my days. Let me see if she'll talk to you."

"*What?* She's *there*?"

"Where *else* would she be? I'm her mother! Who *else* should she go to for solace and succor? Some stupid shrink that would charge her a thousand dollars a minute? That's probably what *you* do! Like it would ever do you a lick of good. You'd probably lie like a cheap rug to them too! Hang on."

Martha Ann slammed the phone on something, probably a wooden table, and walked away calling Maritza's name at the top of her lungs.

"Thank God she's safe!" Olivia said and burst into tears. "Oh! What a relief!"

"Oh God yes! But I'm astonished that she's *there!* How in the hell did she get back into the country?"

"Bob?" Olivia snatched a tissue from a box on the side table, blotted her eyes, and cleared her throat. Then she chuckled, thinking about Maritza and how clever she was. "Maritza is a lot smarter than everyone thinks. Don't let the *magnolia-speak* fool you."

"True. I know. But boy, Martha Ann's pissed," Bob said to Olivia.

"Which means Maritza is beyond pissed. That's her only child, you know." Olivia sank into a chair, thinking about how she was back in the money hole again. But there was just no way she could've worked with Colette. She could work with tough clients, but Colette was *too* horrible. "You can't blame her for taking her side."

Bob's drink was delivered then.

"Thanks," Bob said and had a sip. "I don't. Did you like the way I played the guilt card?"

"About Gladdie? I hate to admit it, but that was a stroke of genius." Olivia looked at the crew member and said, "You know what? I think I'd like a big fat vodka on the rocks as well." Bob had said he would find her work, but where and how soon?

There was a lot of noise coming from the background in Martha Ann's house as though troops were marching through the rooms, but through all the racket, there was no Maritza coming to the phone to speak to Bob. Then it got quiet.

"Just how in the hell did she get the whole way to Mississippi? Was she a stowaway?"

"I have no earthly idea," Olivia said. "I am just as surprised as you are!"

They heard footsteps again through the telephone receiver and the phone was picked up.

"Bob?"

"Martha Ann?"

"She says she doesn't want to talk to you. And *I* don't blame her."

"What do you *mean?* She *has* to talk to me! I'm her *husband*!"

"Only on paper, sonny boy! Only on paper! Maybe you should call another time."

The next thing they heard was the dial tone.

"That old bitch hung up on me!" Bob said.

"I know. Bob, let's not lose sight of the fact that Maritza is alive," Olivia said. "That's what really matters."

"You're right, of course, but can you believe what just happened?" Bob said. "She actually hung up on me!"

"Bob, nobody behaves like they're supposed to behave anymore. People are rude and horrible. Now, drain your glass and let's go tell everyone the good news, especially Gladdie."

"I guess I'll call her back later?"

"After you call the florist down there and fill her mother's house with flowers!"

"Right! She called me *sonny boy*!"

"It could've been a lot worse!"

"You're right. I'm surprised she didn't call me every curse word she knows. Come on. Let's go tell everyone," Bob said. "Thank you, God! I am so relieved!"

"I am too!" Olivia said and meant it.

"I'll tell you one thing, Olivia."

"What's that?"

"If I can get this mess sorted out? I'm going to be a changed man."

"That's good, Bob," Olivia said and hoped it was true. "Maritza is worth changing for. She really is."

"It would be a lot less complicated to just devote myself to her and Gladdie and of course now Daniel and Kitty."

"Yep. It sure *would* be easier and I'm going to tell you something. Marriage is a lot more rewarding and satisfying when you have someone you can rely on. But it has to go both ways."

Bob stopped and looked at Olivia, staring into her eyes as though there was an answer there.

"When did you get so smart?"

"I'm not. Nick is. A good marriage can open your eyes to a lot of things."

They stopped by Ellen and Gladdie's room. There was Maritza's little girl, sitting in her child-sized chair, wearing a ruffled nightgown, rocking a baby doll. She was quiet and very clearly sad. Ellen was reclining on her bed, reading a magazine. There was no interaction between them. Even though Olivia was not a huge fan of Gladdie's undisciplined behavior, she didn't like what she was seeing either. And it was bad enough that Ellen had come so close to ruining Bob's marriage, but she obviously wasn't good for Gladdie either.

"Great news, Gladdie! Mommy is at Grandmomma's house in Mississippi!"

Gladdie jumped up and clapped her hands.

"Really?" Her face lit up with surprise and happiness. "Yay! When's she coming home?"

"I don't know," Bob said. "I think it might be a good idea to go down there and get her! Do you want to come with me?"

"Yes, I sure do!" Gladdie said, sounding like a very determined adult.

Olivia was very nearly brought to tears by the transformation from despair to joy in Gladdie.

"Okay, come give your daddy a hug!"

He leaned down and she all but jumped into his arms, hugging him tight.

"I love you, Daddy!"

"I love you too, princess! I'll see you later. Okay? Sleep tight!" Bob kissed her on top of her head and put her down.

"Well, it's good that you found her," Ellen said. "I'm glad she's safe."

"Thanks," Bob said and turned to Olivia. "All done here."

"Okay," Olivia said, "let's go. Nick is going to *love* this story."

They started walking toward the deck to tell the others.

"I want you to come to Mississippi with me," Bob said.

"Why? I mean, I will, of course, but why?"

"To hedge my bet because she likes you. I don't think she likes me much right now, and I wouldn't blame her if she didn't. I just think I need help with this one. You're my best shot."

"You know what? You just might be right. But I'm not so sure she still likes me."

"Oh, I'm pretty sure you're wrong about that."

When Bob told the story to his guests, they clapped and hooted. The wives were more restrained, but everyone, including Ernest and Betty, was visibly relieved. The horrible thought that Maritza might have been kidnapped and murdered wasn't ever too far from anyone's mind. And the reality was that life could be that fragile. Especially with Bob's net worth.

"This calls for champagne!" Michelle said.

"Yes, it does! Get Jack," Bob said to one of the crew, "and

tell him to notify all the authorities. Ask him to say that she is safely at home. It's not a lie, but at least it won't send film crews to her mother's house. Martha Ann's angry enough as it is. I'm sure they'll think she's in New York."

"Yes, sir! Mr. Vasile?"

"Yes?"

"When I tell the crew, they're going to be so happy that Mrs. Vasile is safe and sound. I know I am. She was always so sweet to me."

"Thanks," Bob said. "Well, folks? I think this vacation is finally coming to an end."

"Wait until I tell Roni this one," Olivia said to Nick.

"Boy, no kidding!" He said. "Who would believe it?"

The plan was to return to Palma and fly back to Teterboro the next day.

"What about Daniel and Kitty?" Olivia asked.

"They can fly home commercial," Bob said. "It won't kill them."

"Have you heard from them?" Nick asked.

"No," Bob said. "They're on the water and probably not watching television, if you get my drift."

Ernest cleared his throat and raised his eyebrows.

"Oh, don't be such an old poop, Ernest," Betty said. "You were young once."

"I imagine so, but *young* seems like a long time ago," he said.

The flight back to New Jersey was uneventful. There was such a sense of relief among them just knowing Maritza was alive. Bob couldn't wait to get to Mississippi and talked of nothing else.

"I called her twenty-two times at least. She still won't talk to me. But she'll have a harder time refusing to see all three of us. I'd fly straight there, but I need half a day in New York. You good with tomorrow, Olivia?"

"Of course! I need to spend a little time in my office anyway. Nick and I can have dinner in the city tonight and stay over."

"Yeah, how's that little pied-à-terre working out?"

"Little is the operative word. It's fine, really. Anyway, Bob, thanks for an interesting few days, even though it feels like we've been gone for a month!"

"It certainly was interesting," Nick said. "Thanks again."

They all said good-bye to one another in the lobby of the terminal. There was a part of Olivia that hoped she'd never have to travel with Dorothy and Michelle and their husbands again. Oddly she would not have minded seeing Betty and Ernest on another occasion. They were superbly nice people with no hidden agenda. Homespun anything had never been so appealing.

Olivia and Nick took an Uber to their apartment on 58th Street, and Roni was there waiting for them. As Olivia was turning the key in the door, Roni was on the other side of the door, opening the chain lock.

"Hey!" Olivia said.

Roni gave Olivia a big hug, and to stay on the right side of decorum, a slightly less enthusiastic one to Nick.

"Hey! Welcome home! How was your trip?" she said.

"How much strength do you have?" Olivia said and began telling her the details of the story, much of which Roni already knew.

"Oh no! How terrible! Listen, at least we know she's okay."

"Yes, and tomorrow I'm flying with Bob and Gladdie to

Jackson, Mississippi, to watch Bob grovel in humble mortification."

"I'd like to be the fly on the wall for that one. Do you think he's really sorry? I mean, will he be able to resist the next skirt that comes along?"

"As long as he stays in love, I think yes, he will. This scared him so badly that he says it changed him. Besides, he's not exactly a spring chicken. That might help."

"Men and their zippers."

"You said it! But I have to tell you when Maritza fell into the cake, I thought she might get up and pitch Colette over the side of the boat, except that Colette is twice the size of Maritza."

"Too bad she didn't."

"I think anyone there would've helped her do it, except her son."

"Funny. But here's the big question. How the heck did she get to Mississippi from Spain without being caught when her face was plastered all over the news?"

"Well, that's the greatest mystery of all, but I'm sure it will come out eventually. So tell me, what did I miss?"

"I'm going to turn on the news," Nick said, "which I'm sure will seem mighty boring after what we've just been through."

"Okay, sweetie, can I get you anything? Coffee?"

"No, sweetheart, I'm fine."

Nick went into the den and closed the door.

"He looks tired," Roni whispered.

Olivia nodded. "It was an eight-hour flight and he's getting older too. Don't say I said it, though."

"Gotcha. Well, remember that woman I told you I met at the Frick?"

"Yep."

"We got the job! YAY! One-million-dollar budget! Her mother said, *Are you kidding me? Just let Olivia do your apartment and quit whining. She's got better taste in her pinkie than you and I have in our entire bodies!* So we've got *almost* carte blanche. I mean, we still ought to give her a presentation, but pretty much we can do what we want."

"Oh! Congratulations! That's wonderful news! Especially since I told Bob's ex-wife Colette to buzz off. I think I need a glass of water."

"I'll grab it. You sit. You told someone to buzz off? Why?"

"Listen, first we're supposed to decorate the Nantucket house. Right? Then we're not. We've got *zero* on the calendar. Then here comes Colette, Bob's most recent ex. She bought this big house in Charleston, if you can believe that for a shining example of six degrees of separation. It needs a total gut and reno. She asked me if I wanted the job, and of course I said yes."

"Well, of course you did!" Roni said and handed her a small bottle of Evian. "It's not like you're living on some huge alimony or a trust fund."

"I know. But when Maritza found out, she felt betrayed."

"That's ridiculous, Olivia. She doesn't own you."

"Yes, but Colette spent the whole wedding torturing Maritza. I mean, every time she opened her mouth, something terrible came out of it. She was so despicable. I mean, she really might be the most nasty and bitter woman I have ever met."

"Girl? That's saying *something*, because we've known a few."

Olivia told her the rest of the story about the cake and the press conference and every detail she could remember.

"You know, I stood there while Bob was on the phone with Maritza's mother just thinking that I was an actual witness to

Bob's complete change of heart and add that to the possibility that he was on the verge of losing his family? Roni, it was intense. And you know what? He does not have a cavalier attitude about this at all. That's why I agreed to go with him to Mississippi. I want to make sure he doesn't blow it."

"It's a real love story," Roni said.

"Yes, it is. A real love story coming from one of the most unlikely romantics I can even imagine." Olivia smiled then thinking of Bob and hoping he and Maritza would find their way back to each other. She would talk to Maritza if it would help. "So, I'm sorry I told Colette to forget it. But I just couldn't work for her."

"Olivia? I don't blame you one bit. Don't worry. Work will find us."

Later on that afternoon when Olivia and Roni had put together storyboards for their new client, they stopped to make cappuccinos for themselves.

"I'm feeling sleepy," Olivia said.

"Well, it's ten o'clock at night for you. Why don't I just take off now and see you in the morning?"

"Probably not a bad idea. I'm not leaving until three tomorrow afternoon. I can get an early supper with Nick and turn in."

"Supper? You mean dinner?" Roni said.

"I'm turning into a southerner."

That night Olivia and Nick walked over to Il Tinello for tortellini Bolognese and a glass of red wine. They were seated at a small table near the front of the restaurant. It was their favorite Italian spot in the city.

Nick said, "I just feel like a bowl of pasta would make me feel better." He wiped his fork with his napkin.

"You don't feel well, sweetheart?"

"It's probably just jet lag, but I feel a little off. You know, not quite myself."

"Do you want to stay in New York longer? I can change your ticket."

"No, no. I hear the call of the wild! The fish are taunting me, even from here!"

"You are so funny, darling!"

"You're pretty amusing yourself. That was some trip, wasn't it?"

"Yes. I have to say, I've never been to a wedding like that. It's incredible to see what greed and anger can make people do."

"Well, I hate to sound judgmental, but this is what happens when a man overstirs the pot."

"Aren't we all our own worst enemies?" Olivia said.

"Yes, we are. You know what strikes me as ironic is the difference between normal average people and super rich people. They do the exact same things to each other, but the super rich seem to have a strange appeal."

"What do you mean?"

"I'm not sure how to parse this, but it's almost as if they give themselves permission to be insanely dramatic or something. If that wedding had taken place down on Sullivans Island and there were the exact same characters and situation, the Bob in that scenario would've taken the Colette in that situation aside long before it got to toppling the cake."

"Oh, I see what you mean." Olivia said. "He might have said something like, *Now Colette, let's remember this day is about our son getting married. It's not about you and me.*"

"Precisely," Nick said. "It seems like there's a devil-may-care attitude that invariably leads to an unwanted spectacle."

"Not enough thought goes into the situation in advance?"

"Yes. But I must say. I loved watching you tell Colette to shove it! Cheers!"

They touched the rim of their glasses.

"Cheers! And it felt really good to do it too. Lord knows, she is absolutely the most odious woman I have ever met. She used to be a lot nicer before Bob left her."

"But not nice enough to keep Bob."

"Well, that's what happens with him. He gets bored. Then he runs around. The wives get mad. He buys them off, but they lose the grand lifestyle. Then they become bitter because they're not wildly rich, just rich. Would you like to split an order of pasta, sweetheart?"

"Sure. Just choose. But your assessment sounds about right," Nick said.

"Look, this job Roni got for us will keep us afloat for a while, and then I'll just start beating the streets and see what I can find," Olivia said.

"Well, I have some news to tell you. You know when we went away, we were at odds about money and you not being completely honest with me about what shape we were really in? Well, this afternoon I received an email from the College of Charleston offering me a position in the history department. It's only part-time, but in addition to my pension and social security, it would help us a bit. I mean, I have to do my part as well. It's not fair for you to have to push all the rocks up the hill."

"Oh, Nick! You are such a darling! Do you care for bread?" Olivia offered the breadbasket to him.

"Sure. Well, as much as I liked the idea of being a kept man, we can only eat so much fish. And to be perfectly honest, I like caviar better!"

"So do I. Shame on me, but so do I."

It was a sweet night for Olivia and Nick, walking hand in hand through the streets of Manhattan. They stopped in front of Rockefeller Center and peered through the windows of Teuscher Chocolates, Olivia's favorite chocolatier. Olivia told Nick a dozen times how much she loved him. He did the same. Then they strolled across the street to have a look in Saks Fifth Avenue's windows. Finally, they began to make their way home.

"It's good to have a walk after dinner. We'll sleep better."

"I don't think we're going to have trouble sleeping tonight," Olivia said.

She fell asleep before he did, but he drifted off while he was memorizing her beautiful face in the ambient light that streamed through the windows of their bedroom.

Nick left early in the morning.

"I'll call you and let you know how it's going," Olivia said.

"It's such a crazy story."

"You know, this morning I remembered that some time ago Maritza told me she knew she was going to have to do something spectacular to make Bob love her again."

"Well, I can't think of anything much more over the top, especially when it was apparently carried out on the spur of the moment. Or maybe it wasn't. It will be fun to talk about," Nick said and kissed her cheek.

"In any case, it looks like it worked. Have a safe trip."

"You too!" Nick was on his way back to the island of his heart.

Olivia spent the next few hours with Roni, going over details of their new job.

"Let's get an exact floor plan of the co-op, and if you could send it to me, I can get busy on scale and an electrical plan.

She's going to love the Scalamandré fabrics for the living room. I know I do."

"I do too. And I love the Old World Weavers brocade the most."

"Yes, it's amazing. Okay, that does it for me. I've got to get out to Teterboro."

"Things have been very dull without you around. I have to admit it. I wish I was going on this jaunt."

"I'll be back on Sullivans Island tomorrow night. I can't wait to give you the details."

"And I can't wait to hear them! Have fun! Tell Maritza I said *Atta girl!*"

Olivia got into the Uber, and all the way to the airport, she thought about Nick and him not feeling tip-top. She didn't like it. When she got to Charleston, she'd find out who the local physician was and make him get a checkup. He would fight her about that, because like most men, Nick hated to go to the doctor. He was sixty-seven and in pretty good shape for his age. Maybe she'd get a checkup too. When they were back in the chips, maybe she'd hire a concierge doctor for them. No one was getting any younger, and maybe a doctor who was on call for them would make them seek out better health. It was something to think about. Then she wondered, passing all the visual blight that was the insult of Route 46, if Maritza was angry with her, if Bob had spoken to her yet, if Ellen was coming along.

They pulled up to the terminal. Olivia got out and took her bag. She had everything with her that she had taken to Spain because she was flying straight from Jackson, Mississippi, back to Charleston. She kept thinking all she wanted was for Maritza and Bob to work out their differences and reconcile. Maybe then they'd buy a different house on Nantucket or Martha's Vineyard and she'd get the job of decorating it. Maybe then her life would become normal again. Maybe she'd get used to the South.

That's a whole lot of maybes, she thought.

She spotted Bob across the waiting area. He was on his cell phone, scowling. Gladdie was sitting quietly on a leather chair, one so large that it made her seem like she was very tiny. It occurred to Olivia then that there certainly was an awful lot of personality packed into one tiny person.

"Well, good morning, little miss! Where's Ellen?"

"Daddy told her to go away." Gladdie looked very sad.

"Really?" Olivia looked up at Bob, who had just ended his call. "Is this true? No more Ellen?"

"Uh, yeah. It's a preemptive move on my end, you know, to make the peace," he said.

"Well, good for you, Bob! That was a very good decision."

"Yeah, I finally realized I couldn't have my cake and . . ."

"I've got the whole picture," Olivia said. "Well, Gladdie? I went to my drugstore this morning and bought something for you. Coloring books and crayons. Do you like to color?"

"Oh, yes!" she said. "Can I have them?"

"What do you say, Gladdie?" Bob said.

"Thank you!"

"Here you go, but why don't we save them for the plane ride?"

"Olivia? That's a good idea."

Olivia laughed because Gladdie sounded like a woman way beyond her years.

"And what's all this?"

On the floor were half a dozen shopping bags from Chanel, Hermès, and Chopard.

"Peace offerings," Bob said. "For mother and daughter."

Olivia did some quick calculations and figured there could be thousands of dollars in value in the bags. Scarves? Handbags? Jewels? Bob didn't exactly frequent John's Bargain Basement or Klein's on the Square.

"Well, you know what I'd call it?" Olivia said.

"No, what?"

"A good start." She smiled.

One of the pilots appeared.

"Is everyone ready?" he said.

"Let's load 'em up!" Bob said.

"We're going to get my mommy and bring her home!" Gladdie said, all smiles.

"Then let's go get her!" the pilot said.

When they were airborne and Gladdie was busy coloring, Bob said, "What if she doesn't come home with me?"

"She will, Bob. She will."

"What should I say to her?"

"Tell her you are deeply sorry for whatever you did—which I don't want the details of—and tell her it will never happen again. Tell her that you love her and you're begging her forgiveness. Tell her you want to spend the rest of your life making her happy."

"When did you get so smart about relationships?"

"It's how I feel about Nick."

"Nick is a good man. He's great company and he makes me laugh like hell. He makes me feel like I'm talking to Shakespeare."

Olivia laughed. "Nick loves language. You should see his old map collection."

"Old maps? What an odd thing to collect."

"Well, map making was a very big deal when countries

were being settled. A lot of the time they had huge errors in them. Those are the ones that Nick likes best."

"Well, one of these days I'll come to Charleston and we'll get together. I'd love to see what blows wind up his kilt! Ha-ha! I'm just always so damn busy. I don't know why I keep working. It's not like we need the money. I guess I just like building businesses."

"It's good for your mind and it puts people to work, which is a very good thing." She was thumbing through an *Architectural Digest.*

Bob, who was a quick as a fox, got a sense that Olivia was giving him a subliminal message.

"Okay, Olivia, time to come clean."

"About what?" She looked at him in all innocence, having no idea what he meant.

"How many jobs have you got on your books? Just tell me."

"One."

"How many did you have six months ago?"

"Maximum capacity."

"What happened?"

Olivia hated telling the details of her decline, but she couldn't lie to Bob. They knew each other for so long. And he really didn't want the details, just the gist.

"It was a cluster you-know-what."

"Like Bear Sterns and Lehman Brothers?"

"Yep. When the markets take a beating, so do I. When Wall Street executives file for divorce, plans are changed."

"And you get shorted," he said.

"Big-time."

"Want to do some commercial stuff for a while? I'm opening up new restaurants all over the place."

"Bob, you are an angel. Let's get you straight with Maritza and then we can talk about that."

"I'm no angel," he said and Gladdie crawled up on his lap.

"I'm hungry, Daddy."

"Princess? Daddy forgot to order catering. Why don't you go see what's in the snack drawers?"

"Okay!"

"I'll help you," Olivia said.

"Thanks! Want to see the picture I colored for Mommy?"

She held up the coloring book and showed them a picture of a mother hen and her baby chicks. Of course the coloring wasn't all in the lines, but the colors she chose were in the spectrum of nature's own. Yellow chicks with orange beaks were standing on green grass. The sky—well, parts of it—was blue.

"You may have a budding artist on your hands, Bob!" Olivia said. "Gladdie, this is very, very good for a young lady your age!" And she meant it.

"Thanks!" Gladdie said and beamed with pride. "Should I do another one?"

"Definitely! Do one for your daddy's office!" Olivia whispered.

"I'm gonna do it right now!" Gladdie whispered back as though she and Olivia were conspiring together to repaint the ceiling of the Sistine Chapel.

"I'll get you a snack," Olivia said and smiled.

Olivia fished out a pack of Oreos, a bag of Doritos, and a tiny box of apple juice with a straw attached to its side. She placed it on Gladdie's table, opening everything for her.

"Thanks, Olivia," Gladdie said.

"You're welcome, sweetheart," Olivia said. "Bob? Do you want anything since I'm up?"

"No, thanks. Okay, maybe a bottle of water."

Olivia took two tiny bottles of Pellegrino from the refrigerator. "Water's always a good idea. So, Bob?" Olivia went back to her seat, handed him a bottle and fastened her seat belt. "Have you noticed how well behaved your little one is this morning?"

"Yes, but I'm afraid to say anything and jinx it."

"Well, I'm going to give you my amateur psychologist opinion."

"Lay it on me, sister."

"Somehow, don't ask me how, but somehow your child knew the other one was a problem between you and her mom. So if she was acting up, maybe she thought she would make the other one look bad and she'd have to go. I'm phrasing it this way on account of because . . ."

Olivia cocked her head in the direction of Gladdie, who was happily coloring and eating her cookies with all the poise of a grand duchess.

Bob turned around and took a look at Gladdie and shook his head. He looked at Olivia and said, "Why are women so much smarter than men? Even at her age, she's got it all figured out."

"I think it's called feminine intuition, Bob, and there's no point in trying to fight it."

"You'd think I would've learned this lesson by now."

"Well, now you've got a daughter and you can witness her female intuition as it grows. It becomes either a useful asset or a treacherous tool."

"I think it would be so much easier if women could just raise their own children," Bob said. "All these nannies are nothing but trouble."

Try exercising some personal restraint, she thought but did not say.

"Well, of course it is better—well, maybe it's not *always* better—but more and more being a stay-at-home mom doesn't fit in with the economics of a normal average family. In fact, most women *have* to work."

"And Nick retired."

"Yup."

"Okay, I've got the whole thing now."

"Bob, I'm going to be okay. Don't worry about me. Especially today."

The plane began its descent and landed quietly in Jackson, Mississippi.

"I've got a car to take us there and he's going to wait. Hopefully, we'll all be on a plane by tonight."

"That would be so great!" Olivia said. "So, she's expecting us?"

"Not exactly," Bob said. "Maybe we should stop at a florist shop on the way in."

Oh, God, Olivia thought, this is going to be dreadful. Bob is going to use Gladdie and me as human shields.

They got off the plane, loaded all their luggage and gifts into the trunk of the waiting sedan, and left the airport. Their driver was a tall handsome African-American man who looked like he could've played pro football.

"Sir? How far is the drive to Cartaret?"

"Just slightly over an hour, Mr. Vasile," the driver said. "Please call me Jim."

"Okay, Jim. Thank you. And you know I need you to wait?"

"Yes, sir, but do you have an idea how long that might be?"

"Could be five minutes, could be a long time. I'm coming down here from New York to get my wife. We had a little spat. She's at her mother's house."

Olivia thought, Bob must be getting nervous because he's talking too much.

"Oh my goodness! Mr. Vasile! I've been in your shoes, brother! I've been in your shoes."

Jim started to laugh and Bob did too.

"I guess I'm not the first guy to ever make his wife lose her mind," Bob said.

"No, sir. You sure aren't. But you'll get it worked out. Just ask the Good Lord to help you."

"That and a florist. Do you know of a good flower shop in Cartaret?"

"If they got one, we'll find it."

"Thanks, Jim."

They rode in silence until they finally pulled up in front of a flower shop. Bob got out and bought everything they had; he filled the front seat of the car with bouquet upon bouquet.

"That ought to smooth the path," Bob said.

"It sure should!" Olivia said.

Minutes later they arrived at Martha Ann's house, which was a gorgeous southern antebellum mansion behind a gate, down a long drive lined on both sides with live oaks dripping with Spanish moss. The front of the house had enormous columns that crossed the portico and four sets of French doors with tall black shutters on either side of a massive front door.

"This is Maritza's *mother's* house?" Olivia said. She was completely stunned. "I thought she was a fry cook in the local diner?"

"She was. Her parents thought she ought to work for her spending money when she was a teenager."

"I didn't know she came from money," Olivia said.

"Her folks own the chicken-processing plant in town. It's the largest one in the United States or the second largest."

"So she's rich?"

"Rich is a relative term," Bob said. "In my world, I'm rich. I'd say her folks get along fine."

"I'd say so *too*," Olivia said and shook her head.

They pulled around the circular drive. Bob and Gladdie got out, carrying armloads of flowers, and rang the doorbell. A few minutes passed and Belle, Martha Ann's head honcho/confidante/majordomo, answered the door.

"Hello, Belle!" Bob said.

"Well, hello, Mr. Bob. Miss Maritza said to tell you she ain't home. Hey, Miss Gladdie! You want some cake?"

"Grandmomma!" Gladdie screamed and ran inside to Martha Ann, who was stationed in the foyer.

"Baby doll!" Martha Ann said loudly.

Gladdie flew into her arms and as instructed, *Bam!* Belle slammed the door right in Bob's face, so hard he thought it might fall off the hinges.

CHAPTER 16

sorry

Bob was stunned. Olivia was horrified. Even Jim their driver was surprised.

They were all standing in the yard at the bottom of the front steps.

"This is worse than I thought," Bob said. "I thought Belle liked me."

"Man, what did you *do?*" Jim said.

The afternoon was very warm and there was a gentle breeze that carried the scent of jasmine that Olivia proclaimed to dislike—at least in candles. She could not remember if she had ever smelled it as it occurs naturally in a garden.

"He was a bad dog," Olivia said. "Gosh, it smells heavenly here. What *is* that smell?"

Jim said, "Confederate jasmine and pine mixed up with the roses from the garden over yonder."

Jim pointed to an area of small boxwoods laid out in an argyle pattern. In the center of the diamonds were stands of old roses and hybrid tea roses. The ancient brick wall that surrounded the property was blanketed with Confederate jasmine vines.

"Jasmine! But I hate jasmine!"

"Maybe you don't," Jim said. "See that bush that's pale, pale pink? That's a rose from the time of Abraham Lincoln! That's how long these folks been here."

"My God. That's incredible. I've never had a garden."

"*For God's sake! Please! Cut the garden commentary and tell me what to do!*" Bob said. What the hell? he thought. I'm practically hysterical, and they're talking horticulture! And why are they so relaxed? "Olivia? Do you know something I don't? Have you spoken to her?"

"No, if I had, I would've told you. You know that! I'm just very taken by this beautiful house and this yard."

"You're sorry what you did, right?" Jim said.

"Very. Look, I can't live without her. I feel like I'm dying!"

"You want to try the back door first?" Jim said.

"That's a good idea," Olivia said.

Bob Vasile hadn't knocked on a back door since he was a delivery boy for his neighborhood grocery store when he was a teenager.

"Yes! Excellent idea," Bob said and started for the back door with another armful of flowers and the shopping bags filled with gifts.

Olivia and Jim followed.

"How long they been married?" Jim said.

"Five years," Olivia said.

"He's got it bad."

"Yes, he does. I've never seen him like this."

"So, y'all go back?"

"Like thirty years."

Olivia thought it was very peculiar that Jim was imposing himself into the situation and being so inquisitive, but she was also amused by it. Maybe it was a southern thing—men sticking together, people asking personal questions or something like that. In any case, Jim could turn out to be more help than she might be because she had a sense that he knew how things worked in that neck of the woods. He knew the history of that rose, didn't he?

Bob went through the screened-in porch and knocked on the kitchen door. Belle opened it.

"What's *wrong* with you?" she said very emphatically, her hand on her hip.

"I've come to tell my wife that I'm *sorry* and that I *love* her and that I want to spend the rest of my life proving it."

"I'm not impressed. Don't you know Miss Maritza don't want to truck no more fool wid you?"

"Belle, have mercy on me. Will you just give her these flowers and gifts and tell her I'm on my knees begging for forgiveness?"

"I can't see nobody on they knees. Y'all 'spect me to lie for you?"

Bob immediately dropped to his knees and Belle looked over to Jim and did a double take.

"Well, look who the cat dragged in! Hey there, Jim, dahlin'! How you been getting along?"

That's how he knew about the rose, Oliva thought.

"Hey, Miss Belle! You sure do look good."

"Thank you, baby. You want a piece of my cake?" she said so sweetly the birds almost fell from the trees.

"You know I do!" Jim said, smiling wide.

"Well, get on in here! Cake is *perishable*, you know."

Belle snatched the flowers and shopping bags from Bob, scowled at him, and opened the door to allow Jim to enter.

Jim looked back at Bob and said, "We used to go 'round together."

"Help me, Jim! This is my *life!*"

"I'll do what I can," he said.

Belle frowned at Bob and she slammed the door again.

"There are other forces at work here," Olivia said to Bob. "Things we don't understand."

"They're playing with me. What do we do?"

"I don't know. Wait a few minutes and call the house. Maybe she'll have caller ID and know it's you. Or maybe we just let them play their game. This has all the earmarks of something that was orchestrated for your benefit. Let's wait a few minutes and see what happens."

"Olivia, listen to me. Look at this situation, will you? My wife is inside. My daughter is inside. My driver is inside. And I'm standing in the effing backyard with you! What's wrong with this picture?"

The back door opened again. Jim stuck his head out.

"Miss Olivia? Miss Maritza wants to talk to you. But just you."

"*Jim!*" Bob said, his hands in the air as if to say, *Come on, man! What's happening?*

Jim put up his hand and waved back at Bob. Then he gave him an okay sign to let Bob know that negotiations were under way. Olivia disappeared inside the house.

Bob wasn't so sure. He moved back around to the front of the house, deciding to look through the windows. Moving like a cat, he got down close to the ground and very carefully peered into the living room window. Nothing—not a sign of life. He moved across the portico in a ninja crouch, stopped under the wood panels of the front door to peep into the glass panels that ran its length on both sides. Nothing but the nasty-tempered miniature shih tzus that followed Martha Ann wherever she went. Bob hated those dogs. They started to bark. All they *did* was bark and try to nip his ankles. Of all the breeds in the world? What was the matter with a golden retriever? Or a Cavalier? He moved on to the dining room windows. No one was in there either. No, because they were probably all in Martha Ann's gourmet kitchen eating homemade pound cake, sipping sweet tea, and having a grand old time, snorting with laughter and getting caught up on all the issues of the day while he was outside crawling around like a snake trying to get just a glimpse of his family he so desperately wanted back! It was outrageous to him. *Outrageous!* But his mother always said something about hell's fury and scorned women. Apparently she was right, he thought.

When Bob left his other wives, he never tried to win them back. This was a first for him and now he knew the bitter taste of regret. Regret was coursing his veins. He was hangdog and completely miserable. In his mind, he could hear Maritza's laughter and he could feel her arms around him, and the same was true about Gladdie.

He finally sat down on the front steps and put his head in his hands. He thought, This is hopeless. Maritza's had it. I blew it. He sat there for a very long time, perhaps an hour or more. As time passed, he got more and more depressed.

I'm a shallow man, he thought. All I've ever cared about was making money, having a beautiful woman on my arm, and living large on my terms. Somewhere along the line I forgot about things that were supposed to matter because, because, because . . . why?

Because he refused to be vulnerable.

Love made you vulnerable. It was too late for Bob because now he *was* in love and she was going to break his heart. Maritza was going to break his heart. He just knew it. He stood up, thinking he'd just go wait in the car. It had to be more comfortable that the hard bricks he was sitting on. As he stood, the front door opened behind him.

"Daddy?" It was Gladdie.

His heart soared!

"Yes, princess?"

"Mommy wants to talk to you," she said.

"Thank God! Thanks, sweetheart!"

Bob scooped Gladdie up into the air and landed her on his hip. They walked into the foyer and he saw that Martha Ann's other housekeeper was setting the table for dinner. Martha Ann came out to greet him.

"Hello, Martha Ann," Bob said.

"Hello, Bob. Thank you for the beautiful gifts."

"You're welcome. Just a token, really."

Bob knew if his gifts were accepted, his prospects had improved.

"Now put my granddaughter down, Bob, and go wait in the living room."

Bob put Gladdie down and she ran to the kitchen.

"Prepare yourself for the Great Chastisement. Maritza is plenty provoked with you as you know."

"I don't blame her."

Martha Ann stopped and stared at him then.

"I'm not that much older than you, Bob, but I know a thing or two that you don't. Good marriages are built on love, mutual respect, trust, and forgiveness. If what my daughter tells me is true, y'all have some work to do to make things right between you again. I know you love her. It just took you a while to realize it. And you wouldn't be here if you didn't. But trust was broken. Now if you can reestablish mutual respect, let's hope there's enough forgiveness in her heart for my granddaughter to grow up with two parents."

"I am certainly going to try," Bob said.

"We'll see. Just remember this, Bob. She's my child and I will always take her side, especially now that I know what you are capable of doing. Now I've said my piece. So *if* you two can mend your fence, I'd *love* to have you all stay for supper. Belle baked a gorgeous ham and fixed a wonderful pot of butter beans with rice and of course biscuits. And we've got some tomatoes from our garden."

"I'd like nothing better than to stay for dinner. Thank you for the invitation."

Martha Ann smiled. "Just because the whole world is going to hell, that doesn't mean we can't have a civilized supper, does it?"

"No, ma'am," Bob said.

"Good. I'll send Maritza to you. I'll be with Olivia, measuring. She's going to redo my den for me. Isn't that wonderful? All the ladies in Cartaret will be just green!"

"I suspect they are anyway," Bob said, reminding himself it was good to suck up to his mother-in-law in one breath and cursing himself for being a suck-up in the next.

Bob walked into the living room across the ancient Aubusson rug and began looking around. He had not been there since he asked for Maritza's hand in marriage. The room was decidedly feminine, furnished in jacquard silk fabrics of green and pink stripes and florals. And there was a lot of fringe trim on almost everything. Bob hated it all, except for the rug and the pictures of Maritza.

There was a large oil portrait in a heavy gold baroque frame of Martha Ann wearing a gown and pearls hanging over the fireplace. It was clearly painted when she was much younger, although she was still a beautiful woman. Landscapes in similar frames that represented different aspects of the South hung everywhere—Audubon prints of egrets wading in the marshes and great blue herons perched on branches. There were paintings of hunting dogs, framed photographs of young Maritza from her debutante ball with her parents and alone in small silver frames on all the tabletops, and a framed letter from a long-dead governor in recognition of some great accomplishment of an ancient relative. It was interesting to Bob to consider the things that people put on display to represent their lives to visitors. Martha Ann's living room was all about her wealth and what she thought was her lofty social position in life. Bob could not have cared any less than he did about what went on in polite society. He didn't want to join a private club or go to charity balls, although he supported plenty of good causes with an annual gift.

Maritza's family had been in Mississippi for a very long time and had distinguished themselves in many ways besides building a business that employed over half of the town. They could trace their ancestors back to the American Revolution. Maybe further. But one of the reasons Bob loved Maritza was because she had shirked her debutante history for the private lifestyle he preferred. She had loved him completely. And he had ruined it all.

Maritza was standing in the room staring at his back.

"Bob?"

He turned to see her and again realized just how beautiful she was. His heart started to race.

"Maritza! Sweetheart! Oh, God! I'm so sorry! I love you so much!"

He was moving in on her to take her in his arms. She held up her hand to stop him, and stop him she did. He came to a screeching halt like a cartoon character.

"Hold it right there, Mr. Robert Vasile! Talk's mighty cheap. You're going to agree to a few things or us making up just ain't going to work."

"Anything! Just tell me!"

"Okay. Number one. No more nannies! You've got enough money that I don't have to work. So what do we need a nanny for? I didn't become a mother to have a situation like we had with Ellen. I'm going to be Gladdie's full-time mother and I want you to act like an equal parent with me. If I say no to something she wants, you have to say no too. We back each other up."

"One hundred percent."

"Good. When we want to go out, I'll get a babysitter, a sitter of my choice whom I hire and fire. When we travel, Gladdie comes with us. I make the call if we're gonna need help on the trip. Agreed? She's not even in school yet. But if we need to go off somewhere when she is in school, my momma is coming to stay with her."

"Sure. That sounds perfectly reasonable."

"Number two. I'm not traveling with Dorothy and Michelle and, God knows, Colette *ever* again—*no* exceptions! You want a boys' weekend with Buddy and Sam? Be my guest. But I don't want those women in my life. Agreed?"

"Done! I don't like them anyway. They're awful. I spit on them. Well, I have to deal with Michelle because of business."

"Buy her out."

"Done!"

"Okay. Just one more thing."

"What's that?"

"This is my life, Bob. This is not a joke where I'm just one of your arms like that Hindu god that has so many arms not one of them is more important than any other. We are going to be equal partners and I am going to be involved in every single part of your life. You will never take my love for granted. And if I ever catch you in a lie again, it's *over.* I will clean your blessed clock. Do you understand? Not even a fib."

"I swear I'm going to be the ideal husband, Maritza. I love you so very much."

"Then I'll be the ideal wife. Come here, you big stinker."

She allowed Bob to put his arms around her. And that grew into an embrace like they had not shared in months, maybe even ever. Bob wanted to weep with happiness, and he was profoundly grateful for the second chance. He kissed the side of her neck and she shivered.

"Oh, Lord, you still got it, you old dog!" Maritza said and laughed. "Now come on, let's get ourselves to the table. Belle's gonna switch our hides. Ain't nothing worse than cold biscuits."

After the most scrumptious dinner anyone could remember, it was time to leave.

"This was so wonderful," Olivia said.

"I'm telling you the truth, Martha Ann. I cannot recall a more delicious meal in my entire life. I did not know butter beans could be so flavorful. And the biscuits? Out of this world!"

"Well, thank you, Bob. It's just plain old southern home

cooking. I think Belle was putting together a peach cobbler for us too."

"If I eat any more I'll die!" Bob said.

"I can cook like this, and when we get home, I will!" Maritza said.

Bob reached out and took her hand in his.

"You know who would love these tomatoes, don't you?" Olivia said. "My Nick! He's just *crazy* about tomatoes! He waits all year for the Johns Island farmers to bring them to market."

"Then I'm going to give you a bushel to take to him. And some peaches. Let's see what he thinks about Mississippi dirt," Martha Ann said with a smile.

"Wow! Thank you! Nick will be thrilled!"

"Gosh, it's just heavenly to be together as a family," Martha Ann said. "Y'all aren't thinking about leaving tonight, are you?"

"I've got meetings in the city day after tomorrow, but I think we can stay the night if it's not an inconvenience," Bob said and turned to Maritza. "Would you like to stay the night, sweetheart?"

"I would, sweetheart," Maritza said.

"Yay! Grandmomma? Would you please tuck me in tonight?" Gladdie said.

Olivia noted that Gladdie's metamorphosis into an angelic child included *please* and *thank you* and a voice at a normal decibel.

"Yes, ma'am! And I can read a story to you too! All your momma's books are still in her bedroom. You can sleep in her canopy bed with all her old stuffed animals and feel like a real fairy princess!"

"My old bedroom is a shrine to my childhood," Maritza said.

"That's so great," Olivia said.

"There's nothing wrong with being so loved," Martha Ann said. "And there's everything wrong with being so missed. I want you to promise me that I'll see y'all more often."

"As often as you can stand us," Bob said.

Olivia said, "You know what? I'm going to call United Airlines and find out if they have a flight to Charleston tonight. Y'all need this time together as a family, and I have a husband waiting for me who needs a tomato sandwich."

"Did you just say *y'all*?" Maritza asked.

"I'm almost southern." Olivia laughed.

"No, you're not calling United. We're going to ask Jim to tear himself away from Belle's company and drive you to Jackson. Then you can take my plane to Charleston."

"*Our* plane," Maritza said.

"I stand corrected. *Our* plane." Bob smiled.

"Are you sure? I don't mind flying commercial," Olivia said.

"Consider this a small bonus for tolerating my insanity all these years. And when you need to come here to do what you have to do for Martha Ann, I'll send it to you. You just have to promise to bring Maritza and Gladdie."

"That's a deal, sir."

Olivia boarded Bob's plane with a box of tomatoes and peaches and a plastic container of peach cobbler. Nick's going to love this, she thought. She was more exhausted than she had ever been. Olivia buckled her seatbelt and thought about the resolution she had reached with Maritza over the working-for-Colette debacle. Maritza understood that Olivia had been put in an impossible position that would cost her either way. In a highly unusual move, Olivia had leveled with Maritza about her financial situation. The best part of the overall conclusion was that Maritza promised she would try to find another house in Nantucket. Meanwhile, Olivia might consider doing some commercial design work for Bob's restaurants.

One thing Olivia decided was that Bob and Martiza's life was too crazy for her. She was so happy when she heard Maritza say what she was going to tell Bob.

The mystery of Maritza was solved. She was not immoral, although it wasn't nice to sleep with Bob when he was married to Colette. But on second thought, the fact that it was Colette almost justified it. Well, Olivia thought, love happens and those two are surely in love.

She couldn't wait to tell Nick about Jim and Belle and Bob on his knees. She chuckled every time she envisioned it. And she was going to plant Confederate jasmine.

And tomatoes. She was going to plant tomatoes, so many that they'd never run out of them. And some basil, rosemary, and thyme.

She couldn't wait to get started. Maybe Martha Ann would give her some tips.

And then she fell into a deep sleep and slept the whole way to Charleston.

When she landed, there was a car waiting for her, another considerate gesture of Bob's. Or maybe it was Maritza who thought of it. It didn't matter. It was after ten o'clock at night and it might have taken a long while for a taxi to arrive. In any case, she was glad to see it. She had been taken care of by Bob, who truly was a new man. At least for that one day. Time would tell, she thought.

When they arrived at her house on the island, her driver carried her luggage and packages to the door for her.

"Thanks," she said.

"Any time," he said.

She didn't ring the doorbell because there was a good chance that Nick would be asleep at that hour. The house was in complete darkness, which was odd. But he did not know she was coming in that night. Or did he? His new habit was to rise early and chase fish. She smiled thinking about that. The door was locked, so she dug through her handbag for her keys and let herself in. It took so long to open the door and finally it opened itself. She took the food to the kitchen and dropped it on the counter and then she took her suitcase to the bedroom, careful not to make any noise that might wake Nick.

To her surprise, the bed was still made. She turned on the overhead light. Nick was definitely not there. Suddenly she was alarmed. Where was he? At this late hour?

"Nick! Nick!" She called his name loudly, not caring then if she woke him up. Maybe he had fallen asleep on a sofa? Or in his leather chair?

He was not in the bathroom or his study or the living room. She turned on lights as she went from place to place. Maybe the porch? She hurried outside, and there he was in his favorite rocking chair wearing his new fishing hat. She was so relieved.

"Nick? Hey, baby! I'm home!"

There was no response. Was he asleep?

She was doubly panicked as she hurried around him to wake him. There was no breath in him. Was he dead?

"Nick? Sweetheart? Baby? Please don't be . . ."

She couldn't bring herself to say the word. But then the horrible reality began to sink in. Nick was gone, no longer among the living. She stood there staring at his lifeless body, unsure of what to do. A few moments passed and she realized she had to call someone. She dialed 911, and within minutes the Sullivans Island Fire and Rescue Department was there with an ambulance from EMS. The island coroner arrived and declared Nicholas Seymour dead of natural causes.

"Most likely a heart attack," the doctor said.

"Oh, no!" Olivia said. Her first thought then was could he have been saved with a bypass procedure? When was the last time he'd had a stress test? She wouldn't sleep until she knew.

"Where would you like us to deliver the body?" the EMS worker said.

"I don't know. We just moved here. Wait. You look familiar to me," Olivia said.

"Yes, ma'am, I'm the guy who helped you on the beach a couple of weeks back. This is your time."

"My time? What do you mean? I think I'm going to faint!" she said and someone helped her to a chair.

But before all these sympathetic and helpful folks arrived she had a moment with Nick's body. He had a stain on his shirt. She kissed the tips of her own fingers and touched the spot tenderly. His fishing hat was lopsided and she gently straightened it. And then she began to weep, wondering if her tears would ever stop.

"Oh Nick, what am I going to do without you? I loved you with all my heart. This is so unfair! What am I going to do now?"

And her Nick was just there, slumped to the side.

Her next-door neighbor's husband just walked in the house saying he saw the ambulance, heard the sirens, and saw the lights. He was asking if there was anything he or his wife could do to help. They had just met Nick earlier that day and he seemed like such a lovely gentleman. Was she hungry? Could he call someone for her? He could make her a tomato sandwich.

"No, thank you," Olivia said.

There were so few people for her to call, but somehow she managed to reach Nick's brother and his wife, who promised to be on the next flight to Charleston.

"Oh my God, how terrible," Rick said. "He was such a great guy. I'm just stunned. He wasn't old enough to die! I wonder if I could have his soldiers? I always loved them."

"Sure," Olivia said and thought, How weird!

She called Roni, who burst into tears. Roni said she would review his address book and try to figure out if there were old friends or other relatives who should be notified. She said she'd help with anything else that needed to be done. Anything.

"Don't worry about a single solitary thing. I'll be there tomorrow before noon. I'll help you get everything organized."

And then she called Bob and Maritza.

"Dear God!" Bob said. "I'm completely stunned! I'm so dreadfully sorry! What a terrible shock! What can I do?"

"I don't know," Olivia said. "I don't know where to start. I don't even know what I need."

"Well, look, if you need money or legal help with the estate or anything, Olivia, you know Maritza and I are totally in your corner," Bob said. "You can't go through this alone and you don't have to. And don't forget we've got *Le Bateau de l'Amour*!"

That wasn't right for Bob to say. It didn't make any sense. In fact, nothing made any sense. But she couldn't stop weeping.

The EMS team asked her if Nick had practiced a faith, and when she said his mother was Roman Catholic, they told her they would take his body to somewhere in Mount Pleasant. A funeral director would call her in the morning to determine whether he wanted to be cremated or buried and to make all the other decisions.

What did he say? Olivia wondered, forgetting his words as soon as she heard them.

If your husband left a will, it would be a good idea to find it. Perhaps his wishes were spelled out for her. They said they were sorry and they told her to go inside the house to a place where she couldn't see his body being taken away.

"Go hide your eyes," a man said.

"What?" Olivia said. "Why?"

Her neighbor gently took her arm and led her to the kitchen and tried to engage her in small talk while simultaneously expressing condolences.

"This is the worst night of my life," she told him. "Please, tell me your name again. I'm sorry. I can't hold anything in my head right now."

"I'm Jack, but it's okay. You've had a terrible shock. Can I get you a glass of water or something? Whiskey? Champagne?"

Jack was the name of the captain of Bob's yacht. It was a nice name with a solid ring to it. And this Jack seemed awfully nice. But this wasn't the time for champagne!

"Yes, thank you," Olivia said. "Water would be nice."

Then he grabbed her by the shoulders and began shaking her, gently at first and then more insistently, shaking her and shaking her almost like she was a ragdoll.

"Ms. Ritchie? Wake up, ma'am. We're in Charleston."

"What? What? What? Where am . . . Oh! God!"

She almost jumped out of her seat. It was the worst nightmare of her life. She was covered in perspiration.

"Are you all right?"

"No! Yes!" She looked at him with crazy eyes of panic and wondered if he was telling her the truth. Her dream had been so vivid! So vivid and so terrifying! "Yes, I'm fine."

She was not fine.

"Here, why don't you just sit for a moment. I'll get you a glass of water."

There was a car waiting for her, another considerate gesture of Bob's. Or maybe it was Maritza who thought of it. It didn't matter. She had been taken care of by Bob, who truly was a new man. At least for that one day. Time would tell, she thought. It was after ten o'clock at night and it might have taken a long while for a taxi to arrive. Wait! Had she not dreamed this? In any case, she was glad to see the waiting car.

While driving to the island she called Nick's cell phone and there was no answer. She left him a message. He was probably fast asleep and the phone was on the other side of the house on its charger or on mute.

It was right before eleven when she arrived at home. Her driver carried her bags and boxes to the door for her.

"Thanks so much! Good night!"

"Any time," he said.

She didn't ring the doorbell because there was a good chance that Nick would be asleep at that hour. The house was in complete darkness, which was odd. But he did not know she was coming in that night. Or did he? His new habit was to rise early and chase fish. She smiled thinking about that. The door was locked, so she dug through her handbag for her keys and let herself in. She took the food to the kitchen and dropped it on the counter and then she took her suitcase to the bedroom, careful not to make any noise that might wake Nick.

To her surprise, the bed was still made. She turned on the overhead light. Nick was definitely not there. Suddenly she was alarmed. Where was he? At this late hour?

"Nick! Nick!" She called his name loudly, not caring then if

she woke him up. Maybe he had fallen asleep on a sofa? Or in his leather chair?

He was not in the bathroom or his study or the living room. She turned on lights as she went from place to place. Maybe the porch? She hurried outside, and there he was in his favorite rocking chair wearing his new fishing hat. She was so relieved.

"Nick? Hey, baby! I'm home!"

There was no response. Was he asleep?

She was doubly panicked as she hurried around him to wake him. He was slumped to the side, fishing hat askew, stain on his shirt. This was her dream. Oh God. Was he dead?

"Nick? Baby? Wake up. I'm home."

As though he had been holding his breath for weeks, here came a long whoosh of an exhale. To Olivia's enormous relief, Nick was very much alive.

"Well, hey there! I missed my woman! Come here to me."

He pulled her onto his lap and kissed her face.

"Oh Nick!" She burst into tears.

"Whoa, Nellie! Hold on there! Whatever is the matter?"

"Oh! I had the most vivid and terrible dream."

"Come on, now. I'm here with you and everything is okay."

"I know, I know." Olivia said and realized again how tired she was. "Thank God you're okay."

"Rough trip?"

"Maritza gave Bob religion. I brought you tomatoes."

"Ah, my lovely girl! Let's go make a sandwich."

epilogue

Labor Day, Nantucket

Olivia would never find better friends than those she had. She knew it and she treasured each one of them, especially Roni, despite her youth, and Bob and Maritza. And life's curve balls didn't always result in a black eye. The first thing that happened in that very tumultuous August was that Roni's mother finally gave up the ghost. Olivia flew to New York and did everything for Roni that she could. To be honest, Roni was more relieved than bereft. Her mother had suffered so terribly for so long.

And things between Roni and Jason had gained sufficient momentum and heat for her to move to Charleston. She found a small apartment in the historic district south of Broad Street and moved in. Next, the old salts on Nantucket who had decided they couldn't part with their twenty-six-million-dollar white elephant changed their mind. Their matriarch who held the deed died too, and suddenly the heirs were screaming bloody murder for their inheritance. Bob picked up the bargain for a mere twenty. The real estate business was good, but it wasn't *that* good.

So Olivia had a gold mine on her books again and the foreseeable future looked pretty darn bright. Immediately following the closing on the Nantucket house, Olivia threw herself into her work. She and Roni were down to punch list details on the New York job, and by Labor Day, with Jason and Roni's help and a lot of expediting, the Vasiles were moved in and able to host a house party. It was to be just family, with the exception of Nick and Olivia, whom Bob had adopted except for the paperwork.

"Think of me as your ugly big brother," Bob said to her.

"You're not *that* ugly," she said with a laugh.

"Oh, thanks a whole lot!"

On Friday of Labor Day weekend, Maritza's mother arrived and so did Betty and Ernest. So of course Kitty and Daniel were there. They were having a barbecue that night and had invited a few locals to come by for a cocktail—the McKerrows, with whom they had become very friendly during the construction and the Philbricks, because Bob wanted to get to know Nat and what he knew about Nantucket.

As unbelievable as it seemed to Olivia, Bob was going to grill the steaks himself, but that was how the idea for his first restaurant came to him thirty something years ago. He said he could grill one helluva steak.

"Well, you *look* like you know what you're doing!" Olivia said and laughed.

There would be steamed corn, the last of the summer, and sliced tomatoes from Mississippi, also the last of Martha Ann's bumper crop. Olivia brought fresh basil from their magic garden on Sullivans Island. Well, she called it that because the rate of growth of her herbs seemed insane. And the tomatoes she planted late in the season were perfection—plump, juicy, and delicious. So she brought tomatoes to Nantucket as well. She, who had never thought of herself having anything close to a green thumb, tended her tomato plants like they were precious babies in an ICU, enlisting Nick to keep them watered when she ran back and forth to Nantucket.

There would be no housekeeper or crew to deal with the aftermath of dinner that night or all weekend. Maritza made the announcement that the Nantucket house would be their family's refuge, not a place overrun with a big staff. Everyone loved the idea of that kind of privacy and freedom to be themselves. Maritza had the novel idea that it might be good for them to have one place to go where they could act like a normal family. Olivia silently applauded it. Kitty and Daniel announced they would take kitchen duty off the hands of all the old folks. And Kitty did make a cake of Old Glory. Even Gladdie wanted to help.

So, at 5:01 in the afternoon, the bar was open and Bob was pouring wine. The Philbricks and the McKerrows appeared. Martin McKerrow was sporting navy Bermuda shorts with tiny kelly green whales on them and Nat Philbrick was wearing kelly green Bermuda shorts with tiny navy blue whales and they couldn't stop laughing at themselves and each other. Maritza took pictures of them standing next to each other.

"I had such a great time with Nick," Nat said.

"Nick's the greatest," Olivia said.

"He is one of the most learned and exuberant historians I have ever known. His students adored him."

"We hear from them all the time."

"I'm not surprised. Well, is he here with you?"

"Yes, he was down on the dock with Bob's son looking at Bob's new submarine" Olivia said.

"Submarine? You're kidding!" Nathaniel Philbrick said.

"No! I'm not kidding! Isn't that the wildest thing?" Olivia said. "Go see! I think they're still out there!"

"Well, now, that beats all!" Nat said and walked away. "That's going to drive the IRS crazy!"

"Sometimes I think they live to torture us," Olivia said, thinking luckily her own investigation had ended before it started, but not before it cost her over four thousand dollars in legal and accounting fees.

Toni McKerrow tapped her on the arm. "Hi, I'm Martin's wife, Toni."

"Oh! I'm so happy to meet you! Martin is so great to work with!"

"He's as much a part of this island as anyone! We've been coming here for generations."

"Oh! How lucky for you!" Olivia said. "I adore Nantucket."

"Well, we think we're lucky! I just wanted to tell you what an incredible job you've done with this house. We've been enjoying parties here for years, and you really brought it back to life so beautifully!"

"Gosh, thanks! So you knew they prior owners well?"

"I sure did. The family's great-grandmother Ethel, who was my grandmother Sarah's mother-in-law, was a real stickler about everything. Even though this house is worth a fortune, old Ethel was a notorious tightwad. She made her children beg for every nickel she gave them. So when she went, that was it! They grabbed their inheritance before the flowers from the funeral even had time to droop!"

"That's so funny. Yes, Bob told me the sale closed in the blink of an eye."

"It did. But again, you did a beautiful job! Congratulations!"

"Thanks so much!"

What a nice lady, Olivia thought, and hoped she'd become a friend to Maritza. Maritza needed friends like her.

Eventually the McKerrows and the Philbricks made their way into the night and Bob began grilling the steaks—prime bone-in rib eyes, of course, brought in from one of his restaurants. Daniel had his eye on Bob, watching him carefully and eventually hanging over his shoulder.

"What's up, son?" Bob said.

"Um, I gotta talk to you about something."

"Sure thing. What's on your mind?"

"Um, I need a job, Dad. Kitty said I have to get a job."

"Why? What's happened?" Bob flipped the steaks on the grill. "You can't be out of money."

The entire gathering on the deck became quiet to hear what Daniel was going to say.

"Um, um . . ."

"Come on, spit it out!"

Daniel whispered in Bob's ear so no one could hear. Bob gasped and then started to laugh.

"Well, I'll be damned! Congratulations!" Bob stepped back, grabbed Daniel's hand, and shook it as soundly as he could.

"I'm having a baby," Kitty said, and burst into tears. She had just stepped outside with the platter of steaming buttered corn. She looked like she might drop it.

"Oh, dear Lord! How wonderful!" Betty practically flew from her seat to Kitty's side. "Let me take that platter, sweetheart."

"Wonderful!" Nick said.

"Congratulations!" Olivia said, thinking, Well, this was inevitable!

"God bless you, sweetheart," Ernest said. "You went forth and multiplied!"

"Darling child!" Maritza cried out. "This is the best news in the whole world! Bob! You're going to be a grandfather!"

"It looks like it!" Bob said. "Maybe we ought to pop a cork on a bottle of bubbles!"

Olivia hurried to the kitchen and pulled a bottle of champagne from the chiller and grabbed a handful of flutes. Bob opened the bottle and filled their glasses.

"To the mother-to-be! Be healthy and may your baby be as beautiful as you are!" Bob said.

"Cheers!" everyone said and took a sip.

"And one more!" Bob said. "Here's to nepotism. To my wonderful son, who is about to embark on a steep and difficult climb from the very bottom to the absolute top of his old man's business! Good luck!"

Everyone laughed and cheered them both.

Finally they sat down to dinner, and a wonderful dinner it was.

"Bob! You're quite the grill man!" Olivia said.

"Thanks!" Bob said.

"This is absolutely delicious!" Nick said.

"Steak is so good, Dad," Daniel said. "I'd forgotten how delicious red meat can be."

"Good, son," Bob said.

Daniel had given up on vegan life and so had Kitty.

"I'm so hungry all the time," she said.

"Feed your baby, sugah," Maritza said. "That child's hungry!"

"Maritza? May I ask you a question?" Betty said. Maritza nodded. "Ernest and I have not been able to figure this out. How did you get from the boat to Mississippi?"

"Yes!" Olivia said. "How did you do it?"

"That's my little secret," Maritza said. "Maybe I'll tell you one day."

"I'll tell you how she did it," Bob said. "She hid in the musician's boat, took a taxi to the airport, got on a commercial flight, flew to Atlanta, and picked up a connection to Jackson, Mississippi. Then she rented a car and drove home."

"What?" Olivia said, shocked.

"Oh really?" Maritza said. "And how did I do that without a passport, a credit card, and a driver's license?"

"Yes! That's the part we couldn't figure out!" Ernest said.

"Because my beautiful daughter is absolutely brilliant!" Martha Ann said, adding, "You know what, Olivia? I think your Johns Island tomatoes are better than mine! Not much, but a smidgen!"

Olivia laughed. "Well, thanks!"

Bob said, "I'll tell you how she did it. She borrowed her friend Jessica's ID."

"Women!" Nick said. "Very crafty!"

"You devil! How did you find out?" Maritza said.

Bob took a sip of the rare 1983 Bordeaux he had opened for the evening. Maritza, Olivia, Nick and he were the only ones drinking it. Martha Ann and Ernest sipped bourbon and the others drank iced tea. Bob put down his fork and knife.

"Because on *Le Bateau de l'Amour*, Captain Jack hands out the mail, right? When he saw your return address in Cartaret, he got suspicious and made her open it in front of him. He called me because he wanted to fire her. I said don't you dare because without Jessica we might not be together. That's how I found out. You're welcome. I saved Jessica's job."

"Oh, Bob! That's so romantic!" Maritza said.

"If you say so," Bob said and grinned.

"It actually is, Bob." Nick said.

"Oh! Olivia! I almost forgot to tell you! We finally got y'all a housewarming gift!"

"You're kidding! Well, that's completely unnecessary but very much appreciated." Olivia said.

"It should be waiting for you when you get back home," Bob said. "I'm pretty sure you're going to love it."

"Bob Vasile? I don't know what you've done but you sure do have a funny expression!" Olivia said.

It was late Tuesday afternoon when Olivia and Nick found themselves back at home on Sullivans Island. There were boxes and boxes from UPS waiting for them. As they began to open them they discovered all the treasures they had put up for auction at Sotheby's.

"Bob Vasile! You rascal!" Olivia said, laughing as she opened each box.

"This is a helluva gift!" Nick said.

"Well, crazy or not, Bob Vasile is a helluva friend."

Nick had gone down the beach to throw a hook in the water. She walked down to the ocean with him, just to see if the dolphins were around. He was so happy to be home. Eventually they had spoken about her terrible nightmare, the one in which Nick died. He had listened thoughtfully while she recounted the dream. Finally, he said to her, *you know, Olivia, chances are that you'll survive me. You know that don't you?* She had replied that she didn't want to think about it. And it was true. She did not want to envision one single day on the planet without Nick, much less one moment without him on the island.

There was something else about that place she couldn't pinpoint, something irrational, really, an inexplicable growing passion in her for the perfume of this particular salted air and the exact land under her feet. It was the most powerful connection to a locale she had ever felt. She was beginning to understand why Nick loved it so. She was coming to feel she belonged to this place that had once felt so foreign. Belonging somewhere was something she had never valued until then. It was Nick who opened her mind and heart to see and then to begin to understand the magic of the Lowcountry. It defied rational thought, but just because you might not believe in something that did not mean it wasn't true.

She kicked off her sandals and sat down on the cool sand. The tide was coming in slowly, washing the shore, while little sandpipers pecked away at the mud and sea gulls squawked. The sounds were beautiful hypnotic music and she could've sat there for days, just watching container ships entering Charleston's harbor, ships from all over the world, bringing dreams and taking dreams away.

As Nick had hoped, the enchanted waters of Sullivans Island had exorcised her urban demons and washed them far out to sea. Nick had transplanted her there, and there she would grow. There were to be no more doubts and second thoughts. About their future? There would be lots of fresh fish, Staffordshire dogs, and laughter. She would work, he would read, and together they would enjoy their sabbatical years. It was unclear what else the future would bring. But she knew this. The Lowcountry was a powerful place, and it was home. There are couples who exist independently of each other in a marriage and those who seem like one person, finishing each other's sentences and so on. They, Nick and Olivia, had always been their own person, but now his happiness was hers. And hers was indeed his. This was marriage at its best. Olivia stood up then and looked out to sea. She watched the afternoon water as its currents ran in ripples to the east. A tiny fishing boat bobbed in the distance. A freighter crept by slowly, coming into port while a container ship inched toward her bound for some foreign destination. There were no dolphins to be seen then, but they would be back. And Nick would be coming home later. They would end this day as they would all those left to them—their love renewed, grateful for each other and happy to be together.

acknowledgments

Using a real person's name for a character's has been a great way to raise money for worthy causes. In this book we raised a tidy sum for the Pink Ribbon Event in Wilmington, North Carolina, thanks to the generosity of Gladys Maritza Vasile, who becomes not one but two characters in these pages—Maritza and Gladdie. I don't know if she has a husband, but I gave her one; Bob is the fellow's name and he's a billionaire. Why not? And Olivia Ritchie from Tulsa, Oklahoma, who made a generous donation to Bishop Kelly High School became a fictional wildly successful interior designer in *All Summer Long* and a spectacular woman I'd like to know in real life. Roni Larini, Ellen Williams, Anne Fritz, and Dorothy Kreyer, who support the Morris Plains, New Jersey, efforts to stop domestic violence, are the Greek chorus in this story and oh my goodness I think I can attest to the fact that the antics of the fictional Ellen, Anne, and Dorothy bear absolutely no resemblance to the behaviors and attitudes of their namesakes! They are bad girls (sometimes very naughty) in this story but almost saintly in reality. You have to have a little wickedness to make a juicy story. Nicholas Seymour? Ah, Nick. I don't know you, but I know the Columbia Catholic School thanks you and I married you to my protagonist because I thought you made such a great couple. And last, thanks to Michelle Bemis for supporting the Tiger Woods Foundation. I married you off to fictional Buddy Bemis, who is a plastic surgeon and a great guy. Again, I have met only a few of these folks and only ever so briefly so I can assure you that the behavior, language, proclivities, and personalities of the characters bear no resemblance to the actual people. I hope they get a hoot out of seeing their names all over these pages.

Thanks to David Fletcher, furniture maker of Kendal, England, for your fascinating work, and always to Faye Jenson of the South Carolina Historical Society for her wonderful advice and guidance.

More truth. Jason, Sam, and Elaine Fowler do indeed own Sea Island Builders and they do in fact build gorgeous houses. I hope y'all will all be pleasantly surprised to find yourselves in this drama. It was fun being reminded of you each time I wrote your names!

And Nicole Bousquet, an actual real estate broker on the island of Nantucket, found her way into these pages via the suggestion of Lynn and Steve Glasser. Tony and Martin McKerrow, formerly of Montclair and always of Nantucket, deserve special thanks for their advice about their island's history and current population. I stumbled onto Nathaniel Philbrick while doing some Nantucket research and thought it might be fun to make him a colleague of my historian character, Nicholas Seymour. Okay, to be honest, I love Philbrick's work, *Mayflower*, in particular, and this story gives me the chance to thank him for opening my eyes to what it was really like for our northern founding fathers to settle this country. Okay, I surrender.

The Philbricks can buy the Franks a lobster roll some sunny summer day! We'd love to meet y'all.

And make sure when you're in the Lowcountry that you do stop in for lunch or dinner at The Long Island Café on the Isle of Palms. Say hello to the owner/chef, Ravi Scher, and tell everyone who works there that I sent you. I really love this charming spot and they do indeed serve the best fried shrimp I've ever had. While you're on the Isle of Palms, have dinner at Ken Vedrinski's Coda del Pesce—best crudo in town!

As always, special thanks to George Zur, who is my computer webmaster, for keeping the website alive. To Ann Del Mastro and my cousin Charles Comar Blanchard, all the Franks love you for too many reasons to enumerate!

I'd like most especially to thank my wonderful editor at William Morrow, Carrie Feron, for her marvelous friendship, her endless wisdom, and her fabulous sense of humor. This is a true story: your ideas and excellent editorial input *always* make my work better. I couldn't do this without you. I am blowing you bazillions of smooches from my office window in Montclair.

And to Suzanne Gluck, Alicia Gordon, Clio Seraphim, Claudia Webb, Cathryn Summerhayes, Tracy Fisher, and the whole amazing team of Jedis at WME, I am loving y'all to pieces and looking forward to more of our brilliant future together!

To the entire William Morrow and Avon team: Brian Murray, Michael Morrison, Liate Stehlik, Nicole Fischer, Lynn Grady, Tavia Kowalchuk, Kelly Rudolph, Shawn Nicholls, Frank Albanese, Virginia Stanley, Rachael Brenner Levenberg, Andrea Rosen, Caitlin McCaskey, Josh Marwell, Doug Jones, Carla Parker, Donna Waitkus, Michael Morris, Gabe Barillas, Mumtaz Mustafa, and last but most certainly not ever least, Brian Grogan: thank you one and all for the miracles you perform and for your amazing, generous support. You still make me want to dance. Not shimmy like Maritza Vasile in these pages, but a respectable dance, like a conga line?

To Debbie Zammit, it seems incredible but here we are again! Another year! Another miracle! Another year of keeping me on track, catching my mistakes and making me look reasonably intelligent by giving me tons of excellent ideas about everything. Thank you so much for all you do!

To booksellers across the land, and I mean every single one of you, I one of you, I thank you from the bottom of my heart.

To my family, Peter, William, and Victoria, I love y'all with all I've got. Victoria, you are the most beautiful, wonderful daughter and I am so proud of you. You and William are so smart and so funny, but then a good sense of humor might have been essential to your survival in this house. And you all give me great advice, a quality that makes me particularly proud. Every woman should have my good fortune with their children. You fill my life with joy. Well, usually. Just kidding. And to Carmine Peluso, who recently joined our family. We love you, son, and we are so proud to claim you! Peter Frank? You are still the man of my dreams, honey. Thirty-three years and they never had a fight. It's a little incredible to realize it's only thirty-three years, especially when it feels like I've loved you forever.

It doesn't seem right to close these remarks without a nod to mark the passing on March 4, 2016, of my great friend Pat Conroy. Pat was an incredibly generous man who changed so many people's lives in positive ways. He was the father you always wanted, the brother you never had, and the confessor you needed when life got out of hand. Like so many others, I loved him. And so many writers would agree that we will miss him every day for the rest of our lives. Rest in peace, you old Bulldog. You were the greatest. (My own father was a Citadel Bulldog, class of 1937.)

Finally, to my readers to whom I owe the greatest debt of all, I am sending you my most sincere and profound thanks for reading my stories, for sending along so many nice emails, for yakking it up with me on Facebook and for coming out to book signings. You are why I try to write a book each year. I hope *All Summer Long* will entertain you and give you something new to think about. There's a lot of magic down here in the Lowcountry. Please, come see us and get some for yourself! I love you all and thank you once again.

about the author

New York Times bestseller Dorothea Benton Frank was born and raised on Sullivans Island, South Carolina. She resides in the New York area with her husband.

Dorothea Benton Frank's most recent bestseller, *All the Single Ladies*, debuted at #6 on the *New York Times* list, where it remained in the top twenty for four weeks. It was also a *USA Today* bestseller, debuting at number ten.

A contemporary voice of the South in the ranks of Anne Rivers Siddons and Pat Conroy, Dorothea Benton Frank is beloved from coast to coast, thanks to her bestsellers, including *The Hurricane Sisters*, *The Last Original Wife*, *Porch Lights*, *Folly Beach*, *Sullivans Island*, and *Plantation*.